THE BUFFALO THIEF

THE BUFFALO THIEF

Yojana Sharma

Doubleday

LONDON · NEW YORK · TORONTO · SYDNEY · AUCKLAND

TRANSWORLD PUBLISHERS LTD
61–63 Uxbridge Road, London W5 5SA

TRANSWORLD PUBLISHERS
c/o Random House Australia Pty Ltd
20 Alfred Street, Milsons Point, NSW 2061, Australia

TRANSWORLD PUBLISHERS
c/o Random House New Zealand
18 Poland Road, Glenfield, Auckland, New Zealand

TRANSWORLD PUBLISHERS
c/o Random House Pty Ltd
Endulini, 5a Jubilee Road, Parktown 2193, South Africa

Published 1999 by Doubleday
a division of Transworld Publishers Ltd
Copyright © 1999 by Yojana Sharma

A catalogue record for this book is available from the British Library.

ISBN 0385 600135

Typeset in 11/13pt Bembo by Deltatype Ltd, Birkenhead, Merseyside
Printed in Great Britain
by Clays Ltd, Bungay, Suffolk.

1 3 5 7 9 10 8 6 4 2

PART ONE

1

DEEPA'S GRANDMOTHER WAS AMMA. SHE COULD SEE FAR MORE THAN WHAT was beyond her nose, and she could see well beyond the furthest horizon. Yet Deepa's grandmother was blind, and scarcely moved from the courtyard house built by her son-in-law before he died on the day she had foreseen.

Before she went blind, long before (in fact she was still young then), the astrological charts that determined the futures of the royal families dominated her life.

Deepa's grandfather had been a court astrologer: a *rajguru*, or sage, to the kings of the northern kingdoms. He would have gone further south, for his reputation had trickled down to those regions by word of mouth. But travelling from East to West was a laborious undertaking, particularly in the summer with its heat and dust, and during the monsoon with its storms and floods. And it was such a fertile period in the history of the royal families of the north, with princes and princesses being born almost every month, he had no need to seek additional rewards further afield. His service in the courts of the north had amassed him a treasure that would be around for the next few generations.

Those adventurous, wayfaring years in Amma's life came to an abrupt end when Deepa's grandfather died. He had been at the court of the remote kingdom of Cooch Behar when his health began to fail him. He was considerably older than Deepa's grandmother, for of course she was just a girl when they married. But it was not old age that had weakened him. It was the heat, the travelling and the *loo* wind that blew treacherously across the Northern Plain.

He had been warned not to set off while the *loo* blew. But Grandfather had received news of another royal birth, westwards, in a Rajput kingdom. The message had reached him from across the great Thar Desert, across the steaming Gangetic Plain, up the lush hills to Cooch Behar. How could he ignore it? His life and his fate were bound up with the lives, the fates, of the princes. It was God's will that he should be in attendance at the birth of a prince.

'And it was God's will that he failed to make it,' Deepa's grandmother said.

It was the end of a partnership that went beyond marriage. Together, Deepa's grandparents had brought these royal children into the world and drawn up their first astrological charts – the charts that would be pored over by all in the royal household, by successive astrologers, by astrologers of other royal families seeking a marriage match, and by astrologers of rival kingdoms wishing to know the best dates for a successful attack. Creation and destruction depended on those charts: births, marriage and wars, all were decided with reference to the princely nativities. There was no room for inaccuracy or any mistake – well, perhaps Grandfather would have died long before if there had been any mistake.

That's what Amma said.

'Not that the maharajas were so cruel,' said Amma. But there was only one way to punish a man who had miscast a horoscope in defiance of fate, and that was to take control of the fate of the one who had erred.

'So powerful were those kings,' Amma said.

'You mean?' said Deepa, wide-eyed as she listened from the homely comfort of Amma's *charpoy*.

'A fate worse than death,' said Amma gravely.

'What could be worse?' breathed Deepa.

'Much worse,' said Amma, 'is when someone other than God can decide how and when you die.'

'That is almost as powerful as God,' said Deepa.

And Amma nodded wisely.

For all the wealth earned at the courts of the kingdoms of the north, there was little visible sign of vast riches. No mansion or estates. Amma led a simple life. The house in Jagdishpuri Extension, by no means large, was not Grandfather's but Deepa's father's. He had been a teacher at the Municipal Boys' College and had been allotted land for a small house in Jagdishpuri Extension on which he built this bungalow intended for a modest teacher's family.

A ruby ring here, a gold and sapphire necklace there from the overflowing jewellery boxes of the maharanis meant that Amma was a widow of some means. But she was not given to ostentation. And, because she lived in Jagdishpuri Extension in relative comfort, for the most part the treasure was largely untouched.

Not long after she had ensured the marriage of her daughter Vimala – Deepa's mother – with a dowry of precious jewels, Amma came to live in the modest house in Jagdishpuri Extension to help take care of her grandchildren, Deepa and baby Kamini.

Into the house, or more correctly into the courtyard, where she was fond of sitting, she brought the aroma of pickles from her array of terracotta pickle-pots, in which she had laid down layers of mango and lime in sweet mustard oil. More importantly for the folklore of Mardpur, it was said that she had also brought with her a box of treasure: priceless jewels from the maharanis, gold and silver ornaments handed down in the dowries of the royal princesses, all made by the most skilled craftsmen who were endowed not only with an artistic eye but also with the gift of patience. To be sure, some amazing jewels surfaced at the marriage of Amma's own daughter, Deepa's mother. But there had been no other evidence of such treasure for many years, and the stories that it even existed began to seem like myth.

As for the cask in which the treasure was said to be kept, Deepa knew nothing of it. She had never seen any such chest. Yet it was not lost on her that, unlike other families unlucky enough to lose the man of the house, Amma was lacking in nothing but her sight, and even that was amply compensated for by her vision.

The suddenness of Grandfather's death notwithstanding, Amma had not been surprised abruptly to find herself a widow. She had had a premonition, a weak one in those days, not yet fully developed. She did not take too much notice of such thoughts when she was younger although she would communicate her thoughts to Grandfather, who would always listen very carefully but check for evidence in the charts before nodding to her in agreement at what she had seen, his glasses, yellow and scratched, sliding down his handsome nose.

Many spoke of Amma's extraordinary powers, although they were barely understood. It was only after Grandfather's death that Amma herself understood her gift, as if during his lifetime she had concentrated only on channelling her talent into his. He took up her suggestions on the fates of the princes and honed them into perfect predictions thanks to the preciseness of astrological science. When he was gone, Amma kept these glimpses into another time to herself, and what she could see grew stronger, more detailed and more vivid. And as the darkness of failing sight closed in on her, her vision became more powerful still.

Deepa was used to Amma's intuition. She experienced it often and had little cause to question it. It was not this that made Amma remarkable in her eyes, but rather the stories of the mysterious treasure.

Deepa would ask, 'Amma, do you really have treasure buried in the front yard?'

'Yes, I have a treasure in the front yard. It is Jhotta the buffalo.'

'How is she a treasure?' Deepa laughed.

'Is she not giving us milk that is keeping us in good health? It is a treasure.'

'No Amma, I mean gold and rubies and jewellery.'

'You are my treasure, more precious than rubies and gold.' And Amma pinched her cheeks.

'I want to know!'

'What will you do with treasure?' Amma said, a smile about her lips.

'Nothing. But I like to know if it is there,' said the earnest Deepa.

'It is there,' Amma reassured her.

But Deepa was not content. She knew Amma could see what others could not, and she wished for once that she, too, could glimpse what was hidden from view.

The treasure also made her the focus of attention at school.

'Does your grandmother sleep with treasure under her pillow at night?'

'Does your Amma have diamonds and rubies hidden in her teeth?'

'Have you seen the treasure? Is it buried under the house?'

Deepa hardly knew how to fend off such questions. She could not say there was no treasure because she herself believed in it, hidden, quiet, to reveal itself when the time came. Yet it seemed to her pointless to dwell on it, because it did not appear that she or Amma needed treasure. They were happy as they were.

2

THE TRAGEDY HAPPENED IN THE YEAR DEEPA WAS SIX, ON A QUIET DAY
when the wind was still and the sun beat down onto the plains, making
the ground ripple, blinding and white-hot.

It was the day Deepa's ma had reluctantly gone to the district court in
Murgaon on the early bus, worrying about her little Kamini, Deepa's
sister, who had woken with a fever. Deepa's father, Dasji, took the sickly
child to the doctor's clinic near the Aurobindo Hospital.

Deepa's ma was an advocate. She often travelled to Murgaon where
there was a district court. Sometimes baby Kamini and an ayah would
accompany her on the bus to Murgaon so that Ma could keep an eye on
the poor child who seemed to thrive only in her mother's presence.
Amma took care of Deepa so that Ma could concentrate on baby Kamini.
It was from very early on that the bond between Deepa and Amma was
formed.

'My poor Kamini!' worried Ma as she prepared to go to Murgaon.

'It is because you did not drink hot milk and eat almonds in pregnancy,
as I did before you were born,' Amma scolded affectionately.

Ma smiled: 'Don't worry, Ma. When baby Kamini grows up, she will
have all her immunities and will never be sick again.'

Deepa's ma was right. Baby Kamini grew into a healthy, extrovert three-year-old, full of energy. Deepa, the strong baby, was the quiet one. Deepa's father, Dasji, affectionately called her *chuhia*, or little mouse, for she was timid, always waiting for someone to reach out to her first before she reached out to them. Deepa remembered that. She remembered that her father had had his own little name for her. *His* own little name, which died with him.

And she remembered how her mother found her quietness a little perplexing. 'Deepa is just like you, Ma,' Deepa's mother would say, referring to Deepa's way of retreating into quiet thoughtfulness.

Amma looked knowing: 'Vimala, she is like you. Quiet and serious.'

'Serious? Yes,' agreed Ma, 'it is baby Kamini who is the jolly one, isn't it?'

Amma nodded, but there was a sad look in her eyes as she held the wriggling Kamini in her lap.

That afternoon, in the shimmering heat which melted the tar on the road from the mill town of Ghatpur, a Tata truck laden with sugarcane crashed into the *tonga* that carried Deepa's father and her baby sister from the clinic. The screaming of the stricken horse brought half of Mardpur out into the street.

The truck lay on its side, its load of sugarcane spilling onto the road, quickly seized by the urchins of Mardpur who initially ran off with bundles of cane under their arms. Then, curiosity getting the better of them, they were drawn back by the demonic screams of the horse. There they stood in a circle around the scene, ferociously ripping with their teeth on the woody outer bark of the cane, the sweet juice running down their grubby chins as they gnawed and chewed and spat out the dried, spent pith.

It was some time before enough labourers and coolies could be found. Sweating and straining on the thickest ropes from Jindal's Hardware Store they managed to right the truck, and found the body of Deepa's father with the child crushed into his arms.

Dr Sharma, who just hours earlier had pronounced that Kamini's fever was 'nothing to worry about', certified them both dead.

Deepa's father and baby sister were wrapped carefully by Dr Sharma in a multi-coloured chequered bed-sheet handed to him by his young son, Govind. He organized for the bodies to be removed from the road. Then Dr Sharma climbed into his battered old Ambassador car, with his dazed and horrified son seated mute beside him, and drove to Jagdishpuri Extension to break the news to Amma.

All morning Amma had locked herself away in prayer. Even Deepa had a sense of foreboding that day, although she was too young then to understand what her grandmother already knew.

'He-ey Mahade-e-va, Mahe-e-sh-wara,' Amma sang slowly as Dr Sharma's car drew up outside, startling Jhotta, the affable, easy-going buffalo in the front yard.

Deepa watched the agitated boy enter and wait patiently beside his father until Amma completed her prayer. She looked up at the doctor, her sight already fading, ready for what he had to tell her. Just a few words were uttered in Deepa's presence, but that moment when Deepa heard the first news of her father's death was one she never forgot.

This was the first time she saw Govind – stricken, aghast, and looking at her with a heart more pained than a nine-year-old boy could bear.

'I saw them,' Govind whispered to Deepa as his father spoke alone with Amma in the room, leaving the two children face to face in the courtyard.

Deepa looked at him astonished. 'All the blood and everything? How could you?'

'No, no,' said Govind quickly, 'covered up. All covered. In a coloured sheet. A sheet of many colours. It was my own sheet, from my bed. I was bringing it back from the *dhobin*, from ironing, and Papa took it from me to wrap them up.'

Govind was babbling now, with shock. 'Such a noise that horse made, screaming, shouting, neigh-neigh-neigh . . .' Govind emitted the inhuman high-pitched sounds, his eyes closed and his hands covering his ears. 'Like a *bhooth* was riding.' His teeth chattered and he looked around as if he expected to see that *bhooth* right there in Amma's house. 'Such a horse-scream – you could even hear it in Jagdishpuri Extension.'

'We probably could,' Deepa said, listening horrified and fascinated at the same time and thinking that was when Amma started her slow prayers, although it was several hours later that the doctor arrived with the news.

Deepa wanted to know everything from this boy who had seen what Amma had seen from so far away.

'The horse. Did he die too?'

'Oh yes. Dead. Gone. Quiet now. *Chup*. Not shouting-screaming any more.'

'And the *tonga*-wala?'

'Yes, dead. All dead.'

'Did she cry?' Deepa persisted, despite the pain on Govind's face. She knew no one else was going to tell her, then or ever. Not with candour or feeling.

Govind was sweating. But he had to speak. He could not keep it inside, pressing on his heart, his stomach, making him feel heavy and sick.

'My sister. The baby, did she cry?'

'No, no,' he said, looking away. 'She did not cry. She went *chup-chaap*. All quietly. Quiet. *Chup*.' He held his finger to Deepa's lips as if to quieten *her*.

Deepa had no sense of time. She could have been standing there with Govind for just a few minutes or for an hour. All she could remember after that was the furrowed face of Dr Sharma as he emerged from the room. And Govind was gone.

That was the only time Deepa heard any details of the tragedy. Only later, much later, she overheard by chance at the temple that the bodies had been cremated together, still wrapped in Govind's multi-coloured sheet.

She did have one opportunity of her own to see where it had all happened. Some days later, on the way to the bus station – she could not remember exactly where they were going and why – Deepa and Amma were forced to make a detour in the bus. A truck had broken down and blocked the road to Mardpur from Murgaon, so they had to approach the bus station from the road from Ghatpur. Deepa peered out of the bus window and could see the wreck of the Tata truck by the roadside, the splintered wood of the *tonga*, still not entirely destroyed for firewood, with its red plastic seat now white with dust.

It was a scene that had the clarity of the pre-monsoon light, even through that grimy window. The dust had been pushed from the air by the rising humidity, bringing the colours and outlines more sharply into focus. Deepa took in every detail.

In the middle of the road a circle of cane bark and dried pith marked the spot where the truck had overturned on top of her father and little Kamini when they fell out of the *tonga*. The people of Mardpur preferred to walk outside this sugarcane boundary; this boundary between life and death.

As she stared the colours seemed to become stronger and the contrast sharper and she could make out tiny spots of blood, brown against the white-baked ground. It was then that the long-expected monsoon broke at last with little warning but a long, drawn-out roar of thunder, splashing huge raindrops against the windowpane.

Deepa turned her head from side to side to peer between the raindrops clinging to the glass, and tried to clear her vision by rubbing frantically with her hand. Then, pushing the sliding window open with both hands, she leant out of the bus and watched the rain hammer the traces of blood into the dusty ground until they mingled with the soil and drummed the pith into the softening ground, until the debris was buried in the mud and once more there was no boundary between life and death. There was only life.

Thereafter, whenever Deepa felt a strange sense of emptiness in her heart, she remembered the pith circle which marked the spot where her father's soul had left his body, and she remembered the face of Govind, stricken with horror. These thoughts brought not sadness, but a pensiveness that recalled images of the death rather than the person that had been alive. It was because of her apparent lack of grief, or any reaction at all, for that matter, that some thought her a little strange, unaffected by things around her.

And Amma? Rather than lose herself in the debilitating grief of tragedy, she got on with her life, consoling her widowed daughter as best she could while her own sight faded and faded, bringing on the darkness that she did not allow her heart to feel.

3

IF DEEPA PUSHED THE MEMORY OF THE TRAGEDY TO THE FURTHEST RECESSES
of her mind, others remembered it in detail for years, for it had scarred the
Mardpur psyche. Of course, people died all the time, including young
children. But not out in the open streets. That made the accident
everyone's tragedy, not like a death in the family, out of sight at home for
just the nearest and dearest to mourn over.

The way the people saw it, unlike the usual cycle of disease and death,
viewed largely as 'God's will', a truck driver, at the wheel of a man-made
machine, had driven into a *tonga*. It was surely man, and not God, who
had wrought this havoc.

They sought to lay the blame on the driver. But he was neither to be
found nor ever identified. On impact, he did not wait to ascertain the fate
of the *tonga*-wala and passengers. He leapt out of the driver's cabin
clutching his tiffin-carrier and cigarettes, and ran as fast as his stout legs
could take him in the direction whence his truck had come, which he
knew for certain led straight out of Mardpur.

Many had seen him running that day, his tiffin-carrier in one hand, his
other hand to his head holding onto his turban-cloth which had become
unravelled and was fluttering like a white pennant behind him, while his
long hair had fallen dishevelled about his shoulders, giving him a rather

wild appearance as he fled. Many saw him thus, but who should stop him? By the time the enormity of the accident became evident, the man was already half-way to Ghatpur where he could blend in easily with the other migrants who flocked to the city to work in the factories.

For months there were rumours and sightings from virtually every town in the vicinity, but as Amma said, why should he stay in these parts? He had probably already returned to the Punjab to do penance at the Golden Temple.

And Deepa said, 'Knowing my grandmother, she was probably right.'

But thereafter, the arrival of the monsoon was special for Deepa. It swept away more than just the heat of summer.

As her mother travelled further and further afield to the district courts, keeping herself occupied with her work, Deepa and Amma sat on the *charpoy* in the covered part of the courtyard, listening to the rain.

'Tell me about the treasure, Amma!' Deepa urged.

And Amma laughed, and began: 'One day when I was just sitting on my *charpoy* like we are doing now—'

'But I was not there . . .'

'No, Deepa, you were not. It was long before you were born. Perhaps even before your mother. But there I was, sitting alone, when Biju came.'

'Biju?'

'She was a simple maidservant in the court of the Maharaja of Mehru, but she was loyal and reliable and her maharani she loved most dearly. "Amma! It has happened at last!" she said. "The maharani is with child. At last she is with child!" Those were her exact words. "For when is the child?" I asked. I was sure she had counted many times and I knew I could believe her when she told me the exact month. I walked to my earthenware pot and found a small silver chain.'

'Silver?' breathed Deepa.

'Yes,' said Amma, pausing to recall the scene again. 'Silver it was. That night we packed our things to travel to Mehru.'

'Straight away?'

'A prince about to be born does not wait. And it was a few months' travel. I was needed to deliver the prince, and your grandfather to bless him with his astrologer's wisdom. We were a rare couple, Deepa. The midwife, the *dai* to the maharanis, and the astrologer. I could signal the exact moment of birth. That was also the secret of the accuracy of your grandfather's predictions and that was why he was such a great *rajguru*! On some courtier or maid he did not have to rely. They did not always understand the importance of being exact. Dates must always be exact.'

'How could you be so exact?' marvelled Deepa.

'The messengers came sometimes months before, and as the time approached for a royal birth I could also feel that we had to be there. I could not rest in peace until we were on the way. And for this we were rewarded. We rewarded our loyal informers, also. If I had to rely on my own thoughts, I would know only very suddenly, maybe with not so much time to spare.'

'Were you late ever?' asked Deepa, caught up in the excitement of it all.

'Late sometimes. It happened in the Gandhinagar kingdom. But never too late. "We must hurry to the Gandhinagar kingdom," I told Grandfather while we were still at the court of Mehru. We had been resting in the palace for a month after the prince was born. If we listened to our informers we had no reason to start for Gandhinagar for two months at least. Grandfather wanted to stay to study and redraw some charts; sometimes those birth charts are fading, even the charts of princes. Some astrologers are using poor inks. Grandfather was never using poor inks, only *pukka* colours. Then there are inaccuracies in the chart to be corrected. Passing events can show that the positioning of planets was not quite as exact as it could be. But there was no time for that. I realized the prince of Gandhinagar was in a hurry to be born, and we should be there in time or he would surely die alongside his mother.

'We arrived just in time. Although we were unable to save the poor maharani – it was God's will, and we were powerless in front of it – the little prince was brought into the world, puny and coughing. But he was the first male heir to survive, and this little prince had been born at an auspicious time. He would live long, Grandfather told the maharaja.'

'But, so sad about the maharani!' said Deepa.

'She could not be saved,' said Amma, shaking her head. 'But without us, the little prince would not have been saved, either. The maharaja rewarded us handsomely in gold. And we felt humble that we were able to give life in this way.'

'Gold he gave you!' gasped Deepa.

Amma smiled. 'And life we gave.'

4

DEEPA'S MA WAS POSTED FURTHER AND FURTHER AFIELD. AND AS DEEPA grew older she and Amma saw her less frequently. Then one day Deepa realized she had not seen her mother for more than a month. Amma, who at first had worried about her widowed daughter, but then realized that Ma could not stop herself thinking about Dasji and baby Kamini each day that she was in Mardpur, encouraged her daughter to go where she needed to, leaving Deepa in Amma's care. For sure, whenever Ma embraced Deepa – and she was not without affection for her elder daughter – her eyes clouded over as the face of Kamini hovered before her.

When Deepa finally plucked up the courage to ask, Amma was matter-of-fact. She said Ma had moved to Vakilpur, a town to the south of Mardpur. To get there you had to change buses twice. Perhaps that was why Ma could not visit so often, Amma said. And then she hugged and kissed Deepa and said, 'Your ma loves you, Deepa, but I need you here with me. See, my eyes are not so good. And you, too, need to be here.'

'To find the treasure?' said Deepa eagerly.

'To find the treasure,' Amma responded gravely.

There was a photograph of Deepa's ma and her father, an ageing print propped up on Amma's trunk near her *puja* corner. Amma had never put it in a frame. Ma, fresh and glowing, was adorned from head to foot with heavy jewellery such as only princesses wear. Amma was in the picture too, wearing beautiful jewellery herself. Deepa had never set eyes on any of this jewellery. It had to be somewhere.

Deepa asked in a more roundabout way, 'Amma, when I marry will I have lot of gold jewellery like Ma had?'

'Of course,' said Amma.

'Where is all this gold to come from?'

'I am keeping it safe for you. You will find it when you need it, Deepa.'

'When will that be?'

'Not yet. Perhaps when I am already gone from this earth.'

'Then I do not want it!' cried Deepa, entwining her arms around Amma's neck.

Amma stroked Deepa's elbow. 'You see, you do not need it now. But when there is a need it will be there for you.'

But Deepa was intrigued. And she often pondered its whereabouts.

'Where is it? Is it in the trunks?'

Still Amma would not say, and Deepa had to content herself with thinking at least Amma had not denied the existence of treasure.

'Amma has never said it is not there,' Deepa told her best friend Bharathi one day.

'People still say there are angels and demons, Deepa,' Bharathi said, 'even when we know they are not there.'

'We cannot see angels and demons, but I can see the treasure. It is in there, in the photograph of my ma.'

'If my grandmother lost something very precious she would not tell me, she would cry by herself,' reasoned Bharathi. 'Maybe Amma just does not like to tell you it is gone. Maybe your ma has it all.'

'She would tell me if that were so,' said Deepa adamantly.

But then she remembered that Amma had not told her the details of her father's death, nor had she told her about her ma marrying again. Still, she believed in the treasure and that one day Amma would bring it out for her. Sometimes, but not very often, Deepa wondered what would happen if Amma were to die without telling her, leaving it to stay hidden for ever.

It was quite by chance that Deepa learnt about her mother's remarriage. It was unthinkable then for a widow to remarry. No one had thought to tell Deepa, or perhaps had not dared, or perhaps did not know how to put such things into words to a child. Not even Amma, who still said when Deepa asked that Ma could not bear to come to Mardpur because it reminded her too much of Deepa's father and baby Kamini.

It was among the trees of the Vishnu Narayan temple that Deepa overheard Sudha-with-Pension and Madhu gossiping. They were Bharathi's aunts, the wives of the brothers Laxman and Vaman, the sari traders from one of the oldest trading families of Mardpur.

'Such a sad face that poor Deepa-girl has always. She never sees her mother now that she is in Vakilpur. Not only has she lost her *baap*, she has become an orphan also,' said Sudha-with-Pension, the older, plump one, who had spotted Deepa in the temple garden. She stood with Madhu, hands full of fruit and flowers, the bounty for the gods.

'Vakilpur? There is no district court there,' said Madhu, the younger, slim one, whose arms jangled with bangles of gold. Her voice was tinged with surprise.

They moved away behind a tree and Deepa did not catch the response. A few seconds later when they reappeared, Sudha was speaking with a voice full of indignation.

'What was the need to remarry? The family has money. Amma has gold. Even Dasji's pension from municipal college is transferable to widow.'

'Maybe love is flowering in the courthouse,' said Madhu, a reader of romantic stories in weekly magazines. She knew, although Deepa did not, that Deepa's ma had married a judge just recently, and had tried to put her family tragedy behind her.

'*Dhut!*' scolded Sudha-with-Pension. 'What are you talking? What is love? You are watching too many movies. It is not good.'

A little later, when Sudha and Madhu returned to the garden having deposited their offerings at the inner sanctum, Deepa heard Sudha-with-Pension refer to Ma as 'that woman with no shame'. Sudha was making no attempt to keep her voice down. Deepa heard them clearly as they wandered among the trees, leaning forward to apply vermilion-powder *tilaks* to the foreheads of the stone deities and then standing back to sprinkle rice.

'But her husband died so tragically,' said Madhu, still referring to Deepa's ma but with more sympathy than Sudha had displayed. 'And who will look after her?'

'She should not be setting eyes on another man,' sniffed Sudha. 'Who would have thought of it? That quiet Vimala with a daughter so quiet like herself to seek another! It is too forward.'

Madhu tackled things with more logic. 'Maybe he is seeing her and feeling sorry for her. And she – well, it is better than being alone.'

Sudha looked at Madhu distastefully. '*Dhut!* Where are you getting such ideas? A man can never feel sorry for a widow!'

'I am guessing only,' said Madhu, standing her ground.

Even Deepa could not know how near to the truth Madhu had got.

'It is not good for that Deepa-with-no-ma to be on her own,' Sudha continued, as if someone was at fault and should remedy the situation forthwith.

'But she has her Amma!' said Madhu, who had never seen Deepa appear anything but content. She was certainly a quiet child, but not unhappy, in Madhu's view.

'Have you not heard about Amma?' persisted Sudha, adopting her patronizing air again to address Madhu, wife of the younger of the brothers. 'It is told there are *bhooths* in her house. It is not good for a small girl.'

'*Bhooths?*' said Madhu, so excited that her bangles jangled. 'I have never seen one!'

'Maybe you have not,' said Sudha with a superior air, 'but there are many who have.'

With just Deepa for company and with her eyesight fading, Amma was regarded with some awe, even fear. The stories of her special powers persisted, but with the passage of time, and because she was rarely seen in the Old Market or Kumar Bazaar, the stories had become distorted. Now it was said that Amma imagined *bhooths* and perhaps could even conjure them up around her, waving and flapping in a breeze of her creation during the hot stillness of summer. Maybe, some said, the house in Jagdishpuri Extension harboured the ghosts of Kamini the baby, Deepa's father and the screaming horse. Could that be why Deepa was so quiet, and why her mother did not like to come to Mardpur?

When the other girls teased Deepa it was often because she was inclined to stay on the sidelines, waiting to be invited into their games, never initiating anything herself. But they also teased her because of Amma. Sometimes when Deepa and Bharathi would not let them join in their hopscotch or share their tamarind seeds, they would jump up and down calling, '*Bhootni Maai, Bhootni Maai!*' and then run off shrieking with mock terror.

Only Bharathi knew Deepa well enough to realize there were no ghosts, although whenever she visited the house in Jagdishpuri Extension she could sense an aura around Amma. It was not so much frightening as inexplicable, just like the smell of pickles in sweet mustard oil which seemed so strong when Amma was around, far stronger than anything a few pots of maturing pickles could possibly produce.

5

THE DAY SUDHA-WITH-PENSION SPOKE OF DEEPA'S MA REMARRYING, SHE had also been scolding Madhu as they completed their temple rituals.

'Don't tell me you have forgotten coconut again? You know coconut is essential. What are you thinking? You are always with head in clouds.'

'Well, no matter, for I am a mother of two sons, it is not necessary to invoke fertility symbol,' said Madhu. It was a vicious rebuke dealt with some force for someone usually more reticent.

Deepa could not see Sudha-with-Pension's reaction, but Sudha could not have been pleased. She had borne no children and had adopted Meera and Mamta, the twin daughters of Raman and the older sisters of Bharathi.

Later, Deepa heard them again.

'Isn't it you and Laxman Brother should be looking for suitable family for Meera–Mamta?' Madhu was saying.

'Yes, and I am saying so too. For what are we educating these girls and teaching music? For singing to us in old age? I am telling my husband. But he thinks it is a joke only. He said, "I like music, even in old age."'

'The men are always waiting for us ladies to organize. Without us they would do nothing. Those girls should marry before their voices are too thick. Who will marry a girl with a thick voice?' observed Madhu.

'Yes, it is time. Why don't you talk to your husband, Vaman Brother, also? Dowry is to come from family kitty.'

'My husband has not spoken about dowry coming from family kitty,' said Madhu, somewhat suspicious.

'You were not long married when our father-in-law died. Discussion then was that sari stores would be given to our husbands, but dowry for girls must come from family kitty. For where is Raman to find money? He is good-for-nothing, lazy, BA third class only. And why are you worried, O mother of sons?' – this in a slightly barbed tone – 'Your boys will be bringing dowry into your home, there is no loss for you.'

'Well, perhaps Raman should be spending some time looking for a match,' suggested Madhu carefully, for she did not know how Sudha would take this.

'Raman?' snorted Sudha-with-Pension. 'Do you think he can be trusted to find good husbands for such beautiful daughters, who have grown up in my home and who are now so accomplished?'

'He can make enquiries,' suggested Madhu mildly.

Sudha-with-Pension brushed this aside with a gesture of irritation. 'Raman cannot be trusted to behave properly in securing a match, even for his own daughters. Too unpredictable, he is. He is not always acting with a clear head. And God knows what gets into his head sometimes. Do you not remember how it was with his own marriage?' Sudha thought she would remind Madhu, even if Madhu did recall. 'We were not thinking that Kumud would be the best match for Raman. Look at her. So thin and without accomplishment.'

'She is not ugly and her skin is not dark,' interjected Madhu, who secretly believed Kumud was the prettiest of the three wives.

'And she is only seventh standard pass,' continued Sudha brusquely. 'In this family, the top sari-trading family of Mardpur, a seventh standard pass only has found a match! And do you know why? It was that Raman! We are not sure about that girl Kumud, *Baoji* said. And you know what he did? In the middle of the night Raman left Mardpur and went there to go and take a look at that Kumud.'

'How could he see her face at night-time?' said Madhu, finding this tale quite romantic.

'By bus he went there, and stayed in the bushes till morning till he could see clearly. Then he came back and said to Father-in-law, "That is the girl I want." Imagine! It is such a disgrace to all the family to have the youngest wife only seventh—'

'Raman himself was not so educated then, even his BA he did not have,' Madhu reminded her, but secretly she was quite admiring of Raman's courage, even if it did display the wilful side of his nature.

'Even more reason for him to listen to the older, more educated members of the family. Do you know, he was locking himself in his room and saying, "Until my marriage is fixed with that girl, I will not come out." We did everything to try to persuade. But once he has a mad idea in his head, it is no use. We even believed he might steal her away in the middle of the night, so adamant he was and listening to no one. So we thought, better have a decent wedding and maintain family honour, so we let him marry according to his choice rather than face any further disgrace. And that is why that Raman is stuck now with a seventh standard pass.'

'Well, she is homely, and that is all Raman needs,' said Madhu pragmatically.

But for Sudha it was not a matter of whether or not Kumud was right for Raman that counted, but that Raman had shown a headstrong, erratic streak that in her view had no basis in logic. Having seen it once, she was determined that it should not influence the marriage of the twins, who she had brought up with such pride. She did not want any midnight antics, or threats, real or imagined, of stealing people away in the middle of the night.

Sudha and Madhu were not the only ones to talk about the marriage of Bharathi's sisters. Rampal, who came to milk Jhotta, said one morning of Bharathi's father, 'That Raman sahib is wandering and wandering in the bazaar, he is always dreaming-scheming. But it is nothing to do with reality. Reality is, he has two daughters to marry soon. What will he give in dowry? He was too no-good in father's sari business. Now he will regret.'

'What is he dreaming?' asked Amma, leaning on the wall listening to Jhotta's milk splashing into the pail.

'Even he doesn't know what! Just dreaming to get away from reality. Well, would you not want to be in another world if you had twin daughters to marry?'

'Did I not also raise a daughter?' she said with a toss of her head. 'Did I run away from reality? Never! I faced my responsibility. Anyway it is the eldest brother, Laxman, who will marry off those Meera and Mamta; a joint marriage, maybe with brothers. Only one wedding is necessary. Much saving. So what is the burden for Raman? None.'

The milk from the buffalo's full udders tinkled into the pail in a gentle stream as Rampal pulled rhythmically at the teats. 'Well,' he said, easing back onto his haunches as the buffalo's let-down reflex suddenly yielded a steady flow of milk. 'He should write down what is going on in his head. If it is so good that it is better than being in this world, then they would be such stories that one day Raman sahib would become a great writer!'

'Ha!' snorted Amma. 'We would all become great writers if we could write all what is going around our heads.'

'And you would be the best writer of all, Ammaji!' said Rampal, who harboured a deep respect and admiration for her.

'Oh no,' smiled Amma, 'I am not on this earth to write.' Her voice softened. It was barely audible over the squirting of the milk. 'I am on earth to see what others cannot!'

'And to assist with birth, Amma! Such an important task, who can do?'

Amma nodded slowly and pensively as if trying to separate the past and the future in her mind. 'You are right, Rampal, everyone has their important tasks in life. Perhaps we should not laugh at Raman. Maybe there is something in that man, but we cannot see it yet.'

'Everyone has good points inside,' agreed Rampal.

6

RAMAN WAS IN A PENSIVE MOOD. HE HAD INDEED BEEN WANDERING ABOUT the town thinking, as Rampal had said.

Raman's wife Kumud was nagging him to think about the future of Meera and Mamta, their eldest daughters. She was already fourteen when she married, she reminded him, and a year later the twins were born. Had he not noticed the twins would be matriculating next summer and what had he done about their marriages? Nothing. One big zero.

'Girls are not marrying so quickly these days,' said Raman mildly.

He had been putting off finding suitable matches for his daughters, not because he had any wish to avoid his duty as a father, but because, quite genuinely, he never thought about such things. He was not a worrier. His view was, why concern oneself until one really had to deal with things head-on? The problem was, Kumud had made it quite clear that now he had to deal with it.

'What are you talking? They are already past fourteen. Looking for a decent match takes time. It is not like going to Kumar Bazaar and seeing who is walking around and bringing him home for wedding,' said Kumud, exasperated at Raman's obvious lack of concern.

'There are new laws against child marriage,' said Raman vaguely.

'What child-wild marriage? Have you seen your daughters lately? They are not babies any longer!'

It was true Raman did not see much of Meera and Mamta; they lived with his elder brother, which made it that much easier to put their future out of his mind.

Laxman ran the Sari Mahal – a large store room lit by fluorescent tubes and stocked high with saris of every hue and design. It was situated at the other end of Mardpur, on the eastern edge of Kumar Bazaar. It was not on Raman's way anywhere, and he had not been there since the wheel of his bicycle was bent in a collision with a bullock that had charged at him from God only knows where in the narrow gulleys of the Old Market. Luckily he had not been hurt. But he had not bothered to buy another bicycle. He could not say if it was out of sheer laziness that he had not gone to Jetco, which sold four sturdy brands, at least one of which might withstand the impact of a bullock, or if it was because Jetco was right beside the Sari Mahal, which would require paying a visit to his brother.

It worried Raman that he was required to take the responsibility of finding a double-match. As if marrying just one daughter wasn't difficult enough! He had always assumed his elder brother Laxman would attend to that task. He had imagined (that is, if he ever thought of it at all) that Laxman would one day inform him that he had found a suitable match for Meera and Mamta with a decent family, that he had negotiated a dowry, and that the priest Satyanarayan Swami had matched the horoscopes and had found them compatible. Did he, Raman, agree to the match? Of course Raman would graciously agree and turn up on the day in a yellow silk turban to perform the rites of giving away his daughters. He had not been expecting to be burdened with the problem of *looking* for a match *and* negotiating the dowry.

Now he realized it would seem surly and disinterested in the extreme if he were to say it was a matter only for Laxman. They were, after all, *his* daughters, even if Laxman had brought them up as his own. And Kumud had begun to worry, which was hard to ignore and made it even more difficult for him to take a back seat.

As with everything to do with money, Raman had hitherto assumed it would be a family affair with all three brothers chipping in. As for negotiations, his brothers, who were involved in business, were used to negotiating all the time; they could hardly expect him to do better in that sphere.

Sudha thought otherwise. She felt that she and Laxman had done their duty by giving Meera and Mamta opportunities they could never have had with their real parents – opportunities for refinement and skill. Once they had surpassed their own parents in accomplishments, something which happened well before they were in their teens, it seemed natural that they should stay with their aunt and uncle to complete their education. In matters of education, too, Sudha claimed to have superior knowledge. Certainly knowledge that was superior to Raman, BA third class, and Kumud, who was only seventh standard pass.

Sudha taught music at the municipal college. She could have taught at the missionary college, she always said, 'But at municipal college seniority is quicker and pension is also good.'

Raman, who never in his life considered the usefulness of a pension, thought she was giving herself airs. 'For what is she needing a pension?' he complained to Kumud. 'When sari business is running so well?'

'What if Laxman Brother should die, what then?' responded Kumud without looking up from scouring the pans from the evening meal.

Raman was shocked. 'Vaman is the younger brother, he must look after. It is his duty.'

'And what if Vaman Brother should die?'

Raman looked aghast at the thought. That would mean, of course, that *he* would be responsible for two widows and their children.

'*Chup!* Quiet. Why is it you are having these morbid thoughts of killing my brothers? You will be casting the evil eye on them by saying such things.'

So Kumud never again stood up for Sudha's right to earn money and a pension. For that matter, she had no reason to stand up for Sudha-with-Pension at all. For Sudha was overweening and bossy, and intent on always showing how superior she was to the younger wives.

The dowry responsibility, Sudha impressed on Laxman, should not be shouldered solely by them or they would have little to live on in old age, for no sons did they have.

'We have the Sari Mahal,' said Laxman mildly, and other property besides, but he did not mention that.

'And you will be selling saris till you are eighty?' mocked Sudha.

'Well, seventy at least.'

'Then?'

'Then what? Someone else will take over.'

'Who?'

This was not something Laxman wanted to think about at that moment. 'Some nephew, I don't know.'

'Like Shanker, the son of Raman?'

What she meant was, if Raman's son ended up with the Sari Mahal because they had no sons, they could not be expected to pay the dowries of Raman's daughters as well. Raman's family would be doing very nicely out of that.

Yes, Sudha-with-Pension had brought up Meera and Mamta to be vocal young girls such as they would never have been allowed to be in Raman's household, and that did not just mean she had taught them to sing. In a gathering, they could talk about all manner of things, including what should be done to improve the country. This made Raman uneasy in their company. What kind of boys would like such girls, he wondered. He felt sure he did not know of any such young men, let alone two of them. Although he read the newspaper, he had developed the habit of keeping his views to himself. He found it most unbecoming when Sudha selected items from the newspaper to discuss. Sudha-with-Pension's newspaper-reading habits did not impress Kumud either. Why did she need to look at the newspaper when she could find out the price of ghee in the bazaar? And how did it help her to know that the rest of India was flooded so long as the water was not at her gates?

'It is always good to know what our *netas* are doing for the country,' Sudha-with-Pension said with a sniff. She liked to remind people that her own father had been a freedom fighter.

'They cannot be doing much, for my life has not changed at all,' said Kumud archly. 'And what they are telling in the newspapers is for people who do not use their eyes to see what is really going on.'

'Still, one must have an *understanding* of the body politic,' Sudha said, trying to confuse Kumud with learned concepts.

'I understand it quite well,' grumbled Kumud. 'The price of ghee is going up and up. If one day it goes down, I will read the newspaper to find out why.'

7

RAMAN HAD LITTLE REASON TO BE IMPRESSED BY SUDHA'S KNOWLEDGE OF what was in the newspapers. He knew quite well what was in them for he worked for the government news agency. The little money Raman earned from the Press Trust of India was regular and enough to buy food and other necessities for his family. What more did they need? Kumud was not one of those women who wanted to own everything she set eyes on, and she made few demands on the family budget. He could not understand why others worked themselves to the bone and still worried about money. That was until he began to realize that not only would he have to find a dowry, he would also have to find two at the same time.

Raman went to the office before eight every morning to check what dispatches had clicked through on the PTI service. He clipped and filed newspapers and made phone calls for the PTI correspondent 'Salt March' Gulbachan, then he came home for lunch and a nap. He did not need to go back to work until five or six in the evening and then it was only for an hour or two, checking the dispatches.

"'TRAIN CRASH IN BADALPUR, PROCEED IMMEDI-ATELY,'" Raman read aloud from the wire that day.

Gulbachan slowly lowered the *Statesman*. He rarely moved fast, whatever the story. 'Will it make a first rough draft of history?'

'No,' admitted Raman, 'but it will be read by the Delhi bureaucrat.'

There were only two criteria for judging the news: that it should contribute to the history of the nation, or that it would be widely read by the bureaucrats in Delhi who were the main readers of newspapers. Since the first never seemed to occur on Gulbachan's patch, the second became paramount. It was enough to galvanize Gulbachan into action. He yawned, scratching his sides as he did so, and took his stockinged feet off his desk, slipping them into his leather shoes.

'Notebook?' said Gulbachan, who could not remember where he had put it. Nor, for that matter, could he remember when he had last used it.

'Under the table,' suggested Raman.

'What?' said Gulbachan, his head appearing under his desk, where he found nothing.

Raman retrieved the notebook from under the table leg where it was keeping Gulbachan's desk from rocking, and banged the dust from it. It had a square indentation in the middle, perfectly formed. It was the hallmark of Gulbachan's notebooks.

'Pen?' said Gulbachan.

Raman checked behind his own ear first. 'Behind your ear.'

Gulbachan transferred it to the top pocket of his bush-shirt. He was ready to go.

In his youth, while the British were still running the country, Gulbachan had tried for the Indian Administrative Service and failed to get in. He never really recovered from that early disappointment. PTI was a poor second, as government jobs went. It had its moments – but they had been long, long ago. Gulbachan's main claim to fame was having interviewed Mahatma Gandhi while on the Salt March. It had been the highlight of his whole career, although not enough to get him posted to Delhi or Calcutta or even Lucknow. If it hadn't been for the pleasant little bungalow that came with the job in Mardpur, and the title Chief Correspondent, Gulbachan would never have accepted the posting.

A Chief Correspondent always has an assistant, if not a whole army of sub-correspondents, but there was no call for that in sleepy, inconsequential Mardpur. When Gulbachan sought an assistant, a sole office junior, he had not wanted some eager young graduate who might show him up. He did not want someone with ambition or aspirations, or pretensions to being a writer. So Raman fitted the bill admirably. Gulbachan, who knew everyone in Mardpur, knew Raman's family well enough to know about

Raman's lack of interest in the family business. Raman had, in effect, already proved himself to be not very ambitious at all.

Although Gulbachan had satisfied himself that Raman was no threat, he took it upon himself to convey to Raman that there was more to writing for PTI than met the eye, for Gulbachan was all too aware that the craft of reporting was easily learnt through observation. Raman should not think that just because he had seen Gulbachan at work he could aspire to the same. 'It is the thoughts, the analysis, that make a good reporter,' he said, tapping the side of his head. 'It cannot be learnt just by watching. Reporting is not a craft, it is a talent.'

Thus Gulbachan impressed upon Raman early on that one should never underestimate a reporter who did not look like he was doing much. There was a lot taking place in the laboratory of the reporter's mind. The writer's mind was thinking and drafting at every possible moment. Not that Raman would ever assume such a thing, for he himself sought to impress on Kumud just that.

'When I am retired,' Gulbachan said one day, 'I will write a book. My job here is just preparation, marking time for the day when I will write a master-work. It is a book-writer I will be.'

'Why?' said Raman, busy stamping dusty newspaper clippings with a cracked rubber date-stamp.

'Why? Why? There is nothing greater than writing a book. It brings out everything that is in a man. That is, if there is anything in a man in the first place.'

'Oh,' said Raman, unimpressed. It did not seem a good enough reason for him. Why would any man need to bring out what was inside? What was in, belonged in.

'And,' said Gulbachan dramatically, 'writers can become very, very rich in a very short time.'

This interested Raman rather more, although if writers were getting very, very rich in a short time, why was Gulbachan waiting for his retirement to begin? It made no sense.

'It is a lot of work, this book-writing, for how much money?' said Raman dubiously.

'What lot of work? Just a little time. Anyone could do it, even you.' Gulbachan laughed drily. 'If you had it in you. As for money, thousands of rupees can be made.'

Raman had long forgotten the details of that conversation. What he *did* remember was that it was something that anyone could do.

8

THE AIR WAS STILL AND HOT, BUT NOT YET OPPRESSIVE ENOUGH TO SILENCE the cicadas. Raman was distracted by their shrill chirp and felt the need to escape the incessant buzz as well as the heat that seemed to rise out of the ground under the trees and envelop the bungalow in the lychee garden in a stifling embrace.

'I am going to the temple,' he told Kumud.

'It is still a few hours before *aarti*-time,' said Kumud. She did not seek to control her husband, but she felt he should have a good reason for everything he did.

'I am going to ask Satyanarayan for his advice.'

'For what?'

Raman thought for a while. He did not know himself.

'For inner peace.' He liked that, it sounded most justifiable, and it made Kumud sound as if she was nagging him.

'After you have achieved inner peace,' said Kumud without a trace of irony, 'please go to the Old Market and get some bananas. I will make raita.'

'Inner peace is not achieved in a day,' Raman told her.

'Then it will be some time before you get raita.'

★

Raman considered himself the most devout of the three brothers. Laxman and Vaman eschewed ritual to the extent of being completely godless. Only Sudha-with-Pension cared about rituals and rites and often went to the temple to offer flowers to the deities. Sometimes she went with the shy Madhu – shy, that is, in Sudha's presence. It was another reason for Kumud to criticize her sisters-in-law.

'Do they not have a *puja* room in their big-big houses, where they can worship? Or is it that they do not want to find time to sweep and clean *puja* room? My small *puja* corner is enough for me – I am not having to go to temple to show the world I know how to pray!'

To be honest, it was not religion that brought Raman to the temple. He sometimes went there for company. Satyanarayan Swami, priest-philosopher-astrologer-Ayurvedic-scholar, always had an opinion on every subject under the sun and usually proffered it unasked. When Raman felt confused because others insisted on making life seem so complicated he consulted Satyanarayan to see if the sage could shed light on the mysterious thought processes of those around him. Not that he always understood what Satyanarayan was getting at – the Brahmin's ideas were often quite erudite. But they filled a vacuum. And right now Raman sensed a very big vacuum – he did not know what to think about the marriage of his daughters. Everyone said he should be thinking about it, but there was not a thought in his head on how to go about it.

The Vishnu Narayan temple was just beyond Kumar Junction. It was a pleasant walk downhill from the lychee garden, even in that heat which glued Raman's bush-shirt to his torso. The trees that lined the dirt road provided some shade, and from somewhere a warm breeze arose, reducing somewhat marginally the weight of the sun's rays on Raman's back. Anyone else would have complained loudly about walking in a furnace, but Raman enjoyed the solitude of the stroll. It seemed to him the loneliest road on the whole Gangetic Plain, when every other road was teaming with men, women and children, buffaloes and bullocks, bicycles and carts, buses and trucks. In the absence of such noise and distraction, Raman could smell the hot dust that swirled lightly around his toes and settled on his sandals. The dust was almost white now, baked and bleached by the sun. He marvelled at how it could change so quickly into warm, thick, dark brown mud when the rains came.

The small white-washed temple with its tall *gopura*, dazzling white against the deep blue of the summer sky, was little more than a shrine set in a small walled garden that bordered on Kumar Junction – the triangle of crossroads around which the central business hub of Mardpur had developed. The temple garden was scattered haphazardly with trees. Although untended by any *mali*, it was a pleasant enough patch. In it, the residents of Mardpur wandered and chatted before and after taking their rounds of the darkened inner sanctum of the temple. In fact, the garden was as much a place of worship as the temple itself. Each tree was surrounded by a platform on which a small stone statue rested. On festival days the platforms were piled so high with fruit and flowers that the gods, themselves overloaded with garlands, could barely peer over them and the devout were hard-pressed to find a place to sit and gossip about the goings-on in Mardpur.

Festival or not, underneath the largest tree – a spreading banyan tree with massive roots – sat Satyanarayan, as if he, too, expected to be worshipped.

Satyanarayan was in his usual place, sitting cross-legged on a reed mat and threading jasmine-bud garlands, when Raman dropped by, trying to look purposeful. The Brahmin pushed a pile of buds towards Raman, carefully threaded a needle at arm's length and handed it to his visitor indicating that he, too, should thread buds. Raman began to push the hardy buds onto the needle, finding it a strangely restful task.

'You are thinking, are you not, what excellent eyesight I have, that I can thread a needle so quickly at my age?'

Raman agreed that that was exactly what he was thinking, although in reality he was not thinking very much at all.

'Seeing is not about age,' Satyanarayan began. 'It is about vision and clarity. To have vision you must know what you want to see. And to have clarity your mind must be free of extraneous bad thoughts. Inner wisdom is the result of years of observation and study and devotion,' he said. And then added, 'Yes, that's it,' as if happy that he had found the right phrase.

Raman was impressed, just as Raman was always impressed with Satyanarayan. Much of what he said seemed to strike a chord with Raman, and was much more eloquently put than either Raman or anyone else around him could put it.

'Do you think to write down your ideas?' asked Raman, pushing the jasmine buds onto the needle. He said this to ingratiate himself with Satyanarayan, and there was a practical reason, too: it would save

Satyanarayan having to repeat his homilies many times every day to whoever came to the temple.

Satyanarayan was a little surprised at Raman's interest in his thought processes, and flattered, too, just as Raman had intended.

'I own neither pencil nor pen.'

'You could dictate,' Raman suggested helpfully.

'And who would write?' Satyanarayan fixed Raman with a penetrating stare.

Raman threaded his buds with deep concentration, only too aware of the Brahmin's gimlet eyes.

'Would you write?' Satyanarayan asked him suddenly. It was not that he thought Raman capable of it, but he wanted to know what Raman's intentions were in suggesting it in the first place.

'I am too humble,' Raman replied modestly, pleased that Satyanarayan should even think of him. 'And of little education.'

'How little?' There was a desire to humiliate in Satyanarayan's voice, though Raman did not notice it.

'BA third class,' he said simply.

'True, that is not enough,' Satyanarayan agreed, dismissing the idea while accomplishing his purpose of showing Raman how ridiculous the notion was. It was not just Raman's lack of education that bothered him, but if the merchant classes were to take up writing en masse – and there was a mass of them – then what need was there for Brahmins, whose whole purpose in being born to that caste was to show the lesser castes what scholarship they could aspire to in a later life? At all costs, thought Satyanarayan, a bania should not be encouraged to take up scholarly work. Education, yes, for there was a need for education in many of the worldly tasks of the modern world. But for scholarship, the high standards set by the Brahmins could never be diluted.

He did not relay this developing discourse to Raman. Instead he said, 'You see, that is my problem. Wisdom is not just speaking and writing. Wisdom is in the mind. It only becomes wisdom when it goes from my mind to yours and serves some useful purpose. Otherwise, it merely remains an innermost thought.'

Raman held up his jasmine-bud garland. Satyanarayan looked at it with approval.

'You have a steady hand, it is a useful thing. But for writing, it is a steady mind that is required. If my thoughts are to be written I need someone with . . . um . . .'

'Status?'

Satyanarayan was surprised to see Raman so skilled with words that he could find the right one so easily. Still, he could not contemplate someone like Raman doing such an important task. It would be the thin end of the wedge – the wedge that could topple the very basis of society which was now so well balanced with the priest-scholars at its pinnacle.

'Status,' said Satyanarayan, savouring the word – it was a word he liked very much – 'status does not come from college degrees and riches. Status is achieved by a lifetime of work. No one can command respect, he must earn it.'

'Some do not earn even in a lifetime,' said Raman without looking up from his buds.

'No,' agreed Satyanarayan, looking at Raman's bent head and thinking he was a good example of one who would not. 'Some do not.'

'And there are some,' continued Raman, warming to the theme, 'who are born with status, such as princes.'

'Do not confuse status with titles,' said Satyanarayan, regaining the initiative in developing the theory. 'Status is acquired when a man rises above others. A prince only has status when he rises above other princes.'

Raman found this interesting. He stopped threading for a moment. 'Does that mean there are Brahmins who have more status than other Brahmins?' As one who came from the trading class, Raman was quite aware of the status that Brahmins commanded for themselves over all others.

'Of course,' said Satyanarayan, drawing himself up and looking pleased with himself. Raman blinked and looked at Satyanarayan with new eyes. It was true this was a Brahmin that stood out from the run-of-the-mill. He felt quite proud that this Brahmin should reside in Mardpur and that he should be talking to him. He was almost willing to forgive Satyanarayan's lack of faith in his writing abilities. Anyone would seem small to a great man.

Raman left the temple after paying his respects to the deities, and trekked through Kumar Bazaar to pay a rare visit to his brother Laxman at the Sari Mahal.

On the way Raman passed Rampal, his *baltis* of milk clattering on his bicycle.

'Oho, Raman sahib!' said Rampal, pleased to see him. 'I am in need of your good services.'

Rampal struggled to pull out a small chit from the pocket of his *kurta*. There were too many other things in his pocket: a large homespun kerchief for wiping his milky hands on, a rope to tie the hind legs of the cow or buffalo, and several screws for fixing *baltis* should they suddenly decide to shed their handles just as a calf was born and extra milk was being produced that would require all *baltis* to be in service.

'Can you read it, Raman sahib? My eyes are not so good,' Rampal said, proffering the chit to Raman.

Raman read: *Owing to selling of land on which we keep buffalo we have also sold buffalo, so your milking services will no longer be needed.*

Rampal looked sad. He clicked his tongue. 'Too many people are wanting to sell land and getting rid of buffaloes,' he said. 'Soon there will be no land left in Mardpur for grazing, and quality of milk will not be good. What shall I reply, Raman sahib?'

Raman thought for a moment. 'You can say: Received your letter and noted contents with interest. Service will be discontinued henceforth. I would be obliged if you would recommend to new landowner my services.'

Rampal was mightily impressed at such eloquence. 'You are one very brilliant writer, Raman sahib.'

Raman helped Rampal write it on the back of his chit, before continuing on his way.

Laxman was always very nervous about Raman's visits, infrequent as they were, as if his younger brother was coming to stake a claim to the sari business. He did not like him coming to the sari shop. He feared Raman would see how much business was being done and how valuable the stock was.

Laxman flapped about, treating Raman like a VIP, getting him tea and biscuits, enquiring after Kumud and the children, which was precisely what Raman had wanted. After they had covered the ground, discussing the health of Kumud and the two younger children, Bharathi and Shanker, they turned to Meera and Mamta.

'They are growing into beautiful young ladies,' Laxman said. 'We will not need too much dowry. Besides, for us it is no problem to provide the boys' family with all the saris they want. Wholesale price.'

He laughed at his own joke and then stopped suddenly, worried that Raman may realize the value of the business and decide he wanted a stake in it if it was doing so well.

'Of course, I will handle dowry negotiations, you don't even need to worry about that, brother,' he added hastily. He did not want Raman to think he was not capable of undertaking negotiations. Raman felt relieved.

Laxman, on impulse, pulled a beautiful chiffon sari from a shelf and handed it to his brother. It was a merry riot of swirling paisleys and plump lotuses in strong hues. Most prominent were magenta and cobalt blue, which offset each other dramatically. It was, Raman had to admit, a very striking sari, one Kumud could be proud of.

'For Kumud,' said Laxman generously; 'she always looked wonderful in chiffon. So slender. So graceful.'

Raman was surprised. He had never considered his wife to be anything special with regard to her looks and bearing. After all, she was married to him: a youngest son and BA third class, too uneducated to put Satyanarayan's words of wisdom onto paper. True, in some senses he had chosen her, but even he did not know what he was thinking so many years ago. He put it down to youth. Young men could be quite hot-headed. He smiled gently as he sipped his milky tea, remembering how he had hidden in the bushes till dawn, waiting to catch a glimpse of Kumud.

'Have you thought of any suitable family, Laxman Brother? Not that I am pushing. I am not in a hurry. Girls are marrying too early these days. But Kumud is worrying. Meera–Mamta are matriculating next year and what then? I am wanting to put Kumud's mind at rest only.'

'I have not considered any suitable family,' said Laxman looking serious. 'I will discuss with Vaman Brother. He is travelling around more than I and maybe he is knowing some good families with sons.'

Raman was relieved. He had succeeded in raising the topic. He could go back to Kumud and report to her that he had done her bidding and that he was not dodging his duty as a father. Laxman, too, was relieved that this seemed to be the main purpose of Raman's visit.

To Laxman, Raman had from the beginning seemed lacking in talent and flair. He seemed not to have the management skills, the business acumen required to run the family's sari shops which had been started by their father. It was their father who had named the shop Sari Palace and when the British seemed about to depart he opened a new one, Sari Mahal, just off Kumar Junction. He would have opened a third, for he always said he would open one shop for each of his sons, but he could never think of a suitable name for a third shop, and died without inspiration. Of course, there was little incentive to establish a third shop when he found Raman so devoid of interest in the sari business.

Laxman and Vaman, as the two eldest brothers, inherited one shop each. But what of Raman? Rather than split up the shops or bring him into the business out of duty towards their deceased father, it seemed easier just to allot him their father's lychee garden.

Although it had been devastated by a drought one year, the lychee garden on the hill still produced kilos of plump, juicy fruit with not inconsiderable market value. And there was a house in the grounds which Laxman and Vaman considered too small for traders like themselves, and too far from Kumar Bazaar, although it was only a ten-minute walk along the dirt road. The problem was, it was uphill all the way from Kumar Junction. You could not get a bicycle up it without dismounting.

'It is so far,' said Sudha-with-Pension when she looked over the property with a sharp eye, soon after her father-in-law's death. She preferred the large old house in prestigious Merchants' Colony. It was where all the Old Wealth of Mardpur resided, although Sudha maintained that was not the main reason for choosing it above the lychee garden. It was in the hub of things and near the municipal college, and she could ask some students to come there for home tuition, she said. How could she ask her students to trek up to the lychee garden?

'It is a beautiful garden,' commented Madhu, who also decided to survey the property to make sure it was not a better option than the house in town which their father had owned and was allocated to Vaman after his death. But she noticed that even the garden was beginning to look neglected.

It fell to Raman, whose wife, Kumud, had always known that someone who was only seventh standard pass could not expect too much from life. For her, it was good enough that she did not have to live in a household with a cantankerous mother-in-law and a hierarchy of wives in which a seventh standard pass would not figure in the upper echelons. She was pleased that, of all his father's properties, Raman was given the small bungalow in the middle of the lychee garden.

She had other reasons to be pleased at the way the father's legacy had been shared out. Laxman and Vaman sent her saris now and then to keep her sweet. True, it was sometimes damaged stock, but the damage was so slight who would notice? All but a tiny proportion of the six yards was hidden from view anyway. Laxman and Vaman knew that their generosity was a good investment. For, while Raman was lacking in spirit, a wife could sometimes be a dangerous power-seeker, seventh standard pass notwithstanding. Who knows what ambitions might lurk in her bosom with regard to the sari shops? What woman could possibly resist anything less than total ownership of yards and yards of the best Kanjeevaram silk, Rajasthani tie-and-dye, Japanese georgette, French chiffon, to say nothing of blouse-pieces of every hue and colour you can think of? The older brothers needn't have worried. Kumud had no wish and no reason to trade the lychee garden for a stake in the sari business.

Thus it seemed to the brothers Laxman and Vaman a fair deal: they got the sari business, which Raman had no interest in, and they housed Raman at the lychee garden where all the profits from the lychees went into his own pocket, give or take a few sackfuls that he distributed to relatives, including his brothers, as a matter of courtesy each summer.

The land and house were never actually signed over to Raman. Laxman, in whose name it was, insisted it was only because he had never got round to it. If Raman really wanted the title deed to the property, of course he was welcome to it. But Raman had never raised the issue. It was an arrangement that kept the family in harmony until the value of the land began to rocket, much much later.

But for now, the ochre-washed bungalow in the lychee garden was a pleasant enough home with verandahs all round, built on a raised concrete platform to keep out the water during the monsoon. The garden, with its few hundred lychee trees plus a row of sweet-smelling lime trees, was kept in shape by the gardener, Raju-*mali*. For the most part Raju whiled away the day smoking *bidis*, squatting on the concrete platform at the back of the bungalow. The rest of the time he slept. Sometimes he divided his time between sleeping and smoking. Raman had long since given up ordering him to prune trees or weed the grass. After all, the lychees, juicy and sweet, arrived every summer without fail, even if nothing was done in the garden. There was even some advantage in Raju's *bidi*-smoking. It kept away the mosquitoes. Mosquitoes were a big problem. It was one of the reasons no one else in the family coveted the bungalow, despite thinking what a delightful garden surrounded it.

Really, the hill and the mosquitoes were not so bad, thought Kumud, if they kept the rest of the family away. True, you needed mosquito nets and had to spray the rooms virtually every second day, but they were not a real plague. It suited Raman and Kumud to keep up the myth of mosquitoes in case the rest of the family realized what an idyllic life they led. Bharathi and Shanker, their younger children, played along.

'You know,' Shanker would tell his older sisters Meera and Mamta while visiting Laxman Uncle, 'I caught a mosquito so big it would not have fitted in my mouth.' He held his hands wide apart.

'How did you catch it?' they wanted to know.

'In a net,' he said. 'If you come to the lychee garden you can hunt mosquitoes with us.'

'I am not thinking that is a good idea,' said Sudha-with-Pension quickly. 'Meera and Mamta do not wish to be bitten by mosquitoes, it could leave scarring and that would raise dowry price.'

'You know, I had a mosquito bite *so-o* big my hand could not fit over it.' Shanker showed them a large scar from when he had fallen on an old iron bed and it had gone septic, leaving a large indentation in his leg. It was very satisfying to see Sudha look so horrified.

'Keep away from those big-big mosquitoes,' she warned Meera and Mamta. And it was rare that the twins visited their parents in their lychee garden.

9

ONCE THE SUBJECT OF MEERA AND MAMTA HAD BEEN TACKLED, LAXMAN expected Raman to find an excuse to leave. But Raman had something else on his mind. He brought it up in a way he thought a merchant would understand.

'Have you thought of starting another business?'

Laxman nearly dropped his tea. Outwardly he kept his face composed but inside he felt his stomach muscles tighten. This is it, he thought, my younger brother has come to stake a claim in the family business. The marriage of Meera and Mamta had just been an excuse.

'What kind of business? The sari business is going well,' stuttered Laxman, battling to maintain his composure. Then, lest Raman should think he was not getting any benefits from the successes of the sari business, he hastily added, 'Not fantastic, of course, we are getting some competition from Ghatpur. Six new sari centres have opened up there in the last year! But Mardpur people do not like to go to Ghatpur. Buses are frequent but crowded. We sell at a good price, so what is the need to change?'

'I was thinking, something like a book business,' said Raman airily.

'A book shop?' said Laxman, incredulous. Raman was not a bookish type.

'Well, book-writing.'

'A publishing house?'

'Yes,' said Raman, although it was not what he meant at all. 'It would not need much capital,' Raman added, knowing that this was what businessmen worried about most with any new venture.

Laxman's heart sank. So that was the crux of it. Raman wanted money.

'But what books will . . . er . . . be published?' Laxman himself had no interest whatsoever in literature, and he could not conceive of anyone in his immediate vicinity who might go so far as to buy books. Despite Sudha-with-Pension's pretensions to being highly cultured, even she could not be described as an avid reader. True, Sudha hobnobbed with various arty and literary types at the municipal college, poets and lyricists mostly. They met regularly for poetry readings, which to Laxman seemed just an excuse for a self-styled poet to utter a few lines about flowers or love and everyone else to shout *wah, wah!* whatever the quality of the couplet. Laxman had always regarded the 'literary' pursuits of such people as mere pastimes. He had no idea what they did with their writings once they had finished airing them at such meetings designed to do little more than bolster their egos.

'Well,' said Raman airily, 'I will have to practise first. I will practise by writing my own book.'

Laxman began to wonder if it had been a good idea after all to banish Raman to the lychee garden, where he had the peace and quiet to write away from the watchful eye and the interruptions of the rest of the family. Aloud he said somewhat distractedly, 'Yes that is a good idea. A very good idea.'

Raman felt elated. His brother had not once hinted that he, BA third class, was incapable of writing a book. Laxman had not doubted his ability for a moment. He had not tried to dissuade him. In fact, he even said it was a good idea. Not long after, since Laxman suddenly seemed unduly preoccupied and incapable of holding any kind of animated conversation on any subject that interested Raman, he left the Sari Palace in a light-hearted frame of mind.

Laxman, by contrast, felt weighed down by what he had heard, and even more so by what he suspected: Raman was beginning to have ambitions of a sort. Worse, they were ambitions that Laxman barely comprehended.

That evening, instead of mentioning his conversation with Raman regarding the twins, Laxman asked Sudha-with-Pension obliquely: 'Are there any book-writers at the municipal college?'

'We have very good writers,' said Sudha enthusiastically. 'Ustaad Malik and . . .'

'He is a poet, no? I am talking of novels.'

'Novels? Why write a novel?' said Sudha. She had echoed Laxman's sentiments exactly. After a little thought she added, 'But there is one.'

'Oh, who?' said Laxman.

'There is one Pundit Sitaram. Sometimes he is writing stories for *Ghatpur Weekly*. I have not read. But he is saying now he wants one day to write a novel.'

'What is his purpose in writing this novel?' Laxman wanted to know.

'Well, he has no other accomplishment,' sniffed Sudha, who still remembered how coarsely Pundit Sitaram sang as he vigorously pumped up the harmonium.

Laxman nodded, a faraway look in his eyes. This analysis could apply just as well to Raman, he thought.

10

IN THE SEARING, RELENTLESS HEAT OF THE AFTERNOON KUMUD HAD TAKEN
Shanker to the doctor to find out why one of his side teeth, which had
fallen out more than a year ago, still had not been replaced. Shanker had
protested, not wanting to walk in such heat. But Kumud brushed aside his
protests.

'You are right, in heat like this. Who will want to see the doctor? That
means we will not be waiting and waiting. Doctor's surgery has a cooler.
It is not so hot inside.'

Raman, too, thought it was extraordinarily energetic to brave the
afternoon heat for such a trivial cause.

'Does it matter if one tooth is missing?' he asked.

Kumud gave him such a withering glance he did not press her for a
response. Kumud instead requested him to supervise Bharathi's homework while she was out. Raman did not mind. It meant he could be at
home without appearing to be doing very little. Earlier, before it got too
hot to sit outside, he had been relaxing on the verandah contemplating
the garden when Kumud, busy as always, came upon him.

'If you have nothing to do and you like to admire the garden, why not
go after that Raju-*mali* to weed the flowers and do some of the work he is
hired to do?'

That was not Raman's idea of a restful afternoon. He did not like to harangue servants. He was pleased that Kumud could undertake her duties quietly, efficiently and uncomplainingly so that there was never any need to get a maid for day-to-day tasks. Not that he wanted Kumud to spend her time in drudgery, but, well, servants were such trouble, they were lazy and incompetent and answered back. He was not inclined to tell Raju what to do for the simple reason that he understood little about gardens.

Raju was kept on at the lychee garden because his father, Prithvi, had served Raman's father. Prithvi had been a lover of flowering plants, and under his loving care the lychee garden had bloomed with colour and scent, making it a most delightful place for afternoon tea on the verandah. Prithvi had carefully tended every herb and bower until it blossomed and flourished, no matter how late the monsoon, and turned the lychee garden into a hill-top idyll. When Prithvi died, Raju stayed. But Raju did not have his father's green hands, nor his father's appreciative master.

'Why not plant some colourful flowers,' Raman suggested less than forcefully. At least he could say truthfully to Kumud that he had not ignored her wishes.

'What flowers is sahib thinking of?' said Raju, looking unusually attentive for one so inclined to slumber.

'Oh, yellow and red and orange,' said Raman, remembering the riot of colour in his father's day.

'For yellow flowers can put marigolds, but red flowers – which are you wanting, sahib?'

'Phlox?' said Raman dubiously, racking his brain for the names of flowers. Only roses and marigolds came to mind easily.

'It is not the season for phlox,' said Raju.

Raman could not think of the names of any other flowers offhand.

'Marigolds I can grow,' said Raju helpfully. 'But we must wait for rain, for the earth is hard.'

Raman looked at the baked, iron-hard earth with the yellowing wisps of grass barely covering it, and decided Raju was right. Nothing could possibly grow in such heat without water. He said nothing and allowed Raju to slip out of sight, knowing the *mali* would soon be fast asleep under a tree and the garden would remain in the same state as it had been since they had moved there.

Raman called to his daughter as he came in from the verandah.

'Bharathi, stop this idling and get out your homework books *phut-a-phut*. Quickly!' He snapped his fingers to hurry her along.

'These are my homework books, Papa,' said Bharathi cheerfully, 'and I have almost finished.'

Raman was a little disappointed to be deprived of an opportunity to assert his authority. He often felt he was too soft on his children, and was well aware that it was Kumud who kept the discipline in the house. He looked over Bharathi's shoulder to make sure her work was neat: he knew they cared about that at the convent school. But he could not fault Bharathi's work on that count.

'Lot of homework today,' he commented, trying to find something of interest to say about her work.

'Less than usual,' said Bharathi helpfully.

'Oho? Why less?'

'Because Mrs D'Souza was away today. Her mother died.'

'Oh dear,' said Raman and clicked his tongue.

'Mrs D'Souza is the English teacher,' Bharathi volunteered.

'Good. Good.'

'She makes us write compositions. Long ones.'

'Why?' Raman remembered his own problematic attempts at writing English composition. He had nearly failed his BA because of it.

Bharathi shrugged. 'I don't know. Maybe it is practising for writing English books. Mrs D'Souza says English people invented the novel. Without the English novel we would still only be writing poetry.'

'We?'

'We in India.'

Was the English teacher denigrating the country? Raman wondered, half regretting that he had sent his daughter to the convent. But there was no better school. It was certainly a lot better than the government secondary school he himself had attended. His father had not lacked money but he was already grooming Laxman and Vaman to take over the business so they were sent to the private school run by the Arya Samaj. He had always said he would transfer Raman to the same school but never got round to it, realizing it might be a difficult task to secure admission for his youngest son, whose academic performance was never spectacular.

When Laxman adopted Meera and Mamta, he sent them both to the convent school, knowing that there was considerable demand in the marriage market for convent-educated girls. Raman decided to send Bharathi there too, though Kumud had complained of the cost.

'We are not running sari business like Laxman–Vaman, how is it you are wanting to spend on most expensive school in Mardpur?' Kumud said.

Raman could not let it seem as if Laxman could educate his elder daughters but he could not educate even one daughter at the convent, and eventually Kumud also came round to the idea. She knew the disadvantages of being a seventh standard pass. For one thing, the best husband you could get was a BA third class, even if BA third class had made a major stand to have her as his wife, and she wished for something better for her daughters.

In the event, Bharathi had no problem gaining admission. Laxman went to talk to the Mother Superior and arranged it all. This act had always impressed Raman. It stood out in his mind as being of far greater generosity than any other his brother had displayed towards him and his family. What impressed him most was that Laxman, in this regard, had no particular advantage over other parents. Mother Superior, or for that matter the other nuns, did not wear saris. Raman never could work out how Laxman had swung it.

At first Raman was a little suspicious of Bharathi's school friends. There was Chitra, whose father was the district collector, Mallika, whose father was a doctor, and Deepa, whose mother was a district judge somewhere out of town and had married twice. Raman had never heard of such a thing: a woman being the district judge *and* marrying twice. The boys at the government secondary school he had attended had all been children of small traders and he had felt quite comfortable with them.

Raman remembered the suspicion with which the boys at the government secondary school regarded Gulab Singh, the son of the local tax collector, who had been thrown out of the boys' Mission school St Paul's for failing his end-of-term exams twice in a row. All the boys feared Gulab Singh had been sent to the school to spy on bania businesses and report back to his father whether they had been paying tax. It was an unfair assumption, but they only realized that later when Gulab Singh set up Mardpur's first imported electrical goods store under the imposing name of Jetco. It was a large two-storey brick affair, right next to the Sari Mahal, packed full of standing fans, refrigerators, imported cameras and electric typewriters. Everyone knew that the only way he could acquire much of this merchandise was from the smuggling fraternity. And it was more than likely he did not declare any tax. It was one of the most successful businesses in Mardpur, particularly during the marriage season when people from the surrounding villages would come to top up their daughters' dowries. No other business in Mardpur was known to have such a wide-reaching clientele. Gulab Singh did not even have a BA, although he did have good English from his days before he was thrown out of St Paul's. And that was a great success because he could translate the instructions on many of the imported appliances. He called it 'after-sales service'. It appeared in small letters under *Jetco: best for electricals, best for after-sales service.* It was a popular slogan which had been put to music and run as a jingle by the commercial radio station so that no one could think of Jetco without humming *best for electricals* . . .

Bharathi clearly did not need Raman's supervision, so he settled down by the window with paper and fountain pen. He was determined to prove Satyanarayan wrong.

'Are you writing a book, Papa?' Bharathi enquired.

Raman was pleased. At least his own children did not think he was too uneducated.

'You are guessing correctly,' he said.

'It was Deepa's Amma who said,' replied Bharathi.

Raman looked puzzled.

'Jagdishpuri Amma, Papa,' explained Bharathi. 'You know, the one who sees *bhooths*? She can see anything. Inside your head. Deepa cannot hide anything from her. It is all found out. That is why I cannot tell her any secret. Because Amma will see it.'

'She can see inside?'

'Everything,' Bharathi assured him.

'Like the world inside Krishna's mouth?'

Bharathi considered this. She did not want to seem irreverent in front of her father. Then she laughed.

'No, Papa. Not like that. She is not seeing real things. But things that have not yet happened. It was she who said if you wrote down everything that was in your head you would be a great writer. Deepa told me. She heard her say it. Maybe it will come true.'

Raman had heard the stories about Amma. He remembered being fearful of her as a child. That was a long time ago, but even in adulthood he felt somewhat wary whenever she was mentioned. If ever the ghost of Deepa's father Dasji had returned, it would be residing at her house, and Raman had good reason to fear that ghost.

After Raman matriculated from the government secondary school where he had not excelled, Raman's father, known respectfully as Baoji, decided to marry off his youngest son and involve him directly in the sari business. But it did not take long for Baoji to discover that if he left his business in

Raman's hands there would soon not be much of a business left. At first he let Raman lounge about in idleness and gave him few responsibilities. Later on however, Raman's father thought his youngest son should at least be equipped for some other calling. Baoji decided to send Raman to college.

It was at the municipal college that Raman was taught by Dasji.

Raman was not a particularly good college student either. That same week six years ago when Dasji boarded that ill-fated *tonga*, Raman had played hookey despite the looming final exams. Raman was angry because Dasji had given him only ten out of a hundred for his English essay. Dasji had marked it up with red all over, and thrown the copy-book back at Raman in front of everyone.

'If you think you will be graduating with essays like these, think again! You will be lucky to get a third,' Dasji had said, impervious to the fact that he was speaking to a student much older than the others. In fact, Raman was already the father of twins. He felt he deserved more respect than the other students who were mere teenagers. Raman was filled with anger and resentment at this humiliation.

On the day of the *tonga* accident Raman had spent over an hour thinking up an excuse for having missed BA revision classes the entire previous week. That was the easy part. Raman did not know how he would explain the fact that he had got up in the dead of night to throw his English copy-book into a ditch on the outskirts of Mardpur, somewhere on the road to Vakilpur. It was an act of irrationality, of impulsiveness. He was surprised even at his own determination to carry out this act of defiance against authority.

The next day he tried to think of several explanations for what he had done, but then decided to say to Dasji: 'In the middle of the night I threw my copy-book into a ditch on the road to Vakilpur. If you want it you can get it, for I have no use for it.' What could he lose? He was going to fail his degree anyway.

In the event, he never saw Dasji again. He scraped a third because his father had been well known in Mardpur. The wives of the Municipal College Examining Board Committee bought their saris from the Sari Mahal and the Sari Palace with hefty discounts. And Raman had made quite a good case during his viva for being 'really cut up' about the death of his 'beloved teacher'. He had said there was no way he could concentrate on the English exam paper while thinking about Dasji and that poor baby, after all was he not a father himself?

★

Raman saw that Bharathi had finished her work and was watching him.

'Have you finished? Then you can help me with writing,' he suggested. He had no idea how to start to write a book.

Bharathi's eyes lit up. She brought her chair and came and sat beside him. Raman put his sheaf of papers in front of her.

'Write,' he said.

'What shall I write? With English composition, Mrs D'Souza gives us a subject,' explained Bharathi.

'No need for that,' said Raman. 'How to start a composition?' He pretended it was a test.

'In English composition you say "one day" or "once upon a time",' said Bharathi.

'Good. Good. Once upon a time. Write down.'

Bharathi painstakingly wrote, 'Once upon a time'. She admired the neatness of her handwriting. Raman admired it too.

She looked at her father expectantly.

'What must come next?' Raman tested her.

'You must have a name of a person. Maybe a prince or a princess.'

'Once upon a time there was a prince,' he dictated and Bharathi wrote this down carefully.

'Then?'

Both were lost for words.

'How is it in English novel?' asked Raman. He had never read one.

'The prince must have adventures. Maybe kill a dragon.'

'Dragon. What is this dragon?'

'Like a flying beast.'

'*Garuda*?'

'No, Papa. More like a demon.'

'What happens after he kills the dragon?' Raman wanted to know.

'Then he goes back home, marries a princess.'

This seemed wrong to Raman. After all Ram first married Sita and *then* had to save her after she was carried off by the demon king Ravana. But it was the English who had invented the novel and who was he to argue?

'Where does the dragon come from?' Raman asked.

'From the sky,' said Bharathi.

'From Lanka?'

Bharathi shook her head. 'I think it is the kingdom next to England.'

Raman knew the answer to that one; after all, he had got as far as his BA. 'That is Germany,' he said, triumphant.

They were both at a loss again. Raman knew nothing about dragons and next to nothing about Germany. In the ensuing silence they heard Kumud and Shanker arriving home.

'Maybe Shanker will know about Germany,' said Bharathi.

'What do you know about Germany? Tell,' Bharathi ordered her brother when he entered, barely giving him time to take off his shoes.

'I am hungry,' Shanker complained.

'I am getting food,' Kumud assured him, and disappeared into the kitchen.

'Germany,' Bharathi reminded her brother.

'Why Germany?' said Shanker, his voice taking on a whine. It was a common affectation with Shanker who since babyhood had attracted attention by complaining loudly.

'I am helping Papa write,' said Bharathi proudly. 'He needs to know about Germany.'

'They make Grundig radios in Germany,' said Shanker, getting interested for the first time. He knew many such facts.

Raman knew his wife and son had been window shopping at Jetco. Kumud often went to Jetco to look around the latest appliances, although she had never asked him to buy anything.

Shanker lowered his voice: 'They are all smuggled.'

'Shhh,' said Raman. 'It is not allowed to say that.'

'Everyone knows,' protested Shanker.

'What do they know?' said Bharathi.

'They go in boats into the harbour and pick up the smuggled things. Then they bring it back to caves for hiding.'

Raman was impressed with this tale. But Bharathi was not.

'Where is the harbour near Mardpur?' she demanded.

'It is secret, underground. With many *goondas* keeping watch. They wrap rags around big-big sticks to give them light underground. Then they wait for smugglers to come silently up the water.'

Bharathi and Raman listened to Shanker spinning a yarn about smugglers and *goondas* until dinner-time.

That evening Raman ate his chapattis in silence. He was thinking about Shanker's story. He would write a book about a smuggler, he thought.

11

DEEPA WAS TUGGING ON JHOTTA'S ROPE. 'COME JHOTTA, YOU WILL FRY IN this heat, and then what milk will you produce? Come to the courtyard where it is cooler. Push this beast, Bharathi.'

Bharathi pushed the buffalo from behind. Jhotta obliged, stomping through the house out to the courtyard, leaving behind wisps of dried grass from her feed that had become caught in her hooves.

In the early morning and evening, when Rampal came for milking, Jhotta passed away the time contentedly tethered to a post in the front yard: a small dirt patch surrounded by a high wall. There may once have been grass, and flowers even, but Jhotta had made the front yard her home, her stamping ground in the literal sense, tramping the dust into a hard, smooth surface.

There was no shade for several hours in the morning in the front yard. In the heat of the summer, when the sun rose fast, beating down unrelentingly before the morning was over, Jhotta was moved to the relative coolness of the inner courtyard. Every morning before school Deepa led her through the house. Jhotta knew very well where she was going. She nuzzled the door-curtain with her wet nose, pushing it upwards over her head so that she could pass through without ripping it, then she lumbered to her usual spot in the cool of the courtyard. There she stayed for an hour or two, languidly watching Amma at her morning tasks and Deepa getting ready for school until Pappu, the buffalo boy, came to take her to graze for the day, to roam and wallow in the choicest ditches and puddles of Mardpur and its outskirts.

Mardpur was not really growing as a town. That would only come later. To the west, beyond Kumar Bazaar, Aurobindo Hospital and the bus terminus formed the limits to the area. To the east beyond the Old Market, various 'extensions' of bungalows fanned out. But even the furthest bungalow was not more than a half-hour walk from the Old Market. Beyond that there was just empty grazing land. Westwards all the way to Ghatpur and Murgaon and southwards towards Vakilpur, it was a buffalo paradise.

Bharathi hid behind Jhotta's rump as the buffalo lumbered nonchalantly into the courtyard. Bharathi was just a little afraid of Amma, although this was not the first time she had come to play with Deepa at the weekend. With all the stories of ghosts, Bharathi always expected Amma to have changed dramatically since her last visit; to have become less human and more ghost-like. But the old woman relaxing on the *charpoy* was no different from any other grandmother, except perhaps she had an air of greater serenity about her.

'You have a friend, Deepa?' said Amma, hearing an extra pair of feet accompanying the familiar sound of Deepa and Jhotta.

'It is Bharathi,' Deepa informed her grandmother, and whispered to Bharathi, 'Go where she can feel you.'

Bharathi, overcome by shyness, had to be nudged again before she would move.

'Come here, girl,' Amma said, gently beckoning in Bharathi's direction. 'My sight is no longer good. But I can feel and smell, and I can see what others cannot.'

Bharathi left the protection of Jhotta's wide flank and approached Amma, still feeling self-conscious. Where would she look when she talked to Amma? It was the initial face-to-face that was the most difficult, not knowing whether to stare back at that vacant glance. Yet each time she was surprised to find Amma's face far from vacant, but animated and vigorous – a face that saw little but understood so much. Bharathi studied Amma's kind and wrinkled features and inhaled her homely pickle smell. She relaxed a little, feeling, after all, that outwardly there was nothing odd about her despite what everyone said.

To Bharathi, Amma exuded the wisdom of one who had been far

afield and the warmth and contentment of someone who had, after long years, arrived home to rest. She sat still on her *charpoy*, but she had an energy that other old people seemed to lack. She displayed none of the cantankerousness and bossiness of other grandmothers, and she had not lost her powers of observing detail even though she could no longer see.

Amma touched the back of Bharathi's hand, feeling the smooth skin of a child. Perhaps because she was away so much when her own daughter was young, she found the company of children pleasant, and she made the effort to make them feel comfortable in her presence.

'Bharathi? You must be the younger one of Raman. I can smell the sap of lychee trees on your skin. But so much dust? The earth must be dry in the lychee garden. Once there were so many flowers there but I smell no flowers on you. Are there none growing now?'

'No, Amma,' said Bharathi. She focused on Amma's lips. 'It is all dry. Raju-*mali* has not planted flowers for many years.'

'Soon there will be flowers. The flowers for your wedding will all come from the lychee garden. But first it will be your sisters who will be married. Tell me, is their marriage arranged yet?'

'Not yet, Amma.'

'It is not easy. But it will be easier when it is your turn. There will be money then.' She put out a hand and patted Bharathi's cheek. Bharathi stood still and let Amma feel her face. Amma's fingers felt surprisingly fleshy, not bony and dry. Once again, Bharathi caught the whiff of pickles.

After Amma had taken charge of the house in Jagdishpuri Extension it had become filled with the sweet smell of mustard oil. More than that, it was a sweet and spicy smell of mustard oil pickles, warm, homely and old – like Amma. It was a mysterious, exciting smell of forbidden fruit. Pickles were adult food. Not for small children. Deepa, when small, could only imagine what these pickles tasted like smeared on salted *parathas*. It is said mustard oil pickles are an acquired taste. But when Deepa was handed her first salt-*paratha* with a sliver of mango pickle from which ran a rivulet of golden, spiced mustard oil, she loved it. It was as if, after years of imbibing the smell, she had already acquired the taste.

Other smells surrounded Amma – the dry, musty smell of earthenware pots, row upon row of unglazed terracotta, large and small pots in which the pickles were stored. Some were empty, and the dry smell of earth was barely tinged with sweet mustard oil. Others, full to the brim with tangy lemon or mango pickle, completely overpowered the earthy smell. It was once said by Rampal, who came away from milking Jhotta every morning smelling of pickles himself, that Amma derived her 'inspiration' from the pickle smell. He said the aroma wafted through her nostrils to the top of her head.

Bharathi drew Deepa's attention to this theory.

'How can it be, that pickle smell going up through your Amma's nose to her brain? Can it be like soda after drinking it and the gas rises?'

'It is nothing like that,' laughed Deepa.

'How do you know?'

'Because,' Deepa teased, 'I can do it too.'

Bharathi looked excited. 'You imagine *bhooths* too?' Then she looked at Deepa's smiling face. 'You are lying. You want to scare me so that you can find out my secrets.'

'I know your secrets, you tell me everything.'

'Not *everything*!'

Deepa felt a little hurt. 'You said you were my best friend, and you are keeping secrets from me.' Deepa folded her arms and turned her back on Bharathi, until Bharathi cajoled Deepa with promises of undying friendship, and together they ran off to the tamarind trees to look for fallen tamarinds to crack open and chew on the sour-sweet pulp.

'What else can you see, Amma?' said Bharathi, sitting on the edge of the *charpoy*, ready to be entertained by Amma's stories. Sometimes if they were lucky and Amma was in the right mood Amma would tell them stories of her adventures in the courts of the kings. But Amma was not thinking of her own past, she was putting her mind to Bharathi's future.

Amma laughed and took hold of Bharathi's hand. 'You want to know?'

'Yes!'

'You will marry a good man, far better than anyone could believe now.'

Deepa and Bharathi exchanged glances, pleased at this prediction.

'Will he be kind?' asked Bharathi.

'Handsome and kind,' prophesied Amma.

'How many children will Bharathi have, Amma?' asked Deepa.

Bharathi giggled, pulling her hand from Amma's grasp to cover her friend's mouth. '*Dhut*, Deepa!' she scolded.

But now Amma was no longer holding Bharathi's hand and the vision of Bharathi the woman became weaker and faded.

'Is it not enough that your husband is handsome and kind?'

'It is more than enough,' breathed Bharathi.

★

Raman relished being at home by himself with no one to comment on how little he was doing. It seemed that however much one did, others always expected one to do more. While Bharathi was at Deepa's and Kumud had taken Shanker with her to the Old Market to buy vegetables Raman decided it was a good opportunity to write. He had crossed out *Once upon a time there was a prince*, written in Bharathi's neat hand, and wrote *Chapter One* instead. Then he sat staring out into the lychee garden for some minutes, conscious of the fattening fruit hanging from the trees. When next he consciously looked down at his paper, he had written two words, *Jagat Singh*, in a flourishing hand. The name had just popped into his head as he sat by the window. He looked at the two words with some satisfaction, spoke them aloud and rolled them around his tongue. Jagat Singh is a good name for a smuggler, he thought. And he must have an accomplice. What would be a good name for an accomplice? Raman toyed with a few names and then hit upon Kanshi. He wrote it down carefully, feeling very pleased with it. Raman sucked the tip of his fountain pen, thinking what kind of adventures Jagat Singh and Kanshi would get up to. But that would be for later. At least now he had his two main characters. Raman put away his paper and pen feeling he had achieved a lot in one day.

'How is your father keeping, Bharathi?' Amma asked.

'He is writing a book!' said Bharathi, barely able to disguise her excitement.

'So! That is unusual. Are there other writers in your family?'

'It is his own idea,' she said proudly.

'Do you know what is in this book?'

'It is about a prince,' said Bharathi eagerly. 'And a dragon.'

Amma shook her head. She began to get a strong sense of this book. 'It is not that book I am thinking of.'

'There is no other book,' insisted Bharathi.

'It is a book about smugglers,' said Amma, concentrating, for details were not always easy to see.

Bharathi fell silent. She was too respectful to contradict Amma. Amma sensed her confusion and took her hand again.

'Whatever it is, it will be a good book. It will make money so you can marry even better than your sisters. Jagat Singh is a good name for a smuggler,' said Amma. 'And there is a *goonda* in the book.'

'How can Papa know about smugglers and *goondas*?' said Bharathi, fascinated.

'Shanker says Jetco is full with smuggled goods,' Deepa pointed out.

'*Chup*, Deepa,' said Bharathi putting a finger to her lips. 'What does Shanker know? He is inventing only.'

'This book-writing is all imagination,' said Amma. 'I can see it already.'

'How do you see it, Amma?' asked Bharathi, curious. 'Is it like seeing the world inside Krishna's mouth?'

Amma laughed. 'Sometimes I am seeing a picture.'

'Like a film?'

'Not so. Like a dream.'

'Can you see inside me?' said Bharathi, drawing up and puffing out her chest as if calling on Amma to look inside her heart.

'Sometimes. I know for instance that you will marry well and stay in Mardpur.'

Bharathi looked wide-eyed. 'Then I can never have any secrets!'

'You can,' said Amma, 'for I will tell no one. See, I have many secrets myself and I am telling no one at all.'

'Like, where is the treasure?' asked Bharathi, emboldened.

'Aah, the treasure,' teased Amma. 'You see I *can* be trusted with a secret. That is my biggest secret. I am telling no one.'

'Not even Deepa?' said Bharathi, exchanging glances with her friend.

'Not even.'

'Your Amma is not so strange like people say,' Bharathi told Deepa a little later.

'They say she is strange?'

'They are saying there are *bhooths* and all, around her.'

'I have never seen a *bhooth* here,' laughed Deepa. 'It is only Usha who is talking of *bhooths*.'

'Even Papa believes there are *bhooths* here,' said Bharathi, 'otherwise how did Amma know about his book-writing?'

'Does your papa think the *bhooths* told Amma about it?' giggled Deepa, and Bharathi laughed too.

'So who is telling Amma about his book?' persisted Bharathi.

'She is seeing it herself,' said Deepa. 'Maybe she is feeling it through you.'

'Me? How can that be?'

'See how much she knew about the lychee garden just by smelling the dust on your hair,' said Deepa.

'A book is different. It is not written yet, it is in Papa's thoughts only.'

Deepa shook her head, as lost for an explanation as Bharathi was. 'I don't know how it is,' she said, 'but what Amma sees will be.'

12

USHA, THE SERVANT GIRL, MAY WELL HAVE BEEN RESPONSIBLE FOR THE rumours of Amma's ghosts. She really did believe in her *bhooths* like Amma believed in Ganesh and Deepa believed in the treasure. Usha's ghosts had never shown themselves but that wasn't because they did not exist. It was because they were waiting for the right time, she said. It did not mean they were not there.

Usha talked about ghosts as if they were around her all the time. Anyone listening to her would immediately imagine that the house in Jagdishpuri Extension was full of them. No wonder people were so wary.

Usha was about fifteen, with two wiry plaits tied neatly with crimson ribbons at the ends rather than one long thick plait down her back like the older girls. It made her seem much younger than she was. She was thin, but her face did not betray any hardship. Like others whose family did not have a trade she accepted poverty as her lot, and as long as she was fed she maintained that she was lucky.

The housework was something that kept her busy during the day; she saw it as neither arduous nor unpleasant. Amma did not nag her nor stand over her like some old women did with their servants. And she did not nitpick about small specks left on the utensils after they had been washed, although if she wanted to she could run her sensitive fingers over the dishes and feel every trace.

Every day Usha arrived just before midday, a spring in her step, with fresh vegetables from the Old Market. She scrubbed the few breakfast dishes, prepared the vegetables and dal, pounded the flour into dough with her lithe hands which displayed a surprising deftness and strength, and swiftly rolled out the chapattis, slapping them onto the griddle with panache. Deepa often watched her efficiently preparing the food, fanning the bucket-stove, or poking the coals alive with a stick. Usha, for the most part, pretended not to notice Deepa – the relationship was easier that way. But sometimes when she had finished all her work she told Deepa her stories. These were the times that Deepa eagerly waited for. She hovered over Usha in the hope of just such a moment when Usha would wipe her damp hands on her *kameez* and begin.

The stories always involved a woman called Baoli – a madwoman. Usha would imitate the madwoman, pulling on her hair till it stood in wisps, holding her head in her hands and stamping her feet as she sat on the floor moaning. There were other characters, mad ghosts, or *baoli booths*, and Jhotta.

'The *baoli bhooth* told Baoli, "Are you *baoli* or am I *baoli*?"' Usha narrated one afternoon when her work was finished and Amma was napping. 'Baoli said to the *baoli bhooth*, "I am more *baoli* than you." *Baoli bhooth* screamed, "Eeeeah! But how can that be? Because I am your *bhooth*, we are the same!" And Baoli said, "But you are only existing because I am *baoli*. So I am the most *baoli* one because only a *baoli* would see a *baoli bhooth*!"' And Usha would round off the tale by pulling at her hair and stamping her feet, singing a kind of refrain:

> *Baoli Maai, Baoli Maai,*
> *Kahan se aai?*
> *Koi jan na paai.*

(Madwoman, madwoman, where have you come from? No one could find out.)

One day Usha told Deepa more about Baoli and Jhotta, the buffalo which Baoli had received as a present from a relative.

'Baoli said, "What will I do with Jhotta?" Jhotta turned round and said, "You must keep me for a few years and milk me." So Baoli kept Jhotta for a few years and then she decided to milk her. But Jhotta was *baoli* and the milk just kept flowing and flowing and Baoli could not stop it. It was flowing out of the pots and the pails and all over the ground. And still it would not stop. Baoli went completely *baoli* because she could not stop it.

> *'Baoli Maai, Baoli Maai,*
> *Kahan se aai?*
> *Koi jan na paai.'*

'Then what happened?' Deepa asked when Usha had stopped stamping the floor.

Usha looked surprised, as if that were the end of the story. Then she thought for a moment and said, 'Then suddenly Jhotta took pity on Baoli and stopped producing milk. But because it was a *baoli* Jhotta it dried up altogether. And Baoli tried and tried but no milk came. She fed Jhotta the best food from her kitchen and even went hungry herself, but there was no milk. And that made Baoli mad.

> *'Baoli Maai, Baoli Maai,*
> *Kahan se aai?*
> *Koi jan na paai.'*

Usha's stories broke up the routine of the day: the morning churning of the buttermilk, the grinding of flour on the two flat stones, the washing and cooking. In some ways the stories were part of the routine.

It wasn't just the ghosts; the treasure permeated everything with a kind of mystique, and Usha wove it into her macabre stories. One story she repeated several times went like this:

'Once Baoli had some treasure: gold and rubies, necklaces and bracelets. She sold two gold bangles and bought a Jhotta. This Jhotta was too greedy and said, "Give me your treasure, Baoli, and I will give you better milk." But Baoli said, "I won't." So Jhotta refused to give her milk and swallowed up her treasure so that it lay in her stomach. Baoli had no milk and no treasure any more. She could not cut open Jhotta to get the treasure because then Jhotta would die and there would be no milk at all. So Baoli went *baoli* trying to think how to make Jhotta give her milk and how to get back her treasure.

'Baoli Maai, Baoli Maai,
Kahan se aai?
Koi jan na paai.'

'Our Jhotta is not like that,' said Deepa emphatically. 'She is kind and loving.'

'That is because she knows you have no treasure,' said Usha. But Deepa knew that Usha also believed in Amma's hidden treasure. It was like Usha's ghosts. It was there but would only become visible to the right person at the right time.

13

AS THE HEAT BECAME MORE INTENSE AND THE HUMIDITY ALSO BEGAN TO rise, Raman's brothers were less inclined to sit all day within the enclosed space of their sari shops with only one ceiling fan stirring the hot air and providing little relief.

Laxman and Vaman started the hunt for a match in earnest by paying a visit to a family in Murgaon – a landowning family, and the oldest brother, it was said, had twin sons now in their early twenties. They had made contact through Satyanarayan who knew the priest at the temple in the village near Murgaon.

'It is a good family my friend Swami Nityanand is recommending,' said Satyanarayan.

'How long has this Nityanand known the family?' said Raman.

'It is a long time since I saw Swamiji,' said Satyanarayan, airily, 'but he is knowing them since they were born.'

Since Satyanarayan was so respected by the brothers they decided it was worth looking into.

Laxman went to see Nityanand, a vague old man whose memory was not really up to it.

'Boys? Two?' Nityanand crackled in a thin, failing voice, forgetting the question as he went. Satyanarayan had said Nityanand had been his guru and his father's guru before him, which made Nityanand very old indeed. How Nityanand had communicated anything to Satyanarayan, Laxman really could not fathom. It was very difficult making sense of the man. After a little coaxing and a little memory-jogging Laxman did unearth a few more details although Nityanand kept contradicting himself and repeating, 'Boys? Girls? No, boys.'

He beckoned his *chela*, or disciple, a young boy of about ten with no expression at all on his face and an equally deadpan way of speaking. He had been fanning Nityanand with a piece of cardboard, which he put down carefully in order to speak, as if he only had enough energy for either one or the other activity.

'Boys, two?' cackled Nityanand.

'Two boys?' translated the *chela*. 'Twins?'

'Twins.' Nityanand nodded violently, so violently Laxman thought he would do an injury to his fragile frame.

'There are Aggarwal twins,' said the *chela*. 'Came for *mundan* hair-shaving ceremony last month.'

'No, no, no, no. Not babies. Big boys.' Nityanand castigated him with a sharp slap on his shin. The *chela* did not react at all, but dutifully came up with the names of several other families who had borne twin boys in the area. There seemed so many of them, thought Laxman in astonishment as he listened to the *chela* reel off the names. Twins were very rare in Mardpur. And, it seemed, so were twin boys in Murgaon until very recently, when there seemed to be a sudden rise in fertility. It must be the water, thought Laxman, reflecting on the phenomenon.

'For marriage,' explained Laxman to the *chela* patiently after yet another family was mentioned which had borne twin sons but only in recent years.

'Boys,' repeated Nityanand.

'There is a good family with twin boys in Murgaon,' translated the *chela*.

'What is the name?' said Laxman, pleased at the progress. He was now sweating profusely. He pulled out a large handkerchief and mopped his brow.

But Nityanand could not remember. He seemed quite perplexed at not being able to recall, as if he could not understand what had happened to his memory.

'What is the name?' prodded Laxman, mopping his head. 'You told Swami Satyanarayan, Swamiji.'

'Satyanarayan,' said Nityanand nodding happily. The name seemed to give him great pleasure.

'What did you tell Swami Satyanarayan, Swamiji?' said Laxman, speaking loudly in case the old Brahmin was deaf to boot.

There was more babble and the *chela* announced: 'He does not remember.'

'Writing,' babbled Nityanand.

'Wait,' said the *chela*, 'it is written down somewhere.'

'Writing. Letter. Good. Boy. Two.'

Even Laxman could understand that. He mopped his brow rapidly in preparation for what was to come. 'Where does he keep his letters?' he asked the *chela*, for Nityanand seemed to have been completely exhausted by his last sentence and stared unseeingly ahead.

The *chela* repeated the question to Nityanand, but got no coherent answer in response. They tried again without luck.

Laxman asked the boy: 'Do you know where he is keeping his letters?'

'Under the mat.'

'Under the mat?'

'The one he is sitting on.'

It was true, Nityanand was sitting on a mat. What should they do? They could not lift the man. Even the two of them together. Although he was unlikely to be heavy, it would be too disrespectful. And why disturb him?

'We will have to wait,' said the *chela*.

'All right,' said Laxman, although he did not know what they were waiting for. He was relaxed and looked around him as he patted his brow with his kerchief. The temple, with its slightly dilapidated air and grey *gopura*, was situated at a crossroads outside the village, and was therefore peaceful and undisturbed – the villagers had to make a special effort to go to it. At one time there had been a water pump nearby, and there had been a steady stream of women with their pots who would fill up at the pump and spend time chatting and praying at the temple. But the well was dry. The pin had rusted and the handle had disappeared. There was no reason to come out here.

Laxman sat and watched Nityanand meditating – or he may have been asleep. The *chela* began rolling cotton wool lamp wicks between his palms, looking up at Laxman from time to time to make sure he was still there. Laxman yawned. He was getting bored. After a while he felt his eyelids get heavy in the languid heat, and his head begin to nod. At that point the *chela* put aside the cotton wool and leant towards Nityanand, whispering something into his ear. Nityanand's eyes fluttered open and he nodded violently. The *chela* helped him up and led him very slowly towards the latrine, throwing a meaningful glance behind him at Laxman and the mat.

Laxman wiped his brow, slowly folded his kerchief and placed it in his pocket. Then he gingerly lifted the edge of the mat. There were a number of rolls of banknotes. Laxman dropped the corner quickly, feeling like a thief. It fell with a plop that blew a cloud of dust into Laxman's face. Laxman coughed and pulled out his damp kerchief to blow his nose. Then he lifted another corner, more slowly. There were two letters adorned with the grey and blue chevrons of the inland lettergram. Laxman looked around, unable to suppress the vague feeling of guilt at trespassing on another's ground. He wondered if he should wait for the *chela* to come back. But that could take a while. He carefully shuffled around the mat so that he could read the inscription on the envelopes by craning his neck. Yes, there was one from Satyanarayan. He picked it up and unfolded it.

> *Thanking you for informing me of the Murgaon family. I think I can find a match here with a very good family of sari traders. Twin daughters. Very beautiful although the father is not as devout as one would like . . .*

Laxman wondered whether Satyanarayan was referring to himself or Raman. It was true he did not consider himself very pious, but that did not give Satyanarayan leave to complain about him behind his back to another Brahmin. Laxman felt peeved; Satyanarayan had already prejudiced his mission even before he arrived. He tried to suppress his resentment and read on. Towards the end of the letter was a clear reference to the Murgaon family, and the address of their ancestral home. Laxman made a note of it. The last line read:

> *It matters little that you have not seen them for many years. A good family is always a good family. If you give me permission, I will convey the boys' details to the father of the twin daughters so that they can pursue a happy union.*

Laxman replaced the letter, letting the edge of the mat drop with a bang and another, smaller cloud of dust. His task accomplished, he was eager to go. Yet he felt he should wait for Nityanand, for the sake of courtesy and because he felt duty bound to guard the Pundit's mat against any marauders who may not be as scrupulous as he.

It was at least another half-hour before Nityanand returned on the arm of his *chela*. At that point, Laxman hurriedly took his leave and set off on the dusty road towards the village in search of some mode of transport that would get him home.

Laxman wrote to the head of the family and got an expansive reply, but one that did not reveal that much about the family itself.

'The only thing to do,' said Vaman scrutinizing the missive, 'is to go and see.'

This they did, armed with a bundle of saris to sweeten the negotiations. Not that they thought negotiations would be tough, but it was best to have a few advantages when one was not negotiating on one's home turf, said Laxman. Laxman had great faith in saris as a smoother of paths.

It went badly from the start. The house was not where the family said it was. Someone else now lived in the big stone courtyard house and they directed the brothers to the nearby farm. The farmhouse was little more than a paddock, although made of brick. But at least they found the person they were looking for, and his younger brother. And the two appeared to be expecting them.

'We went to the big house,' said Vaman pointedly.

'We have let it out,' said the older man abruptly, as if defying further questions. He was sour-looking with a thin face, and wore a yellowing *dhoti*. The younger man was the father of the twins, but the uncle did all the talking. Vaman felt suspicious. He did not know anyone who let out their ancestral home to live in a paddock. There was no sign of any women. Just this old man and his brother. The paddock seemed strangely uninhabited.

For Laxman and Vaman, the experts in sari prices and designs, it was more than just a matter of seeing other members of the family. The brothers were better at sizing up the women than other men. They looked at the jewellery, at the skin on the women's hands, the gloss of their hair, and most important, their saris, and drew conclusions about the family's well-being and lifestyle. But this time they were deprived of such vital clues and that put them on the defensive right away.

The boys' side took the initiative from the start, firing questions at the brothers who barely had time to answer one before another was hurled at them.

'What is the education of the girls' father?' asked the older man, picking the hard skin on his heels as he sat, one foot on his knee, chewing rapidly on some *paan*.

'I am MA,' said Laxman, 'and so is my brother,' he said indicating Vaman.

'You are uncles, are you not? I am asking about father.' The old man paused to spit a stream of red *paan* juice against the wall.

'BA,' said Laxman, wincing as the *paan* juice hit the wall. It was always Raman who let the family down.

'First class?'

'Not exactly.'

'Second?'

Laxman came clean. 'Third. But our father was already very ill. It was difficult to study.'

'And mother is only seventh standard pass?' said the older man.

'Girls are matriculating this year,' said Vaman, trying to steer the conversation in a better direction.

'Dowry will have to be good,' said the older man crustily.

'Lychee garden is available,' Vaman said in a moment of rashness. Vaman could be quite impulsive sometimes. Laxman raised his eyebrows at his brother. This might be problematic. They would have to rehouse Raman and his wife, and Barathi and Shanker, and where would they put them? Raman may want a slice of the sari business then. And Kumud would not be pleased at all. The division of the spoils after Father's death, which had been so amicably settled, could become dangerously unravelled.

'How many acres?' said the older man with little sign of interest, forcing Laxman back to the matter in hand.

'Ten,' said Laxman, his brow still furrowed.

'Twelve,' corrected Vaman quickly. After all, they were responsible for maintaining the dirt road as well.

'Dowry will have to be good,' repeated the older man. 'Half *lakh*, plus goods from Jetco and five hundred saris.'

Vaman's face dropped. Laxman tried to look as if he had not been dealt a punishing blow.

'Father is only BA third class and not in business. Only clerk,' said the older man adamantly after consulting a piece of paper. It was the letter Laxman had written with the family's details.

'He is owning land,' protested Vaman, although it was not strictly true. The lychee garden wasn't in Raman's name.

'Well, only three hundred saris then,' said the older man and spat another stream of *paan* juice into the corner. The eyes of Laxman and Vaman followed the stream as it slammed splat into the wall. Laxman felt quite depressed at the sight of the huge red stain.

'We would like to see the boys,' said Vaman firmly, noticing that Laxman was on the verge of sinking into a morose stupor. He tried to bring things back on track. 'Then we can discuss dowry.'

'Send us girls' horoscopes first,' said the man. He almost spat the words. In fact, as he said it, a small trickle of *paan* juice dripped from the side of his mouth.

'But we are sitting here,' said Vaman, getting impatient. 'We would like to have a glimpse of the boys while we are here. It is some way to come in this heat.'

The two men sensed Vaman's tension. They whispered together for a second. Then the older one said with an air of finality, 'Boys are out of town.'

Vaman was angry. Why had it been suggested they meet on this day when the boys were not even there? But he swallowed his anger: after all, they were only relatives of the girls, they were in no position to make demands. Laxman, perspiring with the heat, thought he felt faint. His mind wasn't on it any more. He would have liked a glass of water, but none was offered. Vaman had to take over. He asked about the exact qualifications of the boys.

'They are still studying,' said the older man dismissively.

'What is the plan after that?' persisted Vaman.

'Business or service,' came the vague reply.

The whole interview was like that. Vaman tried to ask questions, which the older brother was proficient at stonewalling. Laxman and Vaman came away knowing next to nothing about the twin sons except that they were devout and went to the temple often.

'Hah! So devout that Nityanand does not even remember them,' said Vaman as they clip-clopped home on the back of a swaying *tonga*.

'There must be many temples around here,' said Laxman.

'But that is the nearest, the one where Nityanand is residing. It is like our Vishnu Narayan temple in Mardpur, we go there because it is the nearest,' said Vaman.

'Half a *lakh*! Is that the price these days?' said Vaman as they approached the outskirts of Mardpur. For the last half-hour the brothers had been silent, reflecting on the astronomical figure.

'Two girls,' said Laxman, but he, too, was depressed.

'I do not think Meera and Mamta would be happy there,' said Vaman with conviction.

'Even the floor was not swept!' noted Laxman in distaste. But then he added, 'We must not be too choosy. After all, our girls are not princesses.'

'But these boys are not princes either.'

'We did not even get to see the boys!' said Laxman, his voice rising in indignation. 'We came so far and for what? Even saris we have brought back.' The bundle, carefully wrapped in several layers of newspaper, lay at their feet covered in a thin film of dust thrown up by the *tonga*.

'Why waste saris on people like that? But it is good we came,' said Vaman philosophically. 'Then we could really see what kind of people they are. At least we could see it early, before negotiations were advanced.'

'Still,' said Laxman, agreeing with Vaman but unable to rid himself of a sense of uneasiness that it would not be a simple task marrying the girls. 'We must not be too proud or too haughty. We have two girls to marry. And we must marry them.'

'Everyone marries in the end,' said Vaman. 'Sooner or later.'

'It should not be too late. They are not getting younger.'

'How can it be "too late"? We are only starting. Every father is going through the same thing, worrying about a match for his daughter. The only difference is for us there are two. So double worry. But then there are two of us to worry, too.'

'Three – Raman also,' said Laxman.

'Raman? Why should he be worried?'

'With such big-big dowry price, Raman will also have to contribute.'

Vaman considered this with some surprise, but did not allow it to distract him at that point. 'You know what I think, brother?'

'What?' said Laxman.

'I think there are no twin boys in Murgaon. Maybe only one. Maybe that is why they do not want us to see the boys.'

'You think one died?' said Laxman, his eyes open wide. 'But why pretend there are two?'

'Maybe there were never two. They are just trying to get double dowry out of us. Did you hear what he said? Half *lakh*!' Vaman laughed humourlessly at the memory.

'It is not possible,' said Laxman with conviction. 'It would be easily found out during wedding when only one boy is turning up.'

'They will use the same boy to marry both girls,' said Vaman, the arch conspiracy theorist. 'Who is to know?'

'You are inventing, only,' said Laxman. Still, Vaman's story was unsettling, and had put Laxman off the match completely. Yet it made him feel rather less depressed. He peered out of the *tonga* and recognized the first buildings of Mardpur.

Telling Raman was not easy, but impossible to avoid.

'How was it in Murgaon?' said Raman the following day. He dropped by the Sari Palace on his way to PTI. He did not want to get too involved in such things, but he did not want to appear unconcerned, either.

'Not so good,' said Vaman, businesslike and not wanting to go into too much detail. That would be too humiliating. 'Dowry demand is too high.'

'How much?'

'Half a *lakh*.'

'Half a *lakh*! You did not bargain with those thieves?'

'They were not in a mood to come down.'

'Well, that's it then,' said Raman. 'No more discussion, I am not giving my daughters to thieves. What kind of house they had? *Haveli*?'

'Not even,' said Vaman miserably.

'Father, uncle are educated?'

'They did not say.'

'I will not waste my time on such people,' Raman vowed.

'Raman, there are not so many families with twin boys,' warned Vaman.

'Why should it be twins? One older and one younger are good enough.'

'We will keep looking,' Vaman promised. 'We will do our best.' But even he looked worried. None of the brothers wanted a long, drawn-out hunt which exhausted them all even before the wedding preparations started.

Raman broke the news to Kumud.

'We are not interested in Murgaon family,' he said. 'Dowry price is too high, the thieves!'

'How much are they asking?'

'Half *lakh*.'

'Half *lakh*! *Baap ré*!' Kumud was stunned. She sat back fanning herself with the woven-leaves she used to spark the embers of her bucket-stove.

'Two girls,' said Raman, by way of explanation. He held up two fingers and wiggled them.

'Still!' Kumud was quite indignant. 'What do they know about dowry price? They are sitting in a village. And Meera and Mamta are not ugly or dark. There are no scars anywhere on their faces. And they are matriculating! These people are just inventing numbers and expecting us to be fools and accept. You are right, they are thieves!'

'Maybe they are just not interested,' said Raman, trying to soothe her while pleased that she agreed with his analysis, 'and price is set to make us refuse *phut-a-phut*, no beating of the bush.'

'Even if suitable family is asking half that, where will we get such money? I did not get so much jewellery from my *maa-baap*,' said Kumud, 'and your family were not asking.'

'No,' agreed Raman. 'We were quite decent.'

'What to do?' said Kumud wringing her hands. 'And education of Bharathi and Shanker also to pay for. It was your idea to put them in Mission school and convent. They are the most expensive schools in Mardpur!'

'Oho,' said Raman, exasperated that Kumud should turn a discussion about an extortionate demand for dowry into a general moan about overall finances. 'We are talking about dowry, it is not same budget as school fees.' He tried to make it sound as if there was some complex way of arranging the family finances that only the men of the family knew about. He had been quite used to listening to accountants come to his father to talk about the business finances, and they often pigeonholed things into different 'budgets'.

This did not silence Kumud. 'Money is money. From where will we get, and so quickly?'

Raman did not want to say. It had been easy to believe it was his brothers' responsibility to come up with the dowry money. That was before he realized how much money was involved in marrying daughters. He could not be beholden to his brothers for such large sums. He now had another reason to pursue his book-writing project. How else would he find some money towards the double dowry?

14

EVEN JHOTTA BEGAN TO LANGUISH IN THE HEAT. SHE HAD A FEVER. SHE seemed fine in the morning when Rampal came to milk her, although even he remarked on the expression in her eyes.

'That buffalo must be deciding to be ill,' Rampal said. 'Her eyes are not happy.'

By late afternoon, when even the hot breath of the midday breeze had subsided into an oppressive stillness, Jhotta was listless, too tired even to whisk the flies off her back with her tail. The air of bemused boredom had gone out of her eyes. Normally in the mornings she had an interest in her surroundings even if Deepa sometimes suspected it was limited to who was bringing her food and where it would be placed. For the rest of the time Jhotta chewed in contented abandonment, unbothered by the bustle of the world around her.

That afternoon she could not even be bothered to be bored. She lay down in the courtyard, resting her chin on the ground with little expression in her eyes. Her sides were hot and heaving, and she was panting.

'Be happy, Jhotta,' Deepa whispered. But there was no acknowledgement in those sad buffalo eyes. No toss of the head. No nod.

When Pappu the buffalo boy came by to take Jhotta grazing, Jhotta refused to move, even with Pappu pulling and Deepa pushing from behind. The buffalo boy thwacked Jhotta with his stick.

'Hup, hup!' he shouted. But Jhotta barely flinched at the attack. She turned her head away, resting it on the ground.

'Please move, Jhotta,' Deepa entreated.

Finally Pappu turned away in disgust. 'Sell her to the tannery, and let the *chamars* deal with her.' Deepa looked stricken and Pappu relented a little. 'Maybe she is having an off-day. Let her be. She will be missing her buffalo friends only. They will be enjoying.'

'You will miss enjoying the mud,' Deepa whispered into Jhotta's ear.

'No mud,' Pappu corrected her. 'It is all dry. For that she must wait for the rains. But I will take them to the river. That they like.'

Pappu wrapped his dusty turban-cloth around his head, ready to go, when Amma came out, leaning on her stick.

'Leave that Jhotta behind, she is going to be ill with Jhotta-fever. I can smell it in her perspiration. We will not use today's milk,' said Amma.

By late afternoon Amma's prophecy was fulfilled. Amma used some silky buffalo dung ash to rub on Jhotta's forehead with her bony fingers as Deepa looked on, watching carefully for any sign of relief in the buffalo's eyes. Jhotta let Amma massage her head, heaving and panting as before.

'What to do?' Deepa asked Amma.

Amma felt the concern in Deepa's voice and sought to console her. 'It is not serious, you will see, soon she will be better.'

'But I do not like to see her suffer,' said Deepa.

'You are right, why should she suffer?' said Amma, who did not like to hear Deepa so worried. 'There must be some medicine for Jhotta-fever. Rampal will know, he is seeing so many buffaloes for milking, he knows their problems and their illnesses. We must get Rampal.'

'Where is Rampal to be found?' said Deepa. Rampal moved around from house to house in the mornings and no one knew where he would be in the afternoons.

'Hari will know where is Rampal,' said Amma. Usha's brother Hari sometimes came with Rampal for milking. Amma clapped her hands as if summoning someone from afar, although it was only Deepa she was ordering. 'Run to the Old Market. Hari will be there. He can tell you what to do about Jhotta or find Rampal for us.' Then Amma put her arm around her granddaughter's shoulders. 'She is just a buffalo,' she consoled Deepa.

'My buffalo is precious to me,' said Deepa, and added as an afterthought, 'More precious than treasure, even.'

Amma squeezed Deepa's shoulder closer. She knew Jhotta would be long gone before Deepa found her treasure. Until then, Jhotta *was* more precious.

Hari, Usha's brother, had a chequered history. He had been taken in as a servant boy by Father Paul, a priest at St Paul's Mission School. Father Paul had insisted that Hari should have lessons every morning. So Hari attended the morning class of the Mission school, sitting at the back, ignored by the other boys who were the children of businessmen, merchants and teachers. He was not the only 'poor boy', but he stood out because he was quick in lessons, even though the teacher, knowing he was a servant boy, tried hard to ignore him. In the afternoons Hari ran errands for Father Paul, including hunting for firewood. Unlike everyone else in Mardpur who piled on the sweaters and put up with the cold winds that blew in from the Himalayas in the winter, Father Paul had a small grate in his house and liked a cosy fire.

What would have become of Hari was anyone's guess. Many believed Father Paul's aim was to convert Hari and take him into the priesthood, for he could not remain a servant all his life, not after receiving a Mission school education. But the speculation ceased rapidly, for Father Paul died suddenly of poisoning, sitting by his blazing fire in a padded armchair brought all the way from Goa in a truck. Hari was arrested briefly, suspected of the crime. But nothing could be proved and Hari was let go. He returned to the streets doing odd jobs because, with the burden of suspicion hanging over him, no one could quite trust him as a full-time servant boy in their house, only for outdoor errands. In the winter months, when Rampal had a problem with arthritis, he took Hari on his milk rounds.

Deepa slipped on her *chappals* and hurried to the Old Market where Usha's mother sold vegetables. Running part of the way, it took less than fifteen minutes. Pensive with the worry of Jhotta's illness, and keeping to the shadiest parts of the Old Market, Deepa barely noticed the airless heat. A dampness rose from the vegetables which the vendors sprinkled with water to keep them fresh. The vendors fanned themselves but were too hot to cry out their wares as Deepa padded by.

As the streets narrowed it became noticeably congested, the drapery and clothing stalls spilling out onto the street. Bicycle bells tinkled non-stop, and were supplemented by shouts of *Rasta do!* as no one reacted to bicycle bells any more. The odd cow or bull swung its way through, adding to the chaos. Deepa sought out the shortcuts, the narrowest gulleys, but several times she had to press herself against the wall to allow a cow to pass, sharp horns waving this way and that as it purposefully headed towards food.

A little further along, the streets became too narrow for two cycle-rickshaws to pass each other and the congestion eased; people were forced to dismount from their bicycles. The narrowest lanes converged onto an open square which was the vegetable market, its smells of fresh leaves and clean, damp earth from the root vegetables mingling with the odour of rotting produce abandoned at the end of the previous day. The Old Market, narrow as it was, was a great favourite with wandering cows for the scraps that could always be found.

As Deepa hurried through one of the narrow streets a group of ragged urchins attached themselves to her.

'Run, off!' she ordered. 'Go back to your ma!' But they persisted.

'For five *paise* I will find what you are looking for,' promised one small boy.

'Okay, then,' Deepa responded. 'I am looking for Usha and Hari.'

'Hey Usha!' They called into the air, cupping their hands to their mouths. 'Ohey Hari! O hey-O Usha-Hari-hey!'

'*Dhut!*' she scolded. But they followed her for a while, close on her heels, to the vegetable market with its itinerant sellers with just a basketful of goods, who stayed sometimes till late into the night until that one basketful had sold, little by little.

The vegetable sellers were mostly old women with their heavy scales and huge pentagonal five-kilo weights which they barely looked capable of lifting. In the early morning they were busy calling and bargaining. But now many of them had succumbed to the torpid afternoon heat and were dozing.

Deepa spotted Hari idling, with his hands in his pockets, kicking a large, curved triangle of watermelon rind into the open gutter. She was relieved and pleased that it had been so easy to find him. She ran up, causing him some surprise as she planted herself firmly in front of him.

'Do you know where is Rampal? Amma needs him urgently. Our Jhotta is ill.'

'Rampal?' said Hari, wrinkling his twelve-year-old brow. 'I don't know. He is living near Vakilpur in a village. After milking he goes back there.'

Deepa's heart sank. 'Jhotta will die!' she said desperately.

'What is wrong with Jhotta?'

'It is a Jhotta-fever. A panting-sweating fever,' said Deepa.

'You must put cold water on your Jhotta's head. With a cloth, like this.' And he held his hand flat against his forehead. 'This is how to cool fever.'

'I will do that,' said Deepa. She hesitated for a moment. She had come all this way and now she had to run back again in the heat with nothing but advice to put cold water on the buffalo's head. Then she saw Bharathi with her mother. Kumud sometimes chose this part of the day for her vegetable shopping because, she said, it was less crowded in the market and she did not like to be jostled in the morning hours; it ruined her mood for the rest of the day. But it was also because she knew that the vegetable sellers were less inclined to bargain energetically in the heat, and she could come away feeling satisfied at having paid much less than others for her groceries.

'Bharathi!' Deepa called, running up to her. Bharathi's eyes lit up at seeing her friend. But Deepa was not smiling, and said quickly, 'Our Jhotta is ill with fever. What to do? Rampal is not to be found.'

'Ask Swami Satyanarayan,' Kumud suggested. 'He knows many herbs. He will have a *dava* that will cure this Jhotta-fever. Bharathi, you can go with Deepa. I have vegetables to buy, still.'

Bharathi was relieved. She did not like trailing around the market in the hot weather.

Bharathi and Deepa hurried hand in hand through the vegetable market, out towards the spice bazaar, whose stalls were a riot of colour provided by the smooth heaps of red, yellow, brown and saffron spices. They pushed on towards the outer lanes of the Old Market with its dry goods stores crowded with sacks of rice and lentils, beans and sugar and tea leaves. Hawkish customers would run their hands through the grains, detecting the quality in the short time it took a handful of rice to run through their fingers. They would pinch up a small amount, holding it just below their noses to sniff the aroma. Then, and only then, they would begin the loud haggling over the price.

The two girls left behind the smells and noises of the bazaar and made their way towards the dusty triangle of Kumar Junction where traffic had virtually come to a halt for the afternoon nap. At the temple,

Satyanarayan, too, was dozing, his head a little to one side, leaning on the banyan tree. Otherwise, his body kept a perfect lotus posture. Deepa and Bharathi did not want to awaken him so they played for a while in the temple garden, keeping a respectful distance until they saw him stir.

'You must bring the beast to me,' said Satyanarayan, who was not really interested in treating a buffalo. 'I have a remedy.'
　'Will it work?' said Deepa.
　'Is Jhotta not a buffalo?'
　'Yes,' said Deepa.
　'And does she not have a fever?'
　'Yes,' said Deepa.
　'Then my *dava* will work because it is a special *dava* to cure a buffalo fever. You must bring her here, that's all.'
　'How can we do that?' said Bharathi turning to Deepa. 'You said she will not walk.'
　'You must help me,' Deepa told her with resolve.
　'You want to bring that Jhotta-with-fever all the way here through the bazaar and all that? What if she refuses to come? We cannot carry her,' said Bharathi doubtfully.
　Satyanarayan was unhelpful. 'If the beast does not come here, so close to God, then she deserves to suffer fever.'
　'We will bring her,' Deepa assured him, worried that he might change his mind and refuse to treat such a recalcitrant beast.
　Bharathi and Deepa walked slowly back to Jagdishpuri Extension as the searing sun began to relent a little. Remembering what Hari had said, Deepa took a big cloth and a bucket. Jhotta looked a little interested in the bucket, so Deepa allowed her to drink some water. Then she dipped the cloth in the bucket and slopped it onto Jhotta's forehead. The sick buffalo seemed to like this. Deepa ran in to fetch another cloth and Bharathi and Deepa sponged Jhotta down all over.
　All the time Deepa told Jhotta soothingly: 'You must come with us to see Satyanarayan. He has all kinds of herbs. Good *davas*, they will make you feel better.'
　After a while Deepa coaxed Jhotta to her feet.
　'See!' Deepa signalled triumphantly to Bharathi. Jhotta took a few steps. Deepa patted her to encourage her.
　'Good Jhotta. Just a few more steps.'
　Bharathi helped by pushing from behind.

'We are taking Jhotta to see Satyanarayan,' Deepa called to Amma.

'It is a long way,' said Amma. 'And I think she will be fine.' Amma listened to the water being sponged onto the buffalo's head and Deepa's soothing words whispered into Jhotta's flapping ears.

'Satyanarayan has agreed to give her a Jhotta *dava*,' said Deepa.

'Well, it can do no harm,' said Amma. 'Take her, if she will go.'

It took a long time to get back to the temple with the buffalo. Jhotta kept stopping, and she did not like the crowded Old Market. The people had begun to emerge again after their siesta and Deepa, Bharathi and Jhotta were pushed and jostled. But they were in no hurry.

Deepa said to Bharathi, 'If Jhotta will not go, we will sit and wait till she is ready.' As she had guessed, when Jhotta saw the two friends sitting down she was eager to go on. Just like old Jhotta, Deepa thought. And she said to Bharathi, 'Maybe she is not so ill after all.'

Bharathi peered at the buffalo. 'Maybe she will like the *aarti*.'

'Come, Jhotta,' said Deepa giggling, 'you must do *puja*!'

Jhotta seemed to sense that the girls were more light-hearted. She trotted along, blowing at their hair as she went.

15

PROGRESS THROUGH THE OLD MARKET, WITH ITS TANGY–FRESH SMELL OF oranges and limes, mustard greens and radishes, the earthy smells of spices freshly ground, and the aroma of basmati rice and tea leaves, was slow. Nonetheless Deepa, Bharathi and Jhotta arrived at the Vishnu Narayan temple well before *aarti*-time.

'Here she is, our Jhotta,' Deepa said to Satyanarayan.

'Jhotta-with-fever,' Bharathi reminded Satyanarayan when he stared at the buffalo with a look of distaste.

'This buffalo is not allowed into holy temple,' he intoned. 'It is only cow that is sacred. And monkey. Sometimes elephant. But not buffalo.'

'We are not intending to allow Jhotta inside,' Deepa hastened to explain. 'But she is sick and only your *dava* can cure.'

Satyanarayan looked more closely at this earnest, soft-spoken child, and remembered her as the daughter of Dasji who had died so tragically. More importantly, she was the granddaughter of the great sage astrologer, a Brahmin whom even Satyanarayan could not match in wisdom. These considerations led him to take pity on this child who was putting all her faith in him.

He turned to the feverish beast and peered into her eyes, but the buffalo refused to stare back. Then Satyanarayan busied himself with a cure. He lit some incense and prepared some offerings, all the time murmuring incantations in Sanskrit. Coconut, bananas and oranges were offered to the gods, then he dipped some herbs into the flame of a butter-lamp and offered them to Jhotta. Jhotta turned away.

'Oh stupid beast! Can you not even recognize a hand that is helping?' said Satyanarayan, irritated at this rejection. 'What were you? A donkey in your last life? I do not treat donkeys.'

'Maybe she is frightened,' ventured Deepa.

'Of what is she frightened? O donkey, look at me. Am I holding a stick? Am I wielding a whip? Of what is there to be frightened? Can you not tell the difference between one who is harming and one who is helping? Look carefully and learn, for if you know that difference you will also know the difference between gods and demons.' With that catechism Satyanarayan waved the herbs afresh. Jhotta shied away again.

'You must eat the *dava*,' Deepa cajoled softly. 'Let me try,' she suggested, and held out the burnt herbs towards Jhotta. Jhotta nuzzled them.

'Progress,' Deepa whispered to Bharathi, who nodded.

Satyanarayan opened his *Gita* and began to recite from it, swaying back and forth as he sat. The girls listened attentively, keeping a close eye on Jhotta for any signs of improvement. Jhotta seemed happy to listen to Satyanarayan's sing-song, while being stroked and patted encouragingly by Deepa and Bharathi. The incantation was soothing for the girls as well, after running back and forth from Jagdishpuri Extension during the hot afternoon hours. Deepa began to feel quite hopeful when Jhotta sniffed at the herbs. There could be a breakthrough any moment.

Then came an interruption.

'I say! What is this mumbo-jumbo?'

'Papa!' said Bharathi.

It was indeed Raman. But it was not he who had spoken, it was Vaman, who was with him. Vaman was not one for religious ritual.

'Mumbo-jumbo? Mumbo-jumbo-shumbo!' spluttered Satyanarayan in mid-couplet. 'You are disturbing very important healing ritual straight from the Vedas. Have you no respect for our ancient scriptures?'

'Are you saying Vedas are full of buffalo rituals? I am not familiar with this Jhotta-*puja*,' mocked Vaman. 'Nothing is sacred these days. The poor beast: even she must be purified and anointed at the temple or her milk will not be fit to drink!'

'Quiet!' Satyanarayan said sternly. 'Treatment of buffalo is in progress.'

'Jhotta has fever,' Bharathi explained to her father and uncle.

'Aha,' Vaman said. 'Exorcism, eh? Why is it tradition always means going backwards into the dark ages, never forwards into enlightenment, eh, Swami? Were these not your own words once?'

'Ayurveda is a very ancient science,' Satyanarayan said testily. 'There is no reason why living beasts cannot benefit from knowledge that goes back centuries. These herbs were picked from the Himalayas by a very great sage, whose knowledge of Ayurveda is unsurpassed in this day and age.'

'No doubt, no doubt,' said Vaman, 'but the poor buff is suffering. Look at her eyes. Anyone can see it is a sick beast. What she needs, simply, is a vet.'

Satyanarayan snorted. 'Vet? What is this vet? Where is there a vet to be found in Mardpur? Can you show me one? We do not have even enough doctors for our growing population and we are to start worrying about vets?' He had burnt some more herbs and Jhotta, having savoured them once from Deepa's trusted hand, found them to be quite edible and was now devouring them with relish.

During this exchange Raman looked very uncomfortable. To him, Vaman's tone was too disrespectful. Why did his brother take it upon himself to pour scorn on the learned man? Vaman was not so scholarly himself that he could pronounce on the scholarship of others, much less mock it. Raman felt like speaking out in Satyanarayan's defence, but nothing appropriate came to mind.

Satyanarayan decided to ignore the two men, and became absorbed in the buffalo ritual. He addressed Deepa in a stern voice, as if to reassert his authority: 'Girl! How did this beast get into this state?'

'She seemed all right in the morning but then by ten o'clock . . .'

'I did not say when, I said how. How, how, how?'

'I do not know how buffaloes get fever,' Deepa said, perplexed.

Satyanarayan fixed her with a penetrating stare. He was curious to know how the descendants of the great sage astrologer were being educated.

'What standard pass are you?'

'Seventh,' said Deepa, a little shy of talking about herself.

'Which school is that?'

'Convent school.'

'Aha,' said Satyanarayan, 'and you do not learn about buffalo fevers?'

'No,' said Deepa, wondering why Vaman Uncle was laughing so.

Satyanarayan was also distracted by Vaman's guffaws. He rapped his platform a few times with his brass pestle, which he had used earlier to mix and crush the medicinal herbs.

'Imagine! We send our girls to the convent school to learn about buffalo fevers!' said Vaman holding his sides as he laughed. 'Raman, just think, whoever your Meera–Mamta marry, at least they will be satisfied the girls know all about buffalo fevers. They will reduce dowry demand in return for such valuable knowledge, heh!'

Raman pretended to blow his nose so that he was not forced to respond. Meanwhile Satyanarayan decided to take matters in hand.

'Quiet!' he barked. 'Would you carry on this way in doctor's surgery? In emergency department of hospital?'

They dutifully fell silent. Jhotta by then was chomping happily on any herbs held out to her, and appeared less listless than before.

'At least the beast likes the grass, so perhaps no harm is done,' said Vaman in a conciliatory tone. Satyanarayan shot him a withering look for having spoken at all, and returned to the *Gita*, reciting the couplets in a soft drone that even Vaman found soothing.

Just before *aarti*-time, in the red of the dusk, Satyanarayan declared Jhotta cured and began to prepare for the evening prayer. Deepa, while pleased the buffalo had pulled through, worried about getting Jhotta home in the dark.

'Don't worry,' said Bharathi after consulting her father, 'Papa will help you take Jhotta after *aarti* is over.'

It was decided that Bharathi's father would take Deepa and Jhotta back to Jagdishpuri Extension while Vaman Uncle took Bharathi home. Satyanarayan lit the butter-lamps for the *aarti*, and Deepa watched the yellow flames, straight and unflickering as the sun disappeared, leaving the heat and stillness behind. The voices of men and children singing the *aarti* in unison heralded the velvety night.

Calmed by the evening prayer, Deepa and Raman set off for Amma's house. The journey did not seem so arduous without the sun beating down, and Jhotta seemed happy to cooperate. Once, as they passed a small patch of green, Jhotta wanted to graze but Raman would not let her.

'Hup, hup!' Raman shouted. 'It's home we are going. Not eating time.' He smacked Jhotta's rump to egg her on. Only at the Old Market did he allow Jhotta to snuffle through some discarded watermelon rinds and brown, over-ripe bananas, sensing that Deepa was tiring and needed to slow down. He did not allow Jhotta to stray, however.

'Come buffalo, if you do not hurry your Deepa will be hungry for her dinner. What time is your dinner?' he asked Deepa.

'Seven o'clock,' said Deepa. 'But I am not hungry. I must be home to help Amma because Usha is going home at dusk. Amma's sight is not good.'

'Some are saying Amma has a special sight,' said Raman, feeling safe about broaching such subjects in the darkness that enveloped them. He was a little wary of going to Amma's house, as if the ghost of Dasji was hovering there, accusing: 'You are not even deserving BA third class, you are BA fail.'

'She can tell you about the story you are writing,' Deepa said simply.

Raman became alert at the mention of his book. 'The whole story she knows already?'

'She is only seeing a little bit at a time.'

'Few chapters?'

'Maybe few pages only.'

Raman decided to let the subject drop for the time being, although his curiosity was well aroused at this apparent ability of the old woman to see his book. That she knew he was even writing one was surprising enough. Yet he knew children had flights of fantasy. More likely, he thought, Amma had some kind of potion – herbs, like Satyanarayan used, to inspire her to spin a yarn. Satyanarayan had always impressed on Raman that there were herbs for everything. Herbs for memory, herbs for imagination, herbs for improving eyesight. It might be useful to find out what it was that Amma was eating. Several times when he had sat down and tried to write he had found it did not come too easily. It must be the heat, he thought by way of excuse. But now he felt he needed something to overcome that lethargy and inertia. A herb to give inspiration would be ideal. Still, thinking about Amma's herbal potion, it was not clear to him why she referred to her herbal-inspired tale as Raman's story when she spoke to Deepa and Bharathi about it.

When Jhotta saw that they were nearing Jagdishpuri Extension, she broke into a brisk trot. Deepa and Raman were almost running behind her.

'Hup!' called Raman. 'Not so fast!'

'I think she is hungry,' said Deepa. 'All day she has not eaten. Only Satyanarayan Swami's *dava*.'

Sure enough, Jhotta trotted into the front yard and straight to her trough, where she stood munching happily as Raman tethered her to her post.

'Amma!' Deepa called, stirring Jhotta's feed so that the choicest bits, the sugarcane tops, were at hand as Jhotta snuffled through the feed. 'I am back with Jhotta! Oh, and Bharathi's father is also here.'

'I know!' Amma called back from the courtyard. 'Come inside. Food is ready.'

Deepa exchanged a significant glance with Raman. 'You see,' she said quietly, 'she knows many things before they are happening.'

16

'WELCOME. COME INSIDE,' SAID AMMA.

'I must go home,' said Raman, politely bashful. 'She will be waiting.' He did not like to say the name of his wife in front of an outsider.

'I insist, you must eat with us. It is not often I have a visitor.'

'I have eaten already,' he said, rubbing his empty stomach.

'Just a little raita.' Amma held up her bunched-up fingers and indicated towards her mouth. 'Come. Everything is ready.' She turned to go into the house.

'I will not stay very long,' said Raman in feeble protest, following her into the courtyard. It was lit by hurricane-lamps, set in the corners of the courtyard so that the insects that hovered about them would not disturb the meal. It had a slightly eerie feel: the white light coming from the corners, throwing strange shadows across the courtyard.

'Come, come,' beckoned Amma. Sensing Raman's hesitation she laughingly said, 'There are no ghosts here!'

Raman laughed nervously. 'Of course I am not a ghost-believer. I am going often to the temple.' But he looked around for unusual shapes or apparitions and was startled by a large moth that fluttered into his face.

'Deepa, lay out the *thalis*,' said Amma, waving away the moth as it left Raman and flapped around her head, becoming caught in her grey hair.

'Stay still, Amma,' said Deepa peering at Amma's hair and disentangling the moth. She held it by the wings for a second before she let it flit off towards the hurricane-lamp.

Deepa laid out the meal on two facing *charpoys*. Usually Amma sat on the one with the tighter weave. Deepa laid Raman's *thali* on that one, as guest of honour, and helped Amma onto the one with the looser strings. Amma sat with one leg under her and the other hanging down, leaning on her cane and fanning herself with a reed fan. It gave her a stately air. Raman sat opposite, stiff and formal, still wary of ghosts, although Amma's small talk distracted him from thinking too hard about this. He looked behind him from time to time but felt strangely reassured by Amma's presence. She came across as completely worldly; warm and motherly, even.

While they spoke about the heat and Jhotta's fever, Deepa hurried to the kitchen where the vegetables had been placed on the warm embers which had been left glowing by Usha. Deepa stoked up the stove and lifted the lid of one pot and inhaled the aroma of potatoes and spices, realizing how hungry she was. Carefully she doled out the vegetables and the rice and laid out the chapattis on each *thali*.

When Raman breathed in the nutty flavour of *thoor* dal being heated up, hot and sizzling with cumin seeds fried in ghee and flavoured with chilli, he felt his tummy rumble. Ghosts would never appear in such a warm and enticing homely atmosphere, he thought, heartened. Amma looked towards Raman as his stomach gurgled and she smiled a half-smile. Raman knew that the blind often had heightened senses; had she heard his insides? Perhaps she had heard them even before he had got to Jagdishpuri Extension, he thought, and grinned inwardly at his own joke. He would find some way of telling this joke to Kumud if she wondered where he had been at meal-time.

Deepa brought a towel and a goblet of water.

'Begin,' Amma urged, hearing the splash of water as Raman rinsed his hands. Raman needed no further bidding: he had barely dried his hands before tackling the delicious fare before him with such attention that any thought of ghosts was driven right out of his head.

Deepa settled on a small plank and ate ravenously, keeping one eye on the adults in case they needed more of anything.

'We are late,' apologized Raman. 'That buffalo was in no hurry.'

'Yes,' said Amma, 'in the Old Market you went slowly.'

Raman's eyes opened wide. The old woman's powers were indeed unique.

'I can smell the ripe bananas and also watermelons,' explained Amma. 'It must be from the Old Market.'

'I did not let her stay too long in the Old Market,' said Raman apologetically. 'It was already late before we started.'

'You stayed for *aarti*,' said Amma. It was a statement, not a question. She could smell the incense and the soot of Satyanarayan's butter-lamps mingled with the subtle fragrance of dry basmati rice, coconuts and jasmine flowers. She could also smell the more bitter scent of Satyanarayan's herbs underneath all the *aarti* scents and knew Satyanarayan's healing ritual had been completed well before the evening prayer.

'One should always take God's blessing,' said Raman, aware that old people liked to hear such things.

They ate in silence for a few minutes. Deepa jumped up to serve Raman more.

'You are very lucky to have such a granddaughter,' Raman said appreciatively.

'You are very modern, Raman,' replied Amma. 'Usually grandmothers only receive compliments for sons and grandsons. Daughters and granddaughters are seen only as a burden.'

Raman affected a laugh. 'Well, I am lucky enough to have three daughters.'

'And you have a son also!' said Amma. 'I had no sons and I still consider myself lucky. Even one son-in-law, God bless him, did not survive on this earth. But the future will be for our daughters, that is why we must educate them!'

Raman considered this dubious logic, but did not want to seem backward. 'Oh yes, I agree,' he said enthusiastically. 'All three of my girls are going to the convent school. It is essential for securing a good match.'

'Marriages are made in heaven,' said Amma. 'What will be will be, but education for girls is essential for understanding the world. Things are developing so fast around us.'

'Ah yes, Ammaji, but traditions are important too,' said Raman, trying to steer the conversation back to his line of thinking. He was willing to agree with Amma out of politeness, but not if she carried things too far.

'Of course. But traditions will not go away. They are there. It is the future we must prepare our children for,' said Amma.

Raman did not want to appear disrespectful by contradicting Amma.

He nodded his head, forgetting she would not be able to see his assent, and concentrated on eating.

'So!' said Amma when she was finished. She had a small appetite and Deepa did not serve her a large meal. 'It is a long time since I saw you last, Ramanji, and not just because of my eyes,' she smiled. 'How is the sari business these days?'

'So-so,' replied Raman, his mouth still full. 'This raita is superb, Ammaji.' He held the bowl close to his chin and ladled raita into his mouth by the spoonful. Deepa jumped up to refill his bowl. He held it out eagerly, only putting his hand over it to indicate enough when it was almost overflowing.

'It is our own Jhotta's milk,' explained Amma. 'But this is yesterday's yoghurt, before she was ill. I was thinking to keep it for cooking *karhi*, but when I knew you were coming I decided to make raita. It was Usha who made it while you were out with Jhotta.'

'Excellent, excellent,' said Raman, rolling his head for emphasis. Amma was not smiling but he thought her joke an excellent one: she had been expecting him since the day-time! He felt flattered.

'That Jhotta is truly a precious beast. I hope she is better soon so that you can make more raita like this. My wife gets her curds from that sly fox Kalonji. It is not so good. He is always mixing it with water and thinks we do not notice. I tell my wife, do not let yourself be cheated so often. But she says we have always been going to Kalonji and where are we to find another milk vendor these days? They are all cheating.'

Amma laughed. 'Well, Raman, since you like raita so much you can always get it from me. Rampal comes to milk Jhotta every day and her yoghurt is the freshest you will find.'

'You are too kind, Ammaji. I would not take such a liberty.'

'No, no, please. We have too much milk for just me and Deepa. We give it away to the servant girl for her family and others. In our family, because of Jhotta, there are always *rasgollas* and sweetmeats being made, that buffalo gives so much milk. Please come and get raita from me whenever you wish, it will give you inspiration.'

This last point was not lost on Raman. So that was the secret: the inspiration-giving potion that allowed Amma to tell Raman's story as if it were her own. Raman felt a surge of excitement in his breast but kept outwardly calm.

'You are too generous, Ammaji!'

'Not at all. Now, tell me, what is being done about the marriage of your eldest daughters? You are looking, are you not?' Amma settled back, relaxed and enjoying having someone to talk to.

'Do you have some family in mind, Ammaji?' Raman was formal again. He knew elderly people liked to be consulted on such matters; after all, they had little else to do.

'Well, I don't know them myself personally. But maybe you should make a trip to Ghatpur. There is a family there by name of Ramanujan. They are also in sari business. Twin sons. Good family.'

'I appreciate your interest,' said Raman. He thought his brothers must surely know of any family in the sari business in a town as close as Ghatpur, particularly if they had twin sons. Amma must be mistaken, he thought. After all, she does not shift from her string bed day in day out and it must be eons since she went out of town, even to Ghatpur.

'I do not get chance to travel even so close as to Ghatpur,' said Amma as if reading his mind, 'but news travels further than feet. And I am hearing of such a family in Ghatpur from a few sources.'

'I will make enquiries,' promised Raman.

'These things can take a little time to negotiate. Especially with two.'

'Even with one girl, Ammaji,' Raman agreed. 'Dowry is becoming a very complicated business.'

'Dowry was not such a big issue in my time,' said Amma. 'But now everyone is becoming too greedy. They are not looking at the girl any more, only the dowry. They are not caring for the value of education these days.' Her hand found its way to Deepa's head and she stroked her granddaughter's hair lovingly.

'That exactly is the problem, Ammaji,' said Raman seriously. 'Boys' side wants convent-educated *and* dowry on top. It is sheer greed. Perhaps you are right, I should think quickly about Meera and Mamta before this dowry business gets completely out of hand! And then I must still think of Bharathi's marriage after that.' He seemed concerned and ate his second helping of raita in silence thereafter. When he finished, he sat back on the *charpoy* holding his belly and burping with satisfaction. Deepa jumped up and picked up his *thali*, which he had polished clean.

'Bring some *rasgollas*, Deepa,' Amma said.

'No, please. I am full,' said Raman rubbing his stomach. 'It was too good.'

'Just one small one. You can tell me how it is. I assure you, you will be delighted with *rasgollas* from Jhotta's milk.'

Raman allowed himself to be persuaded. As Deepa handed him the bowl with syrup and spongy, creamy *rasgollas* made by Usha under Amma's expert direction, Amma continued on the subject of Raman's daughters.

'It is not so easy with twins. They are a double blessing, but it means also finding double dowry.'

'Well, we are conducting a double search,' joked Raman. 'Laxman Brother and Vaman Brother both are looking.'

'And? What is the progress so far?'

'The greed is incredible of boys' side,' said Raman, his mouth full of *rasgolla*. 'Vaman Brother last week was speaking to one family who is asking half *lakh* in dowry, and that is before even seeing the girls. Imagine!'

'It is a lot,' agreed Amma. 'How can anyone pay? I was lucky. I was having a lot of jewellery. In marriage my daughter was lacking nothing. But what is the normal hard-working trader to do?'

'It is exactly as you say,' said Raman. He enjoyed being called a hard-working trader. 'We have no way of paying such sums.'

'How is your book, Raman?' said Amma.

This was such a turn in the conversation that Raman, who still had his mouth full, could only open his eyes wide.

'Book?' he gulped, excited.

'Your adventure book, the one with Jagat Singh and *goonda* Kanshi.'

Raman swallowed, his eyes even rounder. For Bharathi and Deepa to say Amma was seeing his book was one thing, but to name those names was another. He had not shown those words to anyone. Then inwardly he castigated himself for being led by such child-talk. Jagat Singh and Kanshi were not uncommon names, he convinced himself in the next breath, and yes, they were good names for a smuggler and a *goonda*. Anyone with a bit of inspiration might have come up with them. 'Oh that,' he laughed a little sheepishly. 'I am a little stuck,' he confessed. 'So many things to do.'

'Maybe you should send these characters to some islands,' Amma suggested. 'In the Indian Ocean there are many.'

'Indian Ocean? I am not knowing any islands there. Hardly have I been out of Mardpur,' Raman confessed, but he thought it was an excellent idea. Yes, indeed, he needed to get hold of whatever it was that was inspiring Amma. She was able so cleverly to take up his story where he had left off. What's more he felt a sense of *déjà vu* – had he already been thinking along those lines, or was it his imagination?

'Andamans, for instance,' Amma continued.

Raman could not believe Amma had ever been as far afield as the Andamans. He had only vaguely heard of the islands himself, remembering from some PTI dispatches that there was a jail there.

'Yes, yes. You are right. I was thinking about some island. But you are right, it is the Andamans. I am indebted to you, Ammaji.'

'It is nothing,' Amma said. 'These days I am unable to read but that does not mean I cannot take an interest in books.' And she laughed.

Raman leant forward with interest. 'Tell me more about these islands.'

'The islands I can describe. But I do not want to hold you up too long. Maybe they are waiting for you at home?'

'No, no,' said Raman hastily. He was keen to stay and hear Amma. 'My wife will think only that I am with my brothers. Please continue, Ammaji. My ears are ready.' He settled more comfortably on the *charpoy*. Having overcome his fear of ghosts, there was no reason not to be relaxed.

'All right then,' said Amma obligingly, and she spent almost two hours describing a group of remote islands in the Indian Ocean, just the kind of place a smuggler would want to hide in. Deepa squatted on her plank, elbows on her knees propping up her chin, listening, rapt.

17

IN THE LATE AFTERNOON SHADE, STILL IN HER SCHOOL UNIFORM, HER satchel thrown carelessly on the polished stone tiles of the courtyard, Deepa sat cross-legged on Amma's *charpoy*. She was shelling peas into a metal bowl while Amma chopped vegetables.

Amma was quite adept at such tasks. She preferred to do them herself rather than wait for Usha because it kept her busy. In fact, Deepa suspected Amma did not ask Usha to come in the early morning, like most other servants, so that she was compelled to shoulder the morning tasks herself. Even in the afternoons, when she awoke from her nap, she could hardly bear to let the sun go down without doing anything. What was the point of God giving her hands and fingers if they were not to be used? Amma said. If God intended her to do nothing in her declining years, he would have done away with her hands, not her eyes.

The intensity of the afternoon heat had abated, but the humidity was beginning to rise. Even Amma, who was normally as dry as she was wrinkled, wiped her brow from time to time with the edge of her cotton sari. Yet even in this sultry heat Amma preferred to sit out in the bright courtyard rather than in the dim light of the room with the humming ceiling fan. It was as though the darkness of her inner world made her want to be out in the heat of the sun so that she could feel the light around her.

In the corner of the courtyard Jhotta flapped her ears to keep cool. Deepa, her face hot and shiny, got up to pour some water over the buffalo, who stamped her hooves appreciatively in the puddle that formed on the ground.

Deepa shaded her eyes and looked up at the cloudless sky. 'Soon the monsoon will be here,' she said as much in hope as in yearning.

Amma shook her head. 'When the monsoon is near it draws out the smells of the earth, even if the earth is baked hard like iron. Everything smells stronger. When the smell of red earth from my pots and the pickles suddenly becomes strong, that is when the monsoon is here.'

Deepa sniffed. The smell of red earth and pickles was no stronger than usual.

'The pickle smell is always the same,' she said.

'For you, and for me, because we are used to it, the pickle smell is our very own. It belongs to us,' said Amma. 'Only others are disturbed by the pickle smell. Others will notice the pickle smell as the rains come. But when the pickles are ripe, then you will see . . .' Amma's eyes were bright but she focused on the middle distance. 'Even you will notice.'

'When will they be ripe, Amma?' said Deepa. 'Some have been there already so long.'

'They will be ripe when they are intended to be, Deepa. No one can make them ripe faster or slower.'

'Not even you, Amma?' said Deepa in all earnestness, for she believed strongly in Amma's powers.

'Not even, Deepa. Fate is more powerful than I. We can only wait, like we wait for the monsoon rain; it will happen in its own time.'

'How much longer in this heat?' Deepa sighed, pouring more water over Jhotta's broad back.

'Soon, soon,' soothed Amma.

'What will happen to Jagat Singh?' Deepa asked, returning to the charpoy and fanning herself with her school copy-book. She hoped to distract herself from the heat by listening to Amma's tales.

'That I do not know,' said Amma. 'It is the scenery I am seeing only, and a few other things.'

'Tell me more adventures,' coaxed Deepa.

'That you will have to ask Raman, it is he who is writing.'

'But you are telling him!'

Amma shook her head: 'I am helping him understand only, what is already inside his head. If it is not inside his head, I do not know about it.'

'How is it even he does not know what is in his head?'

Amma paused to consider this. 'Some people are only listening to words and not feeling them. Maybe I am understanding those things in his head that have not yet found words.'

This was quite complex for Deepa; she pondered it for a moment, popping the peas.

'I know you are shelling peas,' said Amma, 'even if I cannot see it, even if you did not tell me. I can hear the peas pop. I can smell the pod, if it is fresh or not so fresh. I can smell if it came from the Old Market because there are other smells – cauliflowers, *brinjals*, potatoes mingling with it – not so strong but they are there. Then when the pod is open I can smell how many peas are plump and big and how many are small and unformed. And I can smell, almost taste, the metal bowl into which the peas are falling.'

'Even I can smell the pods,' said Deepa, 'but the smell of palm trees on an island called Andamans? That I cannot!'

'It is a gift, I have. Yes, it is a gift. Even your grandfather recognized it. It is not so different from what I am describing. I can feel and smell the sea wind, and the palm trees waving, and the waves on the sand. I can tell Raman what I am feeling.'

'But how do you *know*?' persisted Deepa, fascinated.

'Because it is not words, but feelings. Raman does not have to tell me, I have to feel it in his mind. I think this is how it is.'

That evening, when the sun was lowering itself quickly, as if tired from incessantly beating down on the Gangetic Plain, Raman unexpectedly arrived at Amma's house with Shanker in tow.

'Ammaji!' he called from outside, not wanting to encroach on the inner sanctuary of the courtyard uninvited.

'It is Raman,' said Amma getting up from the *charpoy*. 'Welcome! *Ram, Ram*,' she greeted him. 'In this heat you have walked so far?'

'*Ram, Ram*,' responded Raman. 'I am coming only to return your *balti*, please do not trouble to get up.'

Shanker hoisted the vessel, holding it at arm's length as if it were a lantern so that it was fully visible to all.

'Oh, it is not necessary. I have other *baltis* I can use. You did not need to come such a long way,' said Amma, clearly pleased by the surprise visit.

'No trouble,' said Raman. 'It is good to take fresh evening air. We are coming from the temple after doing *aarti*. We want to smell the pleasant smells on the way.'

In fact, there had been the rotting vegetable smells – the evening debris of the Old Market not yet cleared away after the day's trading – fresh cow dung drying on the rooftops, and the acrid smell of kerosene stoves as the women began to cook the evening meal. All this Amma knew in an instant. For fresh air and flowery scents there was nothing like the lychee garden with its blooming night jasmine which filled the air at this time of the evening. And the lychees were getting plumper, giving off their own fruity scent. Soon the first lychees would be ripening, just as the monsoon was about to break.

It was not the smells that brought Raman away from the lychee garden. There was another purpose to his visit, and Amma knew what that was too. She was beginning to sense a great deal about Raman, as if there was some kind of invisible link between them, some gossamer thread along which messages travelled.

'But it is hot for wandering so far!' she said. 'Come, drink some cool water.'

Usha had left early, her evening tasks completed. It was Deepa who ran to fill two tumblers with water from the red earth urn with the spout, splashing some water onto her hot, bare feet. She stood in the cool puddle for a few seconds, savouring the freshness. Then she ran out with the two tumblers.

Raman threw back his head, held the tumbler above his face and poured the cool water from a height into his parched throat. Shanker sat on the edge of Amma's *charpoy* and sedately sipped his water while looking warily at Amma from over the rim of his tumbler, not with fear, but with morbid interest. Maybe she would conjure up a *bhooth*. Then he could proudly tell his best friend Ravindran he had sat in Amma's house and chatted with a real ghost!

'Jhotta is fine now?' Raman enquired as he handed the empty tumbler to Deepa.

'Oh yes,' Deepa said, eagerly pointing to Jhotta shuffling quietly in her corner of the courtyard, chewing slowly with unhurried sideways movements of her great lower jaw, her eyes half closed.

'She is in good health. It was only one small Jhotta-fever she was having,' Deepa said.

'Swami Satyanarayan is an expert in Ayurveda. Only the ancient books have such cures,' said Raman. 'Of course one must have faith, not like Western medicine curing one organ only. It is the whole body, spirit and soul, that is involved. Faith is important,' he added, summarizing Satyanarayan's most recent discourse.

Deepa nodded earnestly. 'Jhotta had faith,' she said.

Raman threw an appreciative glance at the buffalo. 'It is a special beast you have—'

'Please, do take some of our Jhotta-raita for your wife,' Amma broke in.

'Oh no, really. I cannot impose—'

'I insist. There is so much left, for today is Tuesday and it is my fast-day, and how can an old woman and her granddaughter eat so much when this buffalo is so blessed as to be producing so much milk?'

'It is truly a wondrous beast,' said Raman sincerely.

'Then please share with me the fruit of this beast. I know raita is your favourite. Deepa! Fill the *balti*.'

'Then I must come back in the hot-hot sun to return your *balti*,' said Raman by way of protest, mild as it was.

'Keep coming!' said Amma. 'The hot sun will not last for ever. Soon the monsoon will be here.'

Raman looked up at the sky. The light was fading, but there was almost no orange glow in the cloudless heavens except a very fine streak on the horizon.

'There is no sign of monsoon,' he sighed. He knew it was only a matter of weeks at the most. Then, when the rains were over, the marriage season would be in full swing. Before then, a match for his daughters would have to be found. He felt a twinge of urgency in his breast. He had a purpose now for writing his smuggler tale. It was not to practise, nor to impress Satyanarayan, who was difficult to impress at the best of times, but to pay for his daughters' double dowry. Raita gave inspiration and he was lucky enough to find a good source of it. Surely that in itself was a signal from the gods? They expected him to write this book so they presented him with the potion that would enable him to do it. Raman looked at the unblemished whiteness of the yoghurt in the *balti* Deepa handed to him, and was eager to get home to allow it to cast its spell over him.

'Well, we must go. I do not like to disturb your peaceful evening, Ammaji,' said Raman, putting his hands on his knees as if to lever himself up on them.

'I will not hear of it! Keep me company for a few more minutes – tell me about your book-writing.'

Deepa laid out some small stainless steel plates to serve a snack.

Raman knew it would be impolite to refuse such hospitality. 'The book, I have written half already.'

'Half? You mean half a page?'

'No, half the book.'

'You are very diligent,' said Amma, 'but I am thinking perhaps you have completed one chapter?'

'Two,' said Raman confidently.

'So there is much, much more to come.'

Finally Raman confessed. 'First two chapters were easy to write, but now my ideas are not coming,' he said woefully.

'They will come, they will come. They are in your mind. The actions are there, it is only the words that have not yet come,' said Amma. 'Now eat,' she said, waving in the direction of the samosas Deepa had laid out on the steel plates.

Shanker ate disinterestedly; he was beginning to get bored. There was no *bhooth* in sight. All seemed perfectly normal, except that Amma pretended she knew everything even before it had happened. It was a curious affectation, Shanker thought.

Raman bit into the samosa, still ruminating on his book. 'What I am thinking is, Jagat Singh – that is the smuggler – should have one small-small house on the beach from where to plan—' He broke off, surprised at himself; the story was coming out after all. All morning he had sat there fruitlessly, unable to extract any words and put them on paper. He looked at his samosa in wonderment; it looked like a normal samosa to him.

'Kovalam beach?' suggested Amma.

'Kovalam? I have never been there,' said Raman with considerable interest. 'It sounds a good place.'

Amma described a beautiful beach scene. Raman could almost feel the palm fronds brushing against his head, the salt-sea breeze blowing, the sand sinking beneath his *chappals*.

'*Wah*,' he said. 'It is your favourite place, this Kovalam beach? And you who have travelled so much in India!'

'Oh, *I* have never been there,' said Amma quietly. 'I have never been south, only to the kingdoms of the north.'

For an hour Amma spoke, with Raman agreeing and contributing here and there. He was reluctant to tear himself away. But it was dark now,

Deepa had already lit the hurricane-lamps and he knew Kumud would be waiting with their evening meal. Shanker was wandering around restless, ready to go after realizing there were no *bhooths* in Jagdishpuri Extension. Raman took his leave and departed, *balti* in hand, fired with enthusiasm to write again.

'So many places Amma has visited,' Raman remarked effusively as he walked with Shanker towards the Old Market. 'She can describe so well!'

'She said she had not been to Kovalam,' Shanker reminded him.

'She must have forgotten only! How can you describe so well a place you have not visited at least once?'

'You can make it up,' said Shanker. He did not think there was anything special about Amma and he had been watching her closely for any strange signs. It was easy to watch a blind woman closely, because she could not see you staring. He had noted there was no sweat on her brow, but that did not mean she was a *bhooth*. Perhaps she just did not feel the heat. Shanker was disappointed – there was nothing special about her at all. It was too bad; he had been eager to come with his father, a little to Raman's surprise, only because he thought he would have a tale to tell his friend Ravindran the next day at school.

After Raman and Shanker had gone, and Deepa was clearing away the plates, Amma sat mulling over the smuggler tale for a while. There was much she did not have the time to tell Raman. While he had been sitting, jumbled-up scenes like a fast-moving film seemed to emanate from him. In the quietness of the empty courtyard she could see each scene with clarity. She had not been to these places. There were caves where the smugglers hid, and the description of the Andamans which Amma had never visited. The mansion of the rich merchant with its luxurious furnishings, curtains with tassels hanging down and huge staircases.

When Deepa came and sat beside her again, Amma related what she could see. Deepa was pleased. She was fascinated by the tale and wrote it all down, filling page after page of her school copy-book, prompting Amma each time she fell silent thinking about the images she could see. 'Tell me about the little house on the beach where they are plotting to raid the mansion, Amma,' Deepa urged.

Amma folded her hands in her lap and began to describe the house and the beach, an image that began to fade as Raman walked further and further away from Jagdishpuri Extension. Amma realized that she was beginning to struggle to see what she wanted to see and that she could not control the strength of the vision. Finally she realized she would have to stop.

Deepa had been writing it all down with care and concentration exactly the way Amma related it. Only when she stopped speaking, the last image dissipating in a hazy, incoherent mist, did Amma become aware of the scratching of Deepa's fountain pen.

'What are you writing, Deepa?'

'I am writing your stories,' said Deepa.

'It is not *my* stories. I would not know these stories if Raman had not been here. It is *his* stories. I am only telling.'

'The way you are telling me, that is what I like.'

'You are thinking to write a smuggler book also?' laughed Amma.

'I cannot,' said Deepa seriously. 'There is only one smuggler book. It is the book of Bharathi's father.'

'What you have written is what I am telling you in my words. They are not Raman's words,' Amma pointed out.

Deepa had no doubt in her mind. 'No Amma, I could not have thought of such an adventure in *my* head, so how can it be my book? And you are saying these stories are not in *your* head so it is not your book.'

'Could Raman write such a book if we did not help him?' Amma asked.

'I don't know,' said Deepa; 'maybe someone else would help him, Amma.'

'Who can help him?'

'If it is in his head, Amma, anyone could help him if they are knowing how to help.'

Amma smiled inwardly at the maturity of her granddaughter's judgement.

18

RAMAN SAT BACK, SATISFIED. THE TRIP TO RETURN AMMA'S *BALTI* HAD PAID off. Just as he had hoped, Amma had offered more raita. Not only that, she had given so many suggestions regarding the smuggler tale, she could almost be the author herself! All because she had this magical Jhotta-beast in her yard!

In his mind he savoured again the banana–with–yoghurt raita, rolling it around his mouth and letting the cool, sour-sweet nectar slide deliciously down his throat. He had amazed even himself at the number of words that could flow daily from his pen. There was no doubt Jhotta's raita was responsible for this. Wasn't it true the story had begun to take shape only after he had tasted Jhotta's raita for the first time?

Raman spent the next few days occupied with writing on his return from his morning tasks at PTI. He walked briskly up the hill to the lychee garden, barely noticing the muggy heat, and spent the afternoon at his desk overlooking the garden. He had come to know every detail in the garden, so often had he stared out at the trees while searching for a word or a phrase. With each passing day the lychee trees had become heavier with fruit, the laden branches dipping lower and lower towards the hard earth.

Raman enjoyed having a purpose, and now Kumud was taking

Raman's writing more seriously and that pleased him. She thought at first that he was writing letters – proposals of marriage to suitable families – and she left him to do that. But when the writing went on and on she was not quite sure what to make of it. Nonetheless she was respectful of any display of study and allowed him to write in peace.

'Do you want your meal before your writing or after your writing?' she asked.

'It cannot be *after* my writing, for that will be a very long time,' he said with a self-important air. 'I will stop writing now. Only for a little while. Then I must quickly get back to my writing.'

Raman watched his wife lay out the *thalis*. How adaptable she was! He had much to be grateful for, he thought. Any other wife would complain that he was neglecting his family duties.

'Did you supervise Shanker's homework?' Kumud asked when she saw him pause to watch her.

'I was writing,' said Raman proudly.

'That boy is so lazy, you know he won't do it by himself,' said Kumud pointedly.

'I know, I know. I will deal with him when I am finished. And then he'd better watch out.'

'Shanker!' called Kumud. 'If you are not finishing your homework, you had better watch out for your father.'

Shanker appeared, looking evasive.

'He will deal with you when he is finished,' warned Kumud and handed him his school bag. Shanker threw a glance at his father, who was staring intently out into the garden.

'But he is so busy with writing, Ma. He will not be finished till next week.'

Kumud decided to take matters into her own hands. 'If you do not do your homework now, I will not be giving you any food. You will sleep with an empty belly.'

'But then my belly will be rumbling!' protested Shanker.

'Rumbling-grumbling? As if I care!' said Kumud. 'It is only your homework you have to finish. Don't make me angry or I will send you to the kitchen to make chapattis for us all, for it is too hot for me to sit over the stove!'

Shanker reluctantly took up his school bag and delved into it, complaining all the while. 'But I will burn my hands!'

'Let them burn! Did you see my hands? Are they burning from making chapattis every day for you all even in this heat? You will learn how I suffer for you!'

Shanker decided that homework was the easier option and set to it. Really, his mother could be quite authoritarian sometimes, almost as bad as his father. Especially in the summer when the heat made her irritable.

When Raman's writing went on and on, Kumud became curious. It was not easy to see what he was writing. Before his meals and before bed, Raman carefully stowed his papers in a folder and carried them with him. She did not like to ask him what it was all for; *that* would be too impertinent. Kumud always found less direct methods of seeking what she needed to find out.

It was Bharathi who volunteered an explanation as she helped her mother in the kitchen. 'Papa is writing a book,' she said proudly.

'What is the purpose of this book?' Kumud wanted to know.

'So that people can read.'

'Who will read?' said Kumud, genuinely puzzled. Even Sudha-with-Pension was not an avid reader of books, although she spoke at length of her newspaper-reading pursuits.

'There are many who are reading books,' said Bharathi vaguely, not entirely sure herself who these people might be.

'Why should your father spend so much time on this book-writing?' Kumud grumbled to no one in particular. She slapped at her chapatti dough, kneading it with great force, her brow furrowed. Before, her husband had always been so predictable. An open book, so to speak. He was easy to live with precisely because he was uncomplicated. But this book-writing was not so easy to understand. Kumud did not like anything out of the ordinary.

'Books take a long time to write,' explained Bharathi.

'How long?'

'Maybe by the end of the monsoon it will be finished,' said Bharathi.

'But the monsoon is not yet here even! See how I am dying in the heat of this kitchen. Even in the evenings it is too hot!'

Bharathi dipped her finger into the yoghurt and changed the subject. 'Where did this yoghurt come from, Ma? It tastes so good.'

'Not from Kalonji, for sure,' Kumud said, smacking at the dough. 'I have told him if I catch him cheating me again I will go elsewhere. No, your father brought that yoghurt home last night from Amma's Jhotta.'

'So far!' said Bharathi. 'It is a pity, I would like more of this raita.'

Kumud looked worried. 'It is true, the yoghurt of Kalonji is no good and Amma is too far, but where can I get good yoghurt? Your father is asking every day now. He is saying that without raita he cannot write.'

'If he doesn't mind going to Jagdishpuri Extension . . .' Bharathi began.

'Amma is generous,' Kumud said, poking her dough with her thumb and watching it spring back with satisfaction. 'But it is not good that he goes there often.'

'Why?'

'That old woman is strange. I have heard stories from Madhu Sister and Sudha Sister both.'

Bharathi thought if her mother believed what Sudha Aunty said, it would be the first time.

'Really, Ma. There are no *bhooths* there. Even Shanker was disappointed. He said he did not see one *bhooth* when he went there with Papa. Nothing will happen to Papa.'

'Your father goes there and is coming back with strange ideas about books,' sniffed Kumud, cannily making the connection.

'It was his own idea to write a book,' said Bharathi, defending her father.

'For so many years I have been married to him and he did not have this idea,' said Kumud, 'and now suddenly, he has an idea.'

'Maybe he is needing the money for dowry,' said Bharathi.

Kumud stopped slapping her dough and looked at Bharathi suspiciously. Had she overheard her conversations with Raman about money? They were careful to discuss such things only when the children were at school or in bed.

'Writing-rooting will not get money for dowry,' grumbled Kumud, attacking the dough again.

'Writers are very rich,' said Bharathi, guessing wildly.

'Show me one very rich writer,' challenged Kumud, who could not think of any herself.

'Oh, Ma,' Bharathi tried to reason, 'they are not here in Mardpur, they are in Delhi, Calcutta. Rabindranath Tagore was very rich and respected writer. He wrote our national anthem even, *Jana gana mana.*'

Kumud did not want to put her own ignorance on show in front of her daughter. But she wondered quietly, as she turned out a perfect dough onto a *thali*, whether it was true that so much money could be made just from writing a book. Enough to pay a dowry? If so, perhaps she should be more tolerant. Having channelled her irritation into energy to knead her dough, she felt more at ease and was willing to lay aside the whole issue of Raman's writing. Let him write, she thought pragmatically, laying a wet muslin cloth over the rounded, swelling dough. No harm it is doing.

Still, whenever the heat and humidity became unbearable, she found it difficult to rid herself of her suspicions, unfounded or not, about Raman's new pursuit.

19

SO TAKEN WAS RAMAN WITH THE POTENCY OF JHOTTA'S RAITA, HE DECIDED to test the theory of inspiration milk on that great sage Satyanarayan.

'Punditji,' he said the next time he went to the Vishnu Narayan temple. 'I have read somewhere in some Ayurvedic text belonging to my grandfather that raita is very good for writers and giving them inspiration.'

'Really? I had not heard that,' said Satyanarayan dismissively. 'On what principle does it work?'

This caught Raman off guard. He had not considered the mechanics of it. For once he felt irritated by Satyanarayan's air of superiority. How did he know it was *not* true? The Brahmin could not know everything that was in the Ayurvedic tomes. Or perhaps, thought Raman, filling with self-doubt as he often did when faced with Satyanarayan's virtuosity, it was even possible that he did.

'There is some link between the stomach and the brain,' Raman said airily.

'Yes?' said Satyanarayan, waiting for more enlightenment on the theory. When Raman hesitated, unable to develop his theory further, Satyanarayan took on a serious, lecturing posture: 'I hope you are not thinking too much about this book-writing nonsense,' he said. 'Such things must be left to the scholars and sages. Foolish people should not meddle. You must realize once words are put down on paper, they cannot be put back, so they must be well considered. That is why it is too much an important task to leave to those without education.'

Raman felt affronted. Nonetheless he attempted to press his point.

'Books by sages and scholars are only one kind of book, Punditji. In England, they are publishing one hundred books a *week*. Are they all by sages and scholars? Of course it is not possible.' Raman was very proud of this fact from England which had appeared on the PTI wire only that week. The raita was working well, he thought smugly, and was even helping him to think up good arguments to combat Satyanarayan.

But Satyanarayan was undeterred. 'Of course these books cannot all be by sages and scholars,' he said haughtily. 'Can you name one book by an English sage as old as our *Mahabharatha*? There are no books in English written by sages. These books that are being published are only pornography and sex books.'

Raman was embarrassed. He looked around surreptitiously to make sure no one had heard, otherwise people would think they were talking about sex and pornography. At the temple, too! Despite his embarrassment he had to admit to himself that Satyanarayan's argument was a powerful one.

'They are not just . . . er,' he could not bring himself to say the word sex with the same ease as Satyanarayan. '. . . There are also other books, like adventure books for example.'

Satyanarayan sat up straight, fixing Raman with a disapproving stare. 'Adventure? What does it mean, adventure? It means some Britishers went around the world in a ship looking for India then came home to write about it. They are distortions and half-truths. It is these so-called adventures that we are having to rewrite since our independence.'

Raman usually agreed with this kind of nationalistic thinking espoused by Satyanarayan. But this time he felt Satyanarayan was twisting the facts to suit his own argument. And he was refusing to hear anyone else's point of view.

Satyanarayan seemed to sense he was losing Raman's sympathy. He returned to the original point. 'Take my advice, if you want to ingest something that is good for thinking and the brain you should give up this raita nonsense and eat almonds.'

'Almonds?'

'Twenty pieces each day, soak and rub off their skins. It is written in the *shastras*. This can help with thinking and memory. Look at me. I have been doing this for more than twenty years and my mind is clear-thinking at all times.'

Raman did not doubt it, but did it help writing? The only writing Satyanarayan did was of horoscopes. The rest was talking. Almonds clearly helped a man speak more eloquently. Aloud he said, 'My memory is good, Punditji, it is with writing I need—'

'Good memory, you say? Can you recite from the *Gita*?'

'No,' admitted Raman.

'Can you recite from the *Ramayana*?'

'No.'

'So where is the good memory? With almonds, twenty pieces a day, I can recite whole *Gita*, whole *Ramayana*, and from the Vedas I know many couplets also.'

'Well, of course you are using mantras every day,' said Raman. What use had he for knowing the *Gita* or *Ramayana* by heart? For Satyanarayan it was an integral part of his Brahmanical existence.

'So! You say you are not needing to know *Gita* and *Ramayana*, but did you even pass your BA?'

'Yes,' muttered Raman, realizing they were getting onto dangerous ground.

'But it was only third class,' said Satyanarayan, demolishing him triumphantly. 'You see what I am saying – it is almonds that are improving memory. My memory is first class. Tip-top. I am remembering every detail. You think I had forgotten about your BA? No, I am remembering everything about it. Go and eat almonds, then you can lecture me about raita.'

After that, Raman did not feel like staying for the *aarti* and departed towards Kumar Junction and then on to the lychee garden.

Sudha-with-Pension and Madhu arrived at the temple half an hour after Raman left, their hands full of offerings.

Just two days ago Sudha had come alone and found Kumud relaxing in the temple garden. Kumud was waiting for the sun to cool a little before starting out for the lychee garden after an afternoon's shopping in the Old Market. Sudha's favourite topic these days was how many letters she and Laxman had been writing to eligible families. Kumud could not believe so many letters had been written as Sudha said, and yet nothing so far had come of them.

'You know there are not so many with two sons able to marry? This family planning business has really reduced our choice!' Sudha complained.

She had been embarrassed by the visit that week of a family planning worker, a young and sophisticated lady not long out of college in Delhi, trying to convince Sudha in the simplest language of the benefits of sterilization. Sudha-with-Pension had driven her away, her dignity only barely intact, since she did not want to admit to a stranger that she had been unable to bear children.

Kumud had been visited by the same family planning worker and listened to her with great interest. Nonetheless she, too, sent the young lady away with a flea in her ear – had she come ten to twelve years ago instead of now, family planning would have been some use. As it was, Kumud told her, it was too late. There was no way to put grown babies back where they came from. And now, the worker was dead right in her dire predictions, how would they find so many dowries while educating their son?

Kumud thought Sudha was bringing up the family planning issue as an excuse for not having progressed beyond the letter-writing stage after so many days.

Sudha believed letter-writing was most important. First impressions were everything, the Murgaon family apart – they had seemed so good on paper. She took it upon herself to read out some of the best paragraphs, the most fine-tuned and delicately phrased, to impress upon Kumud the value of a good education when it came to sorting out a match for one's children. Of course Sudha claimed some credit for herself for the beauty of such letters.

'There is nothing like education in music for good letter-writing,' said Sudha-with-Pension. 'See this paragraph, such movement, such style, you can hear the *dhun*. And this, written in the morning, does it not flow like a morning *raga*, wakeful and fresh? And here, we are getting aggressive because we did not like the tone of *their* letter, and we have nothing to lose because the boys are not suitable, you see how staccato the phraseology, the beat is *teen tal*. "We are in re-ceipt of your let-ter". You can almost hear it: *dha dhin dhin dha . . .*'

But Kumud did not care for such comparisons. She said to Raman afterwards, 'I do not care if she is writing letters or singing music or mixing the two, only it must succeed in attracting a good family for my daughters.'

★

Two days later when Sudha-with-Pension arrived at the temple with Madhu, she was intent on impressing upon Madhu how hard she was working to secure a double-match.

'So many letters we have written, and so many we have received in return,' Sudha was saying.

'*Wah!* There must be too many proposals. How will we choose?' said Madhu, genuinely impressed.

'There is no suitable family among them,' sniffed Sudha. 'Some are not even of our caste, they are only aspiring to the trading class. They are wanting their sons to be trained in sari business. Everyone knows it is a good business, and we are most established in this industry. We are looking for a good match, after all we are a family of status in Mardpur.'

'So many letters and not one decent boy?' Madhu said, astonished.

'There is. But one suitable boy is not enough. Difficulty is in finding two. You cannot imagine, we are even receiving one proposal for one rich-rich Ghatpur industrialist with textiles factory, but he is having only one son. We are saying no, they are twins. The other family is saying – you will not believe – let him marry both girls! So keen are they on the match.'

'It is not a bad idea,' said Madhu carefully. 'It will be only one dowry.' It did not occur to her to suggest that if the match was so good it should be secured for one twin and then another family sought for the other.

'*Dhut!*' scolded Sudha. 'What are you thinking? Husbands are not for sharing. It is better to get two good husbands and pay double dowry. We have our family name to keep. So,' she sniffed, 'we will pay for it, whatever the price.'

'*Whatever* the price?' said Madhu dubiously.

'If it is a good family, we must all contribute. That includes Raman Brother also,' said Sudha firmly. 'There is no reason why we cannot have the best match.'

'But we must find a good family first,' sighed Madhu. 'And it is taking such a long time. Monsoon will soon be here and marriage season also!'

Sudha was unable to contain herself any longer, even though Laxman had sworn her to secrecy until things had progressed further. She did not want Madhu to think they were not conscious of the urgency of fixing the match, or leave her with the impression that there was no one willing to consider the girls. The twins were accomplished, after all. Sudha had seen to that. Who would not want such girls? At the same time Laxman thought this family, the Ramanujans of Ghatpur, might be a very expensive proposition and he did not want Vaman to veto it even before talks had advanced.

'There is one possibility,' she revealed. 'We are expecting a positive reply any day.'

Madhu looked excited. She had suspected all along that Sudha was hiding something from her. 'Then it is all fixed!'

'Not yet,' said Sudha-with-Pension hastily, regretting a little that she had told so much. 'They have not even seen the girls yet. Let us pray for a good outcome.'

'I will pray for a not-too-high dowry price,' said Madhu eagerly.

'Oho,' Sudha restrained her, exasperated. 'How can you pray for a not-too-high dowry price? It is not God's concern. His concern is a good outcome and a good match.'

Madhu trailed after Sudha-with-Pension, her flowers in her hands, and resolved that she would pray for a good outcome *and* for a not-too-high dowry price.

20

IT WAS AN IMPORTANT DAY FOR RAMAN. HE HAD HURRIED BACK EARLY
from PTI, picking up his pants from the *dhobin* where he had left them for
ironing. For once he did not go straight to his desk to write, as he had
been doing for days. Instead he threw himself into the preparations for the
gathering to be held at Laxman's house that evening.

Kumud, normally so composed, was in a flurry, plaiting Bharathi's hair
for the fourth time to make sure the plaits were absolutely even.

Raman put on his new shirt, with long sleeves and cuffs that Banarasi
Ram the tailor had delivered that morning, having been told only
yesterday to finish the job urgently or expect no more business from that
family. It was no idle threat. Banarasi Ram knew full well not to mess
about with the scions of the sari business. When anyone came into the
Sari Palace or Sari Mahal wanting to know where was the best place to
have blouses made they always recommended Banarasi Ram. He had
become quite prosperous from the connection.

A cuff button popped off and rolled away out of sight.

'That tailor has been cheating us!' yelled Raman. 'A simple button he
cannot even sew! We will not go to him again.'

'He is the best tailor in Mardpur,' said Kumud. 'He can copy whatever
film stars are wearing.'

'Why should I care what the film stars are wearing when I cannot even have a proper button on my cuff?' grumbled Raman. He stooped down to look for it. It had rolled under the chair. Raman could see it lying in the dust, out of reach.

'Shanker! Find the button under the chair,' he ordered.

'But, Papa . . . !'

Shanker was looking neat and tidy; his hair, still wet, was combed back onto his scalp. His mother had worked on him for some time to get such an effect.

'Get the button, you donkey! Am I to stand here all day?'

'Shanker! What are you doing? Your white-white pant will get dirty!' shrieked Kumud as Shanker obediently fell to the floor. She pulled him up, tugging at his shirt.

'Everyone is on at me,' complained Shanker, uncertain what to do.

'Who will get my button?' Raman demanded to know.

'I have a spare button in my sewing box. Leave that button,' commanded Kumud.

'It must be matching exactly,' insisted Raman.

'Of course it will match,' said Kumud. 'Banarasi Ram has been using same buttons for fifteen years, maybe bought cheap in bulk so long ago. I have buttons from your old shirt in my box.'

'I told you that tailor was using cheap-cheap merchandise,' grumbled Raman.

'Cheap-cheap is all we have right now. Let me sew this one and then later you can go and fight with Banarasi Ram.'

'Why should I fight with him? I will only be telling him change your cheap-cheap buttons to better quality or I will be going to another tailor. Where is this button?'

'In a minute, I will get.'

'*Phut-a-phut*, then, or we will be late!'

'First I am finishing Bharathi's hair.'

'It is not Bharathi who is getting married,' said Raman, impatiently.

'Get my sewing box,' Kumud ordered Shanker.

'Everyone is on at me,' complained Shanker.

'Because you are the youngest and have nothing to do,' said Bharathi.

'Even Bharathi is on at me.'

'Did you not hear your ma? Get the sewing box!' roared Raman. 'And stop this complaining always.'

'Where is it?' said Shanker sulkily.

'Must I do everything in this house? Go, find it in the bedroom!' said Kumud, exasperated. 'That boy is such a baby! I must do everything for him.' She had finished plaiting Bharathi's hair and went to get the sewing box. Raman was staring at his daughter. It was the first time he had seen her in *salwar-kameez* instead of a frock. It fitted tightly over her slim body, accentuating her gentle curves. Bharathi was proud of the puffed sleeves – the very latest fashion. Banarasi Ram had said she was the first in Mardpur for whom he had stitched such a *kameez*.

'You like it, Papa?' said Bharathi proudly. 'It is like in the film *Gauri*.'

'I did not see that one,' said Raman, still distracted.

Kumud came running back. She balanced the sewing box on the chair arm; it was really an old *Parle* biscuit tin, with the picture of a plump baby on the lid. She rummaged around matching various buttons to Raman's other cuff, and when she was satisfied she threaded her needle and sewed it on, warning him not to move while she did it.

'I do not want blood from my finger running onto your new shirt,' she said.

Raman stood stock still and Kumud relaxed a little as she sewed.

'Bharathi is looking good in *salwar-kameez*, no?' she confided to her husband.

'Too pretty. Now we will have to start worrying about her dowry,' Raman said in mock sorrow.

'I will ask Banarasi Ram to stitch only *salwar-kameez* for Bharathi now. No more frocks!'

'Not that tailor! He cannot even sew a button.'

'There are no buttons on *salwar-kameez*, Papa,' said Bharathi, pleased at the attention she was getting.

'*My* buttons are okay,' said Shanker, tugging at his shirt.

'Shanker! Stop pulling your buttons. You want me to stand here all day sewing your buttons? Have I nothing else to do?' Kumud bit off the thread and Raman examined the button closely to make sure it was an exact match before doing up his cuff.

At last they were ready. Kumud held a large tiffin-carrier with *rasgollas*, and her smart *chappals* that she would change into when they got to Kumar Junction and could hail a rickshaw. There was no point ruining her best footwear in the dust of the road. Raman also wore his old sandals. He tied the laces of his newly polished brown leather shoes and strung them over his shoulder, which he had carefully covered with a cloth so that polish did not soil his new shirt. Then Raman shot the rusty, squeaky bolt and put a huge padlock on the door, turning the key stiffly in the lock. He was a little at a loss where to put the key, with its patches of rust. He did not want to arrive with misshapen pockets. Kumud saw his dilemma and offered to keep it in her purse, silk-lined though it was.

At Laxman's house a festive atmosphere reigned. Laxman was wearing a new shirt of the finest poplin. Sudha-with-Pension had cleaned and tidied and had hung new silk curtains made from a sari that had arrived damaged by rainwater. The damaged part had been carefully cut away. They were very striking curtains of a turquoise colour with a *zari* border. Kumud thought they looked very chic indeed. But she maintained, when Sudha specifically asked what she thought, that curtains were an unnecessary affectation. What was wrong with bamboo blinds, which kept out the sun and kept the room cool as well?

'Bamboo?' smiled Sudha-with-Pension with a superior air. 'My dear, you must be dusting and cleaning all day. Those blinds! With curtains you are just washing once and it is clean.'

Raman stood up for his wife. 'Bamboo blinds are a good traditional curtain, and what is wrong with it? It is keeping the room cool and pleasant. I will only live in a house with bamboo blinds. I cannot sleep with curtains flapping.'

'Tradition-tradition, you are always going on about,' said Sudha wagging her finger at him. 'So people have always traditionally lived in mud huts, does it mean we also should do so?' and she swept towards the kitchen in triumph.

Raman ran after her to correct her. 'Excuse me Sudha Sister, we are knowing about stone building for centuries, look at Old Fort in Delhi and even Taj Mahal and—'

Laxman called after him, 'Raman, we have things to discuss before they arrive!'

'Where are the girls?' said Raman retracing his steps.

'Meera and Mamta are getting ready. They will take some time,' Laxman said, winking at Bharathi and Shanker with the air of an indulgent father. 'Bharathi, you are looking so pretty in *salwar-kameez*, soon we will have to give you the best saris! But not yet or everyone will be wanting to marry you instead of Meera and Mamta.'

Bharathi giggled.

Vaman arrived with his gold-laden wife and their sons, Shammu and Guru, who ran out into the garden to play with Shanker. Kumud was a little put out by Madhu's appearance, decked all over with gold from her clinking bangles to her toering. Really, it was too extravagant and it would take attention away from her girls, Kumud thought.

Vaman rubbed his hands. 'This is truly an excellent match, brothers,' he said. 'The family is owning three sari stores in Ghatpur and the two sons are the only boys. It couldn't be better. That was a good tip you gave us, Raman. No, Laxman Brother?'

Laxman had to admit this was the case although he was perplexed where Raman had heard about the Ramanujans while he and Vaman, who were in the sari business, had not.

Laxman brought out some scrolls. 'These are the horoscopes from the boys' side,' he said. 'I received only yesterday and I did not have time to show to Satyanarayan.'

He unravelled one. 'But what I can see is good. Money, children, all good sectors.'

The brothers and their wives crowded around, examining every inch of the charts with care.

When the family arrived, everyone was very excited. Kumud and Madhu, with Bharathi's help, bustled around providing food and drink.

'What a pretty girl!' said the mother, pinching Bharathi's cheek.

'Youngest sister,' explained Laxman; 'girls are even prettier.'

'And what class are you studying?' asked the mother.

'Seventh,' said Bharathi coyly.

'And coming first, of course?'

'Of course, of course,' interrupted Raman, adding quickly, 'Please take a seat.'

The two young men, an older and a younger brother, were slim, tall and dressed in bush-shirts and white pants. Bharathi stole a look at them while she handed them juice from a tray.

'So-o handsome,' Bharathi said to Shanker and her cousins as she ran out into the garden.

'Yes, yes,' said Shanker, 'handsome and greedy.' He told Shammu and Guru about the demand for half a *lakh* of rupees in dowry and enjoyed their look of horror.

Shanker turned to his cousins mischievously. 'Are you not glad you don't have sisters? What a burden for us boys! I will have to be working all my life just to find dowry money for Bharathi!'

'Sisters are a burden,' agreed Guru.

'*Chup*,' said Bharathi. 'You are not having sisters but what if you are having daughters?'

'Daughters are a burden,' intoned Shammu.

'Huh!' said Bharathi, unimpressed. 'You boys are so lazy, you need to have girls to make you work. Without us to feed you would have no food all day.'

'That I do not mind!' said Guru. 'I can have more time for playing marbles.' He delved into his pocket and pulled out a handful. The other boys crowded around admiringly.

Bharathi went inside to watch the meeting between her sisters and the boys.

When Meera and Mamta came in with Kumud and Sudha-with-Pension on either side, everyone looked up.

'*Wah!*' said the father of the boys, staring at the saris with wide eyes. 'Banarasi silk, very good, very good. You must tell me who is your supplier,' he said, turning to Laxman.

'Look at this,' said the father turning to his two sons, who had suddenly been taken with an attack of shyness and were looking everywhere but at the girls. 'Learn how to recognize best Banarasi silk. I am having some good silks from Kanjeevaram but it is not the same. No, no, the quality is different. Have you tried to pull Banarasi silk through a ring? You should try some day, it is so fine! And what hues and dyes! Beautiful.'

The mother looked admiringly at the gold jewellery adorning the girls. '*Wah*, fine gold. From Bombay?'

'Yes,' smiled Madhu, from whose collection the pieces came. 'Bombay pieces are the best. Handiwork is good.'

'These days Bombay gold is very fashionable,' butted in Sudha-with-Pension, who did not possess any herself. 'But the old pieces were made by real craftsmen, each piece taking a month to make.'

'It is true what you are saying. I am not possessing much gold myself, but handiwork is good,' said the mother.

'Oh, but Bombay gold is more fine. Look at this.' Madhu pointed to her bangles. 'Where were they doing such fine work before?'

The mother turned to Kumud. 'What is your preference? Bombay gold or old pieces?'

Kumud looked demure. 'We women are keeping only what our mothers are giving us. So we are treasuring it, wherever it is made, no?'

The men talked about saris while the women went on to discuss the price of gold per *tael*. The boys stared hard at the *zari* borders of Meera and Mamta's saris, while the twins giggled and whispered to each other behind their hands.

After some time, when Sudha-with-Pension was bored with the topic of Bombay gold, she announced, 'Now the girls will sing.'

Everyone clapped. Sudha brought out a harmonium, pumped it up, and nodded to the girls. They sang a devotional song, Meera with her eyes heavenwards, her brow furrowed in earnestness, Mamta, her eyes cast down, her brows lifted in sincerity.

'*Wah, wah!*' cried the father, and Laxman clapped enthusiastically.

'It is a traditional song I have taught them,' said Sudha-with-Pension. 'From the repertoire of Meerabai.'

'So much nicer than these filmi songs, don't you think?' said the father turning to Raman. Raman warmed to him.

'Indeed, indeed. It is a part of our culture and has survived so long because it is so pure.'

'It is true,' said the father, thinking a little. 'It is the purity that makes it so charming.'

'Of course,' said Sudha cunningly, 'it is depending also very much on the skill of the singers.'

'Of course, of course,' said the mother and father in unison.

Vaman too was wildly enthusiastic. 'Do you have any requests? They will sing anything you ask.'

The mother looked impressed, but Sudha frowned. She had taught them only two set pieces.

'Oh, no, no,' laughed the father. 'I am no expert in music. Perhaps the boys have a request. Do you have a request, boys?'

The boys cleared their throats and looked at the ground. Meera and Mamta looked at them expectantly: this was something that might reveal their tastes.

'We cannot think of anything at the moment,' said the elder boy finally.

'Cannot think! Come, there must be many songs you like,' said Laxman who was now in a thoroughly good mood.

'Girls have a good repertoire of Meerabai songs,' said Sudha trying skilfully to steer things in the right direction.

'Yes, another *bhajan*, we would like to hear,' said the father.

Sudha started the harmonium before anyone could change their mind and Meera and Mamta took their cue.

'*Wah, wah!* Bravo,' applauded the father when they finished. 'The girls are truly lucky to have a professional music teacher at home.'

Sudha-with-Pension accepted this praise with a modest nod of her head.

'Oh, but talent is also there!' said Raman.

'Talent is definitely there,' concurred the father with a wriggle of his head. 'What do you think, boys? You have not said anything all evening. The family will think you cannot talk! Come, recite some poetry.' He turned to Laxman. 'I am fond of Ghalib, you would like to hear Ghalib?'

'Oh, yes, Ghalib, he is the most lyrical. Please recite Ghalib,' invited Laxman.

The boys started their recitation, stopping now and again so that the men could shout, '*Wah, wah,*' and '*Shabash,*' and other intonations of appreciation and praise. They had clear, fresh voices, deep and mellow, and they recited with expression. Bharathi thought they were wonderful, so handsome, so cultured. The boys were a hit with everyone. When they had finished, there was loud applause from Laxman, Vaman and Raman. Bharathi clapped hard and enthusiastically, too. Even Shanker had to admit that they had recited beautifully, although he considered the poems a little sentimental for his taste.

'What do you expect from Ghalib?' Bharathi scolded him afterwards. 'He is the greatest writer of love poems.'

After the recitation there was another round of food and drink and the two families chatted, relaxed. Then Sudha and Kumud led away Meera and Mamta while Laxman, Vaman, Raman and the father retired to another room to discuss the dowry price.

PART TWO

21

THE MONSOON BROKE AT LAST. RAIN POURED DOWN UNRELENTINGLY FOR more than a week, before it paused for even a moment. The garden was filled with the scent of drenched, ripening lychees, swollen and juicy. Some fell to the ground, battered by the heavy rain, oozing clear, sweet, fragrant juice. Among them hopped the frogs that had appeared suddenly from nowhere, their translucent throats pulsating. Compared with the quiet stillness of summer there was the sound of movement all around: during the day the air vibrated gently with the croaking and whirring of frogs, and at night it shook with the rumble of distant thunder. The gentle drip, drip from the waxy leaves of the lime trees in the lychee garden mingled with the plop, plop of the frogs jumping in and out of the mud-puddles. Occasionally there was the gentle squelch of a ripe lychee as it landed in the soft mud.

All around, everything seemed to be breathing again. With the coming of the rains the lime trees gave off a strong citrus smell, fresh and clean, which could be felt behind the nose, clearing the nasal passages which for so many weeks had been clogged with dust.

The dirt road to the garden was transformed into a sea of mud and the Old Market was awash. It was just the excuse Raman needed not to venture out.

Gulbachan was not unduly surprised when Raman failed to appear for work after the first rains burst upon the Gangetic Plain. He had difficulty moving around himself, although his own home was just a short walk away from the PTI office. The PTI wire was curiously silent for a few days as the most populous parts of the country were veiled in a sheet of water from the heavens. Then it suddenly sprang to life with news of floods, landslips, damaged crops and other huge calamities that people would remember until the following year's rains.

Bharathi and Shanker also stayed at home. Shanker was willing, keen even, to go to school, not so much to turn over a new leaf as a swot, but more to test the mud. He secretly wanted to attempt the journey to school sliding down the muddy hill on his slate. Kumud caught him elaborating on this desire to Bharathi, and, with an eye on getting her children to school in clean uniforms or not at all, gave strict instructions that no one was to poke their nose out of the door without her permission. She would not budge an inch to Shanker's pleadings of an experimental sortie to test the depth of the mud and its qualities as a sledging surface.

So Shanker stayed at home and chased the geckos that suddenly appeared in abundance on the verandah, blinking inertly or racing for the plumpest mosquitoes. His main aim was to whack at their tails with his ruler to see if a new one would grow back before his very eyes. He wanted only to get the tip so that he could create a whole army of geckos with two tails or even produce one with three. The thwack of Shanker's ruler reverberated on the wall causing not a few dents and marks before Raman discovered where the flaking plaster on the verandah floor had come from and hauled Shanker inside by the ear. In any case, Shanker noted without regret, the geckos seemed to be getting wise during the day and had begun to come out mostly in the evening when Shanker was driven inside by the mosquitoes.

It was Kumud who struggled to the market to get their daily provisions and fresh vegetables. She donned an old cotton sari for this trek, hitched up almost as high as her knees, and did not mind if the edges became brown and spattered. She removed her silver-plated toerings and anklets and carried her old rubber *chappals* in one hand and Raman's large black umbrella in the other. As long as she kept to the grassy part, just before the ditch on either side of the dirt road, she could manage not to sink into the mud further than her ankles. She could also clamber over the roots of the trees that provided a bridge over the mud.

Given the struggle to advance even a few inches at times, she was remarkably cheerful. She much preferred the rain to the unmitigated heat of the summer.

During one particularly heavy downpour on her way back from a trip to the Old Market to replenish her pantry, Kumud took shelter at the temple until the torrent abated. And there was Sudha-with-Pension, not wanting to miss her rituals, even in such weather.

'Kumud Sister, it is good to see you so devout, to come to the temple in such rain and through all the mud also! *Arré baapré*, just imagine that dirt road, how did you come down?'

'I am taking shelter, only. I was marketing,' responded Kumud.

'Marketing? Is Raman Brother not doing marketing after work?'

Kumud evaded the question with all it implied about Raman's idle ways. She knew it was a favourite topic of Sudha's. 'Children are also staying home,' she said deftly.

'Oho, it is a problem for you,' said Sudha clicking her tongue in sympathy. 'You should not have come out in such weather, and so much to carry.' She looked with distaste at Kumud's mud-spattered sari.

'What to do?' said Kumud. 'Vegetables must be bought and my husband is also asking for raita, so I must get milk.'

How inconsiderate of Raman to want raita at this time, Sudha thought, but aloud she said, 'He is so fond of raita? I did not know it. It is not good weather for milk. Those buffaloes are eating too much green-green grass and spoiling their milk.'

Kumud knew the effect of the monsoon grass on milk and was herself wondering where she would find yoghurt. She certainly did not relish the thought of going to Kalonji. Her thoughts must have shown on her face, for Sudha appeared to take pity on her.

'Where will you go looking for yoghurt in this weather? Come, take some yoghurt from me. Hari!'

Hari was sheltering under a tree; he came running.

'That yoghurt you are bringing from Amma's house where your sister is working, please give some to Kumud Sister.'

Hari ran back to get the *balti* of yoghurt that he had only minutes earlier offered to Sudha in return for a few coins. The yoghurt had been a reward from Amma for helping Usha with buying vegetables. He had balanced the basket of produce for Amma on his head and helped Usha pick her way through the water which inundated the Old Market and on to Jagdishpuri Extension. On her own Usha would never have attempted that trip, and how would the blind old woman have managed without her? Amma was certainly grateful.

On his return he had taken shelter at the temple and offered the yoghurt to Sudha. But Sudha did not need yoghurt that day and declined.

'It is going sour so quickly in this weather,' Sudha said to Kumud, 'that is why I am not buying.' She handed Kumud the *balti* as if it were her own gift, while Kumud took out her purse and paid Hari. He turned the coins over in his hand, looking pleased.

'Raman is very fond of raita,' said Kumud, delighted at this stroke of luck.

'You can tell him, sister, it is a gift from me,' said Sudha-with-Pension with a self-satisfied air. She turned from Kumud to Hari.

'Boy, have you nothing to do?'

'No, memsahib,' said Hari eagerly. He was hoping there was a job in the offing.

'Good, then you can help me do my marketing. Is Old Market full of water?'

'Yes, memsahib.'

'Then I need you to carry my vegetables.' Sudha-with-Pension turned to Kumud with a superior look. 'Really my dear, you should not trouble yourself so much, ask others to do the work for you.'

'I will remember for next time,' responded Kumud, and hitched up her sari, ready for her return journey, while she watched Sudha depart with Hari. He held Sudha's umbrella high over her head as she gripped her sari with both hands and picked her way around the deepest puddles.

Kumud had barely progressed as far as Kumar Junction when Gulbachan rode past on his scooter. The machine was making an unhealthy putter-putter sound, as if the rain had got right into its inner workings. He stopped when he saw her.

'I say, what a brave lady to venture out in all this rain and mud!'

'It is very difficult,' admitted Kumud, 'but what to do? Food must be bought.'

Gulbachan did not ask why Raman had not been to work. He did not want Kumud to think he was complaining. He liked to appear a gracious boss, particularly to his employee's wife. Gulbachan was nothing if not a gentleman. 'I would offer to take you home on my scooter, for I know it is a long way up that hill. But listen to this putter-putter. I think my engine will not last till your lychee garden.'

'It is not a problem,' said Kumud, who had not been expecting such an offer and had refused to pay an exorbitant price to a rickshaw-wala to bring her home. She had resigned herself to walking.

'Well, walking won't hurt,' said Gulbachan cheerily. 'Did I tell you about the time I went on the Salt March with Gandhiji?'

He had. Many times. Kumud knew it had been an arduous march and that compared to that she could not complain about her short trek to the lychee garden.

'That was some march,' said Gulbachan, his eyes distant as he recalled his heyday.

'You should write a book,' Kumud commented, feeling somewhat worldly-wise about such things since a writer had emerged in her own household.

Gulbachan was pleased. 'It is a good suggestion. It is my intention to do so one day.'

'How long would it take to write such a book?' Kumud wanted to know.

'Oh, no time at all,' said Gulbachan, dreaming enthusiastically. '*Phut-a-phut*. If you have a good typist. Your husband is one such good typist. *Phut-a-phut* he types.'

'One week? One month?' Kumud persisted.

'Oh, well.' Gulbachan tried to look modest. 'It would be just a matter of weeks, I suppose. Of course the reason I did not write the book was sheer lack of time. Independence came and then Nehru, then Tibet, then Siachin Glacier then the Indo-Pak war. One gets quite busy with these things.'

'How much can you earn from writing a book?' Kumud asked, determined to find out as much as she could while she had the opportunity.

'Money? Um, well, thousands, *lakhs* even,' said Gulbachan rashly. 'Yes, one or two *lakhs*.'

'Even if it is not as good as Tagore?' Kumud was proud to be able to quote the name of a real writer to Gulbachan, and she was only seventh standard pass!

'Tagore? Oh, Tagore! He is only read by Bengalis. If you are read by many you can get *lakhs* for book-writing.'

Kumud was satisfied with that.

'I must go, food must be cooked or how will the children eat?' she said happily, and made her way home, leaving Gulbachan completely mystified and startled at Kumud's line of questioning.

'Don't tell me Raman has been soaking up all my stories about the Salt March and intends to write a book about it,' he muttered under his breath as he kicked his scooter to life. It sputtered and stopped, and he had to try again. 'It just goes to show, even the most unassuming dreamer is dreaming about something.'

22

LIKE THE MONSOON RAINS FROM THE CLOUDS, THE WORDS GUSHED FROM Raman's pen.

'So much you have written,' said Bharathi, looking admiringly at the notebooks that lay on Raman's desk. Raman allowed Bharathi to flip through the handwritten pages.

'Like Draupadi's sari it has grown,' said Raman with some satisfaction. 'Like Hanuman's tail before they set fire to it, like . . . like . . .' Raman searched for more analogies from mythology.

'Like Ravana's head growing back when it is chopped off?' contributed Shanker. He was thinking about the geckos he was not allowed to attack.

'Yes, yes,' said Raman enthusiastically before realizing it wasn't quite right.

Later, Raman sat on the verandah with two large bowls – one full of lychees and another for the discarded pips and shells. He was looking out at the rain, which had slowed but still showed no sign of stopping. He had been writing at a good pace and just as he had thought he was running out of steam, Kumud had arrived from her shopping trip with a *balti* of raita. From Amma's Jhotta, she had said. It was definitely Jhotta's milk – hadn't he written so much since eating that raita? What a wife! To go out in such rain just for his raita showed how truly dedicated she was. She had clearly realized the potence of this nectar. Only two days before she had brought it to him he had sat at his desk filled with the urgency of his task and no words had come.

Raman had reached the end of his notebook. He had even written on the back cover and inside back cover. Without raita, thought Raman dreamily, my head is a barren plain, like the lychee garden before the rain. Look at it now, lush and green – not an inch of earth could be seen under such thick-thick grass.

Now even that raita had been consumed, and Raman pondered how to procure more. He needed to find some ruse to take him to Jagdishpuri Extension. He could not impose on Kumud in this weather. Besides, he had other tasks. He wanted to call on Vaman, curious to know if there was any news from the Ramanujans. Surely there must be by now. And just two shops away from the Sari Palace was Ahuja Book Depot. More raita meant that more notebooks were also needed.

He rolled his pants to his knees, found his umbrella, and set out for Kumar Junction.

'This is a pleasant surprise,' commented Vaman, folding his newspaper as Raman entered.

'Busy?' enquired Raman.

'What busy? Who is wanting to buy saris in this weather? Only one customer is coming whole day. And he did not buy. He was not even from Mardpur. He had nothing to do, and was just looking for tea and chit-chat.'

'Why did he not go to a *chai-khana* if he is only wanting to drink tea? The cheek of these people! Do they imagine we hard-working traders have nothing to do all day but make tea for passers-by?' said Raman indignantly.

Vaman did not seem unduly disturbed by such audacity. 'Where can you hear gossip of such quality in a *chai-khana*? There it is a very hit-and-miss affair. People are not knowing anything. Here you ask any question, I can straight away give an answer. I am reading the newspaper, after all.'

'It is the limit!' intoned Raman. 'They should read the newspaper by themselves.'

'He told me someone is wanting to buy the temple land,' Vaman said.

This was something that was not in the newspaper.

'Temple land?'

'Yes, the temple is owning a *mela maidaan*. There is nothing there. Just a few trees.'

Raman realized that Vaman did not mean the temple garden but the part behind the Vishnu Narayan temple which some referred to as the *mela maidaan*, or fairground. *Mela maidaan* was a rather grand title for a small piece of overgrown land that no one could find any proper use for and Satyanarayan was adamant could not be used for grazing cattle. Raman could vaguely remember as a small boy an occasion when a small travelling fair camped there. It consisted of just four rides and an equal number of stalls. He could also remember, somewhat distantly, gathering around an entertainer with performing monkeys, and a snake charmer with his baskets and *bansuri* gourd pipes. The performers came in a procession down the dirt road from Vakilpur, past the lychee garden, rattling their hand-drums as they descended the hill towards Kumar Junction. At Kumar Junction they made towards the temple, gathering a crowd of children as they went, and stopped at the *mela maidaan* for their impromptu performance. But no one had arrived in such a manner since the *pukka* road had been built to Vakilpur, and it just did not seem in the nature of things for wandering performers to travel around on the buses.

'So someone is wanting to buy the *mela maidaan*? Satyanarayan will never allow!' said Raman with conviction.

'If he gets something out of it?'

'The Brahmin is owning nothing, what should he get?'

'It is he who is negotiating.'

Raman simply did not believe his brother. Why should Satyanarayan sell off part of the temple land and reduce the size of his domain? It was out of character.

'That Satyanarayan Swami knows who has power and money,' said Vaman. 'If he is allowing someone to buy *mela maidaan*, maybe they will help him in return.'

'What kind of help is he needing? He is a simple man.'

Vaman snorted. 'He likes people to think he is a simple man. But that Satyanarayan is too clever.'

Raman tried to explain. 'He is of course learned and clever, it is his needs that are simple.'

'Anyone so learned and clever can never have such *simple* needs. They must be complex,' and Vaman laughed a gurgling kind of laugh, as though at his own private joke.

Raman was unsure what Vaman was getting at and dropped the

subject. He could not expect Vaman to be complimentary about Satyanarayan. Vaman had always distrusted the Brahmin, for no clear reason that Raman could see.

Vaman served Raman tea from his thermos flask but apologized for not having milk.

'Rampal has not come today. Usually he comes earlier to deliver. It is lucky there were no customers except one man. I had no tea to offer!'

Raman looked at the dark brew with slight distaste. 'Tea without milk . . . ?' he began dubiously.

'I know, I know,' said Vaman sipping from his own cup and making a face. 'Tea without milk is like a book without writing.'

Raman became attentive; it reminded him of his other purpose.

'I am already needing a new exercise book,' he said. 'Writing is progressing too fast.' He rubbed his hands in satisfaction.

'So it is going ahead then?'

Raman felt hurt. 'Of course it is going ahead.'

'Some people are always talking and boasting about book-writing, but what are they writing? Big zero. That Gulbachan fellow. He is now saying he will write about the Salt March, some thirty years after the event!'

'Oh?' said Raman, with interest.

'Yes, he is going around on his putter-scooter and telling everyone, "I am writing a book about the Salt March."'

'School books are already describing,' said Raman, who had seen it in Shanker's textbooks.

'Precisely,' said Vaman. 'But that Gulbachan is going around telling all because he believes someone in Mardpur is trying to write his story before he can finish it. So everyone will know it is he and not the other person who is writing.'

Raman followed this line of reasoning with some difficulty. 'Who would do that?'

'Gulbachan is not saying. But he said to me few times already so maybe he is thinking it is you and is hoping I will tell you to stop.'

'What did you say to him?' Raman wanted to know, highly amused at this thought. He was capable of writing Gulbachan's Salt March book also! So everyone thought he was capable of writing. Everyone, that is, except Satyanarayan. He sniffed irritably at the thought.

'I assured him you are not capable of book-writing,' said Vaman blithely.

'Oh,' said Raman, deflated suddenly.

'I told him, "Did you not only hire Raman because he got a BA third class and because he had no ambition to be a journalist? Can such a person be a writer?"'

'Why not?'

'Of course, why not. We are knowing that. Anyone can do it. But Gulbachan does not know.'

'Good, good,' said Raman. Vaman was not against him after all.

'Satyanarayan is another one,' Vaman continued.

'What is he saying?'

'The usual. He is saying you must be stopped.'

Well, thought Raman, at least he knew Satyanarayan was talking behind his back. 'What did you tell *him*?'

'Same. It will never happen, this book, I told him.'

'Well, it *is* happening,' said Raman.

'Of course, of course,' said Vaman in a tone that indicated he did not really believe it. Then he looked mischievous. 'It would be too good to complete this book just to show Satyanarayan is wrong. He is always sure he is one hundred per cent right. For one, I will be happy to see it.'

'It is not my intention to annoy Satyanarayan Swami,' said Raman, disconcerted.

'If there is no other purpose to the book than to annoy Satyanarayan, I don't mind at all!' said Vaman. He had pulled out a ledger and began to flip the pages. 'I have already told Laxman Brother we should support you in this endeavour.'

'Good,' said Raman, warming to Vaman. 'What did Laxman Brother say?'

'Oh, Laxman does not understand why you are writing this book. I told him it is purely to annoy Satyanarayan.'

'You told him that?' said Raman aghast, thinking the joke had gone too far. 'He might tell Satyanarayan! He is friendly with the fellow.'

'Let him, let him. I would like to see that Brahmin's face when he does.'

'But Satyanarayan will believe him and really think I am wanting to annoy deliberately.'

Vaman was enjoying himself hugely. 'Let him think.'

'But—'

'What other purpose is there to this book?'

Raman was silent. He did not want to bring up the issue of the dowry. But it reminded him of why he was there.

'Is there no news from Ramanujans?' he asked quickly. After all, the meeting with that family had gone well. Both Laxman and Vaman said as much – and after the humiliation they had suffered in Murgaon they were not inclined to be unduly optimistic. What remained was for the Ramanujans to agree the dowry terms.

'We have heard nothing yet,' Vaman confirmed. He did not seem particularly worried.

'Perhaps they did not like our girls,' Raman said gloomily.

'It is early still,' said Vaman. 'If they are writing too soon they will be seeming too eager. It is not good for *their* bargaining position.'

'What if we should go to another family while they are trying to improve their bargaining position?' Raman wanted to know.

'I am sure they would be hearing about it,' said Vaman mildly, but he agreed it was the best family so far and they should not let the opportunity of cementing the match slip from their fingers. Even Laxman had slackened a little in looking for suitable matches further afield in anticipation of a positive response from the Ramanujans.

'I need a new ledger,' Vaman said as he finished his tea and began to attend to some accounts. Raman had let his tea get cold.

'I am going to Ahuja to get a notebook, I will get for you,' said Raman.

'Drink tea. I will go. It is very easy to get the wrong ledger. And I will get your exercise book also,' offered Vaman.

'No, no, please,' said Raman without much force.

'It is no trouble. All day I have been sitting here with only one customer coming. Now you are here to watch the shop, I am free to step outside.'

'Get two notebooks,' said Raman as Vaman stepped down from the podium, slipped into his leather sandals and picked up his umbrella.

When Vaman was gone Raman read the newspaper. There were floods all over the country. Landslips in the hill areas. Hordes of pilgrims drowned near Badrinath, houses washed away in the swollen Ganges. Everywhere was in turmoil except Mardpur. Considering that, it was surprising there was anything at all in the newspaper about that godforsaken small dot on the Gangetic Plain that Raman called home. It was a short article about the sale of some land beyond the bus station to a Marwari industrialist who owned several mills in Ghatpur. The article suggested that the price of land in Mardpur was beginning to rise 'dramatically'. This did not mean much to Raman, who had no need either to buy or to sell land. But it reminded him of what Vaman had said about Satyanarayan negotiating the sale of the *mela maidaan*. Perhaps a *dharamsala* would be built, or a school. If it was true that Satyanarayan had sold the land, Raman was convinced it would be put to good use.

Raman was disturbed by a clanking outside.

'*Doodh-wala hey!*' came the cracked cry.

Raman looked up as Rampal appeared, *balti* in hand.

'*Ram, ram*, Raman sahib,' said Rampal looking surprised. 'So you have at last taken over your brothers' business?' He laid the *balti* carefully on the sheet-covered platform and adjusted his turban-cloth.

'It is a family business, after all,' Raman reminded the milkman. He did not like the business to be referred to as his brothers' business, as if he were some outsider.

'Are you wanting to buy a sari?' added Raman, businesslike, trying to appear as if he sold saris every day of his life. He looked at the stacks of cloth behind him and wondered where he would start looking if Rampal requested a particular type of sari. But Rampal joined his hands humbly.

'Me? I am a poor man. I cannot afford such saris. Some cotton *dhotis* only my wife is buying sometimes from the hawkers from Ghatpur who are selling straight from the mills, wholesale price. They are damaged goods, but who can see anything? We cannot afford better. I am here only to deliver milk for Vaman sahib's tea,' he said, indicating towards the *balti*. 'In office sometimes there are so many customers and they are consuming much tea.'

'Yes,' said Raman drily. 'Almost as much as the *chai-khana*.'

'*Chai-khana*? That I do not know. *Chai-khana* is having own cows on other side of bus station. I am not selling to them.'

'Not for long,' said Raman, and told Rampal about the land sale. He was proud of having something to gossip about.

Rampal clicked his tongue. 'Soon there will be nowhere to graze the cattle. Only when milk quality is affected, then only they will realize, and they will blame the milk-sellers. They will accuse us of adulterating. But it is not the sellers, it is the cows and buffaloes not having good grass-*ghas* to eat any more.'

'Even *mela maidaan* is to be sold,' said Raman.

But Rampal, who heard a great deal of gossip while going from house to house, knew this already. 'Satyanarayan Swami is wanting to build new temple extension there.'

'Temple extension?' Raman was surprised. It was indeed a noble purpose for the *mela maidaan* but it was far from obvious that a bigger temple was needed. Whenever he was at the temple there was rarely anyone else; he could chatter with Satyanarayan undisturbed for hours.

'Too many people are coming from Ghatpur. They are saying what are these *murtis* under the trees? They must have their own temples,' Rampal explained.

Raman saw no harm in that. 'So all the *murtis* will be put inside. Then what will happen to Satyanarayan, where will he sit?'

'Maybe they will build a temple for Satyanarayan Swami too!' Rampal smiled. He made as if to go, then remembered something and turned to Raman again. 'By chance, are you wanting milk from Amma's Jhotta? It is from Jagdishpuri Extension I am coming and I know you are liking it very much. Amma has already told me this. It is why I am late. The Old Market is full with water. *Baap ré.* Up to my *baltis* the water is already coming. It is good the rain is not so hard as before or I will not be able to go at all to Jagdishpuri Extension tomorrow.'

Raman hid his eagerness. 'You are not wanting this milk for your family?'

'I have milk from other buffaloes, I am not so fussy about having Jhotta-milk only! Take, please. Outside I have on my bicycle, I will bring.'

Rampal went out and unhooked a larger, half-full *balti* from his bicycle. 'I am happy to sell little bit extra,' he said, presenting the *balti* to Raman. 'Many traders are not buying so much because too few customers are coming in the rain. I have too much milk.'

'This is the one from Amma's Jhotta?' said Raman peering into the vessel.

'It is the one,' Rampal assured him. 'It is a good buffalo, her milk is the best and she is eating same as other buffaloes. Such quantities she is giving, Amma cannot even use. It is like a miracle even Satyanarayan Swami cannot perform!'

'Oh, I am sure Jhotta-milk is having magical properties,' said Raman, eagerly receiving the *balti*. What magic it was that Jhotta's miracle milk had been brought all the way to him!

Raman paid for the milk. Rampal saluted and, tucking the money into the top of his *dhoti*, went on his way, leaving Raman with a twinge of excitement in his breast. He did not even have to wade through the water in the Old Market now. He felt like rushing home to continue working on his book. It would all come easily now that he had miracle milk.

There would be no trouble writing! But he needed a notebook to write in, and was forced to await his brother's return.

It was not long before Vaman came back with a smile about his lips. 'You will be glad you did not go to Ahuja Book Depot today, Raman Brother. That Satyanarayan was there, baying for your blood!'

Raman looked concerned. 'Why?'

'He wants to stop your book.' Vaman seemed to find this amusing.

'Why should he care?' said Raman vehemently. 'His job is to do *puja*, not worry about me.'

Vaman handed Raman the two exercise books. 'He is saying you cannot be trusted not to desecrate Hindu culture, et cetera, et cetera. He says he will be doing everything in his power to stop you. We were very entertained by his performance. It was very grand. He made himself seem so important! The protector of the culture, the saviour of our traditions!'

Behind the mockery Raman saw a serious message. He looked worried. 'What can he do to stop me?'

'He is knowledgeable in all kinds of bogus hocus-pocus, like Jhotta-*puja* and buffalo exorcism!'

Raman was not amused. 'I will have to hide,' he said.

'Well, hide the notebooks, anyway,' advised Vaman. 'I mean the fully written ones.'

'Where can I hide them?' said Raman in a mild panic, clutching the empty notebooks protectively to his chest.

23

ONCE THE RAINS HAD COME DEEPA BECAME AS HOMEBOUND AS AMMA, AND
even Jhotta had no choice but to dream about the proliferation of mud-
puddles from the sanctuary of the covered part of the courtyard. It was
Usha who plied between the Old Market and Jagdishpuri Extension,
laden with provisions. She and Rampal brought news of the outside
world which, given the richness of the inner world that both Amma and
Deepa inhabited, did not have to amount to very much to keep them
happy.

With help from Hari, Usha waded through the waters which had
flooded the Old Market. The vegetable vendors doggedly laid out their
wares on the platforms in front of the dank leaning buildings that lined the
narrow streets and tried to convince themselves that each day was a
market day like any other. When the flood was at its deepest, the
platforms hovered just an inch over the surface of the murky rainwater. So
crowded were they with vendors that pedestrians had no choice but to
pick their way slowly through the inundated streets. In dry weather the
vendors took up every inch of the streets and shoppers were compelled to
pass through by stepping along the platforms, dodging old women
chattering and babies with nothing but a black string around their middle
and *kajal* in their eyes.

Usha and Hari did not possess an umbrella. They held a square of cardboard over their heads until it disintegrated in the rain. Hari carried the groceries while Usha gingerly felt her way forward seeking the ruts and potholes with her unshod feet. She moved with a skating motion, dragging her feet through the water so that she did not trip on an unexpected obstacle submerged in the depths. The dead carcass of a rat swept past in the knee-deep water, brushing Usha's leg and making her jump. Hari steadied her. She stopped only long enough to wring out her sopping *kameez* before carrying on. It was not the wet she minded – she expected to get drenched in such weather – but she did not want to be weighed down. Good balance was important for safely traversing the Old Market.

Once they got to Jagdishpuri Extension Usha's clothes dried, infused with the smell of woodsmoke as she got the bucket-stove working. Amma gave Hari a *balti* of milk, fresh from Jhotta that day, for Rampal had managed to come, as he had for so many years, whatever the weather. Sometimes Amma gave Hari flour that she had ground at her stones in payment for his trouble. And often he would eat his breakfast there, before heading back to serve whoever needed him that day. There was a lot of work when the rains came. People could not get about and needed extra hands to run errands or to clear away the rainwater that had invaded their homes and shops.

Hari also did well accompanying people with their shopping, holding up their umbrellas, carrying their loads – which were heavier than usual so that they did not have to come back to the markets again so soon. At other times he ran from shop to shop in Kumar Bazaar foraging for cardboard boxes. If these could be kept relatively dry, they could be put to good use. Hari would throw down a flattened cardboard box on the ground beside a rickshaw almost as soon as it came to a halt, so that the ladies could step out onto it without getting their saris muddied. There were good tips to be had, but the money-making potential was deceptive – the flattened boxes did not have a long life in such weather, and much time was wasted looking for dry replacements.

Amma, as always, occupied her *charpoy*. It had been pushed to the edge of the courtyard to the small covered portion, where a swing had once hung from a large hook. Deepa's father, Dasji, had put it up. Deepa did not know what had happened to the swing – it had just disappeared one day. Deepa could remember even as a very small child, no more than two or three years old, sitting under the covered portion in the monsoon. It was like sitting behind a waterfall.

Jhotta stood chomping grass, looking out distantly into the rain as if she alone could see something beyond that wall of water. Sometimes, unhurriedly, she would stamp her hooves – the only indication that she was impatient (impatient as a buffalo could ever allow herself to be) for some other view of life. This was the kind of weather that Jhotta loved, but Pappu had not come for days. He could not risk letting loose a single buffalo because he was unable to run after them. So he stayed away.

'Tell me more about the smuggler,' Deepa cajoled, sitting with Amma on the *charpoy* and scratching the soft fluff of that buffalo head that waved close to her – it was not such a large area, that covered part. Amma, Deepa and buffalo were all squeezed in together.

Amma tried to oblige. She held an empty *balti* in her hands. She stroked it lightly as if rubbing off the story from the metal.

'There is a march to be described,' said Amma, finally. She had been concentrating hard, trying to make out the details of the hazy vision that had formed and disintegrated like oil on water and formed again, translucent and wavering. She found it difficult to focus her mind on it.

'March?'

'*Morcha*. Demonstration. They are walking barefoot in protest, with Jagat Singh the smuggler as their leader. They are waving their arms.'

Deepa listened fascinated, and wrote it down. She was already writing in the inside back cover. She wrote as small as she could, to get it all in. But there was not much this time.

Amma shook her head. 'I am not seeing clearly,' she said.

'Are you tired, Amma?'

Amma shook her head and smiled.

'If you ask me about the stories of the courts of the kings I can tell you, but Jagat Singh, that I am not seeing clearly.'

Deepa did not mind, there was no more space left in her notebook. She was waiting for the rain to abate and for the water in the Old Market to go down so that she could venture out to buy another one. 'You should rest, Amma,' she said. 'I am disturbing you too much.' She jumped off the *charpoy* and ran to the kitchen, her bare feet slapping the water on the smooth paving stones of the courtyard. In the kitchen Usha, her hair still dripping, was trying with some difficulty to light the bucket-stove from the slightly damp wood that she and Hari had brought that day. She shoved pieces of paper into the stove and flapped her reed-fan but there was only smoke. She bent down and blew into the bucket-stove. The paper fluttered and crackled, but did not burn for long enough for the wood to catch. Usha cleared out the mound of burnt, blackened paper and started again, twisting fresh sheets of old newspaper into long lighters.

'Tell me a Baoli story,' said Deepa.

And Usha, because she had to wait for her wood to dry out, sat back on her haunches and began: 'One day Baoli's Jhotta was standing in the rain and refusing to give milk. "Give milk you *baoli* Jhotta," Baoli said. "I do not like to sit here in the rain getting wet." But the *baoli* Jhotta would not give milk. So Baoli decided she would have to stand in the rain for three days and three nights, and left her in a deep puddle. After three days Baoli came back and said, "Well, are you going to give milk now?" But the Jhotta said, "I have given milk, while I was standing in this puddle, but it flowed away in the rain." And Baoli went *baoli*, because she had lost so much milk.

> *'Baoli Maai, Baoli Maai,*
> *Kahan se aai?*
> *Koi jan na paai.'*

Usha struck a match again. 'So,' she said, getting to the moral of the tale, 'just because you cannot see it, does not mean it isn't there. It can come when you are not looking.'

'Like Amma's treasure?' breathed Deepa.

'Of that I was not thinking,' said Usha, striking more matches in vain.

But Deepa liked to think she was.

The rain slowed. Rapidly the level of the water in the Old Market went down. It was the moment Deepa had been waiting for. After school, that first day back, she hurried towards Kumar Bazaar, to Ahuja Book Depot.

Mr Ahuja, a pleasant, wrinkled man in his late fifties with glasses and a lot of grey hair, wearing Oxford bags and a white shirt, was once a civil servant in Lucknow. He was the kind of man Gulbachan had once aspired to be until he failed to make the grade. Mr Ahuja took early retirement after the death of his brother, who owned the shop, in order to support his widowed sister-in-law and her four children. He kept it open long hours and even all day on Sundays, never employing any help.

But there was another difference between Gulbachan and Mr Ahuja. Mr Ahuja was a patriot; a staunch supporter of the Congress Party and its leaders. He had photographs of Nehru, Shastri and Indira Gandhi on his wall in the book depot and they were often garlanded with fresh marigolds. Whereas for Gulbachan, no leader quite matched up to Gandhiji.

Deepa liked Mr Ahuja; he talked to children as if they were adults and did not allow other adults to talk down to them in his presence.

'*Two* notebooks? Well, you are getting a lot of homework these days,' said Mr Ahuja in his easy, cultured manner.

Deepa laughed shyly. 'It is not for homework.'

'For what, then, may I ask?'

'For writing stories.'

'Writing stories! I hope I am in your story.' His eyes twinkled as he leant over the counter. 'Everyone starts with the story of their own life. And here I am in yours, selling notebooks.'

'No,' laughed Deepa. She enjoyed the way Mr Ahuja made her story seem so important. 'I am writing about a march.'

'March?'

'*Morcha*.'

'Oho! History, then. There were many marches when the Britishers were here. We had to throw them out, you know, *satyagraha*, have you heard of it?' said Mr Ahuja, quite prepared to give her a history lesson.

'Not such a march,' said Deepa.

'Oh? Like labour union march, then? They are going on in Ghatpur. There's a lot of trouble in Ghatpur these days.'

Deepa just smiled and waited for him to bring down the exercise books. He banged them together to get rid of the dust.

'Dust and mud, mud and dust. That is India,' he said cheerily. 'Why should we complain?'

He pulled down a cloth and wiped the dust off the glass counter, shaking the cloth onto the floor.

A shower of raindrops flew into the shop making Deepa jump, laughing, out of the way. Gulbachan entered behind a large black umbrella, which he was shaking into the shop. Mr Ahuja put up his hand to fend off the drops, which fell with a splat onto the just-cleaned counter.

'My goodness me, what a storm!' said Mr Ahuja.

Gulbachan concurred. 'Terrible rain. Did I tell you when I went on the Salt March? It was raining just like this. And now, I am going to write about it.' Gulbachan clicked his fingers at Mr Ahuja. 'Please bring down your best notebooks, Mr A!' He picked up the two notebooks Mr Ahuja was intending to hand to Deepa and immediately threw them down on the counter in disgust. 'No, no. These will not do. It must be smooth paper. Smooooooth.'

Gulbachan's need was clearly more urgent than Deepa's. She stood aside as Mr Ahuja looked under the counter for some newer stock, while Gulbachan drummed impatiently on top with his fingers.

'No time to waste. I must get started before someone else writes about the march.'

'Oho!' said Mr Ahuja. 'So someone is about to steal a march!' His belly quivered and his shoulders heaved in silent laughter at his joke, which was lost on the others. 'Even I have heard that someone is writing about a march.'

'You see!' said Gulbachan triumphantly. 'My sources are always correct.'

'Not only that,' said Mr Ahuja, 'I have also heard that this person who is writing about a march is one very talented writer.' He smiled broadly at Deepa as he said it.

Gulbachan looked hesitant. He would not have described Raman as very talented. He was beginning to wonder if he had seriously under-estimated his assistant.

Mr Ahuja handed Gulbachan three more brands of exercise book.

'This will not do, Mr A,' said Gulbachan, feeling the paper of each book in turn and then flinging it aside. 'Not smooth enough, I said smooooooth. None of these will do. You can't be serious, that's all you have?'

'Sorry,' said Mr Ahuja, genuinely apologetic, 'but this is India, you can't complain.'

'I will take these then,' said Gulbachan, changing his mind quickly. 'I must get started, I cannot wait around for the right notebook.' He dug in his pockets for some change.

'Paper is paper,' agreed Mr Ahuja, wrapping up the purchases; 'if we wait for the country to develop like the West before we buy anything, we would not write anything at all.'

Vaman arrived seconds after Gulbachan had departed.

'You want exercise books, too?' Mr Ahuja said, turning to see who had entered.

'How did you guess?' said Vaman.

'For book-writing?'

'You are excellent at divination, Mr Ahuja. Have you been consulting your astrologer? My brother Raman is indeed writing a book.'

'About a march?'

'I do not know details. But if you want him to write about this, I am sure he will oblige.'

'Oh, it is not me who wants. I was just thinking a march is a popular thing to write about these days,' said Mr Ahuja.

'Is that what people want to read?'

'In newspapers I like to read about it,' admitted Mr Ahuja. 'There are many protests against our government. Prices are going up and up. But they forget these are the people who won independence for us, they should not complain.'

'Independence-walas are already dead, no?' said Vaman leafing through the exercise books Mr Ahuja handed him.

'Spirit lives on in the Congress Party,' said Mr Ahuja patriotically.

'I voted Swatantra Party,' admitted Vaman. 'It is because I like their flag.'

'It is the party of banias,' noted Mr Ahuja, 'while Congress is the party of civil servants.'

'Really?' said Vaman, genuinely surprised. 'There are so many civil servants to keep Congress Party with such a big majority? Then no wonder people are protesting against government. We banias are paying for too many civil servants who are only there to stop us trading. You should understand that, Mr Ahuja; you are one of us now!'

'Oh, but I still vote Congress,' protested Mr Ahuja.

'Then you are still a civil servant at heart!'

Mr Ahuja seemed pleased to hear this.

'Oh, and a ledger I am needing, Mr Ahuja,' Vaman added.

Once again, Mr Ahuja mounted the ladder to root among his stock, only to be interrupted yet again. He looked around, distracted by the commotion. Someone was wrestling with a big black umbrella, apparently stuck in the doorway. He was shouting at the umbrella to close and seemed to expect it to respond to his bullying.

'It is the most busy day I have had for a long time!' exclaimed Mr Ahuja happily as he waited to see who was this latest customer.

Satyanarayan's voice could be heard loud and clear and hectoring as he struggled with his umbrella, finally dislodging it and bringing it down into a neat fold in one swift action. He turned round smartly with his back to Mr Ahuja and held his umbrella out of the door, leaning well forward so that it would not get stuck again as he rapidly opened and shut it to get rid of the raindrops. Only his scraggy legs and big feet in black sandals and his *dhoti* were visible inside the shop as he leant out. Then he walked in, thumping the umbrella on the ground for emphasis.

'I forbid you to sell this man any exercise book for story-writing, Mr Ahuja!' Satyanarayan shouted.

'Oho!' said Mr Ahuja, winking at Deepa. 'A *morcha*. Very troublesome.'

'Satyanarayan Swami!' said Vaman, unable to resist a poke at the Brahmin. 'Surely you don't need notebooks and pens for writing? Isn't it you are knowing everything by rote?'

Satyanarayan stamped towards Mr Ahuja, who was still perched on a lower rung of his ladder. 'Only scholars are entitled to write!' he decreed.

'Well, now. That is a bit strong,' opined Mr Ahuja. 'In fact, Deepa is buying notebooks to write stories, isn't it, Deepa?'

They all turned to look at Deepa in surprise. Deepa shyly nodded.

'About a march, isn't it?' said Mr Ahuja.

Deepa nodded again.

'And Gulbachan of PTI has just departed. He is also writing a book about a march,' said Mr Ahuja. 'The whole of Mardpur is writing marching books, it is nothing unusual. Why are you objecting, Swamiji? Paper is no longer rationed, after all.'

They all looked at Satyanarayan, wondering how he would defend himself against this voice of reason. Satyanarayan spluttered. He glanced at Deepa just as everyone else had done when Mr Ahuja drew attention to her. But whereas the others saw her in terms of her youth, Satyanarayan saw her as something quite different. He recognized her as the granddaughter of the great Brahmin sage Pundit Mishra. As such it was her birthright to turn to writing and other scholarly work. That she had turned to it so young in life was so much the better, he had no quibble with that. But Deepa's pursuits were far removed from what he considered to be Raman's pretensions. Having failed in business, that bania was now seeking to elevate himself through scholarship. By doing so he would debase learning itself!

Satyanarayan was too irate with those ranged against him to articulate any of this in the middle of Mr Ahuja's dusty book depot. They had not yet evolved, poor fools! They did not have the vision and higher learning that he himself possessed to see beyond the obvious and form a greater picture!

The Brahmin calmed down almost as quickly as he had flared up. Poor, stupid fools! It was their karma. They were born the way they were born precisely so that they should not see so clearly. And he, Satyanarayan, was born on earth as a Brahmin precisely so that he could. It was the nature of karma. Why blame these poor mortals for what their past lives had not achieved? He turned smartly and walked out, wrestling with his umbrella to shield him from the pelting rain.

'Causing trouble, that Satyanarayan,' muttered Vaman, feeling triumphant and unable to resist a parting shot.

Mr Ahuja held up a restraining hand. 'Now that Swamiji has *marched* out, we should not speak evil of him.'

He turned to Deepa. 'You are right to write about a march, it is quite a rich topic for discussion. Everyone seems to have something to say on the subject!' He handed her two notebooks.

'And your brother, too, would he like to write about a *morcha*, Mr Vaman? Please tell him he has permission from all of us. Satyanarayan Swami can hardly object when the whole of Mardpur is doing it!'

24

ANYONE ELSE WOULD HAVE BEEN SURPRISED TO SEE RAMAN FACE THE HEAVY rain, the mud and the pools of standing water left behind when the floodwaters of the Old Market receded. Amma was not. She sensed the restlessness that would bring Raman out from the lychee garden and on towards Jagdishpuri Extension. What she could not know was that it was really Jhotta's milk that drew Raman. For all that Amma could read Raman's thoughts and predict his actions, some of the inner workings of Raman's mind were still a mystery. She could not see motivations. She also did not foresee that he would come furtive and nervous, his notebooks clutched to his chest.

'Ram, Ram,' said Amma, 'what a sacrifice you are making to come to see an old woman when it is raining so hard!'

The rain had stopped briefly and Usha had pushed Amma's *charpoy* out to its usual place in the courtyard. There she now sat, like a captain on a ship, her feet well out of the way of the wet courtyard stones. She was enjoying the smell of the damp, swollen wood of the *charpoy* frame which no longer creaked when she sat on it, and the fresh monsoon breezes in her hair which brought to her all manner of smells of life around. With the rains, things had begun to grow, pushing through the rich, damp earth in a riot of blossoming and flowering that pushed aside Amma's homely pickle smell and enveloped her in the scent of fresh, dripping vegetation instead.

'It is no sacrifice Ammaji, I am really here for selfish motive. Just a little yoghurt will send me away satisfied, and I will not have to disturb you again for a few days,' Raman said. He now felt familiar enough in that household that he could be quite open about what he had come for. Quite open, that was, except for the *real* motive of his visit that day.

'But to come in such weather! Now I really know how much you love raita. Well, the rain will not last long. In a day or two it will stop, and our clothes can be dried again outside. Even the chilli powder I ground yesterday has become by today just a lump. Everything is wet.'

'I hope it will not affect your Jhotta-milk,' said Raman, a little concerned.

'Of course, no. Jhotta is a very good milk production machine. We are blessed to have her.'

'It is true,' agreed Raman. 'Our blessings should indeed be counted. There is flooding all over the country. Here only the Old Market is bad. But even that is only one foot and three inches. Imagine, the Ganges has flooded its banks in Bihar, and the situation looks grim.' He was quoting a phrase from that morning's PTI wire. 'It is at least three feet under water in some places!'

'It is a calamity!' agreed Amma. 'Ohey Deepa! Are you getting tea for our visitor?' She could hear Usha on the roof. Usha was taking advantage of the break in the rain to collect Jhotta's dung and pat it into dung-cakes to dry on the roof. The slapping and patting reverberated around the courtyard.

When Deepa brought the tea, Raman rested his cloth-bag on the *charpoy* in order to take the steaming glass. He had been holding it close to his chest, as much to keep it dry from the rain as to shield it from Amma's penetrating vision until the time was right to reveal its contents.

Amma felt the strings of the *charpoy* sag. She sniffed the air. 'What is it you have brought with you, Ramanji? I can smell nothing but dust and paper and ink, some of it quite fresh.'

Raman looked a little uncomfortable, as if hesitant to reveal his intentions. But really his main problem was how to make Amma understand his fear about the notebooks.

'Ammaji, these are my notebooks. All four of them.'

'But why are you carrying them around in the rain, Ramanji? They will be spoilt, the ink will be running. They are so precious to you that you are carrying them all around the bazaar these days?'

'It is not that,' said Raman. 'I am afraid to lose them, if somebody takes them away . . .' His voice trailed off.

'Who should take? It is only book-writing that is going on. You are not taking away anything from anyone.'

Raman sighed. He thought it prudent not to reveal any names. He merely said, 'It may be better to leave my notebooks with you for keeping safe.'

'Of course, of course. It is a good idea of yours to leave them here for keeping safe. Who thinks to look for books in this old-woman house? House of one who cannot see and cannot read! Here they are only looking for treasure, *bhooths* also, but not notebooks!' Amma's voice crackled with laughter, and even Raman allowed himself to smile.

'Deepa will keep them with her school books, isn't it, Deepa?'

Deepa took the notebooks and stowed them in the red trunk where she kept her own school books.

Then Amma ordered Deepa to fill Raman's *balti* from the yoghurt pot. 'Eat raita. It is good for the nerves.'

It was advice that Raman found no difficulty in following. Once relaxed, Amma felt the stirring of Jagat Singh the smuggler stronger than she had felt it for many days. The images she had been struggling to retain in her mind re-formed, clear and detailed as if the figures she imagined were standing before her, bathed in light. It was as though her eyes had opened and her vision was restored – that was how vividly her mind could see. And as they drank their tea she related to Raman what she saw. And Raman thanked God for such a wonderful potion as Jhotta-milk raita.

Deepa could not sleep that night. She lay awake for a while, listening to the rain battering the smooth stones of the courtyard. Then she rose quietly, picked up the lantern with the dim yellow light, and turned it up to full when she got to the trunk room. She held the lantern high with one hand, and with the other opened the lid of the red trunk, leaning it back carefully against the wall so that it would not bang down suddenly. She pulled out Raman's four notebooks and sat down on the ground to look at them.

The writing was almost childish, with well-rounded letters. The pages were easy to read, even though he had crossed out many sentences. But the more Deepa read, the more perplexed she became. Many parts of the story were missing; parts that Amma had already related to Deepa, sitting on the *charpoy* while preparing vegetables or watching the rain; parts that Deepa herself had imagined. Deepa recalled Amma's animated voice as she narrated the tale, and she heard again her own quiet prodding – questions about the scenery or details that were not clear and which filled in the gaps.

Deepa sat back piecing together the story; it was like a jigsaw puzzle – bits by Raman and bits from Amma. As she sat with only the warm glow of the lantern for company, she did what neither Raman nor Amma could do: she imagined the whole rather than the parts.

It was late when Deepa awoke the next morning. Amma let her sleep on and had quietly gone about her tasks by herself: preparing the buttermilk, grinding her wheat and pounding her spices. Even sifting the dal she accomplished, running the grains between her fingers, feeling for any irregular, hard shapes which she discarded. She listened to the tiny stones fall on the ground with satisfaction. At least, she thought, they would not end up in her stomach.

The first thing Deepa noticed was that it had stopped raining. It was sunny and hot. But it was a fresh, steamy heat such as only came with a break in the rains, rather than the dusty, oppressive pre-monsoon heat. The earthy smells mingled with the scent of fresh green grass and dung that had just begun to dry. And rising above these odours, heady and strong, was the smell of pickles and red earth that filled the courtyard.

After a quick breakfast, Deepa brought out Raman's notebooks again and sat down with them on Amma's *charpoy*. 'There are many scenes that are not in the book,' she told her grandmother.

'Maybe he did not have time to write,' said Amma. 'Or maybe they are in other books.'

'No,' said Deepa, 'there are bits missing in between.'

Amma could not explain the gaps either. 'The book I am seeing, the one that will be published, does not have things here and there that are missing.'

Deepa brought out her own notebook in which she had written down some of Amma's descriptions. Then she took one of the new exercise books she had bought at Ahuja's and began to write, drawing from the two notebooks before her. She knitted the two strands together – Raman's and the descriptions of the places that grandmother and granddaughter visualized and jotted down. But that was not the only thing. Suddenly, Amma was beginning to see Jagat Singh strongly again, as if Raman's very presence had awakened the smuggler and left something of him behind when he departed. The story Amma told from this vision also went into Deepa's notebook.

The tale that emerged over some days was quite different from what was etched out in the four notebooks that had found refuge in Jagdishpuri Extension. The new version was still about Jagat Singh the smuggler, but it was more alive, more dramatic: evocative and atmospheric, with bits from Raman and bits from Amma, all stitched together by Deepa into a seamless narrative, so that it was impossible to tell, at the end of the day, whose story it really was.

25

RAIN AGAIN AND YET MORE RAIN. DEEPA LOOKED OUT FROM HER VANTAGE point on Amma's *charpoy* and thought about the story of Jagat Singh. Now it was a real story, not just a collection of scenes and descriptions. She marvelled at how much of it she had missed even while Amma was narrating to her. It had not made complete sense until she had seen Raman's notebooks.

A loud clap of thunder and the heavens opened wider.

'*Baapré*. Only a king could have commanded so loudly that the heavens obeyed!' said Amma.

'How did the kings escape the rain, Amma?' Deepa asked, hoping for another tale.

'In some places the rains are only very short. Like in Gokul,' replied Amma. She was combing Deepa's long hair, feeling the silkiness beneath her fingers as she gathered together the strands.

'Gokul?' said Deepa who had not heard of it.

'It is a principality sheltered by the hills. The Dark Kingdom they are calling it, for it is a principality of forests where the trees are so close, the light cannot get through. At the same time, the subjects are dark-skinned.'

'How did you get there, Amma?'

Amma put the comb down and divided Deepa's hair into three

sections, feeling the weight in her hands to make sure she had divided it evenly. She began to plait them.

'It is a hazardous journey. We were called there because the babies of the *rajkumari* had not survived, and their longing for a son and heir was strong. In the forests are wolves and hyenas and tigers. No palanquin can be carried through such trees, so I tied my sari between my legs and with a long stick I found my way between the roots and creepers. We moved very slowly. We slept in the forest, in huts built for guests of the prince. The prince sent his guides to find us, or we would have been completely lost, there was no one else on the way. What subjects there were lived mostly along the river which cut through the jungle.'

'Why not travel along the river, it is easier than the jungle?' asked Deepa, feeling Amma's fingers move swiftly, deftly along the length of her hair. She was almost at the end now.

'True,' said Amma, pausing to tie the end of the plait with the ribbon Deepa had pressed into her fingers. 'But it was not possible. There were treacherous rapids where the water was fast. The palace was beside the river, deep in the forest, and we arrived in good time. A few days later I was awakened in the middle of the night by Lata.'

'Lata?'

'Sister-in-law of Lekha, a serving maid in the palace. For her I found a silver bangle in my small earthenware pot. She held it to her forehead. I had slept in my sari in preparation for just such a possibility and to the *rajkumari*'s rooms I followed her. There I saw it would be many hours before the baby showed its head. I settled down with the *rajkumari*, massaging her back and telling her stories of the other queens and princesses I had tended.'

'Just like you are telling me?'

Amma nodded. She picked up the comb and began to comb her own hair as she continued. 'All at once there was a commotion outside. A serving maid ran in. "The *rajkumari* must leave," she said. "The forest is burning and the palace is in danger. By boat she must go."

'The *rajkumari* asked where the fire had been seen. I recognized the place-name for there had been a rest-hut there; it was a day's walk from the palace. "We have time," I said; "make preparations to leave." Where all the dark-skinned maids suddenly came from, I do not know. They were packing away so many things that no one could need, while I brewed the special herbs I had brought from Alankar to Alpabad and now to Gokul, hoping to speed the *rajkumari*'s labour. But the child was a stubborn one, just as he would be for the rest of his life, making him a strong ruler – strong enough to steer Gokul out of all adversity.

'Morning was coming with still no sign of his head. The maidservants had stripped the room. The *rajkumari* crying in pain was all that was left, and myself. A maid rushed in. "The fire! The fire! We must go! It is almost at the palace." And I said, "Just a few minutes more." The maidservant was fearful. "No, we cannot, there is too much danger." "We will come," I promised. And the *rajkumari* screamed.'

'The baby was coming?' said Deepa. Her hair done, she was facing Amma now, watching her grandmother rhythmically combing her own hair in long sweeps.

Amma nodded. 'Only very slowly. "The palace is on fire!" cried the maidservant. "Come, please, I am the only one left, and I will surely burn to death with my *rajkumari*." Grandfather ran into the room – there was no one left to stop him. And then I saw the head. A prince was born.'

'But you had to get out of the palace!' said Deepa excitedly, as Amma unhurriedly knotted her tresses into a bun, pushing and prodding it into place.

'I wrapped up the new baby and with him I hurried, while Grandfather carried the *rajkumari* on his back. We followed the maidservant, who found the fastest way out of the burning palace, down to the river. We were stumbling over the bundles and crates of palace valuables, abandoned as people ran for their lives. There, a boat carried us across.'

'The river saved you!'

'The water was golden, shining, and flickering in the reflection of the burning palace. On the other side the court and the subjects were huddled, crying and wailing at the great calamity that had befallen their principality. Only when they saw their *rajkumari* with her baby in her arms did they stop to rejoice – for the birth of a child can affect the emotions that way – despite their exhaustion and their sadness and their night-long work pouring water from the river onto the palace and their own homes. They had worked in long human chains – every man, woman and child – until it was too late. Then they jumped into all the boats they could find to flee to the other side of the river to watch their kingdom burn.

'And so they celebrated the birth of their new prince while that fire raged for a day. At the same time they vowed that their principality would be reborn under the star of the new prince. Grandfather that very day drew up his chart. From our belongings he had saved only some parchment and a reed pen. He dipped his pen into the purple dye that was running from my sari, which had been soaked as we crossed the flaming river. Then, as the fire subsided to glowing embers turning the river red in its light, the *rajkumari* turned from watching the blackened palace, with tears in her eyes, and said, "I have nothing left, but my gratitude." She took the necklace from her throat and put it into my hands.'

There was a long pause as Deepa contemplated the rain and Amma was lost in thought.

'It was a miracle no child ever died,' said Deepa.

'It happened once,' said Amma gravely, and before Deepa could protest at such a calamity, she began: 'Towards the Rajput kingdoms we were heading, through the big desert, when Grandfather fell ill with a fever. "Go on without me," he said. But I knew I could not. My place was by his side. We stayed at a renowned *dharamsala* while he could get better. When he was well enough to travel we went on our way by camel, but the track had been blown over with sand and although we had a guide, we lost our way and had to return back to the *dharamsala* to start again. At last I knew we were on the right road to the palace, a huge fortress in the sand. But my heart was heavy for I knew already that we were too late.'

'Too late!' exclaimed Deepa, sitting up.

'As we approached the gates of the palace in the desert a woman ran towards me, crying and afraid. "It is too late, Ammaji, too late!" The little prince had died.'

Deepa's eyes were wide. 'It could not be!' she said, as if refusing to believe it.

But Amma went on: '"I am Chandra, the sister of Lekha, and I serve the rani," she said, but she could go no further for weeping. I stroked her head and waited for her to calm herself. "Just three hours have passed," said Chandra.'

'It was the storm that stopped you!' said Deepa, then stopped. 'Or the sand. No, it was Grandfather's illness.'

Said Amma: 'Chandra said, "They have taken the small body secretly to be buried. And I must run to the *dai* nearby and find a replacement." And she fell weeping again. "Without a boy, the rani will surely be thrown out of the palace and the raja will marry again." The rani had already borne two girls, so the third must be a boy. But the boy did not live.'

'So that rani, too, must die?' said Deepa.

Amma continued her story. '"Go and find a child, Chandra. I will wait for you," I said, and gave her my anklet which she held to her forehead and kissed before tucking it into her bodice. Gathering her long *chunni* around her, she went running towards the town we had just passed. "We should return home," said Grandfather. "What is there for us to do here? For once it is too late."

'But I knew it was fate that we should not arrive there in good time, and that a small boy unknown to anyone would be given a new future because of this. "Wait," I said. "We cannot abandon the rani now. We have come so far." So we waited and at last Chandra appeared with a small newborn wrapped in her *chunni*, all covered up so that it could not be seen. And we made towards the palace and the guards all stood aside and whispered, "The baby will be born!" when they saw us. And we climbed up to the rani's quarters and just an hour after we entered, it was announced that a boy was born. And there was rejoicing. Only Chandra and the rani could see there was something different, because Grandfather, instead of being hard at work with his reed pens preparing the horoscope, was idle. "There is no horoscope for this baby," he said. "The raja will suspect," said the rani, "draw any horoscope." "I must have the exact time of birth," Grandfather replied. "Draw up a chart as if the time was the time of your arrival," the rani said.

'And with a heavy heart, Grandfather drew up the horoscope for the time of our arrival. And that was the horoscope that was given to the boy. There was no knowing what was his real fate. All we knew was that he was born humble and destined to be a prince. And the rani, so grateful, lavished us with the most beautiful of all jewels, studded with diamonds and emeralds such as I had never seen.'

'It is the treasure, but it is sad!' said Deepa.

Amma nodded. 'That same day Grandfather fell ill with a fever again. A fever so bad he could not discuss the fine points of the horoscope with the raja and the astrologers of the court. "We must leave," I sent message to the raja, "the medicine my husband needs does not grow in the sands but in the lush forests." And he allowed us to depart.'

'And that was how you got the treasure?' said Deepa.

'It is the same treasure,' said Amma.

26

GULBACHAN HAD BEEN A LITTLE DISTANT WITH RAMAN. HE FELT HE HAD A
competitor – and one that was competing on his own turf, for that matter.
He imagined that Raman, cooped up at home while the rain drenched
the streets, was making tremendous headway, the kind of headway that
Gulbachan had always wanted to make in his writing career.

If Raman sensed Gulbachan's broodiness he gave no outward
indication. He went about his tasks energized by the lifting of the torrid
pre-monsoon heat. Gulbachan could not watch him carrying on so busily
while himself having little to do, and while his own ambitions were
coming crashing to the ground, usurped by his assistant.

'Still writing?' Gulbachan finally asked curtly.

The PTI wire had been quiet for over an hour. Gulbachan had read the
Statesman several times over. The telephone had gone dead – probably
something to do with the previous week of incessant rain.

'Yes,' said Raman, wondering why Gulbachan had suddenly become
interested.

'No writers' block?'

'No.'

'No writers' cramp?'

'No.'

'No writers' headache?'

'No.' But by now Raman was worried. Were these all the diseases writers were supposed to have? Perhaps he was not writing enough. He resolved to redouble his efforts when he got home.

'So, from where are you getting inspiration?' Gulbachan wanted to know.

'Raita.'

'What?'

'Banana raita is best.'

'We are not talking about tiffin,' said Gulbachan a little irritably. He thought Raman was straying from the point.

'Yes, yes,' insisted Raman. 'It is from yoghurt I am getting inspiration. Special Jhotta-yoghurt from Jagdishpuri Amma's buffalo. While writing, I am eating raita.'

'And when there is no more raita?'

'No raita, no writer,' said Raman, enjoying his joke.

'And then?'

'I go back to Amma for more.'

'And others are eating this writer-raita too?'

'Only Amma and one granddaughter,' said Raman.

'And they are writing also after eating it?' Gulbachan did not sound too convinced.

Raman pondered this. Perhaps it did not work for children, he thought. And Amma was blind and could not write even if she wanted to.

At that point the telephone rang for the first time in two days. It rang just once and then stopped. Gulbachan held his hand three inches above the receiver, waiting for it to ring again. When it did not he picked it up anyway and held it cautiously to his ear.

'Dead,' he said, replacing it in its cradle.

'Testing, maybe,' Raman suggested.

They waited, watching the phone closely. When it failed to respond after ten minutes, Gulbachan relaxed again. He put his feet up on his desk and leant back in his swivel chair, hands behind his head. He yawned. Then, in a nonchalant yet deliberate voice he said, 'How can I get writer-raita? It has been my dream for many years to be an author.'

Raman looked dubious. Was Gulbachan asking him to share with him his precious yoghurt? He, Raman, had made considerable sacrifice, often going half-way across town to obtain this nectar, and now Gulbachan, with his feet on the table and not enough work to fill a day, was expecting him to just hand it over.

Raman tried not to let his annoyance show. This was, after all, his boss. And to be fair Gulbachan did not expect him to work too hard either. He let him go home in the afternoon and never complained if he did not come back. Raman relented a little at this last thought. 'I don't know if this Jhotta produces enough milk to allow distributing raita among so many people,' he said cautiously. He knew it was not true. Jhotta's milk was distributed to Usha and Hari and Rampal, too. Rampal frequently had milk for sale from Jhotta.

'Why don't you buy the buffalo from Amma?' said Gulbachan suddenly.

Raman looked open-mouthed at his boss. It was not something he had ever considered. Why not, indeed? Then the objections came out in a rush. 'With what money? I have no money – I cannot ask Laxman–Vaman. Where to keep such a beast? It is not for sale. What will Amma do without her Jhotta? I don't think she will want to sell it.'

Gulbachan's response was cool. 'I could not buy the blessed buffalo myself. Where would I keep her? I live in government house and it is forbidden to keep animals. Also, I have no garden. But you have a whole lychee garden for a blessed buffalo to stay happy in. It is the best place for a buffalo, with so many shady trees. And no problem for grass.'

'But I have no money to buy a buffalo, blessed or not,' protested Raman. 'I am on only small part-time salary.' And lest Gulbachan thought he was complaining, he added hastily, 'Not that I am discontented. Oh no. But it does not leave much to spare for buffalo-buying.'

'You have no savings?'

'I am a man with three daughters,' said Raman, his voice coming out in a kind of whine. 'Meera and Mamta are already reaching the age for a decent match. Two at once, just consider! What a burden. I am already having sleepless nights every time I think of it.'

'Maybe you can borrow the blessed buffalo for a while? Until our . . . I mean your book is finished.'

Raman looked dubious. It was true: if he were to keep a flow of writing, he could not keep running to Jagdishpuri with his *balti* in such weather. It would be much easier if he had a constant source of yoghurt nearer at hand. He had to admit, having it right in front of his house in the lychee garden would be extremely convenient.

'I say, Raman,' said Gulbachan deliberately, 'I have a plan. I will be extremely supportive of your book-writing. I won't care that you are writing the book I had always hoped to write.'

Raman thought this was magnanimous of Gulbachan, but he was also a little confused. Gulbachan also wished to write about the smuggler Jagat Singh?

He looked attentively at Gulbachan, and Gulbachan continued almost rashly, 'I will even help you get it published in Delhi. I have many writer friends in PTI. Very powerful. They know all the publishers. But I ask you one thing, only one thing in return.'

'What's that?'

'You organize to borrow this blessed buffalo, and we share the milk. That's all. It is too easy. How can you say no?'

Raman had to admit it was a tempting offer.

'It is not a bad idea,' he said slowly, but before he had time to consider it in any depth the telephone sprang to life, making them both start.

Gulbachan shouted above the ringing, 'Think about it, Raman. It is too simple,' and snatched the receiver from its cradle.

27

WHEN THE FIRST FLUSH OF THE MONSOON HAD PASSED, KUMUD GATHERED the plump fallen lychees from under the trees, discarded those with split skins and served the rest for breakfast. She looked anxiously at the clouds. She wanted the rain to hold for a day or two so that the fruit could be picked before it rotted on the trees. The torrents had abated but each day there were morning showers, and the evening cloudbursts were too unpredictable to organize a harvest.

The mosquitoes around the lychee garden thrived. Raman sprayed the house every day and Kumud examined the mosquito nets meticulously for rips and tears, but still they would be itching and scratching by morning. Raman lay awake at night scratching. It did not help that the two notebooks that Vaman had procured for him from Ahuja Book Depot were virtually empty. Who could write with mosquitoes buzzing? But equally, how could he let Gulbachan down? Gulbachan was expecting it of him, and Raman was not used to others having expectations of him.

When the itching got worse and the sleepless nights became longer, more doubts filled Raman's mind. Would Jhotta be happy in the lychee garden? What if there was something special about Amma's place that enabled Jhotta to produce her magical milk? What if bringing her to the lychee garden would stop that magic?

Kumud, too, was distracted by itching. As she sat in the kitchen preparing the meal, her fingers strayed to her knee where a particularly troublesome bite irked her. 'Oof! Such big-big mosquitoes this year!'

'They are always the same size, Ma,' said Bharathi.

'My teacher is saying it is only girl-mosquitoes who are biting and bothering us,' offered Shanker. 'They should be married off and sent away before they cause more trouble in our house!'

Bharathi took a swipe at him but Kumud was pensive. What was happening about the marriage of Meera and Mamta? The Ramanujans had been, everything had gone well, and since then, nothing. Time was passing and the girls were getting older by the day. Laxman Brother should be writing to the Ramanujans and insisting on an answer, she thought. Sudha-with-Pension, with all her *dhuns* and *tals*, did not seem to know a speedy sort of tune to inject into her letters to the boys' family. And here were they, sitting in silence waiting for the wedding music to start! Something must be done to hurry things.

That night the itching was worse than ever before. The next morning Kumud was tired and Raman was irritable. Even Kumud remarked on it.

'Your mood has not been so good these days,' she said.

'It is the rain,' said Raman evasively.

'The rain is not so heavy since a few days already.'

'It is the mosquitoes.'

'But we are spraying every day now.' Kumud's eyes narrowed. 'Maybe we are being cheated by the spray-seller, that Kavvasji. That spray is not working like before.'

'Spray is from Jindal's,' said Raman. 'Mosquitoes are always breeding too much after the rains.'

'You are worried about Meera–Mamta,' said Kumud coyly, sure that this was what it was about. 'So long since we heard anything. You must ask Laxman Brother what is happening.'

'Oho!' said Raman, exasperated. He felt nagged. 'Laxman Brother will tell me if there is news. Where will I go to see Laxman Brother in this mud-*khud*?'

'They cannot keep us hanging-dangling in air,' protested Kumud.

'Business people are thinking about business.'

'Oho?' said Kumud, her eyes flashing. 'Business people are not marrying? Was your father too busy to marry you or Laxman Brother or Vaman Brother?'

'Few more days, and I will ask,' sighed Raman. 'Maybe there are floods in Ghatpur.'

'What if? Every year there are floods.'

'Anyway it is not this marriage business that is affecting my mood,' he said with an air of finality, as if to close the topic. There was a short silence while Kumud digested this. She weighed up the possibilities in her mind.

'Is it that you are missing raita?' she ventured.

Raman did not respond and Kumud knew she had hit upon the truth. 'I will get you raita,' she said resolutely, 'even from Kalonji who is cheating me.' At least then, with a belly full of raita, Raman could concentrate better on his daughters' marriage.

'Don't bother with that cheat,' said Raman miserably. 'I will organize a good source.'

Seconds later they were distracted by a fight that had built up between Bharathi and Shanker on the verandah. The children were now yelling loudly and Bharathi had grabbed a handful of Shanker's hair.

'She is killing me, Ma! My head she will pull off, and tomorrow is science test!' Shanker shouted.

'What is this screaming-shouting!' Kumud said, running onto the verandah. She had to raise her voice above the din and flapped her hands to try and draw them apart.

'Shanker is always taking my things,' shouted Bharathi, and they attacked each other with such renewed force that Kumud stepped back, helpless. She ran back to Raman, who was still sitting in the room, oblivious of the commotion, thinking about raita as he scratched his mosquito bites.

'Stop them, please,' she appealed to him. 'You are the father. To you they will listen. They are fighting so badly. They will get hurt. *Hai Ram!* They will kill each other and our girls are not yet married!'

Raman got up wearily, not seeing the connection between his battling youngsters and the marriage of his elder daughters. Kumud sat in his chair waving the edge of her *pallav* in her face to cool off and calm down. She could hear Raman on the verandah, shouting and threatening dire consequences if Bharathi and Shanker did not stop.

'The marriage of Meera and Mamta I am trying to arrange and you are shouting on the verandah! How will your sisters marry if you carry on like this, eh? Tell me that!'

When Raman reappeared, he was hauling Shanker by the ear. 'Now you sit quietly and do your homework, here where I can see you.'

'I have finished homework,' whined Shanker.

'Then read. Only be quiet!' shouted Raman. 'I must have peace in this house to organize a marriage.'

Shanker went to his school bag and pulled out a comic book. Glancing warily at his father, he sat down to read it. Kumud had taken Bharathi into the kitchen and silence reigned. Raman watched his son flip the pages of the comic book. He got up from his seat and stood over the child.

'What are you reading?'

'About cowboys in America,' said Shanker in a sulky voice.

'They have cows there?'

'Yes.'

'What else they have there?' Raman sounded like he was drilling Shanker for an exam.

'Horses, buffaloes.'

'Buffaloes, hmm?' said Raman, getting interested. He looked down at the open book. There was a picture of a cowboy on a horse. He had lassoed a large calf. The animal's legs were splayed and its eyes were rolling upwards as it strained to get away. On the opposite page was a picture of a lasso and how to knot it.

'What is this?' said Raman, stabbing a finger at the lasso.

'It is a lasso.'

'Are you learning in school how to make this one?'

Shanker stayed silent.

'Show me how it is done,' Raman ordered.

'I need rope.'

'Ask your ma.'

Shanker got up slowly and went to the kitchen. He came back minutes later with a ball of string.

'It is not rope,' said Raman, 'but it does not matter. It is only for practice. Now, show me how you make this lassi.'

'Lasso,' Shanker corrected him. 'L-A-S-S-O.'

With some concentration Shanker cut off a length of string and knotted it according to the instructions. He looked up at Raman when he had finished.

'Show how to throw,' said Raman.

Shanker rolled up the lasso, held one end and threw it towards the chair his father had been sitting in. It ensnared the arm.

'Very good,' said Raman approvingly. He went over to the chair and examined the lasso, pulling on the string. The chair dragged a few inches over the floor with a high-pitched grating noise. Raman cut a second length of string. Shanker ensnared the other arm of the chair.

'Good, good,' said Raman. Suddenly in a good mood, he ruffled his son's hair. Shanker looked up, surprised. He had not expected his father to be pleased. Usually he got annoyed when he saw him reading comics, although that was often because he was putting off doing his homework.

Raman sent Shanker to the kitchen to get some firewood. Shanker came back with three bits of wood, and Raman chose a long, thick piece, pointed at one end and flat at the other. They went into the garden and Raman drove the wood into the soft ground underneath a tree, still dripping from the morning's shower. He asked Shanker to jump on it to push it deeper into the ground. Then he ordered him to pull it out. Shanker knelt down, getting his knees slightly muddy, and pulled the stake with both hands. It hardly budged. Raman brushed his hands together to get rid of the dirt.

'Now all we need,' he said with some satisfaction, 'is thick, strong rope.'

28

JINDAL'S HARDWARE WAS ONE OF MARDPUR'S OLDEST STORES. IT WAS cavernous and dark, despite all the different lightbulbs for sale inside. Jindal, who wore an old cracked leather apron blackened with age, claimed that in his grandfather's time they used to shoe the horses of the British soldiers. There was no way to verify such an outrageous statement, but he stocked anything anyone in Mardpur was ever likely to need so there was no reason to disbelieve him either.

Mohan Ram Jindal was a genuinely helpful man. He had considerable practical experience and he was always willing to pass on his knowledge. He once jokingly said, after seeing the sign underneath Jetco about after-sales service, that he could do better: he offered 'before-sales service'. That is, he never sold anything to anyone without first explaining its use.

'I am looking for a rope,' said Raman looking around a little furtively, not yet used to the dim light in the store.

'What kind of rope?' said Jindal, clasping his hands and looking extremely ready to help.

Raman looked puzzled. 'Long. Perhaps not too long,' he added, thinking maybe Jindal stocked some very long rope indeed.

Jindal waved a hand at several drum rolls of rope behind him. 'Four ply? Six ply? Coir? Jute? Nylon? Nylon is very expensive. Six rupees a yard. For what you need?'

'For lassi,' said Raman.

'Then small rope will do,' said Jindal, pointing to one of the smaller drums. 'Can wind this one around stick few times.' Jindal made a pulling motion with his two hands, as if churning yoghurt.

'Not that kind of lassi,' said Raman, squinting at the other rolls for the most suitable rope.

'I only know one kind of lassi,' declared Jindal, then corrected himself. 'Actually, two kinds. Salt and sweet. But I am only fond of salt lassi. These days they are even making special fruit lassi. Mango flavour, banana flavour. Have you tried?'

Raman had not, although he got quite interested at the thought of banana lassi. 'Is it something like banana raita?'

'Raita for eating. Lassi for drinking,' said Jindal.

'You cannot drink banana.'

'It is maybe crushed banana they are putting. Very ripe banana people are refusing to buy for eating.'

Yet another way to cheat people into buying substandard produce, thought Raman. The moral fibre of the country was really deteriorating. He would stick to raita.

'Who is drinking banana lassi?' he asked Jindal.

'Maybe children only.'

'Must be,' agreed Raman, and made a mental note to warn his children off the stuff. He pointed to one of the drum rolls behind Jindal.

'That rope is fine. So thick.' Raman held his thumb and forefinger an inch apart. 'Is it strong?'

'How strong you need?'

Raman considered this for a moment.

'Strong enough for horse?' Jindal said helpfully.

Raman thought that would do.

'How long?' said Jindal.

Raman tried to visualize the length. He thought double his own height would probably do.

Jindal squinted at him. 'Five foot seven, yes?'

'Five foot eight,' Raman insisted.

Jindal measured the rope against Raman from top to toe. 'Five foot seven times two is about eleven foot. Three and two-thirds yards.'

Raman made a quick calculation. 'That makes me five foot six only!' he protested.

'Making a round number,' explained Jindal. 'You need more?'

'I am five foot eight!'

'Okay, okay. I make it four yards total. Round figure.'

Jindal measured the rope with a wooden yardstick and showed the length to Raman. 'Okay? Always better to have more.'

Raman calculated: that made him six feet tall. He was quite happy with that. He nodded and Jindal took a knife and sawed the length of rope off the drum roll.

'You see, quite strong,' he said as he laboured with his knife. 'Would take mouse at least a year to bite through. Buffalo even longer.'

'Why longer?' Raman wanted to know.

'Buffalo does not have stamina. Lazy beast. Is stopping and starting. Maybe chewing food in between. No concentration. But mouse, once it is started is chewing on and on till complete.'

'Well I am not intending to tie up a mouse!' joked Raman.

'It is good rope for a tug-of-war,' volunteered Jindal. 'I am hearing you are having one big tussle with Satyanarayan Swami.'

'With Swami?' said Raman, wondering what everyone had been saying behind his back, or indeed whether Satyanarayan himself had been spreading such talk. 'No, no we are on very good terms,' he said quickly. He paid Jindal and hoisted the coil onto his shoulder. It was much heavier than he had expected, quite a weight, in fact. He walked a little way in search of a rickshaw.

Vaman appeared. The Sari Palace was, after all, only a few doors away.

'No news from Ramanujans?' Raman said hurriedly before Vaman could ask him about the rope.

'None,' said Vaman. 'Maybe they are just slow at letter-writing.'

'But with the rains they will have more time for letter-writing. Maybe we should write and ask what is their decision.' Raman felt his brothers should be more concerned.

'I am sure Laxman will handle it,' said Vaman evasively. 'Maybe he has already written and they are negotiating on dowry price.'

'You think they are asking for very heavy dowry?' asked Raman in a dismal voice.

'Sure of it. Boys' side can ask for anything they like,' said Vaman, and then changed the subject. There was no point getting depressed about the Ramanujans' dowry demand when it was the best match he and Laxman could wish for. He fingered Raman's rope as he would a silk sari. 'Good quality, strong rope. How much per yard?'

Raman told him.

'And you are using it for what?'

Raman looked uncomfortable. He was not ready to reveal his intentions. 'Just to tie something to a tree in the lychee garden.'

'Not Satyanarayan, I hope,' said Vaman and laughed uproariously.

But Raman was disconcerted. Had his quibble with Satyanarayan escalated to such an extent? At least in Jindal's mind, and now Vaman's, it had.

29

WITHOUT USING HER HANDS, AMMA COULD FEEL STONE. IN HER MIND SHE could feel it. She told Deepa about the mustiness, the cool, clear smell of water dripping down the cold stone caves, the glistening slipperiness, the acrid smell of bat dung in the darkest corners, and the smoky smell of rag-wrapped torches burning in the underground caverns.

Amma charmed Deepa with her descriptions of fortresses and palaces and underground courses. She had so much to tell and such strong impressions of this imaginary scenery, it was as if Raman's notebooks so close at hand in the trunk in the next room had awakened a deep, hidden memory, except of course it was not a memory. She was looking ahead, not back.

'See, Amma,' said Deepa, with a notebook in her lap, 'Bharathi's father has written here how Jagat Singh is leading his men to a cave where they have hidden the goods.' She read aloud from Raman's notebook.

'He must be shivering down there, for it is very cold and the water is dripping from the walls, tip-tip-tip,' said Amma.

'But it is summer.'

'Still, it is not warm.'

Deepa wrote this down.

'The water is very still. It is clear and full of the reflections of their torches. The light is very yellow,' Amma continued.

'Have you seen such a cave, Amma, underneath the palaces of the kings?'

Amma shook her head. 'I have not seen such caves in the northern kingdoms.'

'Then how can you know so clearly what it is like?' said Deepa, fascinated.

'Even I do not know how I know it, Deepa. Even I am surprised sometimes where it is all coming from. I am just sitting quietly and thinking, that Raman must be coming soon, to get more yoghurt, and then, there is a picture in my head, a cave or a mansion.'

'Maybe the *rajkumaris* were telling you stories when you were in the courts of the kings and you are remembering these?' suggested Deepa.

Amma shook her head again. 'Those princes were all day running off on their horses, going on *shikar*. Bringing back deer they were shooting. Tigers, even! And the *rajkumaris*? They were just staying in the palace hoping and dreaming, they had no adventures.'

'What were they dreaming?'

'They were dreaming about marrying a prince.'

'Did they?'

'Oh, yes, they were princesses, after all. They all married princes. But maybe not always the one they wanted.'

'What happened when they had to marry the one they did not want?' Deepa wanted to know.

'They had to accept,' said Amma.

'They were sad?'

'How can a princess be sad?'

'It is not possible,' Deepa agreed. 'But the princes, were they also marrying the *rajkumaris* they wanted?'

'Oh, yes. They could have anyone they wanted,' laughed Amma.

'I would like to be such a *rajkumari*,' Deepa said wistfully.

'Even if you cannot have the prince you want?' laughed Amma.

'Even then.'

There was much in Raman's notebooks that surprised Deepa. There were fights, stabbings and murders, revealing an unexpectedly bloodthirsty side to the writer. Even Amma remarked on the fighting scenes. Deepa jokingly speculated that Raman was really the *goonda* character in his notebooks, and that he led a secret life of intrigue that no one in Mardpur was aware of.

But Amma laughed. 'Where would Raman have such adventures? He is only sitting in his lychee garden. If he were having so many adventures he would not have the time to write about them!'

Deepa knew from Bharathi that this was true. She pictured Raman sitting in his lychee garden. To Deepa, the lychee garden was like a beautiful forest. She thought dreamily, If I lived in such a garden I would hide behind a tree and watch those princes.

'Then soon Bharathi will catch a prince!' teased Amma. 'For she is playing in the lychee garden every day!'

Then Amma smiled knowingly. 'I like your story, watching the princes,' she said. 'Maybe it will come true.'

'It is not a story, not like the story of Jagat Singh, or Usha's stories of Baoli and the *bhooth*. It is a dream,' said Deepa earnestly.

'Sometimes there is no difference,' said Amma.

Deepa went outside to check if Jhotta's trough needed replenishing. Jhotta contentedly snuffled her sugarcane tops and took no notice of her.

'Just think! If you did not have your Jhotta-fever we would never have known about Jagat Singh's adventures, for Bharathi's father would never have come all the way and talked to Amma,' said Deepa, nuzzling up to Jhotta's downy-soft forehead. 'But I am glad you are better. Don't get ill again.'

Deepa leant her cheek on Jhotta's neck and felt the buffalo's muscles move gently, rhythmically beneath it. It was soothing.

'Have you ever seen a prince, Jhotta, have you? One who lives in a palace like Amma is telling us about?'

Jhotta blew at her. And Deepa laughed, for the soft breath of air tickled. She pushed back a wisp of hair from her face.

'You are right, what would a Jhotta know about a prince? You would not even know if you saw one! And why would a prince come to Mardpur? There is nothing here. Certainly no *rajkumari*!' She rubbed her cheek against Jhotta's neck once more, feeling the unhurried movement of Jhotta's head as the buffalo flapped its ears to keep away the flies, and then kept them still again as if listening for Deepa's affectionate murmuring.

Then Deepa heard the crash. Jhotta heard it too, startling and jerking her head upwards. It was so sudden that Deepa for a moment wondered if she had really heard it. But then she heard a moaning cry from Amma, and Usha's worried exclamations. Deepa ran back inside and out to the courtyard. Amma was lying on the ground, half underneath the *charpoy*. She was holding her waist in pain. A bowl of peas Amma had been shelling was strewn all over the floor, dark green against the light grey stones. Some were still rolling slowly away from the upturned bowl. They squashed, bright green and pulpy, beneath Deepa's knee as she knelt beside her grandmother and gently took her hand.

'Aré baapré baap. Hé Ram meré,' Amma moaned to herself. 'Oh my God.'

Usha was already by her side trying to put a rolled-up towel under her head to make her more comfortable. Deepa looked around to see how Amma could be moved to be more comfortable. But Amma gave a weak signal with her hand to say she did not want to be touched or moved. She was breathing heavily, concentrating on her own inner pain, shut off from the outside world so that she could combat this assault on her senses.

'Where is it hurting, Amma?' said Deepa.

'Oh, I am so stupid. Oh, I am so blind!' Amma cursed.

'Is it your leg that is hurting?'

Usha prodded Amma's leg.

'Hai Ram, do not touch!'

Usha pulled her hand away as if she had touched a hot pan.

'Is it hurting?' Deepa repeated.

'Hai Ram,' moaned Amma, as if she could not hear them.

'I will get water,' said Usha, hurrying to the urn in the kitchen. Deepa looked around and saw the wet patches on the ground, still not dry from the quick shower of the morning. It was on one of these that Amma had slipped and fallen. When Usha returned with the tumbler of water Deepa propped Amma up at the shoulder and Usha held the tumbler to her lips, white with shock.

'A doctor is needed,' Deepa said to Usha as they watched Amma drink a sip or two before pushing the tumbler away, a few drops of water still clinging to her lower lip. Deepa wiped them away with the edge of Amma's cotton sari.

Usha looked shocked at Deepa's mention of the doctor, although it was now obvious that the two girls could do little on their own to ease Amma's pain.

'There is nothing wrong, all is fine,' said Amma hearing Deepa, and she tried to sit up. But the effort made her fall back in pain.

'Hai Ram,' she breathed.

'Be still, Amma,' said Deepa. 'We will find a doctor.'

Deepa looked at Usha. She did not know any doctor. She had been so healthy, and for small ailments Amma took her to Satyanarayan to obtain Ayurvedic remedies.

'Where shall we find a doctor?' she whispered to the servant girl.

It was Amma who responded. 'Dr Sharma has his clinic near the Aurobindo Hospital,' she said.

Deepa shivered involuntarily when she thought of Dr Sharma. His name had hardly been mentioned since the day he had arrived to tell Amma of the death of Dasji and Kamini.

It was Usha who spoke. 'Aurobindo Hospital? It is a long way away. Nearby there must be a doctor?'

'No, no,' said Amma. 'Dr Sharma is a good man. He will come.'

Deepa knew they would have to fetch Dr Sharma, even if he were on the moon. She stood up and looked Usha straight in the eye. It was the first time she had dealt her an order. 'You go fetch Dr Sharma, *quickly*.'

And to her relief, Usha obeyed without a word. She picked up her *chappals* and almost ran from the house.

Deepa felt all alone once Usha had gone. She whispered soothing words to Amma, stroking her grey hair which was usually tied in a tight knot but had now become unravelled about her shoulders. Deepa smoothed the *pallav* of Amma's sari and rearranged it over her shoulder, as if preparing her for a visit from an important personage, not just a doctor.

'The doctor is coming, Amma. Soon he will be here,' she repeated close to Amma's ear from time to time.

And Amma seemed soothed by her voice. She was quiet, only moaning occasionally when she felt a twinge of pain in her dislocated hip.

Almost two hours later Dr Sharma arrived on his motor scooter with Usha holding on tight behind him. Luckily, it had not been so busy at his surgery and he finished seeing his patients before heading out towards Jagdishpuri Extension.

Amma was quiet as he examined her, kneeling among the peas which Usha had not had time to gather up before running out to find him. When he stood up, Deepa saw that a crushed pea had stained his khaki-coloured pants. She wanted to run and flick it from his knee and apologize for spoiling them, but Dr Sharma did not notice and Deepa held back, trying not to be too distracted to hear what he was saying.

'She must come to the hospital for an X-ray,' Dr Sharma said. He looked from Usha to Deepa. Deepa looked calm and Usha looked nervous.

'Do you know what an X-ray is?'

They nodded. Dr Sharma looked around at the house, as if he expected an adult to emerge and take matters in hand.

'I will return with my ambulance-car for I cannot carry your Amma on my scooter,' he said. 'The back seat can come down so that it is like a bed. It is a very special car and your Amma will be very comfortable all the way to the hospital.'

Dr Sharma looked at the two girls again. They were staring numbly at him, not sure what to think. They were a rather forlorn duo and Dr Sharma felt a little concerned.

'How will you manage? You are only children.' He knew Usha would go home that evening, leaving Deepa alone. 'You can stay in my house tonight. It is near the hospital. Bring your bed-sheets. I have given your *nani* some medicine to stop the pain. And soon I will be back to take her to the hospital.'

He had decided not to try to move Amma from the floor. It would be too complicated with only the two girls to help him.

When Dr Sharma had left on his scooter, Deepa rolled together some bed-sheets and went and sat beside Amma, who appeared to be asleep, her mouth slightly open, her lips still white. Deepa was relieved. She hated to think of Amma in pain.

Usha lit the bucket-stove there in the courtyard, so that she could watch Amma at the same time, and insisted on preparing some food. 'Amma will need to eat when she is in the hospital,' she said.

Deepa looked at Usha with big eyes. 'But she is only going for an X-ray and then she will be back again.'

'Did you not hear the doctor say you must prepare your sheets because you will be at his place during the night?' said Usha. She was in control again as she went about her tasks. 'That means Amma will not come home tonight.'

Deepa knew Usha was right. She clutched her roll of bed-sheets to her chest. 'How long will it be before the X-ray is complete? Tomorrow Amma will be home.'

Usha did not pretend she knew. She tackled her dough with hard concentration and said merely, 'Prepare, in case it is longer.'

Deepa got up, found a clean frock and wrapped it in her bed-sheet. When the food was ready she ate a little, and the rest Usha packed away in a tiffin-carrier for Amma.

All the while Amma just lay quietly. And sometimes she said, '*Hai*

Ram,' as if emerging from a dream. But mostly she said nothing. An occasional deep sigh reminded the two girls that there was still some pain somewhere.

The light was already beginning to fade when Dr Sharma returned after dealing with the patients in his surgery. Usha was still there, waiting with Deepa. She would not hear of going home, although Deepa urged her to.

'I can go home even after the doctor arrives, what is there?'

And in reality, Deepa was pleased to have Usha's company. 'Tell me a Baoli story,' said Deepa.

But Usha could not think of Baoli at such a time. She shook her head. 'Sometimes I cannot remember what Baoli is thinking.'

And Deepa likened this to the moments when Amma found it hard to connect with Raman in order to see how Jagat Singh was progressing. Only afterwards, when they were still waiting for Dr Sharma and Usha had nothing else to do, did she start her story to pass the time.

'Once there was a Baoli and a Jhotta. And one day Baoli went to the well on the hill to fetch some water in her *hundia* for Jhotta so that she could produce good milk, but she slipped on the hill and broke her back—'

'Amma's back is not broken,' said Deepa quickly.

'No, but Baoli's is. So then the Jhotta was waiting and waiting for Baoli to bring her water and Baoli was worrying and worrying how Jhotta will produce milk without water. So she called to the *bhooth* she could see, and said, "Take this *hundia* to my Jhotta." The *bhooth* took the *hundia* to the Jhotta and Jhotta produced good milk. But all that milk was wasted because there was no one to take the milk to Baoli—'

'Why did the *bhooth* not take it for Jhotta back to Baoli?' said Deepa.

'Jhotta does not know how to talk to the *bhooth*, and besides, the *bhooth* was Baoli's *bhooth*, it was she who had risen and taken the water to Jhotta after Baoli had died on the hill.

> *'Baoli Maai, Baoli Maai,*
> *Kahan se aai?*
> *Koi jan na paai.'*

Deepa thought about this for a little while. 'It is sad that Baoli died,' she said, 'but it is good that her *bhooth* could take the water to Jhotta.'

'Yes,' said Usha, 'life goes on, even after death.'

Deepa nodded slowly and wondered whether Usha had made up the story just for her, because it was significant. She looked quickly at Amma, but Amma was breathing. Amma is okay, she told herself. Otherwise the doctor would not have left.

Deepa rode in front with Dr Sharma to the Aurobindo Hospital, with Usha squeezed in by the door while Amma lay quietly behind, as if in a slumber. Dr Sharma glanced at the lonely figure of Deepa beside him, clutching her roll of bed-sheets and Amma's tiffin-carrier.

'Your *nani* will be fine,' said Dr Sharma reassuringly.

He drove slowly through the Old Market, where Usha climbed out.

'Do not go to Jagdishpuri Extension tomorrow, just go to the hospital,' the doctor told her. 'There is nothing for you to do in the house with Deepa and her *nani* away, and maybe Amma will need you in the hospital.'

Usha nodded and watched them drive away. The doctor drove past the temple and on to Kumar Bazaar. Aurobindo Hospital lay beyond the large modern shops of the bazaar, close to St Paul's Mission School.

'Someone will need to look after your *nani* when she comes from the hospital. You will have to call your ma to come home.'

Deepa sat quietly, feeling frightened for the first time.

'My ma? She does not need to come!'

'I know your ma,' said the doctor gently. 'She loves you very much and she loves your *nani* very much. She will want to be here.'

But Deepa was not reassured. 'Amma is not going to die, is she?'

'Of course not!' said Dr Sharma. 'Is that what you are thinking? Your *nani* is as strong as a buffalo, she is a long way from dead.'

Deepa sat bolt upright in the soft car seat. It was only then that she remembered Jhotta. Even when Usha had been telling her Baoli story she had not thought of what would happen to the buffalo. Momentarily it distracted her from worrying about Amma. She prayed Jhotta would be all right. Even Usha would not be there tomorrow! Jhotta would be lonely, but she could not come to any harm just for one night. Rampal would come to milk her in the morning, then later Pappu would take her to graze. She hoped Jhotta would not suffer too much from the heat of the morning; there was no shade in the front yard, that was the only worry, and there was no one who might take her into the shade. That had always been Deepa's job.

30

SHANKER FELT HOUNDED. RAMAN HAD NOT TAKEN HIS EYES OFF HIM ALL afternoon since he came home from school. He could not understand why his father had decided to take such an interest in his every activity and was attempting to dictate to him at every turn. Usually Raman left him to his own devices and it was Kumud who kept him in line. Shanker knew how to handle his mother and wheedle what he wanted out of her. But now Raman revealed an unusually oppressive streak that Shanker had not known his father possessed.

'Is your homework completed, boy?' Raman demanded.

'I will do it later,' said Shanker evasively. He did not like to be hounded and it was a standard response. Raman was generally not too harsh with him. But today he slammed a hand down on the arm of his chair and shouted, 'You will do it now. You are always putting off. You have no discipline, lazy buffoon!'

Kumud ran into the room when she heard her husband shout.

Shanker felt his eyes prickle and his nose itch. He wanted to cry. He did not deserve this onslaught. He was being persecuted and he was still only eight years old.

'Take out your books,' Raman ordered. 'Finish your homework *phut-a-phut.*'

'But I always do it later in the evening when it is cool,' objected Shanker.

'He always does it later in the evening when it is cool,' Kumud interjected on Shanker's behalf.

'Enough. I am the head of this family. I am saying it must be done now. So do it.'

Shanker sniffled but went to get his school bag, dragging his feet.

Even Kumud had noticed Raman picking on Shanker earlier in the day. At lunch-time Raman watched his son like a hawk and pounced on him for not eating enough. It seemed an unfair attack. Shanker had come home quite ravenous for once. His mid-morning tiffin had been upturned in the playground during break-time, caught in the cross-fire as Ravinder fought with that bully Arun. Shanker came home and ate three chapattis instead of two and even then Raman had railed at him.

'Why are you not eating? You are picking only like a bird. That is not how to eat. How will you grow? You are so weak.' Raman encircled the top of Shanker's skinny arm with his thumb and forefinger and gave it a squeeze. 'There is no flesh here. Only bone. Eat your rice pudding.'

'I hate rice pudding,' protested Shanker. No one had ever forced him to eat rice pudding before, especially when it had skin on top.

'He hates rice pudding,' confirmed Kumud.

'I am insisting,' thundered Raman. 'My son will grow up thin and weak. People will say what kind of father are you, you do not give your only son enough to eat.'

Raman made Shanker eat the rice pudding, skin and all. Kumud could see the injustice plainly because he left Bharathi alone although she was not eating her rice pudding either. She hated rice pudding with skin on it.

'Bharathi is not eating rice pudding,' wailed Shanker, incensed at the double standards practised in the household that he had had the misfortune to be born into. Bharathi looked slightly guilty. But Raman was not concerned with Bharathi that day. Shanker was essential to the plan he had been hatching, and Raman was concentrating fully on him.

'Girls must not get fat on sweet things,' Raman insisted. 'How will we find a suitable boy for her if she is fat? Double chin means double dowry. I forbid you to eat your rice pudding, Bharathi. In fact, Shanker, you must eat hers.' And he shouted down Shanker's loud protests. 'I am insisting. I will count to ten. One . . . two . . .'

Terrified, Shanker gulped down the second helping of rice pudding, skin and all. He was still feeling humiliated when Raman came after him about his homework. It did not end there. When that was over, Raman ordered him to take a nap.

'I never nap in the afternoon!'

'He never naps in the afternoon,' Kumud supported him. After all it was she who dealt with the children on a daily basis and knew their every habit. Usually Raman took no interest in them, except occasionally to supervise their homework from his vantage point in the armchair overlooking the verandah.

'What is this? He is always tired and yawning in the evening.'

'Be reasonable, please,' pleaded Kumud. 'It is better he goes to bed early so that he is fresh in the morning for school. Early to bed, early to . . .'

'Silence. Tomorrow is Saturday. No school.'

'It is sports day,' Shanker announced triumphantly.

'Are you taking part, boy? Running or what?' Shanker had always been hopeless at sport.

'Three-legged race and sack race,' said Shanker proudly.

'I will give you sack!' shouted Raman. 'There will be no sports day unless you take a nap now.'

Shanker's face crumpled. He had been looking forward to sports day. For one thing he had agreed to swap his dented tiffin-box for ten cricket star cards and his friend Ravinder had promised to bring the cards tomorrow.

'Go and lie down for a little while,' Kumud urged Shanker in a whisper, trying to signal that it was better to placate Raman than to enrage him further. She could see Raman was not going to relent.

'It is what your father wants.'

She helped Shanker settle on the sofa and covered him with a sheet. He threw it off immediately, watching it slide to the floor. Raman fixed his eye on him, like a hawk.

'I am watching you, boy,' he said in a threatening tone. 'Your eyes are still open.' Shanker squeezed them shut. When he opened them again after a few seconds, Raman was still glaring at him intently. Shanker turned round and faced the back of the sofa, making himself cross-eyed examining the checked upholstery so near at hand. He could hear Bharathi singing in another room and he squeezed out a few tears of self-pity at being picked on in his own home. If they did not watch out and insisted on treating him this way he would throw himself under a train and then they would all be sorry. But perhaps he would wait till he had exchanged his dented tiffin-box for ten cricket star cards. Perhaps he could even wangle twelve out of Ravinder. After all, the dent was only a small one. Okay, so it was difficult to fit the lid on securely but Ravinder only wanted it for his centipede collection. And wasn't it Ravinder's favourite colour – metallic blue? For sure, it was a very beautiful tiffin-box. Ma would have to buy him another just the same. Only bigger. Soon Shanker was breathing regularly. Raman got up quietly and covered his son's skinny shoulders with the sheet, then sat back in his chair, brooding about his plan for which he would need Shanker's cooperation. No, not cooperation, Shanker's absolute obedience. He would not allow his truculent son to wreck his plan, hence the need to keep a firm hand even before the plan was in operation.

When Shanker awoke it was obvious that his ordeal had not finished. Raman insisted he drink a glass of hot milk. Shanker hated hot milk. It always had skin on it.

'What is wrong with hot milk?' Raman raged. 'It builds strength in a body.' He held the glass to the boy's mouth.

'Too hot,' objected Shanker.

'Nonsense. How am I holding it if it is too hot? Am I burning myself? Blow on it.'

'But that will make more skin.'

'Stop this nonsense behaviour at once.'

Shanker took another sip. 'Too hot.'

'Drink!'

Shanker sipped again. 'Too hot.'

'Drink, I tell you!'

Father and son continued in that fashion until the milk was consumed. The afternoon was less tense as Raman went off to PTI to finish his afternoon tasks, returning home in time for supper.

Everyone was on guard at supper-time, especially Shanker. He watched his father warily but Raman seemed lost in thought and ate slowly and silently. Nonetheless his heavy presence pervaded the meal and his wife and children did not want to appear too cheerful in case it attracted attention. Kumud put only small helpings on Shanker's *thali* in case he was not hungry and Raman was in the mood to force him as he had done at lunch-time. She hated to see another scene.

After supper Raman spoke decisively and commandingly: 'Right, boy, put your sandals on.'

Everyone jumped because this was the first thing Raman had said throughout the meal apart from a few grunts while being served by Kumud. There was something ominous about the command, not just because it was highly unusual to go out after the evening meal, but also because he had made it clear that only he and Shanker were involved.

'Surely you are not thinking of going out at this time of night?' said Kumud, alarmed. 'It is muddy, you might slip or fall in the ditch even. And it looks like it will rain again.'

'The sky was clear when I went to work,' said Raman. 'And there has been no rain since this morning very early.'

'The boy will be tired!'

'He has had his nap. Are you tired, boy? Answer me!'

Shanker did not dare say no.

'Be reasonable, leave him behind,' said Kumud.

Raman trained a glinting eye on Shanker. 'Do you want to stay home or come? It is your choice.'

Shanker did not see that he had a choice while his father was in this mood.

'Well? I am waiting for an answer. Are you coming?'

'Yes,' said Shanker in a very low voice.

'It is settled, then,' said Raman. 'Sandals on.'

Raman had his rope, the one he had bought from Jindal's, slung over his shoulder. With all the protests no one had thought to ask him *where* he was going with Shanker. As she watched them walk towards the gate, Kumud vaguely wondered about the rope but did not think it appropriate to ask.

31

FATHER AND SON HEADED TOWARDS KUMAR JUNCTION. THE STEAMINESS OF the day had subsided and the night was clear with stars glinting in the dark sky. A large moon bathed the damp ground in silvery light, making it glow white. The mud gave underfoot but was not so soft that their feet sank right in. Shanker trod warily and kept silent. If he had not been so nervous about his father's intentions, he would have enjoyed the walk more. After all, he was more than a little excited at being allowed to roam around at that late hour.

Perhaps they were only going to visit Vaman Uncle, Shanker thought at first. But then, instead of turning towards the Sari Palace, Raman turned smartly in the direction of the Old Market. Shanker felt quite nervous as the streets began to narrow and the odour of rotting vegetables, swept into the gutters, met his nostrils.

'This is the Old Market! The market is closed,' he said, more to himself than his father. Raman, grim-faced with intent, ignored him.

Shanker dragged his feet as they walked away from the Old Market. They had no relatives in that vicinity, there was no bazaar, no shops, should his father want to buy something at this late hour. Shanker could not hold back any longer.

'What are we doing here?'

Only then did Raman reveal his purpose. 'We are going to visit Amma.'

'Oh,' said Shanker, relieved. Was that all? What was the secret about that? It was certainly an odd time to pay a call. But grown-ups kept odd hours. And perhaps Amma, who was blind, could not tell the difference between night and day.

When they arrived at Amma's house it was in darkness. There wasn't even the low glow of the turned-down lantern usually put out in front at that hour. There was no sound from within although it was still early for Amma to have retired to bed. Jhotta, her back glistening in the moonlight, was thoughtfully chomping at her grass. If she was a little surprised that no one had come to bring her into the courtyard, she did not let it spoil her evening feed. She had spent an enjoyable afternoon wallowing in the mud-puddles around Mardpur, so she was quite happy to stand a little longer in the cool light of the moon.

Raman listened for a few minutes.

'Shall I call Amma?' said Shanker.

'Shhh,' said Raman. He walked swiftly towards the moonlit buffalo, circling her warily, throwing his long shadow around the yard as he did so. Jhotta flapped away the flies with her ears and carried on eating, her jaw muscles moving rhythmically and unhurriedly. She cooperated well while Raman undid her rope and tied one end of his lasso around her neck. She had no reason to fear this man, whom she had seen before. It was easier than Raman had imagined. Not knowing much about buffaloes, he had come fully prepared to have to chase her and then ensnare her in the manner of the cowboy in Shanker's book. Or at least he would have asked Shanker to do so, since the boy was more skilled in that quarter. All that proved unnecessary; Jhotta followed willingly when she saw Raman fill a sack with dry grass from her trough.

'Charming beast,' murmured Raman, 'so cooperative.'

They set off. Jhotta rambled at an easy pace. Perhaps she imagined she was heading for another mud-puddle, Shanker thought, running along-side in the darkness of her plump shadow. He was still baffled by his father's desire for secrecy but with the house so obviously empty he assumed Amma had gone away and had asked Raman to look after the animal.

'Can I ride?' Shanker asked.

Raman was relaxed now. He helped his son onto Jhotta's back. The buffalo trotted along at a good pace, purposefully even, away from

Jagdishpuri Extension. Shanker patted her and held onto the rope around her neck, digging his heels into her sides and clicking his tongue as if she were a horse. He waved one hand, pretending he was holding a sword. I am a *rajkumar* riding into battle, he said to himself, and stabbed his sword at the invisible enemy with a thrust that could leave no enemy standing. He stabbed and gouged and parried and clashed swords at a whole army of enemies, finally defeating them just as they got to the Old Market. This was handy because Shanker found he needed both hands to hold onto Jhotta to prevent himself sliding off over her head as she bent to nuzzle at the rotting vegetable matter. She was not interested in the sack of dry grass Raman proffered to tempt her away. Raman was not in a hurry and he did not wish to attract attention by battling with a recalcitrant buffalo, although the only people out at that hour in the Old Market were a few vendors returning home. Without the familiar market bustle, the old houses hugging each other around the market square came more sharply into focus. The buildings were alive with chatter and the sound of radios blaring out. Children cried, dogs barked from within. But no one came out to see who was walking at that hour with a young boy and a buffalo.

Shanker surveyed the scene, perched atop the buffalo. This was fun. Wait till he told Ravinder. He would be so jealous! He was sure Ravinder had never ridden a buffalo through Mardpur in the middle of the night.

The buffalo was so well-behaved, Raman warmed to her. It is truly an enchanted buffalo, he thought, and began to dream of a perfect future with this beast in his hands. With as much raita as he pleased, his book would soon be finished and then he could marry off his daughters with ease. There was a spring in his step as Raman approached Kumar Junction. Mardpur was quiet at this hour – it was not a town that stirred much after a fulsome evening meal. Then, as Kumar Junction came into view, Raman froze. A shadowy, *dhoti*-clad figure stood in the middle of the road, defying them to proceed any further.

32

SATYANARAYAN LOOMED DARKLY IN THE MOONLIGHT, HIS LEGS SLIGHTLY apart, leaning on his black umbrella.

'It is late for buffalo-walking,' he observed as Raman brought Jhotta to a halt in front of him. Raman patted Jhotta proprietorially.

'Is it Jhotta-fever again?' enquired Satyanarayan.

'No, no,' Raman assured him pleasantly and attempted to look as if taking a buffalo for a long walk during the night was a very natural activity. 'Buffalo is very healthy, producing good milk every day.'

'My *dava* will keep this beast in good health for long time yet. I can guarantee. Can any Western doctor give you such guarantee? Where is it written on their *davas* and pills that it is guarantee for cure? Have you ever seen such guarantee?'

'No,' admitted Raman.

'But I do not remember advising night-walking for buffalo,' Satyanarayan continued, perplexed. He walked around the buffalo as if examining it for any clue as to this unusual behaviour, then stopped in front of the animal and stared first into Jhotta's left eye and then her right. Jhotta flicked her ears as if trying to get rid of an irritating, buzzing fly. She wanted to move on; the night-time trip had proved to be quite pleasant so far, and by peering into her eyes so closely Satyanarayan was spoiling her view.

'Buffalo is healthy,' Satyanarayan pronounced.

'I am thinking, a little walking is helpful for good health. It is – um –' Raman searched for the words, '. . . helpful in circulating oxygen. Best milk is produced that way.'

'If it gives you pleasure you can do night-time walking with the beast, but it will make no difference to the milk,' responded Satyanarayan, the expert.

Raman bowed to his superior expertise. 'I should have consulted beforehand,' he conceded. 'Then I could have avoided tiring walk. But I am a simple man with no knowledge of the *shastras*.'

'Ayurveda is a very ancient Hindu science,' Satyanarayan lectured, stabbing the ground with his umbrella for emphasis. 'It is unsurpassed in whole world. Those who do not accept this are only sowing mischief and wanting to destroy our country.'

'Why do they want to destroy?' said Raman, genuinely perplexed at such dire motivations.

'Destructive force is coming from inside. It is not *explosion*, it is *implosion*, destroying first the person inside and *then* destroying everything outside.'

Raman listened with interest. Only that week he had read on the PTI wire about the country's atomic bomb test. The dispatches had discussed the merits of the technique of implosion as distinct from explosion, so he knew what Satyanarayan was talking about. In fact, everyone had been talking about implosions all week. Raman thought it quite interesting that Satyanarayan had seized on this topic of modern science.

'This *implosion* theory,' said Raman with an innocent air, 'is it also written in the *shastras*?'

Satyanarayan seemed about to implode himself, Shanker thought with some satisfaction. He watched the Brahmin closely – it would be interesting if he did, not something Shanker wanted to miss. But years of yoga and meditation had instilled into Satyanarayan a level of self-control that seemed almost superhuman. He pulled himself up to his full height, some four inches below Raman.

'I know you are of limited education, Ramanji, but what are they teaching you in school? Did you do no science?'

'I know, I know,' said Raman, predicting what Satyanarayan would say. 'Without mathematics invented in India there would be no science. But was it not one English gentleman, this Mr Rutherford . . .'

Satyanarayan exploded despite himself. 'Rutherford–Mutherford! That is what these Britishers are brainwashing you with!' Satyanarayan wagged his finger violently. 'Do not forget, Ramanji, where we are coming from. Centuries of culture and learning. Every single scientific principle on earth is based on Hindu philosophy. We have *always* known about implosion because it is there in the *shastras*: every action has equal and opposite reaction!'

Raman wrinkled his brow. That piece of philosophy was something he had heard of even though he had never read the *shastras*.

Shanker, too, had heard of it. 'That is Einstein!' said Shanker excitedly, rocking on top of Jhotta and looking like he might fall off in his eagerness to show off his own knowledge. 'He is one German fellow! Germany is next door to England.'

Satyanarayan looked up at Shanker as if noticing him for the first time. He did not correct him, instead, he said, 'You are out late, boy. It is written also in the *shastras* that early to bed, early to rise, makes a man healthy, wealthy and—'

'We were just hurrying home,' interjected Raman. He had been quite happy to talk of implosions because it had occupied Satyanarayan completely and distracted him from thinking about their late-night exploits. He did not want Satyanarayan to return to the subject of night-time buffalo walking.

'Of course it is very late,' said Satyanarayan, peering at his wristwatch, turning it this way and that, hoping to catch the moonlight in order to see the watch-face more clearly. But he could not find enough light to see the hands and while he was thus occupied, Raman decided it was time to make their escape.

'Come,' said Raman, and he stepped forward purposefully.

'Well, go then, I am not the one who is holding you up,' said Satyanarayan standing aside and waving them away. Raman, the buffalo and Shanker surged forward towards the dirt road to the lychee garden. Shanker looked back and watched Satyanarayan attempting to read his watch again. Then, finally giving up, he pointed his umbrella straight ahead as if to remind himself in which direction he was intending to go, then ambled off towards the temple. As he retreated, Shanker could just make out Satyanarayan's umbrella swinging from side to side like a pendulum, the tip of it emerging first from one side of the Brahmin and then the other.

Early the next morning Raman was woken by a fearful bellowing from the garden, and Kumud, who came running into his bedroom.

'Come please, there is a big-big buffalo sitting in the garden. It has invaded and is eating all our lychees. I am always reminding you to call Mistry to fix that perimeter fence. But you did not listen and now it is too late. *Hai Ram meré!* That beast will eat everything without stopping. And listen to her! She is showing such anger. I dare not approach even with stick! We are facing danger even in our own home!' Kumud opened the window and waved her arms at Jhotta.

'Hup, hup, beast.'

'Leave her,' said Raman, yawning and scratching his sides under his vest. 'She is not dangerous. Look, she is tied to the ground with one strong rope.'

Now that the immediate danger was over, Kumud laid her fists on her waist. 'And who brought that beast here? That is what I am asking!'

Raman did not look her in the eye. He scratched his sides again, this time somewhat sheepishly. 'Vaman asked us to look after her. Few days only,' he lied.

'I see. And are we the keeper of Vaman Brother's buffaloes? Does he not have a house two times bigger than this small bungalow? Do I not have enough to do already?'

Raman let her rail on. He knew she would calm down eventually.

'Big-big house he has, but our lychee garden is bigger,' he said mildly.

'And I have nothing to feed to this buffalo. She will be eating up our whole garden. What will this beast be eating, have you been thinking? Rice pudding?' Kumud continued.

Raman affected a laugh. 'Rice pudding! Ha, ha. That is a good joke! All that rice pudding that your son will not eat, you can feed to this buffalo. Shanker! I will not be making you eat up your rice pudding. Buffalo is here now!'

Shanker appeared looking tousled and bewildered. 'Buffaloes don't eat rice pudding, Papa.'

'No?' Raman said good-humouredly. 'What is it they like?'

'Grass.'

Raman looked at Kumud triumphantly. 'Then there is no problem. There is too much grass-*ghaas* in the garden. It is a buffalo paradise here.'

'So why is she making such a noise, if she is so happy?' Kumud persisted although her anger had evaporated.

'She is bellowing because she needs milking.'

'But I do not know how to draw buffalo milk!' said Kumud, worried now.

'We must find someone.'

'I will get Rampal.'

'No!' said Raman. He was sure Rampal would recognize Jhotta. 'We can get much cheaper milking boy. I will send for Hari. He has learnt milking from Rampal.'

'Oho!' said Kumud, her hands on her hips. 'When it is raining all day I am having to go in mud-sud to do shopping. No one was calling Hari then to help. But now we must look after Vaman Brother's buffalo, Hari must come running. Buffalo is getting better treatment than me even!'

'The buffalo is for you only,' said Raman soothingly. 'This way you will not have to go through mud-sud to find yoghurt for me.'

Kumud relented a little. It was not that she had any objection to the buffalo *per se*, it was just the shock of seeing it there that morning without any warning. How was she to know Raman was thinking of her and regretting that she had to traipse through all the mud for his raita? She had been under the impression he did not even notice. Well, he had noticed the raita, but had not, she thought, acknowledged her own effort or thoughtfulness.

She went to the kitchen to finish preparing the breakfast. It was a special breakfast – stuffed *parathas*, to give Shanker energy for his sports day. Raman watched the children playing with the buffalo while he put on his bush-shirt and pants.

'Looks just like Amma's Jhotta,' Bharathi was saying.

'You mean same stupid look? All buffaloes look the same, *yaar*,' said Shanker, unable to resist teasing her.

'Amma's Jhotta is gentle-looking, like this one,' said Bharathi, holding her hand above Jhotta's nose for the beast to blow at. Jhotta seemed to enjoy the attention, but more than anything she enjoyed the shady bowers and the grass-smells of the lychee garden. It was indeed a buffalo paradise, and Jhotta was as ecstatic as any buffalo would allow herself to be in between feeds. There was no reason for her to miss Jagdishpuri Extension. Not yet, anyway.

'Maybe they are sisters, twins like Meera and Mamta,' suggested Shanker sneakily. He was enjoying being in on the secret.

'I don't think so,' giggled Bharathi, 'or Vaman Uncle and Papa will surely be worrying about arranging their marriage!'

Shanker pushed some grass towards Jhotta with his toe. So! Perhaps Jhotta was to be part of Meera and Mamta's dowry – he could see no other use to them of a buffalo. In any case he could not reveal too much to Bharathi to solicit her opinion about the presence of the beast.

'Under no circumstances must it be revealed where buffalo is from,' Raman had said in threatening tones the night before as he was tethering the beast to the stake under the tree. 'If you are telling anyone, I will tie you with this rope to this stake and you can sit like a buffalo all night eating grass.'

This was enough to silence Shanker. He had no desire to spend the night in the garden with the mosquitoes.

33

GULBACHAN HAD NEVER EATEN AT RAMAN'S HOUSE — THERE WAS NEVER
any occasion for it — and he himself did not invite Raman to his own
home. Not having a wife to cook and welcome people, Gulbachan often
dined at the various stalls and tea-houses around the bus station, puttering
along on his scooter just before midday every day. So when Raman
invited him to the lychee garden to see for himself how the buffalo was
faring, Gulbachan graciously accepted, enquiring whether the dirt road
was in any fit state to use his scooter.

'My scooter is not well. Did you not hear it going putter-putter? I am
not sure it will make it up the hill.'

'The mud is still soft, cycle-rickshaws are refusing to go. Such
laziness, can you believe? It is the limit! Just for a slight incline they
are making a fuss,' said Raman. 'But perhaps walking is better. I am
always insisting my children should walk and take oxygen. My wife
also.'

Gulbachan was not used to walking, but he did not mind, under the
circumstances. It was such an unusual invitation. And he felt taking
oxygen might do him some good.

Raman meanwhile combed the market for Hari. When he found him
with not very much to do, he sent him to the lychee garden to milk the

buffalo and to give his wife the message that he would be bringing his boss home for lunch.

'But do not go telling the whole world that Raman has a new buffalo,' Raman warned him. 'Or I will cut out your tongue.'

Hari thought this was a bit drastic, but as someone who had already been accused of the murder of a Christian priest, he did not fear Raman's threat. Nor was he one to question why Raman was making such threats. Employers were funny, secretive people. They distrusted servants and errand boys so much that they often made dramatic threats of dire consequences if any of their business was divulged. Hari was quite used to this manner of speaking from those who hired him, and he prided himself on being completely trustworthy.

Kumud had been busy all morning, preparing sweetmeats. Hari had milked the buffalo, and with that milk Kumud had begun to prepare a whole variety of delicacies. She even found time to arrange the house and spend some time on her own appearance. Raman nearly toppled over when he saw his wife. Instead of her usual sari she was wearing a dramatically embroidered *salwar-kameez*. She had applied make-up with care, and had painted her nails and toenails and wore an extra-large *bindi*, with matching lipstick. She looked extremely glamorous.

'Please come into our humble home, Mr Gulbachan,' she welcomed them. 'I have freshly squeezed lime ready. It is very hot outside, is it not? And you must be tired from walking up the small incline. Rickshaw-walas are so lazy these days. Such a small incline and they do not want to come. They will go as far as Kumar Junction only.'

'Oh, it was nothing. Not steep at all. I like to take some oxygen from time to time,' said Gulbachan, mopping his brow with a large hand-kerchief. He took the lime juice from Kumud's tray. Raman looked at her admiringly; such sophistication to use a tray!

'You put yourself to so much trouble. Water would be sufficient,' said Gulbachan.

'No trouble,' said Kumud, 'limes are growing in the garden only.'

'What a wonderful garden! Such beautiful lychee trees. And lime trees also! You are truly blessed. And what a comfortable bungalow. My government bungalow is not so pleasant, although for me it is adequate, and I am not a fussy fellow.'

Raman was enjoying his wife's hospitality. He rarely gave her the opportunity to play hostess. And when they went to his brothers',

Sudha-with-Pension and Madhu would push Kumud into the background, so eager to show off they were: Madhu with her gold, and Sudha with her music and other trappings of high culture. If only they could see Kumud as she really was. She was the pleasant-faced, pretty one. Looking young for her years, despite four children, and graceful in movement, unlike that plump, waddling Sudha and that thin Madhu. Raman felt proud of her.

'Lime juice is okay?' he enquired of Gulbachan. 'Not too little sugar? People are drinking with less sugar these days, it is the new taste. I am not so keen myself. I am a traditional fellow. I like the old way. But I do not like to force others to do as I do. Do take more sugar if you wish.'

'It is perfect!' said Gulbachan. 'Any lime juice made by your wife's hands is bound to be perfect. How can I complain about sugar when it is just right?'

Nonetheless Kumud, on cue, had brought the sugar pot and Gulbachan helped himself to another spoonful, stirring it into his lime juice vigorously. Raman also added another spoonful of sugar.

'Such nectar!' exclaimed Gulbachan, and downed the lime juice in one go, wiping his mouth delicately with a large white homespun handkerchief, which he then carefully folded again and returned to his pocket.

'Why people are buying these soda-sada drinks imported from the West, I do not know,' said Raman conversationally, still sipping his lime juice delicately. 'I myself think there should be nothing but lime juice and lassi.'

'Oh, yes, lassi,' Gulbachan agreed. 'I am very partial to sweet lassi. But I am also fond of rose nectar.'

'Yes, rose nectar is a good Indian drink. There should be nothing on sale but lime juice, lassi, and rose nectar,' said Raman.

'Yogis are making a very good drink with almonds, it is good for the brain. For the memory, they are saying.'

Raman duly added this to his permitted list, although not without thinking of Satyanarayan.

'And coconut milk. Very good in south,' Gulbachan continued. Raman was just about to amend his mental list when Kumud saved him.

'This is our daughter Bharathi,' Kumud broke in, just at the right moment. 'Come here, Bharathi, say namaskar to Mr Gulbachan. He was on the Salt March with Gandhiji. He will tell you all about it.'

Gulbachan beamed. 'Yes indeed, I was on the Salt March. How did you know? It was a long time ago!'

Kumud was now serving tea. 'Sugar?' She held a small tray in her hands with a silver sugar pot and a silver milk jug perched on it. Raman had never seen such silverware in his house before but he had to admit they were very elegant. His wife certainly had style.

'Sugar? Yes, please. Now, as I was saying, the Salt March. Well that was way back, young lady, you weren't even born . . .'

'Samosa?' offered Kumud.

Kumud breezed in and out with various offerings, treating Gulbachan like a king. He enjoyed the attention. Since his wife had died so many years ago he had fended for himself. He did not have relatives nearby, and it must be said, however efficiently he managed his household on his own, it lacked a feminine touch.

Finally, while Gulbachan was still telling the story of the Salt March, they sat down to eat. Bharathi brought in the hot chapattis one by one and pressed Gulbachan to take one more than he really had room for in his stomach.

'No, really!' said Gulbachan, holding his hand over his *thali*. 'It is all too good, but I have eaten more than I can manage, and I am having to walk home this evening. If I eat more I will be sinking into the mud and Raman will have to come and save me!'

'What if!' joked Raman, now in a thoroughly good mood. 'I am strong.'

'Do you want to carry me home on your back?' teased Gulbachan.

'Well now I have a buffalo, you can go on her back,' said Raman.

'It is a fantastic buffalo,' opined Gulbachan.

'A blessed beast,' agreed Raman happily. It was an intoxicating feeling, being able to joke with one's boss in this informal way.

After the meal, while Gulbachan was washing his hands, Raman whispered to Kumud, 'I have not seen that silver pot and jug before.'

'From Vaman Brother I got them.'

Raman normally would have criticized his brother for spending on such fripperies when they lived such a simple life, but he was more bothered about whether Kumud had also been talking about the buffalo. He began to regret that he had lied to his wife about the buffalo belonging to Vaman.

'I told them buffalo was okay here,' said Kumud before Raman could mention it himself.

Raman froze. 'What did he say?'

'Oh, Vaman Brother was not there. Only Madhu Sister. She said Vaman Brother did not tell her anything. He tells her nothing at all. She is always in dark. "You can keep buffalo," she said. "As if I care. I will also not tell him I have lent you silverware for your husband-boss party. Women can keep secrets too.'"

At that point Gulbachan came back and Kumud ran back to the kitchen to bring out various sweetmeats and a large bowl of plump lychees. By now Gulbachan was in a terrific mood. He was telling them all – Raman, Bharathi, and Shanker, who had arrived back from school – of the time he was sent to the Himalayas and billeted with the troops. From those remote regions he sent back dispatches about the war with China.

'So cold it was and me only in my vest! I had no time to pack.'

'Was there snow?' asked Shanker.

'Yes, big-big pieces.'

'Did you see any *Chini*?' asked Bharathi.

'Oh yes, they were all there. It is a big country. With one billion people. That is more than one *crore*. It is bigger than India.'

'We are also more than one *crore*,' said Shanker proudly.

'They are one hundred *crores*,' said Gulbachan.

'One hundred *crores*!'

'How were you writing?' said Raman, wondering about the technicalities.

'My fingers were frozen. No gloves even. But yaks provided milk and butter,' said Gulbachan. 'So we drank tea to keep warm. Imagine! In the middle of nowhere we are drinking tea. But it was nothing compared to the Salt March. There we suffered real hardship,' and Gulbachan began again to recount his favourite story.

At last, after several hours of eating and storytelling, Gulbachan left, satiated and contented.

'Will he give promotion, pay rise?' said Kumud when he had gone.

'He seemed quite pleased, Papa,' said Bharathi.

'God, and I had to listen to that boring Salt March story. It went on and on. And I am knowing it already. In school we are studying,' complained Shanker. 'I only didn't yawn because I thought you will lose your promotion if I did!'

'You did well,' said Raman, worried that his family now expected him to be promoted. It was better that he did not try to explain to them the only purpose for inviting Gulbachan was so that he could see Jhotta. 'But there is something more that he will want.'

'What more can he want!' exclaimed Bharathi. 'I never saw one man eat so much!'

'He wants raita every day,' said Raman a little nervously, wondering how Kumud would receive this.

'Oh, we have been blessed with our new buffalo. It is no problem to make raita every day now,' said Kumud happily. 'What luck that Vaman Brother decided to lend us this beast just at this time! Tell your brother we do not mind to look after his buffalo, I am quite happy about it.' And she went off to change out of her glamour outfit into something more practical.

34

THE SUN STREAKED THROUGH THE SLATS OF THE WOODEN SHUTTERS. DEEPA awoke and lay quietly, watching the dust dance and swirl in the white light. Suddenly she was bathed in light as someone opened the shutters and attached them to the wall on either side of the window so that they would not bang against the house.

Deepa sat up, blinking. Dr Sharma's wife had laid a mat in the living room for her to sleep on. Although she had come with her own sheets, the one she had been lying on was not one of hers, it was multi-coloured, with a chequered pattern. The marble floor was clean but scratched, and had lost its sheen. And the morning sunlight revealed walls that had not been painted for some time. Yet it did not seem a neglected house; it was pleasant and homely, cheerful and lived in.

The living room was sparsely furnished with a large dining table, a sideboard and a cane sofa with chairs piled with mirror-work cushions. There was a formica-topped coffee table with tapering legs. Some dusty magazines lay on it: *Femina*, subscription copies of the *New Scientist* from several years ago and the *Illustrated Weekly*. A string of grapes hung down from the fruit bowl on the sideboard, already going brown near the stalks. On the dining table was a vase of roses of different colours, which were beginning to shed their petals over the crocheted cotton doily.

Deepa carefully folded the sheets and rolled up the mat, stowing it by the wall. Then she went to the window seat, waiting for someone to come. Somewhere at a distance she could hear voices calling, chattering, answering, but they did not seem to be coming any nearer. She looked out at the small garden full of weeds and saw the rose bushes, scores of them, growing out of control but with large, beautiful blooms on them. Clouds of white and pale yellow butterflies flitted aimlessly amongst the roses. There was no one in the garden and no sign of the person who had opened the shutters. The walls of the ochre-washed bungalow were not in very good condition – black with monsoon fungus, and cracked here and there. But the worst cracks were covered by purple bougainvillaea which climbed up the house and crawled over the flat roof to the back verandah.

'Did you sleep well?'

Deepa turned around. A boy in his teens, tall and slim in a white shirt and white pants – so dazzling white that it made Deepa think of the picture on a soap-powder box – was standing by the door. His hands in his pockets, he was leaning against the doorframe as if he had been there a while, not at all self-conscious at being caught staring at Deepa. His face seemed familiar: thin with high cheekbones, and a sad, sensitive air.

'I have seen you before,' said the boy. 'Do you remember?'

Deepa did not respond.

'Always when there is some mishap,' he went on, stepping out of the direct glare of the sunlight. His clothes no longer seemed so dazzling.

Deepa felt he was exaggerating. Amma had fallen down, that was all. She had been taken to hospital but she would be coming out soon. Why was this boy trying to make it sound so melodramatic? The boy smiled wryly.

'But this time of course it is not so bad, like before.'

Deepa looked at him curiously. It came to her in a rush that this was the boy who had come with Dr Sharma to tell Amma about the death of her father Dasji and sister Kamini. He was almost a man. Without inhibition she scrutinized his face, looking for the familiar. So many times she recalled that day her father had died. So many times the face of the boy, intense and troubled, came to her mind. When she remembered her father, she also remembered this boy. But the face before her, as she sat by the window, was relaxed and confident compared to their last meeting. Oddly, it seemed younger than the face troubled by her father's death, the one she remembered so vividly. He let her stare at him, as if he realized she was calling on her memories as she did so. Finally she dropped her gaze.

'You are just the same,' said Govind. 'I have not forgotten, so passive.'

He pointed to her bundle of sheets she had stowed by the wall. 'They wrapped him in a sheet like that.'

Deepa looked at the sheet. It was as if they were talking of an incident that had happened just weeks before, not years.

'Both of them, they wrapped them in such a sheet.'

'I remember,' she said. It was the first thing she had said.

'You remember? How could you? You were not there to see. I saw it. I saw them wrapped in the sheet.'

'I remember that you told me,' said Deepa, a little confused by his tone. But she felt a bond with this boy. It was as if they were carrying on their conversation where they had left off so many years ago. These were the unresolved issues between them that had to be dealt with and laid aside before anything else could be broached.

Govind walked towards the window and sat down beside her on the window seat. He sat hunched, his hands still in his pockets; his thoughts seemed to go back, back to the day he had come to Amma's house.

'When Papa said you would be staying in our house, I wanted to see what kind of person you have become. Why have you not changed? Your father died, your sister died, and yet you seem just the same. *I* have changed very much since that day. I am not the same person.'

What was she supposed to have become? Deepa wondered. She could remember her own feelings of helplessness at the time. She had felt: what was the point of wanting anything, if God was so strong he could take away people you loved? I will not ask God for anything, she had promised herself after that. He took away my father without me asking. He will never listen to me.

Govind seemed to be waiting for her to respond.

'How should I change?' Deepa asked.

'I think I would be more angry than you are.'

'Anger? At what?'

'Anger at – at – what? At the blows fate has dealt you.'

'But I am fine. I have Amma. There are others more unfortunate.'

'That sounds like something my *nani* would say,' said Govind irritably. 'What is more unfortunate than losing your father?'

Deepa thought how serious Govind was. Melancholy. He seemed to have all the burden, the heaviness of her loss, when if anything it was she who should be suffering!

'It is good you are fine,' said Govind in his odd, stilted, adult way. 'I often wondered what it would be like to lose my father like that. I wondered what would become of you. Now I know.'

They sat in silence for a few seconds.

'Are you hungry?' Govind said suddenly and stood up. He made it sound like a chapter had closed. And maybe it had.

Deepa shook her head.

'We are about to have breakfast anyway. Here is my sister, she has come to find you.'

Mallika had just walked in. She was a year younger than Govind. Deepa had seen her at school; she was good at sport.

'Don't bother the girl,' she admonished Govind. Then she took Deepa's hand; she had a mature, kindly air. 'Are you sad?'

Deepa shook her head.

'Good. Papa says your Amma will be fine. So now we should have breakfast. But first, do you wish to bathe?'

Deepa followed her to the bathroom of polished stone with a large tap and two buckets and a cracked sink. Deepa had never seen such a big tap before. She had to use both her hands to try to turn it and it wouldn't budge. She was contemplating washing at the sink when Govind called from the other side of the door, 'Are you having a problem with the tap? It is sticky sometimes.'

She undid the bolt and stood aside as Govind entered. He turned on the tap. Deepa noticed he also had to use two hands. 'We have to keep it closed like this otherwise it drips all day,' said Govind.

Deepa nodded.

He looked as though he wanted to say something more to her but could not find the words. Deepa waited. Then Govind went out and she bolted the door behind him.

She looked in the mirror.

Why have you not changed? What kind of child had she been, she wondered, before her father's death? What kind of child was she now? It was true, when her father was alive there were more people to run to for attention, there were more of them to be concerned about her. But it was also true that after his death, she had stayed in Mardpur, the place she knew best. If I had to go away from here, she thought, then I would change. Even Amma would die one day. Only Mardpur would remain.

'Are you finished, Deepa?' called Mallika.

'Nearly,' said Deepa, and hastily splashed her face with water. She washed the rest of her body quickly and put on her clean frock. It felt too short and tight. There was no comb so she just patted her hair down with a little water. When she had finished she unbolted the door and peered out. There was no sign of Govind. She was relieved, having half expected him to be standing there waiting for her. She emerged with the damp towel over her arm.

The doctor's family ate breakfast sitting at the large dining table, not sitting cross-legged on *charpoys* like Amma or on wooden planks on the ground like Bharathi's family. And they did not eat from steel *thalis* but from china plates. They were eating English toast, topped with butter and masala-peas. Mallika sat next to Deepa, and next to her sat Govind. There was another brother, a year younger than Mallika, almost Deepa's age, called Shyam, and a younger girl called Nalini who was about eight. They called each other by name rather than saying *didi* and *bhaiya*. They talked and joked, even with their mother, in a way which made Deepa seem quite shy and inarticulate.

Mrs Sharma was a plump, cheerful woman who good-humouredly allowed herself to be bossed by her children. She sat with them at breakfast but did not seem able to keep much discipline or even attempt it.

'Well, doctor sahib is late again,' said Mrs Sharma to no one in particular. 'We will have to start without him.'

Every time the maidservant brought in some toast the children would lunge at the plate without consideration for the others. It was not so much bad manners as a game they had all been playing since early childhood. They were expert at securing supplies of toast just when they needed it. Mallika, who had taken it upon herself to look after Deepa, bagged some for Deepa. That seemed to surprise Nalini, who emerged the loser for not being as swift as her elder sister. She stared at Deepa hard.

'Are you an orphan?' she wanted to know. Shyam giggled and stared at Deepa too.

'No,' said Deepa.

'So where is your *maa-baap*? Papa said you have to stay here because you have no one.'

'My ma is in Vakilpur.'

Mrs Sharma looked interested. 'Which is your ma?'

Deepa told Mrs Sharma her mother's full name and Grandfather's full name. It was a kind of formality; she felt sure Mrs Sharma already knew. Mrs Sharma looked approving.

'Good Brahmin family. Old-old family,' she said.

'That's your only criterion, Ma!' teased Govind, clearly used to this. He seemed more relaxed than when Deepa had seen him earlier.

Mrs Sharma looked good-humoured. 'Nothing wrong with that,' she said.

'What if I were to marry a bania?' squealed Nalini, joining in the fun.

'What if?' said Mrs Sharma.

'He will have to be rich,' said Mallika, buttering her toast.

'Silly owl,' said Shyam. 'You would have to make him fall in love with you first.'

'Who would fall in love with you?' Mallika teased Nalini. 'You have honey all over your face!'

'I have not!'

'You have!' shouted Shyam and Mallika together.

'Quiet, quiet,' said Mrs Sharma mildly.

Only Govind was dignified in his silence. He did not join in the teasing of his sister.

'Anyway,' said Nalini, determined to have the last word, 'anyone can fall in love with anyone. Her ma did a love-match!' She was pointing to Deepa.

'Nalini!' Mrs Sharma shrieked, flustered, and hurriedly steered the conversation away.

Deepa realized they knew more about her than they let on. But then Mardpur was a small town, and a doctor's surgery was a good place to pick up gossip.

35

AFTER BREAKFAST, DEEPA JOINED NALINI, SHYAM AND MALLIKA IN A GAME of *carrom*. Govind hovered over them.

'Do you like him as much as your papa?' Nalini said to Deepa.

'Who?'

'That man. The one your ma married.'

'Nalini!' Mallika warned, but she did not stop her.

'I have not met him,' said Deepa, who had no reason to be embarrassed by this line of questioning. Mallika, noticing Deepa did not mind, let Nalini carry on. And carry on she did.

'Never?'

'Never,' said Deepa.

They seemed to find this strange.

'What if your Amma dies and you have to go and live with your ma again?' Mallika said.

'Then I will go and live with her,' Deepa said matter-of-factly, aiming carefully at the red queen.

'If you are married before your Amma dies then you will not have to go and live with that man,' said Mallika.

'It is not in my hands,' Deepa laughed, flicking the striker and triumphantly taking the red queen.

'You cannot just wait passively until things happen to you.' It was Govind who spoke.

But Mallika seemed to side with Deepa. 'Why worry till it happens?' she said. 'But still, I would not like to go and live with strangers.'

'My ma is not a stranger,' said Deepa, and smiled at the notion.

'But you have not seen her for such a long time!' said Mallika.

'No,' Deepa agreed. 'But she is my ma.'

'And if she has changed?'

'My ma is my ma,' said Deepa, and the doctor's children seemed satisfied with that.

'What about your brothers and sisters?' Nalini started up again as they got a new game going. This time Govind took the place of Shyam, who did not want to play any more.

'My ma has two girls, but I have not seen them,' said Deepa.

'Two sisters you never see or play with!' said Nalini.

Deepa shrugged. 'Sometimes you do not see your relatives often but you make friends quickly when you do.'

'It is like our cousins in Kanpur, Nalini,' said Mallika. 'We have not seen them in many years, but when we see them at weddings, we feel close to them.'

While they were playing, Dr Sharma arrived. Nalini jumped up, abandoning the game, and the others followed.

Nalini threw herself at her father.

'Oof! You are too heavy to carry, Nalini!' said Dr Sharma. 'You are not a baby any more.'

'Baby! Baby!' teased Shyam.

Mrs Sharma fussed around her husband, taking his bag and taking the tea from the maidservant to hand to him herself – it was served in a cup and saucer. Dr Sharma sat in one of the cane chairs, after plumping up the mirror-work cushions. The sunlight was pouring more obliquely into the room than when Deepa had woken up and the mirrors glinted and sparkled. Dr Sharma sipped his tea and bit into some biscuits, which he offered to Nalini. His youngest daughter shared his chair, determined to stay as close to her father as possible. Mrs Sharma and Mallika sat on the cane sofa with Deepa between them, with Govind resting one leg over the arm of the sofa, the other supporting his weight on the floor. Shyam occupied the other cane chair but he seemed restless; he preferred to play in the garden. It was as if a meeting was about to begin. When Dr Sharma had drained his teacup and replaced it in his saucer, he looked at Deepa.

'Well, what will we do with you?'

Dr Sharma was about to put his cup and saucer on the coffee table, but Mrs Sharma took it from him before he could put it down.

Deepa wanted to ask how Amma was and what was happening to her, but felt it would be too impertinent to address Dr Sharma in front of the whole family. He was looking thoughtful.

'Your *nani* has a small fracture. She will have to stay in hospital. Your ma will have to come and get you. But it may be a few days before she can be here.'

Deepa felt frightened. Her life was being organized by people she hardly knew. She did not want them to deal with such large issues, she merely wanted them to allow her to see Amma. Deepa had an odd thought: if only she could tell Govind this, she felt, he would understand what she was thinking. Despite his oddness, his melancholy, there was something about him that made him special to her. Perhaps because he had opened himself to her. But short of appealing to Govind with her eyes, she had no recourse.

It was not Govind who came to her rescue but Nalini. 'Oh, but Papa, Deepa cannot go away with her ma just like that! She has not seen her in many years! And she will have to play with her two sisters who she also has never seen!'

Dr Sharma was a little startled. He threw a glance at Deepa but she did not seem to mind Nalini speaking out in this way.

'Deepa must decide for herself, after all it is *her* ma. She may want to go with her. How do you know she doesn't?' He looked at Deepa as if expecting her to speak, but Nalini jumped in again.

'But Deepa wants to stay in Mardpur, she told us!'

It was Govind who spoke. 'What will happen to Deepa's *nani* if she goes away? She is blind, no? She may need help. Who else is there to help her?'

Deepa looked at him; it was as if he had read her thoughts.

'Did you ask Deepa's *nani* what should happen to Deepa?' Mrs Sharma said.

'All right, everyone,' said Dr Sharma. 'It is clear you know better than I what Deepa wants. I will not call Deepa's ma. Is that all right with you, Deepa?'

Deepa's nod was almost imperceptible.

'But you cannot stay alone in Jagdishpuri Extension. Even with the servant girl.'

'She can stay with us for a few days,' Deepa heard Mrs Sharma say. 'She is in the same school as Mallika and Nalini, they can go together. She is a nice Brahmin girl. Old Mardpur family, like us.'

'Oh, Ma!' groaned Shyam.

'It depends on the girl,' said Dr Sharma. 'What do you think, Deepa? Do you want to stay with us?'

'We will take you to Aurobindo Hospital every day so that you can visit your *nani*,' said Govind.

'Well?' said Dr Sharma.

What alternative was there? Deepa thought fleetingly about Jhotta being alone. But she knew Rampal would be there every morning to milk her and tried not to worry. Rampal would organize something. Please get better soon, Amma, she prayed silently. Then I can go home. Deepa realized how much freedom she had in her life with her grandmother. She felt hemmed in at the doctor's house, as if everything she did or thought needed to be explained to the family so that they would not worry about her.

'She does not know what to say,' said Mrs Sharma, gauging the situation accurately. 'Where else can she go?'

'It is settled, then,' said Dr Sharma. 'After breakfast you will come with me to the hospital and we will tell your *nani* not to worry, you are fine with us.'

'Don't feel shy,' said Mrs Sharma. 'We are like your own family.'

'She does not know what it is like to have a family,' Deepa heard Govind whisper to his mother. Mrs Sharma looked slightly stricken and then looked at her with pity.

'Mallika will look after you,' Mrs Sharma said to Deepa kindly. 'She will be like a sister. And Govind and Shyam are like your brothers.'

Shyam wrinkled his nose, Deepa thought in embarrassment. Deepa knew the doctor's wife meant well and was quite sincere in her own way, but she found it strange to be suddenly handed all these brothers and sisters. Please get better soon, Amma, she prayed.

Dr Sharma had another cup of tea, then went back to his surgery. Govind and Shyam were in the garden practising cricket.

'Do you want to play badminton?' asked Mallika. She brought two rackets and they played in the shade of the verandah as the butterflies flitted among them. Deepa caught one with her racket and it fell to the ground, twitching. Mallika picked it up and stroked it. 'It will go to the butterfly hospital,' said Mallika.

'Butterfly hospital?'

'We are helping the butterflies get better,' said Mallika. 'Shyam likes to collect butterflies in his net, then he kills them and pins them on a board, but Govind and me, we like to save them.'

'Why does Shyam kill them?' said Deepa.

'He likes things which look beautiful. But Govind and me, we think of the butterfly's soul.' She took it inside. 'Let it rest,' she said. 'It has had a shock.'

Deepa found it difficult to concentrate on badminton after that, worried that she would catch another butterfly with her racket.

'You must be worried about your *nani*,' said Mallika as Deepa missed another shuttlecock. 'It must be difficult to be all on your own like that with a blind grandmother.'

Deepa had never thought of it that way at all. Being with Amma was for her the most natural thing in the world. 'Don't you have a grandmother?' she asked.

'Oh yes, I have a *nani*, but she is an old bat. She cannot hear anything and she is always saying we are spoilt. Her favourite is Govind. He cannot do anything wrong for her. She still thinks he is only six years old. She treats him like a baby. He hates it!'

'But you must love her.'

'Of course,' shrugged Mallika. 'But she is so bossy! She bosses Nalini worst of all. We have to dress in our best clothes when we go to see her and even then we are not pretty enough for her. I think she just does not like girls. Only boys. She thinks girls are stupid. Where will you go to college?' Mallika asked Deepa suddenly.

Deepa had never considered this.

'I will try for IIT, for engineering, like Govind,' Mallika said, not waiting for her to reply.

'Girls don't do engineering,' Deepa said, surprised.

'Of course they do!' Mallika said with a toss of her head. 'You are talking like my *nani*. I am more clever than Govind, why shouldn't I?'

'What does your Papa think?' Deepa was becoming curious.

'Oh, he is supporting me. It was his idea.'

'So far from home!'

'It is far for Govind, too.'

'Won't you be frightened with so many boys there?' Deepa felt it was quite daring to be asking her this.

Mallika laughed. 'Why should I be frightened of them?'

Deepa warmed to her. 'What will happen when you finish studying?'
'Maybe I will go abroad.'
This was too exciting to contemplate. 'Will you not be married?'
'What is the hurry?' said Mallika with a nonchalant air. 'Nani is determined to marry us all by day after tomorrow, a nice Brahmin boy she is always looking for us. But Papa says girls should not marry too early.'
'Why not?'
'Because then they have too many children and cause overpopulation. Too many children are not good for children's health, either.'
Deepa had not thought about issues like these before and decided that she liked Mallika a lot.
'And Papa says we should choose ourselves who we should marry.'
'You mean love-match?' said Deepa, her eyes opening. Imagine one's parents sanctioning that!
'Not quite, but finally it is our own decision if we like someone. Is your ma strict?'
Deepa missed the shuttlecock again and ran to pick it up before responding. 'I don't know.' Deepa had never considered this. She supposed it was true, since it would be her mother who would arrange her marriage. 'But I do not mind. I will accept her decision.'
'Sometimes it is not good to be too accepting,' warned Mallika. 'We girls can sometimes spot bad things in boys that our parents cannot see. Mothers seem to think their boys are perfect; look at my *nani*. For her, both Govind and Shyam are perfect. Only we girls are not perfect. But we know that Govind is too serious and Shyam is too critical.'
'I will remember that,' said Deepa. 'But if you reject too many proposals you will become difficult to marry off.'
'Huh! Nani is always saying that too. But I tell her she would not want us to marry the first person we see. We must gain experience in looking before we make the final choice, and how can we do that unless we reject a few first!'
'What does your *nani* say about that?'
'She is always trying to persuade Papa to stop me saying such things. But Papa is proud of us girls, he stands up for us.'
For the first time in her life Deepa felt envious of someone else's father. 'You are lucky to have a father like that. I will remember what you said.'
'Yes, always be choosy. Do not just accept.'

36

EVERY MORNING DEEPA AWOKE TO THE CLANK OF THE SHUTTERS BEING opened from the outside and the living room filling with white morning light. Sometimes it was Mrs Sharma who came in with fresh blooms for the dining table. Sometimes it was Mallika, to see if Deepa had everything she needed. Mrs Sharma cleared a corner of the sideboard so that Deepa could keep her school books near the dining table where she did her homework in the golden, late-afternoon light that poured through the living room window. They treated her with utmost kindness, but Deepa never really felt at home there.

Deepa visited Amma every evening. Sometimes Dr Sharma brought her to the hospital, and sometimes Govind escorted her, leaving her with Amma while himself going off to attend to other errands. Deepa was more at ease with Govind now, but she felt that he regarded her as a rather strange, pathetic little orphan-figure. He constantly wanted to know what was going on inside her head, as if searching for clues to her reticence. But the truth was, Deepa's world was much smaller than that of the doctor's children. She did not ponder social issues the way they did, or analyse every move of the government. The doctor's children were inquisitive and energetic. They knew all sorts of interesting snippets about the world gleaned from their books and newspapers. Govind and Mallika read the *Hindustan Times* which was delivered to their home every morning. Deepa did not possess any books aside from her school texts which she, like others in the class, dutifully memorized. She had never thought to question beyond them. It never occurred to her to read a newspaper or listen to the radio. Amma never did, and she knew so much about the world beyond the courtyard.

'Do you not have any ambitions?' said Govind on the way back from the Aurobindo Hospital one evening, after questioning her closely on what she wanted to study in college, with little success.

'What will be . . .' Deepa started to say.

'Goodness! You are beginning to sound like my *nani*,' said Govind, stopping her in exasperation. 'It's not like that any more. These days you have to know what you want. My father wanted me to be a doctor like him, but when he saw I really knew what I wanted he relented and let me sit the exams for IIT Kanpur.'

'IIT Kanpur?'

'Indian Institute of Technology. God, don't you know *anything*? Maybe you are too alone with that blind grandmother of yours.' He did not mean it rudely, it was just an observation on his part. 'What do you do all day in your grandmother's house?' he continued.

Deepa became thoughtful. Amma did the household chores and told the stories that came into her head that she saw in other people. She herself did her homework and worked on the stories. Usha worked hard and told stories. They all had their fantasy worlds to sustain them. Did they really need ambitions? What would Usha do with ambitions? She certainly had no chance of getting educated, even if she wanted to. Amma probably had ambitions; they were that her daughter and granddaughter should be happy and cared for. And she, Deepa? The future was not something that concerned her. What was the point of thinking what would happen when Amma died? Perhaps she would go back to her ma and lead a different life. She could not even imagine what kind of life that could be, so why dwell on it? Deepa knew only to be happy for the present, because the future was a complete unknown. She did not know how to communicate any of this to Govind.

Govind was used to her not answering his questions. But his concern about Deepa was genuine enough. As a child who had nightmares about the dying horse and the dead man with the child crushed in his arms, Govind was always left with a sense of horror at how nonchalant Deepa had been that day when the news was broken to her. It was Govind who had mourned in her stead, barely eating for days afterwards, lying awake at night, wondering at the meaning of life. It was the first real tragedy he had witnessed and it had made an important impression on him. It was then that he had decided he could never be a doctor like his father and break the news of such tragedies to the families of the deceased.

Amma seemed very tired and not very talkative during her granddaughter's visits, although she was pleased to have Deepa's company. Deepa did not mind. She only wanted to be close to Amma, listen to her breathing, study her deep wrinkles and smell her very faint pickle smell, barely discernible since Amma had come to the hospital.

'I will have to write to your ma,' Amma said. 'You cannot stay with the doctor for such a long time.' She said this gravely, knowing it was a difficult course of action for both her and Deepa. 'We cannot be a burden on Dr Sharma, he hardly knows us! He is too kind.'

'Please don't, Amma,' Deepa said, shocked. 'Ma will surely take me away from here, and then who will watch after you? Ma will be so worried about you, also.'

Amma sighed. 'Your ma misses you. But I have been selfish and have wanted to keep you close to me. I want your ma to be happy and I know it would make her happy to have you with her.' She held Deepa's hand in hers. 'We must think of your ma sometimes, too, you know. I think of her often, although I do not see her. And she thinks of you, although she does not see you.'

Deepa nodded, but felt torn. What would make her happy? It seemed she could not be with both Amma and Ma at the same time. She threw her arms around Amma's neck. 'Let me stay just a little longer, Amma. Surely Ma won't mind that. It won't make her sad.'

And Amma stroked Deepa's hair and said, 'I want Ma to be happy, she is my daughter. But also I want you to be happy, Deepa.'

'I am happy with you,' said Deepa, her voice muffled.

Amma did not mention Ma again that evening. Instead she tried to cheer Deepa up. 'Are you taking dancing lessons?'

'No Amma,' Deepa said, thinking it was an odd turn in the conversation. She had not spoken about dancing at all.

'I can see you dancing,' Amma said. 'While I am lying in this bed I can see it. Maybe you should learn dancing.'

Deepa brushed this aside as unimportant when Amma was talking of calling her ma and throwing her whole life upside down. But she was also pleased. It was a sign that Amma felt much better. Before, the pain had made her shut off from the outside world and concentrate on what was happening within her body. Even her acute sense of smell was not as good as it normally was. That she was beginning to have visions again pointed to a recovery.

Back at the doctor's house, Deepa pondered Amma's point about being a burden on the doctor's household.

'How long will Amma stay in the hospital?' she asked Mrs Sharma at supper-time.

'Oh, you poor child. You must be feeling homesick. I will ask Dr Sharma,' said Mrs Sharma and redoubled her efforts to make Deepa feel at home. 'You can bring your friends to play here,' Mrs Sharma said. 'Then you will feel less lonely.'

But loneliness was not Deepa's problem. The doctor's household was animated and lively. True, she missed Jhotta, but Jhotta could not be brought there, she knew that, and anyway Jhotta was fine. Usha had said so. Jhotta's milk was being delivered to the hospital every day by Hari so that Amma did not have to drink cows' milk, which she was not used to.

Usha did not go to Jagdishpuri Extension. Without Amma and Deepa, there was little for her to do there. Instead she had asked her brother to make sure the buffalo was all right, and to get milk for Amma. After all, Hari understood about buffaloes and knew how to milk them.

Hari consulted Rampal.

'What to do? There is no sign of Jhotta,' he said, 'and Deepa is wanting to know if she is all right.'

'*Hai Ram,*' said Rampal. 'That Jhotta is truly lost. Carried away by a *bhooth*. Even her *avatar* has not appeared. How will I tell Amma? And I am responsible for milking that buffalo! I have already told Pappu we are looking for one Jhotta, mysteriously disappeared, but even Pappu has seen nothing. Tomorrow I will go to the temple to pray that Jhotta should return. But wait. Tell Amma nothing or it will delay recovery. She will be more sick to find out her Jhotta is gone.'

'But Amma is asking for Jhotta-milk every day to make her better,' said Hari.

'*Hai Ram!*' said Rampal. He lifted the lids of several *baltis* to check how much milk was there, but there was none to spare. All the milk was spoken for. Jhotta was such a prolific producer, without her he had no extra. It was Rampal's turn to say, 'What to do?'

Hari said he knew a good source, a buffalo he was milking every day. Perhaps some milk could be spared for Amma.

Rampal, normally so inquisitive, was so wrapped up in the problem of the missing buffalo that he did not think to question Hari about the buffalo he was milking. Instead he said, 'It is a good idea. But what if Amma can tell the difference? Jhotta-milk is something special, and Amma – well, Amma has such talents. She can taste, even smell. It will not make her better if she is knowing it is not her own Jhotta's milk. It will make her worse!'

'We can say Jhotta is not so happy without her and that is why she is not producing good milk,' suggested Hari.

Rampal pondered this for a moment, but he saw there was little choice. 'Let us try. It can do no harm. We cannot burden Amma at this time by telling her the buffalo is no longer on this earth.'

So Hari dutifully informed Usha that Jhotta was fine, and saved a small *balti* of milk from his daily milking round at the lychee garden.

37

WHEN GOVIND ACCOMPANIED MALLIKA, NALINI AND DEEPA TO SCHOOL, Bharathi noticed immediately.

'Who was that you were walking to school with?' said Bharathi, wide-eyed.

'Mallika.'

'And what about Mallika's brother also? I saw you talking to him!'

Deepa told Bharathi she was staying at Dr Sharma's house and this made her eyes open even wider.

'Will you marry Govind?'

'Silly, soon he is going to IIT Kanpur to study.'

'Do you love him?' Bharathi's voice fell to a whisper.

'Go away!' Deepa said, annoyed.

'You always said you would tell me all your secrets!'

'There is no secret.'

'If you don't love him, you are as blind as your Amma!'

'*Chup*, Bharathi. I need your help,' said Deepa. She had far more important matters to consider. 'You are my best friend, Bharathi. Can you help me get away from Dr Sharma's house?'

'You don't like Govind any more? I think he likes you, I saw him looking at you.'

'Please stop it, Bharathi. Amma is saying I am a burden on Dr Sharma's kindness and she wants to write to my ma to tell her to come and take me away.'

Bharathi looked horrified. She understood Deepa's predicament very well. She abandoned all thought of romance between Deepa and Govind. 'What can you do?'

'I can come to your house, Bharathi. You are my best friend.'

'Yes,' said Bharathi, sincerely wanting to help. 'I will ask Ma and Papa and we must also ask permission from your Amma.'

'We will go together after school to ask,' Deepa said.

That afternoon, after school, Bharathi went with Deepa to the Aurobindo Hospital, buying some fruit on the way. Amma was sitting up and drinking a glass of milk. Usha stood by the bed holding the *balti* she had got from Hari.

'What would I do without my Jhotta's milk?' Amma was saying. 'It is unmatched by any other. It is good your brother can go so far each day to Jagdishpuri Extension, to get this Jhotta-milk.'

'Amma, my friend Bharathi is here,' said Deepa.

'Come Bharathi, let me hold your hand. This hospital is so full of noise I cannot feel anything unless I touch. What a sweet smell of lychees in your hair! They are all ripe. You must be harvesting them soon.'

'They are still on the trees, Amma. Papa is waiting for the rain to stop and then we will pick them.'

'There will be more rain. You still have a little time. But then you must bring those lychees in quickly or they will be lost! Take Deepa to help you gather them.'

That was Deepa's cue. 'Amma, I would like to stay in Bharathi's house. I have been at the doctor's house for too long now.'

Amma was thoughtful. 'Will your *maa-baap* agree?' she asked Bharathi.

'Of course,' said Bharathi, although she had not asked her parents yet. 'I will ask them today, then I will come and get you tomorrow, Deepa. That is,' her voice fell to a very low whisper, 'if you can bear to be parted from Govind.'

'*Dhut!*' Deepa castigated her.

'Be good and help Kumud Aunty in the kitchen,' Amma said to Deepa, as if it were already arranged. Deepa herself felt a burden had been lifted and she was in good spirits. At the doctor's house she neatly folded together her school uniforms and stacked up her textbooks in anticipation of moving the next day.

That evening Mallika had her weekly dance lesson in the living room. Govind and Shyam pushed the long dining table against the wall just as Ustad Khan, a tall, lean dance teacher, arrived with his son Ahmed carrying a suitcase.

Ustad Khan carefully laid the suitcase flat and unpacked it, pulling out two cloth-bags drawn at the top with a drawstring. He loosened these strings and the cloth-bags fell open, revealing the *tabla*. Ahmed, barely ten years old, played the *tabla*, looking over his right shoulder, his lips pressed inwards in concentration. He did not watch Mallika while she was dancing, but kept up with her rhythm by listening to the sound of her feet and Ustad Khan calling out the steps. Deepa watched Mallika twirl and stamp. Mallika was not particularly graceful, but she had a proud, somewhat haughty style, which made her dancing seem quite striking.

Govind was also watching his sister, beating time on the ground with a pencil. When she had finished and Ustad Khan had packed away his *tabla* and departed, Mallika sat down beside Deepa to remove the bells from her ankles.

'Oh, no. They are knotted again. It is always like this. If I don't tie a knot they fall off and hurt my feet. Help me with this, Govind.' She held out a foot to her brother. He held it in his lap as he knelt and wrestled with the knot.

'You will have to sleep in these *ghungrus*, then every time you turn in your sleep you will awake the whole house,' said Govind. He bent his head to prise open the knot with his teeth.

'Silly!' said Mallika, aiming a playful slap at his head. Then, turning to Deepa, she said, 'Would you like to dance?'

Deepa looked shy.

'Come, you are graceful, Deepa. Just try. Govind, put the *ghungru* on Deepa,' said Mallika as the string of bells fell free from her ankle. Govind shuffled towards Deepa and before she could protest he pulled at her foot and wound the bells around her left ankle. Mallika tied the other one of the pair to Deepa's right ankle.

'Now, watch me,' she said, calling out the steps as she moved. Deepa self-consciously tried to follow her movements.

'Too stiff, Deepa,' Mallika said. She stood in front of Deepa and told her to repeat the steps she had just taught. 'You are naturally graceful,' said Mallika, 'and expressive. Isn't she, Govind?'

'Yes,' agreed Govind.

'Do you not want to learn to dance?'

'Yes,' said Deepa, barely audible. She was trying to remember her movements more accurately this time. She repeated the steps a third time.

Mallika clapped. 'Why don't you ask Amma to talk to Ustad Khan? He has a bicycle. He can go to your house in Jagdishpuri Extension when you go back.'

Deepa, flushed, flopped down beside Mallika and began to take off the bells. She was not used to having strong wishes and desires, still less realizing them.

'I can ask Amma for you if you are shy,' offered Mallika.

'No, no,' Deepa protested. She felt a little guilty that they were so concerned about her when she was attempting to flee their household.

'You cannot get anything if you do not ask,' said Govind, as if he did not believe she would summon the courage.

'Of course she will ask,' said Mallika, standing up for Deepa. 'Then we can practise together, Deepa, you and me, even after you have gone back to your house.'

Later that evening, Deepa was doing her homework alone at the big dining table, now pushed back to its usual position. She was a little tired after the rowdy evening meal, during which the children teased and shouted and laughed. Shyam, the aloof, broody one, had got angry over some trifle and was accused of being spoilt. Nalini was told to shut up for being too outspoken. Mallika was faulted for being vain and rebellious, and Govind was told he was lacking in humour. Deepa did not want to be criticized, but by being left out of their banter she felt she did not belong. She was pleased when they disappeared to their rooms to do their school work, leaving her alone with her own books. As she worked, she could hear some distant chatting and occasionally laughter, Mrs Sharma shouting orders to the maidservant, and the sound of the radio news. Deepa barely looked up when someone entered the room. Then she heard his voice. It was Govind.

'Maths, is it?' said Govind looking over her shoulder.

'Yes,' said Deepa, distracted by his presence.

'Do you need help? I am good in maths.'

'No, it is not a problem,' said Deepa self-consciously as Govind watched her work through some more sums. She was not the top of her class, but she was nowhere near bottom either, and never felt she was struggling with her work.

'Ma said you are going to stay with another friend tomorrow.'

'Yes,' said Deepa, who had informed Mrs Sharma that day.

'You did not say anything to us,' said Govind.

Deepa looked at him, wondering if he was angry with her. But he did not expect an answer. Instead he sighed: 'You are so used to being on your own, you do not think of others. In fact, I do believe you do not think of yourself much either.' Govind took her face in his two hands and stroked her cheekbones with his thumbs. 'You must know what you want, otherwise you cannot get it. And what you get may not be what you want.'

She was forced to stare into his face but he seemed not to be seeing her, Deepa as she was now, but Deepa the six-year-old whose father and sister had died horribly. He had the same stricken look on his face.

'You must not suffer because you do not care what happens to you.' He let go of Deepa's hot face. His hands rested gently on the table.

'I do care,' said Deepa, thinking it was only one more evening and tomorrow she could leave. 'I do know what I want,' she said.

Govind stood up. She watched him leave the room, bewildered by his behaviour. Why was he so intent on analysing her, on worrying about her? she wondered.

When Deepa finished her school work, it was quiet. The younger children were already asleep but she could still hear the radio faintly. She could not be sure whether it was Mrs Sharma waiting for her husband's return from the hospital, or Govind who slept later than the others. She went to the bathroom with a small towel and a brass *lotta* that Mrs Sharma had given her after she had noticed the trouble Deepa was having with the large tap. Deepa looked at her reflection in the stained mirror as she brushed her teeth in the poor yellow light of the bare bulb, and imagined she could see the imprints of Govind's thumbs on either cheek, just below her eyes. Her face flushed red as she thought of him in his white shirt and white pants and serious face. Then, hurriedly dipping the narrow-necked *lotta* into the bucket, she poured water onto her hot face and tried to scrub the imprints from her mind.

38

RAMAN RETURNED FROM A QUIET DAY AT PTI TO THE INTENSE SCENT OF ripening lychees bursting with sweet juice. Riots had broken out in the neighbouring town of Ghatpur and Gulbachan had departed complaining that that very day he had intended to start writing his book.

The lychee smell wafted in through the window netting and filled the house, clinging to everything and leaving behind a startling aroma. Bharathi, Shanker and Raman opened their tiffin-boxes at school and at work and breathed in the smell of lychees even before the homely smell of Kumud's freshly baked *parathas* reached their noses.

Even the geckos were immobile on the walls, inhaling the scent, and the frogs, drunk from it, no longer hopped about the garden but sat motionless under the trees, their throats throbbing with delight at having found a garden so sweet.

Kumud said, 'We should bring in the lychees or they will be spoilt. While the rain has stopped, they should all be picked.'

'Well, is Raju-*mali* not attending?' said Raman lazily.

'There are too many trees. If it is to be done quickly, we need more than just Raju-*mali*.'

'If we are to do *anything* in the garden we need more than just Raju-*mali*,' Raman grumbled.

'Vaman Brother has already agreed to come tomorrow with Guru and Shammu, and if you can ask Gulbachan for a little time . . .'

Raman could see she had it all planned in advance and was merely telling him of her arrangements. 'Gulbachan has departed for Ghatpur,' he told her. 'There are riots there.'

'Then it is no problem,' said Kumud, pleased at this turn of events. 'Look how fat are those lychees.'

Raman looked out and could just catch a glimpse of Jhotta's large black head, her horns in curves more graceful than her body, chewing cud underneath the trees. She had been happy and she had been producing good milk. The abduction had been successful, but for one thing: he had not written a single word since she had been there.

'It is good your brother is coming. Maybe he has news of the Ramanujans,' Kumud continued.

Raman began to feel pressured. 'He will tell us if a letter . . .'

'I know,' said Kumud, used to his excuses. 'But it is some days since you spoke to your brother. There may be news. Even a *sadhu* does not keep silent so long.'

'Maybe Ghatpur post office is closed, because of the rioting.'

'Oho,' said Kumud, her hands now on her hips. 'A messenger can be sent. Such an important matter as two girls marrying two boys and they have to wait for post office to open! I will go there to Ghatpur and get it myself if Vaman Brother has heard nothing. We cannot sit here with two girls and know nothing for so many days. Marriage season will soon be over!'

Kumud had become quite heated. Raman knew it was the tension of not knowing. Raman, too, felt tense. But it was the tension of not being able to write. As Kumud departed for the kitchen, he took out a new notebook and opened it at the first page. He stared into the near distance, he stared into the middle distance, and he stared into the far distance, but nothing helped. No words came to mind. It was four days since Jhotta had been tethered in the lychee garden providing Raman with all the milk for raita he could wish for, but Jagat Singh and the *goonda* were not in an adventurous mood. Raman was puzzled. The exact opposite had happened from what he had expected: the more raita he ate, the less he seemed to be writing.

Raman felt distracted by the household again. This time it was Bharathi. She had been hovering for some time, in fact since she had arrived from school. Once she saw she had caught his attention, she sat on the arm of his chair and came straight to the point, before Raman could send her away for disturbing him.

'Deepa's Amma is lying in hospital, Papa. Can Deepa stay with us? Please can she come, Papa? Ma has already said yes.'

'She said yes?' said Raman, annoyed at being pre-empted.

'Ma said Deepa can help to bring in the lychees tomorrow. Everyone is coming to help, Papa, it will be such fun!' said Bharathi, unable to suppress her excitement.

'If your ma says . . .'

'Oh, wonderful Papa!' said Bharathi, cutting him off in mid-sentence and throwing her arms around his neck. Only when Raman had disentangled himself from her tight grip was he able to think more clearly. Deepa would surely recognize Jhotta immediately she set eyes upon her in the garden and would wonder how she came to be there. Raman was not in the mood for complicated explanations. He tried to back out.

'How will she come up the hill from Kumar Junction with so much mud on the ground? Did you tell her no rickshaw will agree to come?'

'It is not raining so,' said Bharathi, sensing that her father was wavering.

'She will not be able to go in or out,' he said. 'It is not a good idea.'

'But I have been going to school, and Shanker too, and Ma was coming and going to market even in very bad weather.'

'It is different. We are used to it.'

'Oh, Papa! Where will she go if she cannot come here? She is my best friend. Don't you remember when her papa died? The whole of Mardpur was feeling sorry for her.'

Bharathi did not remember any of it herself, for she had hardly known Deepa then, but it was a useful ploy that she hoped would bring her father round.

'I will think about it,' Raman said evasively, realizing he would have to first think of a plan to spirit Jhotta back home.

'But I have already told her you said yes!' said Bharathi. 'Deepa, I said, you can count on your best friend, my house is your house, your Amma will not worry when you are with us, that is what I said.'

Any thought of writing had completely flown from his mind. Raman had more urgent things to think about.

'Later we will discuss,' he said vaguely, then stood up and slipped into his *chappals*, laying aside his empty notebook.

39

AS RAMAN WALKED DOWN THE HILL TO KUMAR JUNCTION IN THE CLEAR, hot, dust-free sunshine typical of those rare days during the monsoon season when there was no rain, he pondered what to do about Jhotta. Having acquired the buffalo at such risk, he was not inclined to give her up so easily. On the other hand he could see that there would be some explaining to do if Jhotta was standing in the lychee garden when Deepa arrived.

By the time he began his ascent towards the lychee garden, with a bundle of sacks from Jindal's, he had reached the conclusion that the buffalo would have to go back. Anyway, he said to himself, what use did he have for the buffalo? Gulbachan had gone to Ghatpur and did not need the milk of inspiration for a few days at least. Meanwhile it had become only too clear to him that raita made from Jhotta-milk, if it had any potent force at all, had now lost it. Had he not been eating raita every day, morning and evening, since he had procured the buffalo? And he had written nothing at all. Much as Raman loved raita, he began to have a niggling feeling that maybe, after all, there was no connection between raita and writing.

Once he got home, Raman went outside where Hari had just finished milking Jhotta. There was a pail of fresh buffalo milk standing beside

Jhotta. But what was this? Raman's eyes opened wide. Hari had kept aside a small *balti* of milk. Raman, tense from considering and reconsidering his options, rose to anger. Bhup! He cuffed Hari on the ear.

'Are you cheating me, you rascal? Where are you going with that *balti*?'

Hari held the side of his head and wailed. 'It is for Amma, sahib, she is needing it in Aurobindo Hospital for getting better.'

Hari continued as Raman glowered at him.

'Sahib, Amma is asking for milk every day. I am taking just little-little because this beast is giving too much milk and it is too far to go to Jagdishpuri Extension each day.' He said nothing about Jhotta's disappearance at that point.

'Is Amma knowing where this milk is coming from?' asked Raman, looking closely at Hari.

'No, sahib. Of course Jhotta-milk is best. This milk cannot be as good, but what can I do? Jhotta has disappeared!' Hari's voice rose to a wail. 'She has been taken away in the night by *bhooths*!'

Raman's eyes narrowed. He wondered who had been watching them that silvery night.

'Fine,' said Raman, thinking quickly. Hari clearly did not think this buffalo and Jhotta were one and the same. 'Now, you will take this buffalo to Amma's yard in Jagdishpuri Extension.'

'But—' Hari looked completely bewildered.

Raman held up a finger to silence him. 'By eating Jhotta's grass at Amma's place this buffalo will produce better milk for Amma. And then after one day you can bring this buffalo back here. That way Amma will be happy, she will get better milk, and we will be happy too.'

Hari blinked, trying to understand the scheme. In any case he had to obey. He was not taking any chances after Raman had boxed his ears without any provocation. He undid the rope and tugged at it. Jhotta did not budge. She had no reason to leave her buffalo paradise.

'Here,' said Raman, getting businesslike. 'Fill the sack with grass and leaves. The beast must have something to eat on the way. If she is starving, she will not be giving good milk.'

Hari did as he was told and tugged on Jhotta's rope. Jhotta looked up languidly and continued chewing. Hari waved some grass before her eyes and she happily went after it, slowly progressing towards the gate.

Raman went indoors, rubbing his hands with satisfaction. Shanker barely noticed him enter – he had his head bent over his homework – and Bharathi and Kumud were preparing the evening meal, as evidenced by the sizzling aromas that came from the kitchen. None of them had noticed that the buffalo had gone.

Raman followed the scent of cumin seed frying in hot oil. 'Bharathi!' he called, peering into the kitchen. 'You can tell that Deepa-friend of yours she can stay here till Amma is better.'

Bharathi was pleased. She jumped up from her plank and threw her arms around her father's neck. 'You are the best papa I ever had!' she said.

'Oho!' said Kumud, waving a hot ladle. 'This is no place for excitement, you have nearly upset all my dal!'

'It is still all in the pot, Ma,' said Bharathi, looking down.

'Only just,' said Kumud disapprovingly, but secretly she was just as pleased to have another hand to help with the lychee harvest.

The following day Raman rose early, still feeling pleased with himself. He stretched and sniffed the fresh morning air; it was free of humidity and dust. There were not so many mornings like that in a year, not on the dusty plains where the Ganges meandered. He went out to the verandah to savour the coolness of the garden, the sweet smell of ripening lychees, and the quietness of the hour; from inside came the sounds of his family stirring.

Then Shanker came running. He was looking concerned.

'Papa! Where is our buffalo? I was looking out of the window and I saw she is not there.'

'Buffalo?' Raman looked out into the garden, shielding the sun from his eyes with his hand to his forehead. '*Baap ré baap!* Someone forgot to tie her to the stake. That Hari! How can you trust that son of a swine? He is always eating my head with his excuses. Lazy buffoon! And that Raju-*mali* is sleeping again. I will whip him if I catch him with even one eye shut!'

Bharathi came running when she heard her brother shout and they both hurried out into the garden. There was no sign of Jhotta among the fragrant trees, which were heavy with fruit.

'I told you to call Mistry to fix that perimeter fence,' accused Kumud when she heard the news from the children.

'She has run away!' wailed Shanker.

'What if?' said Raman, irritated at the commotion his son was making over the mere disappearance of a buffalo. It did not merit such attention. Shanker was making it seem like a major tragedy.

'What will you tell Vaman Brother? That his buffalo is gone from under your nose?' said Kumud.

'What will I tell? Vaman Brother is not like these mad children beating their chests over a buffalo. He is thinking about more important things like the marriage of Meera and Mamta. Buffalo is not fitting in with his scheme of things!'

'Still, it will require some explanation.'

'What explanation? Tell Vaman Brother the beast did not leave any explanation behind, no message when she left!'

'But what will we tell when he asks? He is coming here today with Guru and Shammu also for lychee picking!'

'Okay, okay. I will go to Vaman Brother myself and break to him the sorry news of the disappearing buffalo, so that you are not embarrassed to tell anything when he comes to pick lychees, okay? After that I do not want anyone to mention one word to him because I know you will all just try to blame me.'

'But still he may ask.'

'I will be telling him not to ask. Not to say one word about the buffalo. We will all be *chup*. No one will mention.'

'I was going to make *rasgollas* today,' said Kumud regretfully, although resigning herself quickly to her buffalo-less household.

'Still you can,' said Raman pointing to the pail of milk Hari had left on the verandah the night before. 'Hari did milking before she ran away.'

'So convenient!' said Kumud, and went to get the pail. It was cool on the outside and wet with dew. With the low humidity of the night it was still quite fresh. 'I am beginning to like that buffalo–character. Maybe we can get another one.'

'Maybe,' said Raman noncommittally.

Raman ate breakfast and went to fetch Vaman.

'By the way, in my house you must not mention the topic of the buffalo,' said Raman as the two brothers headed towards Kumar Junction.

'The buffalo?'

'One buffalo we had. She escaped and they are all very upset. If you mention that word buffalo Kumud will be weeping only.'

'Oh, I would not want her to weep!' said Vaman. Besides, he had more important things to talk about. The Ramanujans had at last come up with a match proposal, but he pretended not to know anything about the dowry details.

'Laxman is dealing with those negotiations and maybe it is not yet fixed. We are all wanting it to go ahead, it is a most decent and suitable family. If you agree, we can set the wedding date for the beginning of the winter wedding season and I will go to Satyanarayan to ask for a suitable auspicious date.'

'But there are *hartals* going on in Ghatpur. Rioting. It is all in flames there!' said Raman. He felt panicky. The wedding was going ahead just when he had discovered that Jhotta's raita was not working. How would he finish writing? How would he pay the dowry?

'So? Does it mean no wedding can take place?' said Vaman.

'Let them wait a little,' Raman urged. 'With the troubles in Ghatpur they may not be in a mood to think about a wedding.'

'Only last week you were worrying because we had heard nothing from Ramanujans, and now you are saying it is too quick!'

'I am worrying about the situation in Ghatpur,' lied Raman. 'On PTI this morning I am reading terrible news.'

'Yes, I am reading it also in the newspaper. And Akashvani news is telling of burnings, but all that will be over soon,' said Vaman confidently.

Vaman and Laxman had expected protests from Raman, but they expected them to be over the dowry price, which was why they agreed to keep it secret for the time being. But Vaman was not sure why Raman was keen on a delay. As for the dowry demand, it *was* high. Even Laxman had to admit that. 'Let everything be finalized first,' Laxman advised nervously. 'Dates and everything. Then we will mention to Raman.'

There was a good reason for accepting the high dowry demand, which they had failed to haggle down. The brothers had discovered that the Ramanujan family was a major controller of Rajasthan tie-and-dye saris in several districts around Mardpur and Ghatpur, helped by their connections with the Marwaris of Ghatpur. Rajasthan tie-and-dye saris were all the vogue in the big cities. It was only a matter of time before the women of Mardpur would be clamouring for them. When that new film was released in which the heroine Lata was clad in each scene in tie-and-dye, every mother, wife and daughter would want the same. Luckily, Mardpur received films rather later than the other towns, and Laxman and Vaman had been working frantically looking for a supplier. Only later they discovered the Marwari mafia of Ghatpur had the business around the area sewn up, and they were charging huge middleman fees. If they could not find an independent supplier, Laxman and Vaman knew they had no choice but to pay the extortionate fees.

'The future is in tie-and-dye,' said Laxman. 'Silks, chiffons, even georgettes are getting expensive. And there are not weddings every day that everyone will keep on buying silks always. We cannot ignore tie-and-dye.'

'But the market is being protected,' said Vaman. 'I can go to Jodhpur, Jaipur even, but what good is it? Those Ghatpur Marwaris have paid producers not to sell to outsiders.'

An alliance with the Ramanujans seemed their only hope. Vaman told Laxman to go ahead with the marriage whatever the dowry demand, and promised he would try to persuade Raman that this was the best thing that could ever happen to his daughters. Somehow they would all find the money for the dowry. The survival of the brothers' sari business depended on it.

When Raman and Vaman arrived at the lychee garden, Deepa was already there. Vaman's sons Guru and Shammu had also been there since morning, fighting a guerrilla war using rotting lychees as ammunition, much to Kumud's consternation.

'What will your ma say?' she cried. 'Look at your clothes! Madhu Sister will say I don't know how to look after you!'

'We will say the lychees dropped splat onto our clothes,' grinned Guru.

'She will never let you come here again for lychee picking,' said Kumud, as the boys ran off screeching and rat-a-tat-tatting among the trees, delighted with their unexpected holiday from school which they agreed should be devoted to jungle warfare.

Deepa and Bharathi were standing demurely on the verandah keeping out of the rotting-lychee fire when Hari appeared with Jhotta in tow, just as he had been instructed by Raman.

'My beautiful Jhotta!' cried Deepa, throwing her arms around the beast as she trotted happily into the familiar territory of the lychee garden. Jhotta headed straight for the tree where she had been tethered before and waited for someone to tie her to the stake and provide her with a bag of rich, luscious leaves and grass.

'Deepa,' said Raman, before anything could be said on the subject of the buffalo's morning antics by his daughter, 'I thought you would like Jhotta to be kept here. She can sit in the lychee garden eating grass all day. That is a pleasant life for a buffalo. I would be jealous if I were a buffalo!'

'It is the best surprise I ever had, Raman Uncle,' Deepa said, and meant it. 'I have been missing my Jhotta for so many days.'

'Well,' said Bharathi. 'This morning only we lost one buffalo and this afternoon we have Jhotta. Papa,' she said looking worried, 'is the perimeter fence mended?'

'Oh, Jhotta would not run away anywhere!' said Deepa. 'Not while I am here.' She had already heard the story of the mysterious runaway buffalo from Bharathi and knew what Bharathi was feeling. Why, she would be quite upset too if Jhotta were to take off. But she knew Jhotta; she was not the type to go wandering. Deepa told Raman as much.

'When these buffaloes take it into their heads to run away, you cannot stop them,' said Raman. 'The other one, we never thought she would run off.'

'Maybe Vaman Uncle's buffalo ran back to Vaman Uncle's house,' said Deepa.

'Oh no, no. I asked Vaman Brother already,' said Raman, quickly looking around, but Vaman was inside the house being quizzed by Kumud for details of the Ramanujan proposal.

'Mysterious,' reflected Bharathi.

Kumud soon appeared on the verandah, like a shrill army general, handing out an assortment of buckets and *baltis*, bowls and bags, assigning everyone in pairs to a section of the garden. Raman with Raju-*mali* to keep an eye on him, Vaman with Shammu, Guru with Shanker, although the potential for too much play and not much picking was there. But Kumud realized that she should not make it feel like hard work in this heat or they would wander off and refuse to do any picking at all. Bharathi and Deepa of course were teamed up, Bharathi expertly climbing the trees she had grown up with and throwing down plump lychees into Deepa's frock, which she held up to catch them in. And she, Kumud, worked the patch nearest the house with Hari.

For hours they worked, chattering and laughing, the newly harvested lychees piling up on the verandah, filling the whole house with their fragrance. The boys juggled with them, threw them up into the air and tried to catch them in their mouths, saving the split and rotting ones as ammunition for later games. Deepa and Bharathi tried to see how many they could hold in one hand without dropping even one, a game which Kumud joined in for a little while, and even Vaman and Raman vied against each other to see how high each could climb into a tree. Shanker had a better idea. He got a head start by clambering onto Jhotta's back, then urging her to move from tree to tree. The problem was, Jhotta kept heading out for the open ground where the unshaded grass was greenest. In every corner of the garden trees were being shaken, prodded with sticks, climbed and fallen out of. And it goes without saying, in every corner of the garden lychees tumbled from the bowers like hailstones in the Himalayas.

Kumud broke off earlier than the others to lay out the food for lunch, which she had decided would be just before midday, when the sun was at its hottest. Everyone came in sweating and hungry and queued up at the bathroom to wash the dust and earth and sticky lychee juice away before sitting down to a big meal prepared that morning by Kumud.

After lunch Kumud brought out the *rasgollas*.

'These are too good!' said Deepa.

'Yes, they are made of milk from buffalo that ran away this morning,' said Kumud. 'Shame it is. She was a good buffalo, looking very much like your Jhotta, even also with scar on her rump.'

'*Dhut!*' said Raman, irritated. Vaman had gone to wash his hands, luckily, and had not heard the conversation. 'Why do you keep going on about that other buffalo? Of course Jhotta is looking like that buffalo, what else is she supposed to look like? Hanuman?'

'But it's true, Papa, now that you mention, Ma, there is also a scar on Jhotta's back,' Bharathi broke in.

'So they are having the same scar! What if? Just because these two buffaloes are going grazing with the same buffalo herd who bang them on the back in the same place with the same stick. Next time you will be saying their milk is tasting exactly the same.'

'I hope so,' said Kumud.

But Shanker decided to tease his father a little. 'Papa, tell me what is *different* about them . . .'

'*Dhut!* Are you saying I am blind or what?' said Raman belligerently. 'I tell you, I have had enough of this Jhotta and Jhotta-*avatar*. If one more word on this subject is falling on my ears I will send that Jhotta away back to Jagdishpuri Extension. And that will be that! I will not be repenting.'

'Oh Papa!' said Bharathi and Shanker in unison.

Deepa looked stricken and Kumud said mildly, 'I was planning more *rasgollas* for tomorrow, plus raita.'

'Not a word,' warned Raman sternly as Vaman reappeared with clean hands.

They had only a short rest, because Kumud noted the clouds appearing on the horizon. Kumud herself sat on a small stool on the verandah sorting through the fruit, while Hari and Raju collected them in Jindal's sacks.

The others flitted among the trees laughing and chatting, picking the lychees, eating some and throwing down the rotting ones. They worked more slowly as the humidity rose and from time to time they would stop and listen to the distant rumbling. The cloud-cover made it muggier but it was not so hot that they could not bear to be outside, and as long as it was not actually raining there was no reason for distant thunder to stop the lychee harvest.

The storm broke without warning – or perhaps they were all so happily engrossed with picking that they barely noticed the first drops. One minute the thunder clouds seemed so far away, the next minute they were upon the little group of lychee harvesters, bearing heavy rain.

Kumud, her arms full of lychees, ran to the verandah laughing, for the rain was warm and pleasant. It ran in rivulets down her parting and onto her nose.

'Come in, come onto the verandah,' she shouted, holding up her sodden sari so it would not trail the ground. 'It is raining.'

'We can see that!' laughed Shanker.

Guru and Shanker and Shammu were dancing up and down like demons, sticking out their tongues to catch the rain, their hair plastered to their heads.

'Come in, Guru! Come in, Shammu! What will your ma say?'

'We have an umbrella!' Guru shouted back. It was true, they did have an umbrella but it was open, the tip stuck into the ground and the umbrella itself piled high with lychees.

'Don't throw the lychees in the mud!' shouted Kumud. 'Leave the umbrella. And *run. Hai Ram*, these boys! Do they ever listen?'

Deepa and Bharathi were doing their own little rain dance. Deepa, delighted, held out her arms and let the warm rain pelt her face. Her frock was stuck to her legs, but she pirouetted on her toes, which dug deliciously into the cool mud. Kumud caught sight of Deepa with her bare, wet legs and thought there was something very pleasant about her look of gay abandonment, and something extremely graceful about her movements. Deepa's ma would not have any problem in marrying off Deepa.

The sound of the boys laughing uproariously carried through the rain, now coming down in a sheet, obliterating the view from the verandah. Kumud's eyes searched for them, and found the outline of Raman banging the bottom of an empty bucket, and Vaman, emerging from the trees, flapping his elbows and bellowing rhythmically as he did an exuberant *bhangra* dance. The boys fell in line behind them, jumping and flapping, clicking their fingers over their heads, banging their hips against each other, feeling the slap and the squelch of their wet clothes. Even Kumud had to laugh as she watched them. Despite herself she joined in, clapping to Raman's beat, her wet hands ringing to the rhythm.

Deepa and Bharathi joined the group as it reached them and they all chanted and sang, and swung and jumped, until they reached the verandah. Then Raju and Hari, grinning, took over the instrumentals, banging buckets and *baltis* while they all pranced, rivulets running down their legs. They laughed and slid and slapped each other on the back, while lychees rolled hither and thither, pushed in all directions by their feet.

That night, after they had all bathed and feasted, and Vaman and his sons had departed for home, Deepa slept soundly in the bed she was sharing with Bharathi, tired but happier than she had been for weeks. Not for her the heavy analysis of the doctor's children intent on saving the souls of butterflies and, it would appear, Deepa herself. This was the life she wanted, with its freedom and exuberance, and with no thought spared for the future.

40

WHILE THE LYCHEES WERE BEING HARVESTED, THE PTI WIRE WAS TICKING through frantically with news of a major disturbance in the neighbouring town. Mardpur was abuzz. People stood at street corners, tuned into Akashvani news, wondering whether the violence would spread to sleepy Mardpur. But as quickly as the riots flared up, they were put down again.

Two days later, Gulbachan returned from Ghatpur in tremendous spirits. 'It was all ablaze,' he said, his eyes glinting. 'There was no rain even to put it out, that night of the fire. And the *morcha* – how they rushed and the police charged back!'

Gulbachan was like a child describing his first visit to the movies. For days he talked about the Ghatpur riots, and not once mentioned the Salt March. His audience, which was just about every trader and shopkeeper, listened wide-eyed, and shuddered lest such calamities should reach their town. Gulbachan mistook this wide-eyed fear for wide-eyed awe at his adventures. He began to exaggerate and embellish, until it was all around Mardpur that nothing less than a revolution was taking place in their neighbouring town. It was only when the riots subsided that the people realized that whatever it was that had caused the unrest so close to home was being resolved, leaving Mardpur completely unscathed.

Now, instead of being encouraged for more details of the riots, Gulbachan came up against a wall of disbelief every time he spoke of it.

'But it is being resolved. Discussions are taking place,' said Mr Ahuja. 'It was in the newspaper.'

'I am sure they will come to agreement, after all what good is it to fight? Traders must trade,' noted Jindal.

'They have come to their senses. No more fighting-shooting,' growled Satyanarayan.

And as the interest in the riots faded, so it appeared did Gulbachan's feeling that history was in the making. Ghatpur had awakened some of the feelings he had experienced on the Salt March, but after all, in the clear light of day, what was it but a few petty squabbles stirred up by merchants with competing commercial interests? He could never hope for anything as momentous as the Salt March, stuck in this small town on the Gangetic Plain, even as Chief Correspondent. Even when there were riots breaking out.

'So it looks like the riots will not spread to Mardpur,' Raman said with relief.

'It was a dispute between the worker unions and the industrialists who are paying indecent wages. What is there here in Mardpur? No factories, no industrialists. Big zero. So what is there to fear?' said Gulbachan.

'Mardpur is uneventful,' agreed Raman. 'But that is good.'

'Maybe, Raman, for once, I am beginning to agree. The times when I could follow Gandhiji up and down the country are over. This must be my last great story as a reporter. I must realize that and retire gracefully.'

'Your book you can finish writing,' said Raman by way of encouragement.

Gulbachan yawned. 'I wanted to tell you before, Raman, but for me that writer-raita did not work. Not one word have I written so far.' He leant back in his seat dreamily. 'If I had written my Salt March book a long time ago, I could have enjoyed some money, status as a historian. What is the point now? PTI pension is fine, I am a simple man with simple needs. After all, I have no daughters to marry off. Better enjoy the memories, instead of working hard writing them down.'

Then he put his hands behind his head and leant back so far in his chair that Raman thought he would sink to the floor altogether. He had to strain to hear what Gulbachan was saying. 'Go ahead, Raman, write the

Salt March book. I do not mind any longer. There is no competition between you and me.'

'Salt March?' said Raman, incredulous. 'I am knowing nothing of history. I cannot write such an important book. I am writing small-small adventure story only.'

'You mean fiction?' said Gulbachan, sitting up with a bounce.

'Yes,' Raman admitted humbly.

'*Wah!* Tip-top idea! All the time you were writing this adventure?' Gulbachan now felt he had wronged Raman by suspecting him of competing with him. He leant his elbows on the table and looked at Raman with new interest.

Raman nodded.

'*Wah!* Then you can count on my support. Now, when are you needing it to be published? I will ring my friends in Delhi!'

But, Raman thought, it was not Gulbachan's support he needed but inspiration. And soon. Now there was another problem. Gulbachan had added to the doubts in Raman's mind. He could no longer believe in the magical properties of Jhotta's milk. The whole time she had been encamped at the lychee garden, Raman had not written one word. Raman knew the story of Jagat Singh was in him, because Amma had seen it there. But how was he to bring it out?

He had spoken to Deepa about it after the lychee harvest.

'Have you written about the *morcha* in your book, Raman Uncle?' Deepa said. 'Amma is telling me about the *morcha*.'

'But she is seeing more than I have written.'

'She is seeing what you *will* write.'

'Even if I have not written it yet?'

'Yes,' said Deepa, 'even if you have not written it, it is there in your mind.'

'But if I am writing nothing or I do not write for some time, how can she see?'

'Perhaps you are resting,' said Deepa. 'Amma did not say there is no more book. She is saying there is a *morcha* in the book that you will be writing.'

'I see,' said Raman. 'What if I stop writing altogether, this book? She can continue seeing what should be written?'

'Oh, no,' said Deepa. 'Only if you stop *thinking* about the book you are writing. Or if you stop *wanting* to write it.'

'How will she know if I stop thinking?' said Raman, bemused.

'I think she needs something of yours like . . . like your *balti* or . . . or your notebooks. Then maybe by just touching or smelling these things of yours, she knows what you are thinking.'

That's when Raman began to wonder if it was not the raita after all, but the *balti* in which it was brought. The *baltis* that went back and forth between himself and Amma, sometimes via Rampal, gathering smells and traces and thoughts and *feelings* on their outer surface.

41

THE DAY AMMA CAME OUT OF HOSPITAL DEEPA RETURNED HOME, LEADING Jhotta by her rope and carrying a bag of lychees given by Kumud as a parting present.

'Your Amma will need fruit to eat to get better. Whenever you want, just send Hari here and I will send lychees,' said Kumud, pressing the fruit into Deepa's hands and giving her a quick hug.

'It is like having another daughter,' she smiled, thinking of Meera and Mamta. They did not live with her, she did not see them often, but she felt a mother's concern and bond.

'I will think of you, Deepa, like I think of them.'

And Deepa remembered her own mother and felt secure in the thought that perhaps Ma was thinking of her like Kumud thought of her twins, and Amma thought of Ma.

Jhotta ambled through the Old Market with Deepa's small bundle of belongings strung around her neck. Hari urged Jhotta from behind with a small stick, but she hardly needed urging. Once she recognized the Old Market, Jhotta broke into a brisk trot all the way to Jagdishpuri Extension, swinging her large head from side to side. Hari and Deepa had to run to keep up with her.

'She knows she is going home!' cried Deepa happily, although breathless and hot with running.

While Hari tethered Jhotta to her stake in the front, Deepa ran into the courtyard and into her grandmother's arms. The smell of the pickles, the red earth and the water pump with the water from deep in the earth was almost overwhelming to her after so many days away. Deepa closed her eyes and inhaled. She buried her nose in Amma's shoulder, breathing in the familiar scent. It was as though in just the few hours that Amma had been back, the aromas from the pots and the pickles had risen up and swirled around her and embraced her, welcoming her home.

'Why, Deepa, so long it has not been since you saw me in the hospital! Too tight you are holding me!'

Deepa loosened her grip, but with her nose still buried in Amma's shoulder she said, 'Amma, you are different when you are here.'

'I am still the same,' laughed Amma.

Deepa shook her head. Amma's presence was stronger when she was at home, the many layers of her past adding to the aura around her.

'I missed you,' said Deepa.

And Amma laughed and held her granddaughter to her, rocking back and forth and inhaling the scents of the lychee garden from the top of Deepa's head.

With Amma still unable to walk, Usha now came early in the morning and stayed till dusk, tending to Amma's needs and doing all the other chores Amma used to do. Only the grinding wheels Usha could not master by herself. Deepa would help her, as she used to help her grandmother. They sat on low stools, their hands on the handle of the top stone, pushing and pulling until the pitted grey stone, white with flour, began to move. Deepa only then realized how strong Amma had been.

'Amma turned these stones and we are two and cannot even turn as fast!'

'She was turning them with magic,' said Usha with conviction.

'Magic? But she was also holding the handle and turning like we are doing,' puffed Deepa.

'The *bhooths* were helping,' said Usha knowingly.

'Let us get a *bhooth* to help us also,' said Deepa, stopping to rest.

Usha shook her head. 'Not everyone can know how to talk to a *bhooth* and not every *bhooth* will help.'

Deepa laughed at the ease with which Usha sidestepped the challenge. 'Tell me a story, Usha,' she said.

'About Baoli?'

'No. This time, tell me a story about a *bhooth*.'

So Usha began: 'One day when Baoli woke early in the morning, she found that Jhotta had already been milked. "Who is milking my Jhotta?" she said. But the Jhotta was a *baoli* Jhotta and did not want to tell. So Baoli went *baoli* wondering who did it. Then one morning she got up before the sun was up. She could hear the sound of milk splashing into the pail. So she went out to look and she saw the milk from Jhotta splashing into the pail but no one was milking. "What is happening?" she cried. And the *baoli* Jhotta replied, "You were always late in getting up, so I asked a *bhooth* to milk me." And that is how Baoli went *baoli*.

> *'Baoli Maai, Baoli Maai*
> *Kahan se aai?*
> *Koi jan na paai.'*

Deepa laughed. She felt she had really come home.

42

GULBACHAN HAD SPRAINED HIS ANKLE FALLING OVER A STRAY DOG. THAT was his story. Others said he had been bitten while trying to kick out at it. Still others said he had been bitten while trying to kick out at it, *and* fallen over it. Whatever the truth, he hobbled into the PTI office with a neat bandage on his foot and a pained expression on his face. He went straight to his desk, without once mentioning the Ghatpur riots, and picked up the *Statesman*.

Things did not improve when Raman looked at the message wire: 'HOW ARE MERCHANTS COPING? PROCEED TO GHATPUR SOONEST.'

Gulbachan did not react immediately when Raman handed him the slip of paper.

Raman, not sensing any urgency, took a large pair of shears. He tested them by clacking them together. Then, kneeling on the floor, he began to cut out the articles that Gulbachan had marked in the *Statesman* to be kept in dusty files in the battered metal filing cabinets, which neither he nor Raman ever consulted.

'Well, Raman, it looks like *you* must go to Ghatpur,' said Gulbachan finally.

Raman looked up after carefully turning the page with a square hole directly in the middle where he had extracted an article on yoga and longevity that Gulbachan wanted to keep.

'It is still early. You can catch the ten o'clock bus. That is not so crowded like the early buses,' Gulbachan continued after a pause. He had somehow hoped for a more dramatic response from Raman.

Raman banged the large rubber date-stamp on the violet ink-pad and from a great height, *bhup!* He brought it down on the Brahmin demonstrating how *singhasana* improved the circulation of the blood. He examined the violet imprint with satisfaction.

Gulbachan reached out for the petty cash box. 'For your fare and expenses. Find out all you can.'

Raman, with an expression of anger, was looking at the Brahmin branded on the forehead by a violet date-mark. He peered at the stamp with a look of disgust, wound the rubber to the next number, and repeated the action. *Bhup!* Only then did he look up.

'But I do not know how to do reporting,' he said.

'I will guide you,' said Gulbachan, enjoying the role of mentor. 'A man who can write a book can surely do a report. You have watched me. It is not a difficult task.'

'But how to conduct interview? I am not properly trained.'

Gulbachan stopped himself rolling his eyes heavenwards; his job was to encourage and train a possible successor, he reminded himself.

'Interview! What a big word. Interviewing is just chit-chat, *baat-cheet*, bazaar talk. The only difference is you write it all down.' Then by way of encouragement he added curtly, 'Just do your best.'

Raman had made the point that Gulbachan should not expect too much from him. He picked up the wad of notes, counted them carefully and put them in his pocket. Then he searched for Gulbachan's yellowing notepad. Gulbachan generously lent him his pen.

Raman hired a cycle-rickshaw, aggressively haggling over the fare to the lychee garden. To his surprise, he got his way. The rickshaw-wala could sense that Raman was not in a mood for compromise. But that was as far as Raman's luck went. As the clouds began to rumble and with the very first drops of rain the rickshaw-wala insisted he could not go all the way to the lychee garden. How would he get up the hill in such mud? The rickshaw-wala began to grumble. He knew that hill. Many rickshaw-walas had told him it was very steep. And then, once at the top, how would he come down? His brakes, he said, were not perfect. And when it rained they were really bad.

'Down the hill I do not want to be rolling.'

'It is a few drops only,' protested Raman.

The rickshaw-wala pedalled furiously and while the rickshaw was coasting, he wiped the sweat from the back of his neck with a cloth that hung from his shoulder. Then, twisting his body so that he could watch Raman's reaction in the back seat, he said, '*Huzoor*, one tyre is flat already. Even as far as the temple I cannot manage.'

He steered the rickshaw in a rakish zig-zag, as if to prove his point.

Raman looked anxiously at the front wheel then leant over the sides to check the side wheels. They looked suspiciously healthy and well-blown. Raman could see the rickshaw-wala was trying to get rid of him there and then. He wanted to get home, the lazy rascal, Raman thought. Raman played for time, trying to make the most of the ride. He knew in this weather it would be difficult to persuade any other rickshaw to stop when hailed, let alone go as far as the lychee garden and then back down again to the bus station.

'Why did you not check your tyres before?' Raman asked, annoyed.

'*Huzoor*, I did that. But what can I do? There is no pump.'

Raman was unsympathetic at such laxity. 'What happened to the pump?'

'*Huzoor*, my pump I sold it to my rickshaw-wala brother.'

'Why did you sell it?'

'My daughter was married last month, *huzoor*, and pump was sold to raise dowry.' Raman did not want to hear any more. 'Okay, okay,' he said, cutting him off, 'take me to Kumar Junction, from there I will walk. But I will pay you no more than two rupees. I did not ask for a ride in a rickshaw with flat tyres.'

'*Huzoor*, two rupees fifty,' said the rickshaw-wala pedalling hard. 'Two rupees is only for Vishnu Narayan temple. Kumar Junction is further.'

Raman knew he had no choice. The rickshaw-wala would just dump him unceremoniously at the temple. He waved to the rickshaw-wala to pedal on. What was the point of arguing? Everyone was after money these days. Everyone, it seemed, had daughters to marry off.

At Kumar Junction he climbed out, paid the rickshaw-wala two rupees fifty, and hoisted his umbrella as he started up the hill.

Kumud happily packed his lunch into his tiffin-carrier. Although Raman had said nothing on the subject, she was convinced this mission was evidence of the promotion they had all been waiting for since Gulbachan had paid them a visit. She bustled around him, seeing to his every need, and then came to the gate in the light rain, to see him on his way.

At Mardpur bus station the crowd at the ticket counter took Raman by surprise. He held his tiffin-carrier tight and plunged in. Caught up in the swirling crowd, he pushed his way towards the front. This crowd was worse than he could ever expect. It seemed like the whole population of Mardpur was trying to leave at once. Squeezed and jostled, he began to worry that he would never make it to the counter.

Then he heard a familiar voice just behind him. 'Sahib, are you needing Ghatpur ticket?'

It was Hari at his elbow.

'What?' said Raman, gasping as he was jolted by a coolie pushing past with two large leather suitcases on his head. Raman checked quickly that his tiffin-carrier was still safe and had not fallen to the ground, spilling his lunch under the feet of the crowd.

'Sahib, I can get ticket!' Hari shouted.

Raman pulled away from the crowd and followed Hari. Once away from the mêlée he felt able to breathe again.

'I have ticket-friend,' said Hari, nodding towards the crowd milling around the counter. Normally there were at least four ticket booths but today just one was open, causing chaos.

'Why is only one ticket booth open?' grumbled Raman.

'People are saying that number one ticket-wala is attending daughter's wedding. And number two ticket-wala is attending son's wedding,' volunteered Hari.

'Why is everyone marrying on the same day? It is the limit! So many weddings are happening all the time. They cannot organize on different days?'

'I am asking that also, sahib. Number one ticket-wala's daughter is marrying number two ticket-wala's son.'

'It is too inconvenient,' complained Raman.

Hari grinned, 'And then there is number three ticket-wala—'

'What excuse is he using?'

'He is the father of number one ticket-wala and has to attend wedding. Also, he helped number two ticket-wala to get ticket-wala job to improve prospects for son-in-law.'

Raman groaned. 'There is no limit to what people will try to get away with.' Then he added, 'Well, at least number four ticket-wala is still working. There is one honest man.'

Hari was enjoying himself hugely. 'Sahib, number three ticket-wala is paying number four ticket-wala good fee to come to work, otherwise other three cannot take holiday all on same day!'

'Oho! So *baksheesh* is being paid!'

'Yes, sahib, because number four ticket-wala is also asking for holiday today.'

'Why?'

'Sahib, number four ticket-wala's father died,' said Hari, rolling his head tragically.

'It is a tragedy,' observed Raman. 'He should be allowed to mourn. But if everyone is always taking holiday because of marriages and deaths and all, there would be no buses running ever.'

Hari nodded, looking wise beyond his thirteen years. 'They are having to pay number four ticket-wala to come back from mourning.'

'Oh? When did his father die?'

'One month before, sahib; only three ticket booths are open all month.'

Raman groaned.

'But I have ticket-friend. And I am not charging commission, sahib.' Hari grinned. 'But for small *baksheesh*, sahib, I will find him.'

'This country is full of scoundrels,' muttered Raman as he placed a rupee in Hari's outstretched palm.

43

RAMAN SAT UNDER A PEEPUL TREE AND WATCHED SEVERAL CLIENTS consulting a fortune-teller. Just as he was trying to make up his mind whether to have his palm read, Hari returned. He was carrying a bag and a white-haired man in his fifties with bandy legs and a large moustache was following him.

'Sahib, Ghatpur bus is full. No more tickets we can get,' announced Hari with an air of finality. And by way of alibi he pointed to the man beside him. 'Even Uncle cannot get.'

'Why is everyone wanting to go to Ghatpur when there are riots there?' grumbled Raman, not unduly put out by Hari's news.

'Not enough buses, sahib. Always like this,' volunteered Hari.

The grey-haired man took his bag from Hari and sat down beside Raman. Raman was not sure what he was waiting for if there were no tickets left to Ghatpur. Perhaps the old man would sit here all night and the next day until he got on a bus.

'Riots are over in Ghatpur, but much damage is there. Even where I am working in Ravi Printing Press, it was burnt,' Uncle said by way of explaining the rush to get to Ghatpur.

'Uncle is working in *Ghatpur Week* printing press,' Hari offered. '*Phook!* All burnt down.'

Raman had already read about it on the PTI wire. *Ghatpur Week* had taken the side of the mill owners and that had angered the workers.

'Not only printing press. Also sari shop next door,' said Uncle. 'Sari stock: silk, brocade, chiffon, georgette, valuable stock all gone.'

'Nylon saris were all sticking, like *Chiclets*-gum,' said Hari cheerfully, as if he had witnessed it himself. 'Melted sari is looking like this.' He made a gesture with his hand as if holding a fistful of molten plastic.

'Only because of Ravi Printing they were burnt,' said Uncle with some sympathy. 'Sari merchants have no problem with workers at Rustomjee. Only Ravi Printing because of *Ghatpur Week*. We all are too close to Rustomjee Mill. Many trouble-makers at Rustomjee. Big-big union and many workers.'

'Who is the owner of the sari shop?' asked Raman.

'Ramanujans,' said the old man.

'The one with twin sons?' said Raman, hardly believing what he was hearing.

Uncle nodded.

Raman was quiet for a few seconds. 'What is to happen to shop?'

Uncle shrugged. 'Sahib, compensation will have to be paid, but who knows when?'

'Sari-walas will get compensation?' said Raman. 'How much can they get?'

'In the bazaar they are talking *lakhs* for compensation,' interjected Hari.

Uncle shrugged. 'They can get, but when? It is taking years. No compensation for stock. Only for building. It is bad luck. Some old *zari* pieces also burnt. Very valuable.'

'Are many people claiming compensation?'

'Everyone! Some are even removing stock from their shops and lighting small fire to claim,' Uncle said.

'But *sarkar* is knowing because everyone could see who was burning and who was not on the night,' said Hari, knowingly.

'We are more lucky. Paper stocks are not kept here. Only one edition of *Ghatpur Week* is lost. Damage is mostly to roof. Printing machine is tip-top. Others are not so lucky. Merchants are angry. Very tense situation now in Ghatpur Bazaar. Mood is still not good. In bazaar area there can be unrest again. *Hartal*. Riots.'

Raman tried to draw the conversation back to the sari merchants. 'So they are ruined if entire stock is gone?'

'Almost. Only good thing is boys are marrying in three months' time and big-big dowry will be paid. With that they can build up again.'

'In three months!' echoed Raman.

'Yes. Astrologer has already fixed the date. I am knowing because we are printing wedding invitations.'

'Invitations?' said Raman in a daze. 'They were all burnt too?'

'No. We are sub-contracting. Delivery date will stay same. When such a good match is there, we cannot make problem with invitations. Dowry will be more than one *lakh*, I am hearing. Twin girls for twin boys. Very perfect.'

'More than one *lakh*!' Raman felt faint. He did not want to hear any more. But Uncle was distracted. The bus to Ghatpur, the one for which both he and Raman had failed to get tickets, was ready to leave, full to bursting.

'Quickly Hari, take my bag, I must get on the bus.'

'But you have no ticket!' exclaimed Raman, then realized they were already out of earshot. Hari and Uncle were running towards the bus, taking advantage of the chaotic jostling and frantic shouting of vendors around the vehicle to clamber on board. Vendors of peanuts and roasted chickpeas, candy-floss on sticks and sticky *jalebis*, their baskets on their heads, were running alongside the bus calling out. It was as if they would only make a sale when the bus was about to move – the last chance for passengers.

Swift as a monkey, Hari shimmied up the ladder to the top of the bus with Uncle's bag, and quickly tried to wedge it securely amongst the other luggage. Uncle, too, was hanging onto the back ladder, scaling it at a more sedate pace, nonetheless agile for a man of his age.

Raman watched them, somewhat astonished at their determination. But he would have none of it. If he could not get on the bus the normal way he would not try. He rose from his seat and left the bus station as the bus, rattling and belching thick, black diesel fumes, impatient to leave, was moving forward. He missed what happened next.

All at once, the bus lurched to a halt. Hari, close to the edge, lost his hold and was thrown from the roof. He was extremely fortunate in landing on a vendor's basket among the peanuts. Pods were thrown in the air when he landed, like drops of water when a huge boulder is thrown into a pond, scattering in all directions. There was a huge commotion. Vendors rushed away from the bus, thinking it was tipping over and fearing all the luggage would rain down on them, or even that they themselves would be flattened by the keeling vehicle. A bus station official banged on the side of the vehicle and shouted at the driver to stop, convinced a child had fallen from the roof and been killed. The bus company would surely lose its licence in such an event.

The peanut vendor, oblivious of the dangers that others seemed to perceive, rushed hither and thither to retrieve his precious merchandise, stretching spider-like from a squatting position to reach under the bus, intent that not a single pod should be lost. He was more concerned with gathering together his peanuts than with the fate of Hari, bunched up in his basket like a hen sitting on eggs. Hari flailed about, finding it difficult to extricate himself without sinking further into the peanuts. Amid all the shouting and bother and his attempts to get up, Hari became aware of a long, drawn-out peal of laughter.

The laughter came from a well-dressed man, young, smooth and wearing real leather boots up to his ankles. He stood gracefully with one foot on the stump of a tree and his elbow resting on his knee as his boots were being polished. He had a proud air and even though he was laughing uproariously, he maintained a dignified posture. Surely this was a prince, Hari found himself thinking in some surprise. A prince of regal bearing.

Hari grinned wryly when he realized he was the subject of the regal-sahib's mirth, although he did not think it was funny. He could have been badly hurt. He found it an odd thing for the regal-sahib to laugh at.

After the initial shock, when everyone realized it was not a child but a servant boy that had been thrown and that he had landed without injury, the vendors crept back and the bus passengers descended to see what all the fuss was about. Hari finally rolled out of the basket unharmed and they turned on him, chided him for endangering himself, the bus, and all the passengers, and suggested that next time he held on tight. Then they climbed back on board and urged the driver to start moving. Uncle, who had also clambered down from the bus to make sure Hari was all right, ran after the belching, sputtering vehicle as it moved forward and leapt onto the back ladder. He hung on, swaying, as the bus picked up speed, and slowly scaled one rung at a time, his *dhoti* billowing white in the wind.

Hari was momentarily distracted by the peanut vendor entreating him to empty his pockets of peanuts which may have fallen in. He was a poor man, the peanut vendor wailed, and could not afford to lose half his stock, even if the circumstances of the loss were highly unusual and unlikely to be repeated. As he emptied his pockets Hari's eyes were on the regal-sahib, who was still chuckling loudly.

'He is the one, Man Singh,' the regal-sahib said to the plump, older man beside him. 'None the worse, eh? Made of rubber these boys!'

Hari must have been staring hard, taking in his smooth features and garb, for the regal-sahib addressed him, not unkindly: 'Okay now, boy?'

Hari nodded.

'What is your name, boy?'

'Hari, *huzoor*,' said Hari.

'You have work here?'

'No, *huzoor*, I'm freelance,' Hari said, using an English word he had learnt from Father Paul.

'Freelance! You hear that, Man Singh? He's freelance! You speaka English, boy?' he said in mock-broken English.

'Little-little,' said Hari in English. He was beginning to enjoy the attention of such a man who seemed like a foreigner in his bearing, although he spoke and looked like an Indian.

'Little-little! I could use a boy like you. You know Mardpur well?'

Hari beamed. 'I'm born in Mardpur, *huzoor*.'

'Good, good. We need someone to show us around.'

44

RAMAN STAYED AWAY FROM WORK THAT DAY. HE WENT HOME TO MULL over the significance of what he had heard, but also to avoid having to admit to Gulbachan that he had never got any further than Mardpur bus station. The following day, he arrived early at the PTI office and laboriously typed up a passable dispatch on Gulbachan's old typewriter with its faded ribbon and dust-encrusted rods which stuck together in bunches before even getting to the paper. When he was satisfied, after several attempts, Raman laid the single sheet of paper in Gulbachan's in-tray and returned to clipping the newspapers. He was still clanking his shears when Gulbachan arrived.

'"Tempers are still frayed in Ghatpur. The mood is volatile, the tension high. Deep in the bazaar, unrest could break out any moment."'

Gulbachan was effusive. '*Wah!* Raman. Not bad. You have captured the um . . . the . . .' Gulbachan searched for the word. 'Yes, the mood! All this without raita, too!'

Gulbachan enthusiastically set about cleaning up the dispatch, setting it in journalese – the kind of language the Delhi bureaucrat would like and understand. Not long after, it ticked through on the PTI wire as an 'eye-witness report' from Ghatpur.

Both Gulbachan and Raman sensed something had changed in their relationship. Raman was no longer just a dogsbody. Quite apart from book-writing, he had attempted and succeeded in writing a very creditable dispatch. Gulbachan pensively watched Raman clip back-issues of the *Statesman*. When Raman had finished and was looking around for something else to do, Gulbachan joined his hands together under his chin and leant forward on his desk to make his announcement.

'I have been thinking, Raman. I will be retiring soon – early retirement,' he added, as he saw Raman's look of surprise. 'There is no one in Delhi who wants to come to Mardpur for this posting.'

Raman was not surprised. 'What is the need for a Mardpur correspondent?' he said, then added hastily, 'With your experience it will be hard to follow on.'

'They are thinking of keeping only sub-correspondent,' said Gulbachan. 'After all, PTI house is here. They have to appoint someone. But there is not much to report. The riots were unusual. A senior correspondent is not necessary.'

Raman wondered who would want to be a sub-correspondent in Mardpur.

'I am thinking of putting your name forward,' said Gulbachan, a smile lingering about his face. He watched Raman's reaction with some satisfaction. 'Your work in Ghatpur was good. I will put your name forward. I will say you are a well-known writer. They should be honoured to have you as sub-correspondent.'

Raman did not know what to say; he was truly touched by the faith Gulbachan had in his abilities. 'I . . . er . . .'

'It is nothing,' said Gulbachan, waving him aside. 'You are the ideal person to follow on.'

'Compared to you, I am nobody,' said Raman humbly. 'I have been nowhere. I only know about the Salt March from you.' That, at least, was entirely true.

'Yes, the Salt March . . .' said Gulbachan dreamily. 'It was a long time ago. Of course you will never be a *great* correspondent, but you will learn fast. I will still be here to guide you. And that is the best thing about this arrangement of ours. If you are my successor, I can keep my PTI bungalow in my retirement. For you are not needing it. Such a beautiful bungalow you have of your own in your lychee garden. I saw with my own eyes. It is an idyll. PTI bungalow will hold no attraction for you. So it will be good for me and good for you.'

'You are wanting to stay in Mardpur for your retirement?' said Raman lamely. He realized he was the man of choice out of expediency rather than talent or even friendship.

'Why not?' said Gulbachan. 'PTI bungalow is free, and I can come here every day to read the *Statesman*. They won't object in Delhi as long as they have someone on the payroll assigned to Mardpur.'

Raman wondered what it would be like to have Gulbachan wandering in every day looking over his shoulder. In fact, he could not imagine himself taking on such a responsibility at all. The thought of communicating with the PTI editors in Delhi filled him with dread.

'It is a good offer,' Raman said slowly, not wanting to seem ungrateful. 'I will think about it.'

'What is there to think?' said Gulbachan, astonished. He was handing Raman the biggest opportunity of his life, and this fellow was not even sure he wanted to take it. Anyone else would be touching his feet. He had misjudged Raman, his assistant really *was* unambitious. Gulbachan bit back any hint of sarcasm. He wanted to be pleasant and friendly towards Raman, and persuade him gently to take the job.

'My daughters' wedding is coming,' said Raman lamely. 'There is much to do. Also, I must finish writing . . .'

'Of course, of course,' said Gulbachan. 'After all, I am not retiring tomorrow. Next week I will draft a letter to Delhi. I will say first I am interviewing many, many candidates. Only later I will propose your name. And, from today I will give you a raise.'

Gulbachan went to the cash box where he put the money he saved out of his budget. He had never passed on to Raman the salary rises he claimed in the budgeting forms he sent to Delhi every year. He pulled out a handful of notes.

'Buy a bicycle. When you are a sub-correspondent you will need one.'

Raman took the money without counting it. Gulbachan wagged a finger at him. 'You must buy a bicycle. This money must not be used for your daughters' wedding. Tomorrow I will take you to Jetco on my scooter and you will choose one. Atlas is best.'

Raman tidied up quickly and then left. Gulbachan lowered his newspaper when he heard Raman go and scratched his head in bewilderment. Raman was a most unexpected fellow, he thought. You could never tell what he was thinking.

Raman was extremely thoughtful as he waited for a rickshaw, but Gulbachan's offer was not prominent among those thoughts. There was no getting away from it, his daughters' marriage would go ahead.

★

Laxman greeted him effusively when Raman appeared there half an hour later. 'Sit, brother,' said Laxman. 'Meera, Mamta, bring your father tea!'

Sudha-with-Pension bustled between the kitchen and the living room, laden with sweetmeats and delicacies. It was calculated to put Raman in a good mood. But Raman felt uneasy. Laxman had called a family meeting but would not reveal the substance of the conference in advance. Hence Raman had been on edge all the way from the PTI office. It did not help that it had taken a while to hail a cycle-rickshaw. Raman arrived half an hour later than the appointed time, convinced they must have started without him.

'How could we start without you?' said Laxman, greeting him at the door. 'You are chief guest. Vaman also is not here yet.'

Almost an hour later, when Laxman and Raman had long exhausted the small talk and retreated behind the newspapers, Vaman arrived. Madhu accompanied him, with heavy gold jewellery at her wrists and throat.

Sudha-with-Pension threw a disgusted look at Madhu's show of ostentation. 'What is the need for wearing so much jewellery? This is only family meeting. We all had jewellery given in marriage. I could be wearing too, but this is not the time or place,' she grumbled to Meera and Mamta while preparing tea in the kitchen. But she still came out to talk to Madhu about prices in the market and to complain about how they were all being cheated.

'Not everyone is cheating,' said Madhu. 'It is inflation.'

'Inflation? What fine words you are learning,' sneered Sudha, not liking to be contradicted.

'I am listening to Akashvani news every day,' explained Madhu, ignoring her tone.

'Akashvani radio I don't need, I am reading newspapers,' said Sudha.

'What are you paying these days for ghee?' said Madhu.

'Fifteen rupees.'

'Fifteen rupees! You are being cheated, sister.'

'It is better to pay few more rupees to be sure it is pure,' said Sudha-with-Pension. 'That cheap-cheap sugar dealer you were recommending mixed white stones to make it heavier. You cannot trust anyone.'

'With me he is never doing that,' said Madhu defensively. 'You should be watching while he is taking sugar from the sack.'

'You think I am standing there with my eyes closed?' said Sudha heatedly.

'Now we can start!' said Laxman, flapping his newspaper for emphasis. Meera and Mamta hurriedly took a seat, as if a show were about to begin. They arranged their saris carefully, showing off the pleats at the front to their best advantage. They fiddled with their *pallavs* so that they hung neatly over their left shoulders, showing off the beautiful *zari* borders of fine gold thread woven into delicate paisleys and lotuses.

Laxman waited till they finished arranging their silks, savouring the beauty of the shimmer with the eyes of one who had picked them out himself from the best of his stock. He stood up to make his announcement.

'I have good news.' He coughed and shuffled, and then decided sitting down was better. 'I would like to announce that the Sari House in Ghatpur has been burnt down in the riots that took place there last month.' Laxman had a smug look on his face.

'That is good news?' said Vaman astonished, his voice rising above the buzz of female voices of surprise. 'What is good about that?'

Raman, to whom the news was less of a surprise than to the others, was also nonplussed by Laxman's rosy view. Why should this be a cause for joy? Surely they should all be commiserating with the Ramanujans on their misfortune?

'What's good about that? I'll tell you: it means that now those Ghatpur Ramanujans are equal to us. Two sari stores of theirs and two of ours. And so –' Laxman rubbed his hands with glee and his words came out in a rush, so excited he was, '– and so, they are willing to negotiate on dowry for Meera and Mamta.' He smiled fondly at his adoptive daughters. They sat demurely and fiddled with their saris, knowing that their marriage to the Ramanujan boys was almost certain.

'Pour tea,' Sudha-with-Pension whispered to them with a small push at Meera's arm, which was nearest to her. They moved gracefully with a swish of pure silk, Meera taking the teapot and pouring tea into Raman's cup and Mamta adding sugar.

'I have not finished,' continued Laxman when he saw the puzzled faces of his brothers. 'Not only have they expressed willingness to negotiate on dowry but they have indicated that their starting price is *half* what they spoke of initially. I am confident we can negotiate them down further.'

He looked around pleased, unaware that even the half-sum was likely to shock Raman, once he found out how much it was – just as it would shock Sudha-with-Pension, who, while wanting the match, had grave doubts about the sums of money required to ensure it.

'Well,' said Vaman finally. 'That is highly suspicious.'

'Why?' said Laxman. It was his turn to be puzzled. He had imagined that all that remained was for the family to congratulate him on his acumen. 'I am already reading about it in the newspaper. Dispatch from PTI is reporting. It is all true.'

'Number one: if they have lost one shop, then they will be looking for *more* money to re-establish business,' said Vaman, who did not doubt Laxman's facts, merely his interpretation of them. 'Number two: we must know which shop is lost. If it is the one the boys were to inherit, then we are not making such a good match after all.'

'Of course I have made all enquiries,' Laxman lied, but he was clearly put out by such considerations. 'And there is no problem of that nature.'

The prime consideration for Laxman was to move forward as fast as possible to take advantage of the situation.

'So,' summed up Vaman, 'we must go to Ghatpur when the riots are over and negotiate.'

'When it is all over?' said Laxman with a frown. 'No, no. We should not wait. While they are in bad position we should move quickly.'

'But it will be dangerous for us to travel there now,' protested Vaman, who knew it was usually he who travelled on behalf of the brothers.

'Well,' said Laxman, 'one of us must go.'

Sudha-with-Pension at once began to massage Laxman's legs as if to press the point that it would be too much for her husband. Raman looked around and realized no one was looking at him. His two elder brothers were glaring at each other. Clearly he could not be trusted with dowry negotiations, even when the brothers were in a stronger position than the other side.

'Okay, okay,' grumbled Vaman, crumbling finally. 'I will go.'

'Tip-top!' gushed Laxman, pleased. He indicated to Sudha to stop pressing his legs now that the danger was past.

'Now,' said Laxman, turning to Raman with a gracious sweep of his hand, 'we only need your consent, brother, for this marriage to go ahead. It is a good match. Dowry will be a bargain. You are the father, your consent only is needed.'

They all looked at him in anticipation. The demure eyes of his twin daughters, glowing and expectant, searched his face for assent.

Raman gave it. Everyone clapped. Laxman patted him on the back. Raman reciprocated. After all, Laxman had achieved an admirable feat, making it appear as if the marriage would not have gone ahead or a date been fixed had it not been for the 'bargain-price' dowry they could now get. Yet no exact price had been negotiated still and he was being asked for his assent on what was in effect a blank cheque, even if it was half the sum of before.

Vaman stood up and then sat down again, and voiced what was in Raman's mind. 'Perhaps it is a good idea, brother, if we discuss dowry now.'

Laxman, thoroughly businesslike, stood up again. 'I must ask the ladies to withdraw.' He wanted no recriminations afterwards. Money was a man's matter.

Sudha-with-Pension, Madhu, Meera and Mamta swept out of the room.

'I suggest . . .' said Laxman, getting straight to the point in order to retain the initiative, 'I suggest we split the dowry three ways.' He made it sound as if he had only just thought of it.

Raman had been afraid of that, and came straight out with his response: 'And with what will I pay a share? My book is not written yet!' Raman was seriously worried. He had not put a single word on paper in more than a week.

'Well, we cannot wait,' said Laxman, irritated. 'We must take advantage of Ramanujans' weak position before they can build up again. You had time enough to complete.'

Raman realized he had no room for manoeuvre. Although his brothers had not mentioned it, he was well aware that the date was set. Invitations were being printed. All that had happened that afternoon was that Laxman had skilfully obtained his consent for a virtual blank cheque of a dowry, dressing it up as a 'bargain', and told him to pay one-third.

45

LAKHAN BHAI, THE POTTER FROM THE VILLAGE OF JATAK, SOUTH OF Vakilpur, came to Mardpur with his handcart full of pots, large and small, smooth and round, all smelling freshly of the earth. He beat his pots rhythmically with a reed, producing a haunting tune which was hollow, reverberating and mysterious.

'*Handia-wale-e!*' he called in a sing-song, rasping voice, as dry and dusty as his pots.

Lakhan Bhai's father and uncles had been apprentice potters in the court of Jaipur, where the pots were transformed by artists using them as their canvas. His father, the oldest brother, came back to Jatak by the river and set up the pottery kiln there. Lakhan Bhai carried on the craft, despite hard times, as villagers and townspeople alike took to the shining beaten-brass pots available in the markets which were unbreakable and carried intricate designs. True, they did not keep the water as fresh and as cool, but who was thinking of such things these days? To add to his woes, the good red clay from the riverside at Jatak had become exhausted. Lakhan Bhai had to pay more for women to bring the clay from further down river now that his wife was not as strong as she used to be. Lakhan Bhai, though old, pushed his handcart for miles along dusty roads to find buyers further and further afield.

Arriving at Jagdishpuri Extension, Lakhan Bhai left his handcart in the front, just out of the way of Jhotta's horns in case she took it into her head to tip it over and smash weeks of hard work. He joined Amma in the courtyard for tea, sniffing appreciatively at the red-earth smell that pervaded the place. He, more than others, could smell beyond the pungent warm mustard oil and fermenting mangoes and detect the old, old smell of the pots from the days when the red clay was abundant and moist, and easy to dig up and carry away. He could smell the more recent pots from the not-so-good clay, which were drier and more brittle and needed more care when spinning on his wheel. He felt at home drinking tea with Amma.

'How is business, Lakhan Bhai?' said Amma drinking from her saucer. Visitors were so rare that she savoured every moment she could spend with him, hearing about the wider world.

'Not good,' said Lakhan Bhai squatting on the ground, sipping the hot tea. Years of squatting at his potters' wheel made him quite unable to sit on a seat of any kind. If he could not squat, he would rather stand. But he knew Amma would not mind, as long as she knew where his voice was coming from. It bothered her not a mite if he sat on the floor.

'There is a new hand-pump installed at Beejli village and they are buying new pots there. Big-medium-little,' he said, indicating with one hand above the other, the way the women and girls stacked up the pots on their heads, forgetting that Amma could not see. 'But mostly little, because there are many young girls in Beejli. I was not knowing this, so now I have many large left over.'

'Good,' said Amma. 'For it is large pots I am needing.'

'If I had an unmarried son I would be sending him to Beejli for a wife. There is a lot of choice there!' he joked.

'Why so many girls, Lakhan Bhai?'

'The boys and men have all left. What is there to do in Beejli? No *pukka* road, no electricity, only the chilli harvests and chilli-drying. And that is women's work.' Amma knew the dirt road to Beejli well; it was lined on both sides with red, yellow and green chillies, all drying in the sun on muslin *dhotis*. Amma used to go regularly to Beejli to bargain for the best chillies for her pickles. She knew many of the women who gathered in the chilli harvest and waited for the chillies to dry in the sun before selling them to the merchants from Vakilpur, who sold them to the merchants of Ghatpur, and from there to a middleman in a big town and perhaps to Delhi, and who knows, even to foreign countries these days.

'Then there is no business this year in Jhula village,' Lakhan Bhai continued sadly.

'Why is that?' Amma asked, surprised. In Jhula village quite a large handloom industry had grown up around the villagers' special weaving skills. The dyeing industry that supported it required a constant source of water from the river nearby, much of it brought to the courtyards of the weavers on the heads of the women of the surrounding villages.

'They have grown rich in Jhula village. Panchayat council is strong and villagers have persuaded *sarkar* to give them waterpipe from the river. They are not using pots any more.'

'They had been talking of a pipe for a long time but the government never obliged them before,' observed Amma.

'No, they are getting big-big money from the Well Bank in Amrika. There is a tap in every village house. Brand new. I have seen with my own eyes.'

'So much money they are getting from Amrika!'

'Yes, the Amriki Well Bank is deeper than any well here!'

'At least the waterpipe will make the women's lives easier.'

'That it will not,' said Lakhan Bhai with certainty. 'Who will employ them now? Before they were getting a few annas to feed their children. They may have been illiterate but they knew how to use their heads!'

'You are right, Lakhan Bhai, it has completely altered everything, this coming of the waterpipe. What will become of the water-haulers?'

'Ammaji, come to Jhula village and teach them how to make pickles. For that they will be needing pots and it will bring a little income. There are many-many mango trees also around Jhula. There is an Amriki social worker trying to find things for them to do. But she is wanting them to do sewing. Who can buy a Singer machine? Why, girls are saving for sewing machines in dowry, not buying for themselves!'

'It is a good idea, Lakhan Bhai, but I am an old woman. And pickles need time to mature. I will not be living so long.'

'Ammaji, may you live a hundred years more! You are young like me!'

'I have done my duty. I married my daughter well. Only for Deepa, I worry. But her fate is not in my hands. There are many things she must go out and learn that I cannot teach her. But I have provided well for her, she will not be lacking in anything. I had enough treasure from the courts of the kings for my daughter's dowry and my granddaughter's.'

'What will happen to all your pickles?' said Lakhan, waving his hand towards the rows of pots high on the shelves in the kitchen. To him the pots were a far greater treasure than the trinkets Amma spoke of. Each pot was formed lovingly in his hands, like magic, each lump of clay willing itself to be a pot.

'They will be for my granddaughter. With pickles here, she will have a reason to keep coming back after I am gone!'

'Your pickles are the best in the district, Ammaji; who would not keep coming back for them!'

'Now tell me, Lakhan Bhai, how many large pots do you have out there? And you must give a good price to an old woman who cannot see what is being sold to her!'

'Amma, I give you only the best. There is not much market for these old pots now. And what is the use of my hauling them back home to Jatak? I do not want a heavy load, for I am getting old, too.'

When Deepa arrived from school and threw down her school bag Amma was priming the new pots with warm mustard oil while Usha was slicing the unripe mangoes, ready for pickling.

'Sit, Deepa, we will write. Usha! Ohey Usha! Bring a *lotta* and soap for me to wash my oily hands.'

'I am here, Amma,' said Usha from beside her and ran off to get the water.

'What is the hurry for writing, Amma?' said Deepa. 'I have not yet started my homework.'

'We have still much to do, Deepa. And I do not have much time in which to complete. My days are coming to an end.'

Deepa stood stock-still. It was the first time Amma had spoken thus. Deepa tried to ignore the seed of fear that had been planted, but she could not.

'Oh no, Amma, it was a small accident only, you are recovered already.'

'My time is coming soon. Only we must finish writing.'

Deepa said nothing. She hardly knew what she felt; there were so many things she was thinking all at once she could not extract a specific thought to say what it was. The seed of fear began to grow. Deepa went to get the notebooks from the red trunk while Amma washed her hands. She stood there in the dim light for a few minutes, breathing deeply and trying to push Amma's words to the back of her mind. But the fear overtook passivity; she wanted to fight, but fight what? Fate? It was a battle she would lose, and she knew it. Then, because she had no choice, she gathered the notebooks in her arms and took them to her grand-mother.

'What will happen to me when you are gone?' said Deepa quietly as she sat on the *charpoy*. She held the notebooks in her lap but did not open them. 'It will not be like your accident, when I went to Dr Sharma's house and then Bharathi's. I will be sent away from Mardpur, and then I will never be able to come back here.'

Amma reached out and found Deepa's hand. She held it between her own two hands, softened and aromatic with mustard oil. 'Your ma loves you, Deepa.'

'I love this house. I want to stay.'

'Without me what will this house mean to you? You will not want to stay alone.'

'I have lived here for so long!'

'This is your father's house. It belongs to you to keep if you want it.'

'Even if the house is here, will I be coming to it? My ma never comes here.' Then Deepa added sadly, 'Maybe for her there are too many bad memories here. But for me, they are all good memories. They are my only memories. I have no others.'

'Only when you find the treasure and take it away with you will your link with Mardpur be broken,' Amma promised.

A tear dislodged itself from Deepa's eye and rolled down her cheek. 'The treasure is not real, Amma.'

She remembered how she went around the house with Bharathi when they were younger, knocking on the walls to see if they could find a hollow spot, and the times she had tried digging in the front yard with a spoon but had given up before getting very far. Jhotta always tramped down the dirt, so there was hardly any trace of her attempts.

'There is treasure here,' said Amma gently. 'You will find it when you are ready.'

'There is no treasure!'

'It is for you.'

'Then where is it?'

'Everyone must work hard to find something even if it belongs to them. Life is never so easy.'

'What if someone else finds it first?'

'It is your fate to find it.'

'Don't go, Amma! I don't want the treasure if you are not here.'

'Shh, child. I still have some time. But we must work quickly. Have you got your notebooks? And Raman's?'

Deepa handed her Raman's notebook. Amma fingered it, going quiet with concentration, and gave it back to her granddaughter.

'Read,' she said.

Deepa obediently opened the notebook and tried to read the last few paragraphs. But the writing became blurred by her tears, which began to drop one by one onto the page in front of her, merging with the blue ink that spread across the page in spidery, watery splodges.

46

AMMA, WHO WAS ONCE SO STRONG AND ROBUST, NO LONGER WENT TO HER grinding stones. Now she was too tired, and the stones were too heavy. Instead Deepa and Usha heaved those stones when flour was required for their daily chapattis.

There were other small changes. Amma did not make so many minute observations as before. She was less inclined to articulate what she could smell, hear and feel, but seemed instead to be withdrawing into herself. She did not follow Deepa's every move around the house with her chatter, her interpretations of Deepa's daily actions. Deepa noticed it was much quieter. If it were not for Usha, who came much earlier now, it would be quite lonely. Deepa sensed Amma's exhaustion and was alarmed. The seed of fear that Amma had planted in her breast was growing, and Deepa did not feel as carefree as before, burdened as she was now with the unknowns of the future.

Yet there were times when Amma was quite animated. Every afternoon, after her nap, Amma was at her most alert, waiting for Deepa to come with Raman's notebooks as if she were drawing strength from somewhere to continue the story of the smuggler.

Amma sat cross-legged on the *charpoy*, distant in her thoughts, and sometimes with her palms held to the sides of her head to concentrate better. Then she spoke. From her mouth came the most wonderful descriptions of coves and caves, beaches and islands: places that Amma had never been to, but which she visited through her visions. And Deepa visited them with her, wandering in the same dreamland and turning it into words.

Sometimes Amma held one of Raman's notebooks in her hands, as if drawing out the words from within it, although of course the words she was drawing out had not yet been written. And sometimes she sat with a *balti* in her lap – one of those she had sent to Raman with yoghurt in – and she would gently rub it, as if trying to rub off Raman's thoughts, turning the *balti* around and around in her lap to find a spot where the thoughts came strongest.

'Best is a watch or a pendant,' Amma noted one day, feeling that the pictures were not coming to her mind with any kind of clarity. 'Something that belongs to Raman. In the old days, when I wandered the kingdoms of the north, it was the pendants of the maharanis, the bangles I was wearing, that linked me to them. Every piece they gave bonded me with them. Maybe that was how they were always able to find me in good time.'

'You must have been seeing so much all the time,' said Deepa in wonderment. 'What confusion!'

'It was not like that,' said Amma, thinking back. 'The important messages were always the strongest. And I must be listening. If I am not listening, what will I hear? Now I am listening for messages from Raman and these are the ones I will hear. But it is not always that he chooses to send messages to me.'

Deepa laughed. 'It is a good thing, then, that we have his notebooks. Then we do not always have to wait for his messages.'

Amma ran her fingers along the notebooks. 'Before my accident he was reaching out to me – I know, I know, he liked Jhotta's yoghurt. But whatever the reason, he was reaching out in this direction. Now he is not looking towards me, and I have to find him some other way.'

All this seemed perfectly logical to Deepa. 'Shall I ask Bharathi to bring me something of his?' Deepa suggested.

Amma shook her head. 'Let things take their course.' Then she put her fingers to her temples to try again.

'*Handia, Handia-wale!*' called Lakhan Bhai, rapping out a mournful but melodious tune on his red earthenware pots.

Kumud had her hands full of flour. But the tune of red pots reached her ears. 'Ask him to stop,' she called to her husband. 'We need pots for the wedding of Meera and Mamta.'

'Let him come inside the gate,' said Raman lazily.

'Oho, gate is too narrow for his cart, how can he come? Outside he must stand.'

Raman went to the gate. Lakhan Bhai was leaning on his handcart, mopping his head. 'I am no longer young,' he said, throwing a glance in the direction of Kumar Junction as if to measure how far he had come. 'Or that hill has become steeper.'

'Maybe you have too many pots this time,' suggested Raman.

Lakhan Bhai looked at the pots on his cart and said sadly, 'You are right. Every year I return to my village with more pots on my cart.'

Raman looked sympathetic. 'Is no one buying in Mardpur?'

'Only Amma,' said Lakhan Bhai.

'There is no wedding in *her* family,' said Raman, faintly puzzled.

'Amma is making pickles, best in the district. So aromatic. One smell and it is going to the top of head like this.' Lakhan Bhai traced a line from his nose to the top of his head. 'Only in red–earth pots can such pickles be made.'

'Amma is very fond of pickles, I know. But what will she do with so much?'

'Pickles take some years to ripen,' said Lakhan Bhai.

'It is true,' said Raman. 'But there is enough mango pickle in Jagdishpuri Extension to feed all of Mardpur.'

Kumud came out wiping her hands on her sari.

'You have a good selection this time, Lakhan Bhai. Sometimes you were coming from town and there is nothing left.'

'That was in old days,' said Lakhan Bhai sadly. 'Now there is too much left.'

'Well, you are lucky, Lakhan Bhai, for my daughters are getting married and for the wedding *mandap* I need some pots.'

Lakhan Bhai looked pleased. 'That is seven pots for each post of the *mandap* and some extra in case of breakages.'

'Do you have so many?' asked Kumud. 'Without cracks and marks? For a wedding they must be without blemish.'

'If I do not have, I will come back just for you, *bahenji*,' said Lakhan Bhai happily.

'No, no. For that I do not have time. I will take what you have here.'

Kumud began to examine the pots. 'These are the only medium-size ones left, but all are having black-black marks,' she said, frowning.

Lakhan Bhai examined them. 'Wedding-time flowers will cover, *bahenji*,' he said. 'These days red earth is not such good quality as before. From far we are getting. I will give you good price, why should I take them back to the village with me?'

Kumud looked hesitant; she scratched at the black marks.

'It is good red clay, not dust. Some are using ordinary mud and painting red only,' said Lakhan Bhai. He rapped on a pot with his knuckle and it let out a melodic resonant sound. 'Not brittle, will not crack.'

Kumud knew he was right. She selected her pots. 'Help me carry them in,' she said, and Lakhan Bhai unloaded the pots.

When they had paid Lakhan Bhai and offered him water to drink and a bag of lychees to take home, Raman surveyed the terracotta army on the verandah.

'What will you do with so many pots when the wedding is over?'

Kumud made it clear she was not thinking of such things just yet. 'Lychees we can store in pots instead of sacks,' she suggested.

But Raman looked dubious. 'Not enough air is circulating.'

'Then we will save them for Bharathi's wedding,' she said. 'By then, no one will be making such pots. Lakhan Bhai is already old.'

'They will just gather dust,' grumbled Raman.

'Oho, why do you worry? Is it the biggest problem on your mind? You can ask Raju-*mali* to plant flowers inside, see how they will grow!'

'I can think of nothing to put in such pots,' said Raman flatly.

47

'I HAVE HAD OFFER OF PROMOTION FROM GULBACHAN,' RAMAN FINALLY
revealed to Kumud just as she was about to go to market.

'He is giving you sub-correspondent post?' said Kumud happily. Even
Raman was surprised how much pleasure it gave her.

'Now we will be able to buy decent jewellery,' Kumud said. 'Before, I
was thinking, *Hai Ram*, how can we do it?'

'You already have jewellery,' said Raman disingenuously. 'You
brought so much when we married. Those bangles also.' He pointed to
her gleaming wrists.

'My *maa-baap* were generous,' said Kumud, somewhat wistfully. 'We
must do the same for our daughters.'

'But Laxman . . .'

'Laxman has his duty, but a *maa* and *baap* have theirs. And now the
marriage is approaching. Sudha has told me the date.'

So even the women knew! Everyone except himself. Raman
pretended he had been in the picture all along. 'I was waiting to verify
date with Satyanarayan before I told you,' he said, trying to salvage some
status.

'Maybe that is why Gulbachan is giving your promotion now,' said
Kumud, who was not one for recrimination. She was more taken up with

the urgency of the wedding preparations. 'He knows you have your duty as a father.'

'I will spend every *paise* on jewellery for our daughters!' vowed Raman. He found himself wanting to do good by Kumud. He was rewarded with her glow of pleasure.

Kumud was smiling gently to herself as she tidied a few things around him, fussing with a cushion here, wiping a speck of dust there. It was as if she could not bear to go out without finishing all her tasks. When she was ready, Raman accompanied her to the gate. He stood there, on the damp earth, watching her slim figure swaying gracefully as she walked over the hill on the long, tree-lined road towards Kumar Junction, her bangles glinting in the clear, bright morning sunlight.

Raman became engrossed in writing a fighting scene between Jagat Singh and his adversaries. The fighting scene developed into a bloody massacre. Raman found that once the details of a fighting scene had been etched out, it was that much easier to push the hilt of a dagger that much further, to draw the ends of a rope that much tighter around a neck. There was not much more, it seemed to him, to killing than there was to fighting.

By the time the sun had reached its highest point of the day, Raman had filled an entire notebook with mayhem. He seemed surprised himself at the amount he had written. As he screwed the cap on his pen, he heard someone's feet scraping on the verandah. It could not be Raju-*mali*. He would never be walking around at this hot hour, if he ever walked around at all.

'Who is it?'

'It is Hari, sahib,' Hari called back through the netting door.

'Ohey, Hari, what are you doing here? I did not call you. Did she call you?' said Raman, referring to his wife.

'No, sahib, I am sent by Amma,' said Hari.

'Come inside, boy. Why are you making me shout at the walls?'

Hari carefully removed his *chappals* on the verandah before entering. He wiped the sweat off his forehead with the back of his hand. It was quite a climb up the hill in this sweltering post-monsoon heat, and Hari had stopped from time to time underneath the mango trees that lined the road. But he was also fearful that, in such heat, the contents of his *balti* would go sour, so he pressed on.

'Sahib, Amma is sending yoghurt. Fresh today. She said it is to celebrate that you are writing.' He held up the *balti*.

Raman was no longer surprised at Amma's talent for seeing from afar. And he was pleased to have the yoghurt, although he no longer believed in its magical powers.

Somehow the link had been re-established. While Amma had been in hospital there had been no progress on Jagat Singh. But that had passed, and Amma was once again able to see what was in his mind, and once again he, too, was beginning to generate the ideas she wanted him to generate.

'Sahib, there is one little thing,' said Hari holding up his index finger.

'What?'

'I am to take back *balti*, please, but only if convenient for you, Amma said.'

Raman went into the kitchen to tip the yoghurt into some other receptacle and bring back the *balti*. When he returned to the room, he noticed his notebook on his desk.

'You are going back directly to Jagdishpuri Extension?' he asked.

'Yes, sahib. To return Amma's *balti*. Then I will attend my new *malik*.'

Normally Raman would have been curious and would have asked who Hari's *malik* was, but he was distracted, thinking about the link with Amma. He picked up the notebook.

'This is for Deepa. Carry carefully. Do not let it get wet.' It had been raining that morning, although now it was quite dry and hot.

'No, sahib,' promised Hari, and shoved it under his vest.

'Now go,' ordered Raman.

Hari saluted briskly, shuffled into his *chappals* on the verandah, and headed back down the hill, swinging the empty *balti* in one hand and pressing the palm of his other hand against his vest to make sure Raman's notebook did not slide to the ground.

When he had gone, Raman sat thinking. He was beginning to understand. Amma needed something of his. He had touched the *balti* that Hari would take back to Jagdishpuri Extension and Amma could feel something of him when she in turn touched it. Definitely, that was it.

There was a major commotion at Kumar Junction when Hari arrived there at a leisurely pace. A white Ambassador car, hooting aggressively, had frightened Pappu's herd of water buffaloes, which had been gently ambling off for a day in the fields and ditches on the outskirts of Mardpur. Panicking, the buffaloes had scattered all over Kumar Junction running this way and that. Worse, the bellowing and shouting had brought out

Satyanarayan, who had tried to take things in hand but only succeeded in creating more anarchy as he distracted Pappu by shouting at him.

'You donkey, son of an owl! Have you not learnt to control these buffaloes? Around a sacred temple you let them run amok!'

Vaman came running up with a yardstick to help round them up, and other traders and vendors had come out to watch, wanting to ensure that no beast entered their shop and created havoc there. Pappu, clutching his trailing head-cloth, ran hither and thither, calling to first one buffalo by name and then another.

The regal-sahib, meanwhile, finding his vehicle blocked by a particularly lazy-looking buffalo, stopped and got out, watching with some amusement the disarray he had caused.

'One would think these buffaloes had never seen a car before,' he said to no one in particular.

Vaman was standing right by him, leaning on his yardstick. He looked at the regal-sahib curiously, summed up the quality of his fine poplin shirt, and responded, 'They have not.'

'Who would believe this town is so close to Ghatpur. It is so backward!'

'You should not judge a town by its buffaloes,' responded Vaman, and surged forward to tackle one large beast who seemed to want to head towards the temple.

Satyanarayan, who was flailing his arms in all directions, hoping to drive the buffaloes away from the general direction of the temple, looked very briefly grateful as he saw Vaman head the beast away. 'No matter what you do, they head for the temple,' he grumbled.

'Maybe they think it is time for Jhotta-*puja*. They know you are doing such a *puja*!' said Vaman, patting his rescued buffalo and holding tightly onto its rope so that it would not take it into its head to run off again.

Satyanarayan looked angrily at Vaman. It was surely in bad taste to be joking in this way when there was a crisis in hand. He began flailing his arms again.

'It's no good,' said Vaman, 'I don't think those buffaloes can see you.'

'You think buffaloes are short-sighted, or what?' said Satyanarayan.

'No, they are just not looking in your direction.'

Satyanarayan stopped flailing. 'It is not my job to round up buffaloes,' he snapped.

'No,' agreed Vaman, tugging on his buffalo who seemed to think it was time to head off again. 'But buffaloes don't distinguish between castes.'

At this the regal-sahib let out a guffaw of laughter. Vaman and Satyanarayan both stared at him, Satyanarayan in disgust, and Vaman with curiosity. Satyanarayan decided he did not have to put up with such people and moved away.

'I think you annoyed him,' said the regal-sahib.

'It is not difficult,' said Vaman light-heartedly. 'Satyanarayan is a great man and we are not good enough for him.'

'It is easy to be a great man in such a small place as this,' observed the regal-sahib, watching bemusedly at the chasing and shouting that was going on in one corner as a number of vendors made after a stray buffalo.

Vaman turned to the regal-sahib, once again noting the quality of his out-of-town, possibly foreign, garb. 'Don't underestimate Satyanarayan Swami. If Mardpur grows, Satyanarayan will grow powerful with it. It is in his nature always to be on top.'

'A man to keep an eye on, then?' said the regal-sahib.

'Certainly you cannot ignore,' concurred Vaman.

'If that is the case, he is the only one in Mardpur that rises above the ordinary!'

Vaman smiled wryly, for he knew that this outsider's perception of his home town was probably quite accurate. But he had no time to reflect on it at length. He was on guard again as he spotted another buffalo breaking free from the herd that Pappu had managed to gather together, which looked to be heading towards him. Then the regal-sahib did something that Vaman found very strange. It bothered him for many days afterwards, and long after he had forgotten about the buffalo uprising itself. The regal-sahib stooped down and picked up a rock. He hurled it at the oncoming buffalo with a swift over-arm motion, graceful as a cricketer. Fortunately, the buffalo changed direction before the stone could hit it between the eyes, on the soft, furry part of its forehead. Vaman was shocked. Boys hurled stones at stray, rabid dogs, but he knew of no one who would attack a gentle buffalo in this way. He instinctively moved two steps away from the regal-sahib and kept his distance thereafter.

Satyanarayan had meanwhile spotted Hari. He shouted at him to ensure that no buffalo went heading in the direction of the lychee garden and Vakilpur, where it would be lost for ever. Hari smartly blocked the path of one smallish buffalo by waving his arms in front of her face, forcing her to lumber towards Satyanarayan. Satyanarayan stepped smartly aside, losing his balance and almost landing slap into a newly fallen buffalo pat. It was only because of a judicious twisting movement by his body, made supple by years of yoga, that he prevented himself from falling in it. He got to his elbows, eyeing the pat distastefully.

'Owl!' he shouted at Hari, as if it were somehow his fault. 'Dare you push a holy man into a pile of dung? Have you no eyes in your head? And what are you staring? It gives you pleasure to see a priest lying in the dirt, or what?'

Hari rushed to amend matters by helping Satyanarayan to his feet but the Brahmin was having none of it, waving him aside angrily. Nonetheless, Hari managed to haul him to his feet, receiving for his pains a cuff on the ear from Satyanarayan once he was upright.

'Ow-wow-wow!' howled Hari, cupping his ear and jumping up and down in agony, for Satyanarayan had a firm hand.

'That will teach you, son of an owl, to send those buffaloes in my direction. Be off with you!'

And Hari, who felt it unfair to be blamed for the buffalo break-out, took off, determined to put some distance between himself and Satyanarayan.

The Brahmin was brushing himself down angrily with brisk strokes that started at his stomach. When he reached his knees, he stopped as he noticed the notebook on the ground where it had fallen from Hari's vest. He picked it up gingerly and banged off the dust. Shoving it into the waistband of his *dhoti*, he hurried back to the temple, noting that Pappu seemed to be in control of the errant herd now, backed up by Hari's expert assistance.

48

BY THE TIME RAMAN REACHED KUMAR JUNCTION, THERE WAS NO SIGN OF the buffalo bedlam that had afflicted the area just half an hour earlier. Raman traversed the junction, which was quiet except for a few tinkling bicycles, a scooter and a stray dog, and headed for Sohan Lal & Sons, the jewellers.

It was easy to miss Sohan Lal & Sons. There was no shop window. It was reached via a rickety staircase on the side. The board saying Sohan Lal & Sons was large enough, but many visitors, not finding the entrance, assumed it was an old board and the jewellers long since moved away. It never occurred to them that the staircase was the way in.

Madan Lal and Mohan Lal, his father, and Sohan Lal, his grandfather, had been Mardpur's jewellers for generations. Anyone seeing Madan Lal in the street with his round glasses, bald pate and walking stick could have mistaken him for Mahatma Gandhi except that his back was more bent and his attire less scanty. He was quite unassuming, and there was nothing about him to suggest that he dealt in anything more valuable than tin. But Madan Lal was extremely knowledgeable about the pieces he sold. They were not just trinkets to him, but works of art. It caused him some grief that clients were no longer interested in such detail. All they wanted was sparkle and show, and this was provided by the jewellers of

Ghatpur with their modern designs and brightly lit, glittering show-cases.

Madan Lal opened the ageing shop on the first floor of the leaning wooden building for only a few hours in the afternoon. Sometimes customers, pressed to do their business in the morning hours, would go to his house, a once-proud but now dusty and unkempt bungalow in Merchants' Colony, where the shutters were rarely opened since his wife had died fifteen years ago and his only son had left to study abroad. Madan Lal would emerge, coughing and shuffling, and obligingly accompany them back to his Kumar Bazaar shop, and show them some of the most beautiful pieces ever produced on the Gangetic Plain, pieces that even the Ghatpur jewellers did not know how to reproduce – not that they had tried, for they insisted that the kind of heavy jewellery sold at Sohan Lal & Sons was not what women wanted to wear these days. Maybe it was true, but those who had never seen the older pieces at Sohan Lal & Sons did not know what they were missing.

When Raman appeared shortly after lunch, Madan Lal was dozing fitfully behind the counter. He woke up with a start.

'When is the wedding?' enquired Madan Lal, polite and refined as always.

'In few weeks only,' said Raman. At least here was one person who had not been told before he himself knew. 'A father must do his duty, but of course I have no idea about brides' jewels.'

'It is all a matter of taste,' said Madan Lal helpfully.

'What is popular these days?'

'Popular, or fashionable? It is not the same thing,' said Madan Lal, already beginning to busy himself with his trays. He had a technique, which was to start with mediocre pieces and move on to the more dazzling ones, as if to give the impression that he always had something better to show. He knew at this stage money was hardly ever talked about, and that what people wanted was to see the kind of range that could be found at Sohan Lal & Sons.

'Well, both,' said Raman, to be on the safe side.

'What is fashionable are the modern pieces made in Bombay. I have none of those here,' said Madan Lal. 'But I have old-old pieces, from the courts of the kings. Many people are looking for these pieces.'

'That means that their value will rise faster than Bombay gold?' said Raman.

Madan Lal nodded, pleased at Raman's grasp of the economics of scarcity.

For the next half-hour Raman looked at the jewellery brought out by Madan Lal.

'When you see so many beautiful pieces, it is very difficult to choose,' Madan Lal said, admiring them himself, although he had seen them many times before.

Raman agreed.

Madan Lal went on: 'Of course they are not fashionable now, but later maybe they will be popular, when your daughters are giving them to their daughters.'

Raman nodded distractedly. He was not concerned about his daughters' daughters at this stage. He found the old pieces pretty, but heavy and ostentatious. And they did not gleam as yellow as the present-day gold.

'That is the trick of the Bombay merchants,' explained Madan Lal. 'They are knowing that what people are wanting is the shine. So they are producing that. There is no art, no skill. It is like a factory. This old jewellery, every piece is individual, made by craftsmen with proper tools. There are very few these days who can appreciate.'

'Of course, I know nothing about these things,' said Raman hastily. 'But it is my duty.'

'It is mainly the women who decide,' acknowledged Madan Lal. 'Women are sometimes saving secretly some money for such jewels for their daughters.'

Raman knitted his brow, but he did not think Kumud had been setting money aside. 'Let my wife choose, then,' said Raman gaily. 'Then payment will be after my approval.'

Raman felt he had given Madan Lal the impression of being an involved father.

'Of course,' said Madan Lal effusively. 'We men cannot be expected to know what women like. It is they who have to wear, why should we interfere in their choice?'

At that point there was a clattering on the stairs. Both Madan Lal and Raman looked up expectantly. Raman stared at the stranger who had walked in, tall, suave and beautifully dressed. Raman's eyes came to rest on the regal-sahib's shiny leather shoes. Such leather he had never seen in Mardpur.

'Come, come,' said Madan Lal, looking pleased. He came out from behind his counter to welcome the regal-sahib and directed him to a padded bench.

'Sit, please,' said Madan Lal. 'Tea has already been ordered, you must partake with us. Ramanji here is of very old distinguished sari trading family of Mardpur. Experts in silk and all kinds of *zari*. Real gold thread. They are often in my shop. Very knowledgeable about jewels. He is my best friend.'

Raman felt flattered at being honoured so, although it was far from the truth. He wondered if he should withdraw, but Madan Lal pre-empted him.

'Let my friend Ramanji advise you, he is an expert in matters of taste. Now, what is it you would like to see in my humble jewellery shop?' And he rubbed his hands and looked expectantly at the smooth features of the regal-sahib.

The regal-sahib had asked Hari where to find old things, old paintings, old furniture, old jewellery. Hari had to think hard. He did not know of any painters. Mardpur was a town of merchants; true, they sold on the wares of the artisans of the surrounding villages, but as far as Hari knew none of these villages specialized in painting. As for old furniture, that was usually broken up for firewood. However, Sohan Lal & Sons seemed the kind of place the regal-sahib might be interested in.

'Show me your oldest pieces,' said the regal-sahib without any preliminaries.

Madan Lal sent Hari to find tea in the bazaar, then looked at the regal-sahib through his heavy, scratched spectacles. 'Old, as in traditional designs, or old meaning from old days?'

'From old days. I mean antique. More than one hundred years old.'

'These days people are not so fond of such old pieces,' Madan Lal commented as he put away some of the jewels he had brought out to show Raman. Then he pulled out a large bunch of small keys, unlocked padlocks, and boxes, and shot back the bolts. He ran his finger along the rows of neatly stacked velveteen boxes. He had not touched these boxes for some years.

'I have some old-old pieces from Jodhpur, from the court of the maharajas,' Madan Lal said, blowing the dust off the velveteen as he brought out the boxes. 'Very good pieces. Very valuable, made by the best Rajput craftsmen.'

Madan Lal opened the first box with a flourish. Nestling among the dark blue satin was a large, exquisitely designed necklace with a peacock pendant set in sapphires and emeralds.

Raman gasped at such beauty. He suddenly began to understand what people meant when they referred to treasure. There was no other way to describe such brilliance. These pieces were not just jewels.

'They are not so popular now because people want gold only,' said Madan Lal.

The regal-sahib drew in his breath, clearly enchanted by the sight. 'Beautiful,' he breathed. 'Just beautiful.'

'They all have the craftsman mark,' Madan Lal pointed out. 'Genuine. From Jodhpur.'

'Do you have more?' said the regal-sahib without taking his eyes off the sapphire-and-emerald peacock.

'I have some more pieces, also pieces from royal households,' said Madan Lal. He opened the second box to reveal a breathtaking necklace and earring set, swirling with a paisley design set in rubies and some kind of violet semi-precious stone. A smaller velveteen box housed a necklace among the cream-coloured satin with a leopard pendant of diamonds set with sapphire spots. Its pointed teeth of ivory were bared ferociously as it leapt into three strands of diamonds.

'These are the very best, each piece is unique. And worked with devotion,' said Madan Lal with some pleasure. He stood back to admire the wares himself.

Raman had never seen such jewels in his life and thought they were the most beautiful pieces he had set eyes on.

'How did you acquire them? These are not everyday jewels,' said the regal-sahib, unable to take his eyes away from this glittering array.

'They are very special, no?' said Madan Lal. 'There is an old woman in Mardpur. She is blind now. Her husband was the astrologer in the courts of the maharajas. He was a *rajguru* in ten states – such a scholar we had here in Mardpur once. These pieces were given as payment for his services. When the time came to marry off her daughter, she came to me to sell these pieces to pay for the dowry and the wedding. And also to pay for the education of her granddaughter, when her son-in-law died. I have not seen her in many years, for there has been no wedding recently. Maybe the next time will only be when she pays for the dowry of her granddaughter. That is the story of how I come to have these pieces.'

Amma! thought Raman, wide-eyed. So Amma did have treasure! This was it. It was all sold to Sohan Lal & Sons.

Madan Lal brought out some more old pieces. 'This from the court of Cooch Behar, and this from Gandhinagar, as you can see, made also by the finest of craftsmen.'

'What a treasure trove,' said the regal-sahib, sitting back. He was overwhelmed by the magnificence of the hunting scene in different precious stones set as a necklace. At the head of the hunt were the dogs, then the bearers with guns, then the elephants with their *howdahs* and *rajkumars* on top, with more bearers bringing up the rear. The regal-sahib admired the way the stones were set to imitate the flow of the turbans. Every detail was reproduced in glittering stones.

'Yes,' agreed Madan Lal. 'And there are many stories about the old woman's hidden treasure. No one knows where it is kept or how much there is.'

'There is more?' broke in Raman.

'Who knows how much there is? The *rajguru* was truly a great man. Many rewards he collected from the kings. There may be more, but no one knows where.'

'Surely she is not the only one who has such pieces as these?' said the regal-sahib, now truly fascinated.

'Outside the royal families? I think so. Some people were receiving only few small pieces, and not so valuable.' These were some of the pieces that Madan Lal had shown to Raman before.

'What does an old woman need such jewellery for? I will buy it all from her!' said the regal-sahib.

'Whether she will sell, I do not know,' said Madan Lal doubtfully.

'Money is no object,' said the regal-sahib. 'Man Singh can find cash like this,' and he snapped his thumb and forefinger.

Raman was impressed at anyone who could find money like that. But Madan Lal was not so easily influenced by people's professed affluence.

'Man Singh?' said Madan Lal.

'My financial adviser,' said the regal-sahib loftily. 'He advises me on all my investments.'

'It is true, it is an investment, these jewels,' Madan Lal said. 'But money, I don't think Amma is in need of it. Take what I have in stock and later maybe you can add more.'

But the regal-sahib's appetite had been whetted. 'These here I can buy any time,' he said dismissively. 'Who else in Mardpur can afford such jewels?'

'It is true,' said Madan Lal, 'Mardpur is not so rich. Even the traders of

Merchants' Colony are not making money like the traders of Ghatpur. I have had these jewels since Amma sold them to me at the time of her daughter's wedding. No one has shown any interest in such jewels.'

'I am not surprised,' said the regal-sahib. 'These are jewels fit for kings. They would look out of place on the women of this town.'

'It is an investment,' repeated Madan Lal. 'But people here are not thinking of such things.'

'Yes, yes,' said the regal-sahib impatiently, 'now tell me how can I find her, this old woman with the treasure?'

49

WHEN THE WHITE AMBASSADOR CAR STOPPED OUTSIDE THE HOUSE IN Jagdishpuri Extension, Deepa was in the front yard. It was the evening milking time and she was watching Jhotta's milk squirt against the pail as Rampal leant against the buffalo's flank.

Deepa looked up, curious, thinking at first it must be Dr Sharma. Who else would come in a car? But it was a stranger who emerged from the vehicle. He was youngish, well dressed and confident. Deepa was quite taken by his appearance.

'Is this the house of Amma?' he called. Deepa was peering out from behind Jhotta. She had a clear, fresh face. Anyone analysing Deepa's features would find them to be well-proportioned though not exquisite. But the regal-sahib was not thinking about that. He saw only a child peering out from behind a lazy-looking buffalo being milked by an older man in a dusty yet pleasant yard.

Deepa ran inside to alert Amma, while Rampal looked at the stranger and smiled to himself. For so long Amma went to the princes, now a prince has come to Amma.

Deepa was excited. 'It is a stranger to see you, Amma,' she said urgently.

'Who, *beti*?'

'I don't know. He looks like – like a prince. Did you not know he was coming?'

For once, thought Deepa, who sensed that this was an important visit, Amma's powers had failed her.

Amma smiled and straightened her *dhoti*, bringing the edge of her *pallav* over her head and tucking the stray wisps of grey hair under it. 'If it is a prince, then I will be happy to receive him. How many princes have I brought into this world? I cannot even count! Let him come into our humble home. Usha! Put on the water for tea. Come on, child! Move!' said Amma, sensing that Usha had not responded either in word or in movement. Usha suddenly found her feet and ran.

'Is it Amma?' said the regal-sahib, pushing aside the door-curtain and finding his way into the courtyard, uninvited.

'It is,' said Amma, who as always was enjoying having a visitor. 'Please sit. I cannot offer you a more comfortable seat than my old *charpoy* but you will forgive me for that, otherwise you would not have come here!'

'Oh, I am not bothered at all,' said the regal-sahib and perched himself on the edge of the string bed. He found her blindness convenient. It meant he could look around without seeming in the least impertinent.

Amma turned her face towards him and leant forward slightly. She could smell his youth, his eagerness, his determination that nothing should get in his way. She caught the cleanliness of his morning ablutions conducted with great care and attention, and his fresh shirt of the finest poplin thread. And she caught the sideways movement of his head as his gaze wandered right and left, taking in every aspect of the house. That he was distracted with looking around suited Amma as well. It meant she could form a more detailed picture of the man, drawing in his scents, savouring and analysing them. There was an underlying smell of something darker, more elemental, possibly even violent, in this man, of someone used to getting what he wanted even in a world where the privileges of the princely families were fast disappearing.

The regal-sahib continued to look around, and sniffed as he caught the aroma of Amma's pickle-pots. He wrinkled his brow, trying to think what it was. It was not unpleasant.

Deepa stared at him shyly, half hiding behind her grandmother, admiring the fineness of his white shirt with no creases or wrinkles, and his pale, glowing skin.

'What is your name, and why have you come to see me?' enquired Amma genially.

'Will you still talk to me if I do not give you a name?' said the regal-sahib good-humouredly.

'If that is your wish,' said Amma, unperturbed at this unusual request.

'Well then,' said the regal-sahib. 'I have come to ask you for a favour.'

'Ask it,' invited Amma.

'A few days ago I went to Sohan Lal & Sons to buy some old jewellery and Madan Lal showed me some very special pieces from Jodhpur that he said were coming from you. I have come to ask whether you have more of these precious pieces.'

'What will you do with them?'

The regal-sahib hesitated very slightly, but it was a hesitation that Amma, with her heightened senses, did not fail to catch.

'I am a collector of beautiful things,' he said carefully.

'These days such pieces are not considered to be as beautiful as the gold ornaments that are coming from Bombay,' said Amma artfully.

'True. But it is not those pieces I seek. It is the old pieces. Do you have more of these?'

'I have many, all are beautiful. All are the treasure of kings. Yes, each one has a story behind it, of the birth of a prince or a princess. It is the treasure of giving life. I can tell you such stories, maybe of how your father was born or your uncle or . . .'

But the regal-sahib seemed not to be interested in stories of the past; he kept brutally to the point. 'I would like to buy them. Of course I will give you a good price.'

Amma shook her head. 'These pieces are intended for my granddaughter's dowry.'

'I will be paying you enough for a very big dowry indeed,' said the regal-sahib.

'What is money? It will be spent. Jewels are different. For a woman, jewels are everything.'

The regal-sahib seemed impatient. 'Show me these precious jewels you have, the jewels of kings, so that I may know what I am missing.'

'Are you an expert in such jewels?'

'Not exactly . . .'

'Well, then I have no need for any evaluation. Madan Lal I trust, and his word is good enough for me.'

'Still, one must see to appreciate.'

Amma shook her head. 'It is not possible. They are hidden.'

'In the house?' The regal-sahib looked around as if he expected to find some possible hiding place. He caught the strong, heady pickle-scent as he turned his head. He also caught Deepa's eye. She had been listening to the conversation in some astonishment. From where had this man come to ask her grandmother such searching, personal questions? The regal-sahib's glance lingered only momentarily on Deepa, this quiet child with nothing special about her. Then his mind wandered on, dismissing Deepa as being of little importance. He doubted that she knew anything about the jewels. He turned back to Amma, searching for an answer, but Amma said nothing.

'Buried?' said the regal-sahib.

'The secret will die with me.' Amma had become adamant. She had hardened as she felt a flickering in her breast that reminded her of the sandstone fortress in the desert where the jewels had come from. Then she sensed his refusal to give up. His confidence that anything he wanted, he would have.

'There is only one way that you can come to these jewels.'

'What is that?' said the regal-sahib, rather too eagerly.

'That is if you marry my granddaughter, for she is the one who will find these jewels.'

The regal-sahib shot a glance at Deepa, who had gasped as Amma spoke and dropped her eyes quickly when she realized the regal-sahib was looking at her.

'She is just a child!'

'I am not offering you my granddaughter in marriage,' said Amma, her mocking tone almost imperceptible, 'for, yes, she is just a child. All I am saying is, she is the one who will get them. Anyone else can only get them from her.'

'I see,' said the regal-sahib, no nearer his goal. 'I do not think such a marriage is very likely, do you?'

'Well then,' said Amma, matter-of-factly, 'it will never be possible for you to have the jewels.'

'There must be a way,' said the regal-sahib.

Amma shook her head. 'No way is as powerful as fate.'

50

RAMAN STEPPED OUT OF SOHAN LAL & SONS INTO THE BRIGHT SUNLIGHT. HE blinked for a few seconds in the direction of the white Ambassador that had departed just minutes before, and turned towards the Vishnu Narayan temple.

Satyanarayan sat under the banyan tree, his head bent over some reading matter in deep concentration.

'Ohey! Punditji,' Raman called, not sure whether he should disturb the Brahmin in his studies.

Satyanarayan started and with a quick, surreptitious movement hid whatever it was that he was reading under his mat.

'Is this a bazaar, that you have to call like this?' grumbled Satyanarayan, although he was quite relieved that Raman had given him advance notice of his arrival.

'*Ram, Ram,*' Raman greeted him. He sat down opposite the priest. 'What is new in Mardpur, Punditji?' He wanted to put their past rancour aside, and equally he was hoping Satyanarayan would come straight to the point and mention the wedding of his daughters, the date of which he himself had fixed, or even discuss with him the finer points of the Ramanujan boys' horoscopes.

'Such trouble we had today at Kumar Junction with buffaloes,' Satyanarayan replied.

'Oho?' said Raman, by now thoroughly convinced that, in general, buffaloes were more trouble than they were worth. They could be devious, too. Had not that Jhotta bluffed him into believing her milk had magical properties? 'There was not one buffalo there just now. What is causing so much trouble?'

'It was a white Ambassador car that was hooting and frightened them in all directions,' Satyanarayan continued.

'Aha!' said Raman. 'I know that white Ambassador. It is belonging to one princely fellow. What brings him to Mardpur?' He was beginning to forget his primary purpose in talking to the Brahmin.

'Why should he not come to Mardpur? We have land here,' said Satyanarayan in his usual brusque manner.

'Everywhere there is land,' said Raman with a sweep of his arm; 'there has always been land. But no one has come before to take interest in it. It was of interest only to our buffaloes.'

'It is called progress,' Satyanarayan said loftily.

'It is surely not progress to go around in these vehicles frightening our holy animals who give us milk,' said Raman smugly. He thought Satyanarayan would appreciate this line of thinking.

'Why not?' said Satyanarayan, frowning. 'Cars are progress. We should maintain our traditions, but we should not be backward. It is not the fault of the car, it was the buffaloes who should not have been there.'

'They are not used to cars,' said Raman, confused. Whenever he tried to adopt Satyanarayan's own philosophies on the value of tradition, the Brahmin moved the goal posts. Raman felt frustrated.

'Why is our land suddenly of interest?' said Raman, returning to that point.

'It is close to Ghatpur, and not so full of workers. There is space here, it is not so congested as Ghatpur. Look at all the land we have. It is wasting. Only the buffaloes are roaming on it.'

Raman blinked. Buffaloes needed somewhere to roam, after all. He thought. 'Wasting? What about the *mela maidaan*?'

'*That* is different,' said Satyanarayan. 'It is land belonging to the temple. A new temple will be built on it.'

'A new temple! What is wrong with this temple? Hardly anyone is coming here.'

'Precisely. A big new temple will attract more people.'

There was a tiny pause, then Satyanarayan looked straight at Raman and said, 'Have you thought, Ramanji, you could sell some of your lychee garden land? A good price you can have for it.'

Raman did not want to admit the truth about the lychee garden, that actually the deeds were still in his brother's name and any proceeds would go to Laxman to divide or keep as he thought fit.

'It is a family estate,' said Raman cautiously. 'I cannot sell without the consent of my brothers.'

'Then how,' said Satyanarayan rapping the ground with his pestle, 'do you intend to pay your share of dowry? Only three months you have to find money.'

Raman looked a little shamefaced. He had to tread carefully, for he hardly dared to antagonize Satyanarayan after all the things others had been saying about the rift between them. The Brahmin had at least been talking civilly to him, and he did not want to destroy that.

'My book, Punditji, I am hoping . . .'

'I have been hearing all about this book,' Satyanarayan interrupted animatedly. '*Goondas* and smugglers and *morchas* and whatnot. Have you not thought what such a story would do to Mardpur? I will tell you. Once these crooks are hearing of the *goondas* and smugglers in your book they will all be flocking here. They will be thinking, this Mardpur must be a good place for *goondas* and smugglers, they have even made a book about *goondas* and smugglers there instead of flinging them into jail. Let us all go there.'

'But it is all from imagination, everything in my book,' protested Raman.

'How can it be from imagination, Ramanji? Have you ever been to the Andamans? No. So some *goonda*-type must be telling you, for you are writing it too realistically not to believe.'

'I am writing too realistically?' Raman echoed, surprised at Satyanarayan's detailed knowledge of the text.

Satyanarayan looked sly. 'That is what I am hearing, Ramanji.'

'I am writing too realistically?' Raman repeated.

'Yes, yes, all this palm trees and salty wind and . . . and . . . what is it?' Satyanarayan tried to remember what he had just been reading. '. . . Oh yes, dry smell of coconut coir. It is too realistic to be imagination.'

Raman looked at him intently. These were the exact words he had written in his last notebook. Was Satyanarayan another mind reader like

Amma? One of those in Mardpur was surely enough.

'Well,' he said nervously, for he did not know how Satyanarayan had got his information, 'it is good that it is realistic . . .'

'You are missing the point,' said Satyanarayan curtly. 'What I am saying is if this book is published, all the world's *goondas* and smugglers will descend here. I want only to protect our town.'

Raman looked crestfallen. He found Satyanarayan's argument quite persuasive. As Satyanarayan portrayed it, he, Raman, was responsible for the upkeep of the moral fibre of Mardpur. It was a great responsibility on his shoulders.

'I am wanting only to pay this big-big double dowry,' said Raman sadly.

'That is what I am saying to you. Look at the lychee garden. You can raise money from it to pay dowry, wedding, wedding jewellery and what all. Have you thought of it? Then you will not need this book.'

'The lychee garden is not for sale,' Raman repeated.

'No, not sell,' said Satyanarayan patiently. 'Raise a mortgage.'

'Mortgage?'

'Let us say your lychee garden and bungalow is worth two *lakhs* of rupees,' Satyanarayan began patiently.

'Two and a half *lakhs* at least,' said Raman quickly. He had no clue what the lychee garden might be worth. It had never occurred to him to value the land and the bungalow.

'Two and a half *lakhs*, then. Of course it is on top of a hill where no rickshaw will go, and there is no *pukka* road going past. It reduces the value. Still, you can raise a loan of, say, one *lakh* until your son is married and brings in a dowry himself.'

'That will be at least ten-twelve years,' said Raman.

'Or you can pay back the loan in instalments.'

'I see,' said Raman. 'How long will it take to raise such a loan?'

'Few days only. I am knowing one rich-rich Rajput, very honourable, who can give cash. I am always willing to help the old families of Mardpur when they are having little financial problem.' Satyanarayan's tone became almost kindly.

Raman began to see how the arrival of a white Ambassador could be construed as progress for Mardpur. Such loans had never been available in the past. One had no other recourse but to borrow from one's family and then too many questions were always asked.

'Will he ask many questions?' said Raman dubiously.

'I will be telling him of your good character and your family's standing in Mardpur. He will ask nothing and he will tell no one.'

'He will need the papers,' said Raman thinking of the title deeds.

'Of course you will sign a legal document. But there are advocates in Ghatpur who will notarize. No problem. It happens often that the title deeds are lost. Just a small adjustment can be made in the legal documents.'

Raman fell silent. He was far from being convinced, but he was still motivated by the need to repair his relationship with Satyanarayan. The Brahmin let him mull over it while he prepared for the evening *aarti*.

Vaman appeared just before *aarti*-time. He was holding his hand to his heart, opening and closing his fist to indicate how fast it was beating. 'These cars are destroying Mardpur!' he exclaimed. 'Just now a white Ambassador is almost running over me.'

'Have you not learnt to look left and right before crossing Kumar Junction?' said Satyanarayan unsympathetically. 'Some discipline is necessary.'

'Last time I was looking left and right there were buffaloes coming from all sides. It was a great danger. I could skip aside for I am faster, but these cars? It is no use to skip aside.'

'Cars are progress,' intoned Satyanarayan, lighting the first lamp. 'We cannot always be moving at such a slow pace like buffaloes ourselves.'

'Mardpur is progressing,' echoed Raman, putting aside his initial misgivings. He had begun to feel some pride in the changes. Satyanarayan always understood these processes better than lesser mortals such as he, Raman thought. The Brahmin was right. One should aim for progress and welcome the arrival of cars and loans.

'Progress?' said Vaman. 'What progress? The road to Vakilpur past our lychee garden is still a dirt road.'

'*Om jai Jagdish hare*,' sang Satyanarayan, beginning the *aarti*, and the two brothers fell silent, their faces bathed in the flickering light of the oil lamps.

After the evening prayer the brothers returned to the Sari Palace.

'It was about the wedding that I came looking for you,' said Vaman after apologizing for not offering tea. 'There is no fresh milk, Rampal has not been while I was away.'

Raman looked attentive. 'I am hearing a date is already fixed,' he said, trying not to sound as if he was accusing his brothers.

Vaman looked at him obliquely. 'Satyanarayan has told you already?' Then, as if he was carrying on from a discussion they might have been having before, he continued: 'We are thinking it may be better to hold the ceremonies in Laxman Brother's house.' Vaman stole a look at Raman to assess his reaction and when he saw none he carried on. 'We want to make a good impression. They will be thinking our girls live in a house which has only a dirt road leading to it.'

Raman had no objection at all. 'For making a good impression it is important,' he agreed. 'Lychee garden is worth only two-three *lakhs* while Laxman's place in Merchants' Colony is worth double,' he said, inventing the figures. 'People from Ghatpur notice such things.'

'Two-three *lakhs*? The lychee garden is worth four *lakhs* at least,' said Vaman. 'But the dirt road . . . that will not be good. They do not have dirt roads in Ghatpur.'

Satyanarayan could not have known the full extent of the orchard, thought Raman.

'*Doodh*-wala, hey!' called Rampal, tinkling his bicycle bell.

'It is the milkman,' said Vaman looking at his watch. 'Ohey Rampal, why so late today? Already it is past five o'clock. I am drinking my tea at four. You are lucky only that I was not here at that time.'

'Evening milking at Jagdishpuri Extension is late,' apologized Rampal, using his shoulder-cloth to wipe the drops of milk from the bottom of the *balti* before posing it on the platform.

'But all those buffaloes running wild at Kumar Junction were rounded up hours ago. Don't tell me Amma's Jhotta took off again!'

'No, sahib, but it was my payment day and I am waiting for Amma to come out. I am waiting because Amma is having a very important guest. *Pukka* VIP.'

'Who?' said Vaman, knowing Rampal was only too keen to tell.

'Nothing less than a *rajkumar*. Rajput only,' said Rampal, knowing it would have an impact on his audience. He was rewarded with looks of amazement from both Raman and Vaman.

'A prince? Oho! Not that one who caused all the trouble at Kumar Junction and then pretended he had nothing to do with it?' exclaimed Vaman. 'He was a smooth fellow. Even his shoes were shining in the dust.'

'He was looking at jewels in Sohan Lal & Sons,' said Raman, convinced there could only be one prince in Mardpur at any given moment in time. Mardpur was not the sort of place that princes flocked to, even with the kind of progress that Satyanarayan had referred to.

'What is he wanting with Amma?' Vaman wanted to know.

Raman kept quiet; until he had seen the jewels at Sohan Lal & Sons he had been among those who barely believed in Amma's treasure. Now he was as convinced as the regal-sahib that it must exist.

Rampal could hardly contain himself for the gossip he was about to divulge. 'Her granddaughter she is offering to this prince in marriage,' he said.

The eyes nearly popped out of the brothers' heads.

'A Brahmin girl marrying a Kshatriya, even a very rich one? Never!' said Vaman. 'What is happening these days? Caste system is breaking down altogether!'

But Raman was nonplussed. 'Deepa is only a child.'

'It is true! I heard with my own ears while milking Jhotta,' insisted Rampal, holding onto his earlobes to emphasize the point. 'Amma was saying, if you want my treasure you will have to marry my granddaughter, for it is all for her.'

'Treasure!' exclaimed Vaman, who had heard the rumours but never really believed them. 'So the treasure is to be used to secure a prince for the granddaughter. It is a good use for treasure. But why should a prince want it? These princes are already having so much treasure.'

'Even *rajkumars* do not have enough treasure of their own these days,' said Rampal, shaking his head. 'They are getting greedy. If you have money you want more and more. If you have no money you are thinking only how to feed your belly and the bellies of your children. Look, you can see in Mardpur already, these Marwaris are buying so much land here. Is it that they have no land? They have too much! Still they want more.'

'It is true what you say,' said Vaman. 'Satyanarayan has a temple, still he wants a bigger one. Even my wife sometimes is complaining our bungalow is too small,' he joked.

Raman listened with some surprise. Was he alone in considering that his home was perfectly adequate for his needs? And as for Kumud, she had certainly never complained.

51

BHARATHI AND SHANKER WERE QUIETLY DOING THEIR HOMEWORK WHEN
Raman arrived home. To his surprise Kumud was not yet back from the
market. Raman peered over Shanker's shoulder.

'Oho, mathematics. "If one man takes four days to fill a bath using
three buckets how many days will it take three men to fill the bath?"'
Raman picked up the book to take a closer look. 'We are not needing to
fill baths. It is a British habit. Even in our textbooks we cannot escape.'
He could see he was neither as eloquent nor as convincing as
Satyanarayan, and his enthusiasm for the nation's cultural superiority over
the West was beginning to wane since Satyanarayan no longer thought
tradition was supreme in all cases.

'People are bathing in the Ganges at Banares,' Shanker pointed out.

'It is different. It is taking a holy dip.'

'No,' said Shanker adamantly, 'they are washing, with soap.'

'*Dhut!*' said Raman, who never liked to be contradicted by his son. 'I
am telling you, it is *ritual cleansing.*'

'Maybe it should say, "How many women would it take to fill three
hundias at the well,"' interjected Bharathi.

'So backward we are not,' said Raman, ignoring her question. 'Villages
now are having pumps and taps.'

'These fellows are using buckets,' Shanker said, looking closely at his mathematics text. But Raman had moved on to Bharathi, who was tackling compound interest.

'"A bank loans four-thousand rupees at twenty-five per cent interest per annum, how much . . ." Twenty-five per cent seems very high interest,' said Raman.

'Does it, Papa?' said Bharathi looking worried. 'I wrote it down correctly.'

He looked at her calculation.

'*Baap ré*. So much he will have to pay back after only eight years!'

Bharathi looked at her calculation, thinking she may have made a mistake. 'It is correct, Papa. But with simple interest it would be less.'

They all stopped what they were doing when they heard Kumud return. Bharathi threw down her pen and rushed to the verandah to greet her. Kumud entered looking crumpled and tired, but happy. She put her small matching purse on Shanker's desk, partly covering his mathematics exercise book. He looked up at her and did an exaggerated double-take.

'You have been to the wedding of Meera and Mamta and we have all missed it!'

Kumud ruffled his hair. 'Such nice saris I have from your uncles, sometimes I must wear them. I am only dressing nicely to look at jewellery for Meera and Mamta.'

'I too went to Sohan Lal & Sons,' said Raman, the dutiful father.

'Sohan Lal? That old place! I am not going to Sohan-shohan for my daughters. For them I want only the best,' said Kumud proudly. 'With Sudha and Madhu I went to Ghatpur Bazaar.'

'Ghatpur!' said Raman with amazement. His wife had never shown such a taste for adventure before. Going to Ghatpur was a major undertaking. He had not managed it himself. And here his wife had dressed in georgette and had gone out of town without saying anything to him!

'Ghatpur!' said Bharathi and Shanker together.

'Quiet!' Raman silenced the children.

'The pieces in Ghatpur are beautiful, but expensive,' Kumud pronounced.

'So why go all the way to Ghatpur? Buses are always full and crowded.'

'One must always compare,' replied Kumud.

'Well, you have found out what I knew already,' said Raman with some relief, pleased to be able to assert his superiority. 'We will buy from Sohan Lal & Sons.'

'It is not the fashion,' sighed Kumud.

'Gold is gold. Old pieces are heavier, with more gold. These Ghatpur jewellers are selling less gold for more money. We will buy from Sohan Lal & Sons, he will give us a good price, so long we have known him. Who do we know in Ghatpur? We will be cheated only.'

Kumud, ever practical, knew that he was right. She nodded her assent. 'Let us buy from Sohan Lal & Sons then.' She gave him a significant look. It was for him to make sure the jewellery was bought in time for the wedding. She had merely gone to see what was available.

'I must tell you that there is a prince who is wanting to buy Madan Lal's entire stock of old pieces,' Raman said later.

Kumud looked surprised. 'Prince? In Mardpur?'

'It is one Rajput,' said Raman. 'I am hearing he is so greedy for such jewels he is even wanting to marry Deepa to get hold of Amma's treasure.'

'Deepa marry a *prince*?' cried Bharathi in astonishment. 'Not Govind?'

'Wow! A real *rajkumar*?' said Shanker. 'You should buy all those old jewels, Papa, and then the prince will come here asking to marry Bharathi!'

'*Dhut!*' Bharathi castigated him with a toss of her head. 'Why should I care for a prince?'

Kumud was laughing. 'We are already worried about dowry for Meera and Mamta, and you are thinking of catching a prince for Bharathi!'

'If Deepa is getting a prince, soon you will be wanting,' teased Shanker, skipping aside to evade the blow Bharathi was aiming at him. 'You girls are always wanting what the other one has.'

'Let Deepa have her prince,' pouted Bharathi, and ran out into the garden.

Only Raman took Shanker's suggestion seriously. He found it a strangely interesting notion that buying the jewels could secure a prince for his daughter.

That evening, when the children had gone to bed and Kumud was completing her evening chores in the kitchen, Raman knelt down in his bedroom and, using his weight against his shoulder, pushed the heavy timber *palang* with its frame for the mosquito net. Pushing and shoving, he managed to move it the few inches he needed to expose the loose tile. Raman prised it up with a knife. Underneath was a brick with a piece of frayed rope around it. He eased up the brick by the rope, for it was a tight fit. Under that was another brick. He could just get his thumb and forefinger around it to prise it up. A large cavity was now exposed, containing a small strong-box. The box contained only a wad of banknotes – Raman's meagre savings – and a gold watch from his father. He removed the money and placed it directly in the hole. Then he hid the empty box at the back of the wardrobe. There was a great deal more room in the cavity now.

52

SEVERAL DAYS LATER, RAMAN GOT UP VERY EARLY AND HEADED DOWN TO
the PTI office. To his surprise Gulbachan was already there. Gulbachan
had, for the last week or so, sought to avoid Raman by coming in very
early and leaving on some pretext just before Raman was about to arrive,
leaving behind chits on which he had written a number of tasks for
Raman to do. It had become clear to him that Raman was not about to
give him a quick response on his job offer, and the more Gulbachan
mulled over his options the more nervous he became.

When he heard Raman walk through the door at that early hour,
Gulbachan hid behind the *Statesman*, tense from thinking Raman had
come to inform him he was about to turn down his offer. Raman was one
person who might conceivably do so. All those other eager graduates at
the municipal college would have leapt at the chance to be a sub-
correspondent. Possibly they would have long ago engineered their way
into such a position. Yet Raman seemed positively uninterested.
Certainly, Gulbachan could not understand why it was taking Raman so
long to decide. He found it easier to avoid the issue by burying himself in
the *Statesman* and speaking of anything but the matter which preoccupied
him most.

'So much land they are buying and look at the prices! Even PTI bungalow must be worth at least one *lakh* these days. Who has such money?' Gulbachan commented.

'With a mortgage you can buy,' Raman said, studiously watching the PTI wire as it ticked through the latest economic statistics.

Gulbachan slowly folded the newspaper and looked at Raman. 'Mortgage? It is not easy to get, even if you are knowing the general manager of the State Bank of India. Who has cash? You are lucky if you can get.'

Raman said nothing.

'And then you will have to go to Ghatpur for notarization, on top. It is too much trouble.' Gulbachan hoped Raman would say something about the sub-correspondent's job. All this talk of property made him nervous. It reminded him of how difficult things might be for him if he did not have the PTI bungalow to retire in. The PTI pension was not large, after all. How would he manage? He could not think of renting a small place with some Draconian landlord always over his shoulder keeping an eye on his every move and action. He had been independent for too long.

After he had completed his PTI chores Raman muttered something, but Gulbachan waved him away. He was glad to see him go. Raman hurried to the temple, arriving there at the scheduled time. Satyanarayan was talking to a gentleman Raman had never seen before.

'This is Mr Man Singh,' said Satyanarayan. 'He is very experienced in raising money for mortgages. He will even do it for the royal families of the north!'

Raman looked at the Marwari. But the financier barely looked back at him, he was shuffling his papers. Man Singh pushed the sheaf of papers towards Raman without any preliminaries.

'We will complete the papers and then you will sign. Satyanarayan Swami will sign as witness. Don't worry about the rest. I will go to Ghatpur and have everything notarized for you. Within a week the money will be in your hands. It is lucky there is a town like Ghatpur nearby.'

Raman took a deep breath. He had expected an interview; a discussion; social niceties like tea-drinking and small talk. But this was very businesslike. Presumably, Satyanarayan had already told this Man Singh what needed to be told. Raman had no choice but to painstakingly go through the documents with this man who would loan him the money.

Raman hesitated under the section entitled *Legal Owner of the Aforementioned Property*. 'I am not sure exactly in whose name,' he said.

'You mean when your father died the deeds were never formally transferred?' said Man Singh without looking up from the previous sheet of paper. 'It happens all the time.'

Raman nodded, although he was not even sure this was the case. He had a niggling feeling that, in fact, the property was in Laxman's name.

'Leave blank,' suggested Satyanarayan, but Man Singh was far from happy with this.

'Then who will be responsible for payment?' he said.

'When my book is finished, I will,' said Raman warily, hoping not to antagonize Satyanarayan by the very mention of the task.

'Oho! So the writer of the book, so-called, will be responsible for payment,' sneered Satyanarayan, convinced it would never be so. Once Raman had a loan there would be no reason to continue writing. 'Okay, okay, let us say that the house belongs to the writer of the book!' said Satyanarayan heavy with sarcasm. To him, that was equivalent to leaving the space blank.

Man Singh wrote this down. 'We can come back to it later,' he said. 'We can file an amendment with the notary. But you must understand that the owner of the property is responsible if payments are not made. He will forfeit . . .'

'Yes, yes, we understand all that,' said Satyanarayan, irritable at being talked down to in this way as he was used to being looked up to as the fountain of all knowledge. Raman saw Satyanarayan's discomfort and forgot the vague sense of uneasiness he had felt at not knowing what 'forfeit' meant. This man, this Man Singh, had no respect for learning. He had treated the Brahmin as if he knew nothing.

Finally, Raman signed the documents under Satyanarayan's watchful eye. Then, in what Raman thought was a rather odd gesture, Satyanarayan and Man Singh shook hands. He was about to hold his own hand out to Man Singh but the financier was busy gathering up the papers and did not even look at him.

'You are lucky. In actual fact the mortgager is a prince, and not a bank. Man Singh has arranged it all. It is better to deal with honourable people than with banks,' said Satyanarayan. Raman could only take his word for it.

'Yes, I have many dealings with the royal families,' said Man Singh. 'I am their trusted financial adviser.' And he laughed a rather strange, humourless laugh. Raman did not know whether to trust him or not. But he pushed such thoughts from his mind. Satyanarayan would not deal with someone who was not trustworthy. The Brahmin was too learned for that.

53

SEVERAL MORNINGS LATER, WHILE KUMUD WAS PREPARING BREAKFAST, Raman pushed aside the *palang* and retrieved some of the money he had received from Man Singh. The bundles of notes filled the hole almost to the top. He tied the notes in a muslin cloth and placed the bundle in a cloth-bag, which he placed under the bed as he heard Kumud call him to the kitchen to eat.

The children had already left for school and Kumud was in a pleasant mood as she fried Raman fresh *parathas* for breakfast.

'There is a big-big rat running left and right. I saw him in my kitchen yesterday. We must kill him,' she said chattily.

'But you have a rat-trap. From Jindal I bought it,' said Raman whose mind had been far away from such mundane matters.

Kumud slapped at her dough. 'It is clever rat. Knows which is trap. Maybe another rat is telling it.'

'How can other rat tell it? As soon as one rat was caught, I took it to the garden. You think it ran back to tell?'

'They are getting wise, these big-big rats. How else can they survive? They need to be clever. We need poison. It is available in Jindal's.'

Raman ate slowly. 'I have no time to go to Jindal's,' he said.

Kumud looked at him in surprise. 'So much there is going on in PTI?'

'Now that I am promoted, there is more to do,' he lied.

She seemed satisfied. She slapped another *paratha* onto the griddle. 'You should buy a cycle,' she said as it began to sizzle.

Raman tried to concentrate on what she was saying. 'What is the need of a cycle? Soon you will be saying I will need scooter next.'

But Kumud was practical as ever. 'Oho,' she said, 'scooter is for Chief Correspondent only. I am saying only cycle. So many things must be done before the wedding. Every day I cannot go running to the market and also to Jindal's. If you have a cycle, you can go. In Jetco you can buy good-quality Atlas cycle,' said Kumud. 'All sub-correspondents are having one.'

He nodded. 'Gulbachan has already given money from PTI kitty to buy,' he said.

Kumud looked pleased. 'Then you should buy. Today you should buy.'

'I will,' he promised, 'and I will go to Jindal also to get rat poison.'

After breakfast he retrieved the cloth-bag and headed down the road towards Kumar Junction as if he intended to go to work. But instead of turning into Kumar Bazaar, he hailed a rickshaw and made his way to the Sari Mahal.

Laxman was quite shocked to see his brother. He did not know what to say to him and could not even begin to guess the reason for Raman's visit. It must have something to do with the wedding, but what? He was entirely unprepared for what came next.

'Brother,' said Raman, a little nervously, 'I have come to pay my share of the dowry. For this wedding should not be held up because of me. I know I have never worked hard. But my wife is keen on this match and it should go ahead.'

Raman held out the bag. Laxman sat back, quite stunned. He had been worried about the dowry. He had even toyed with the idea of getting a loan against the bungalow in Merchants' Colony. But the banks asked for too much money and the moneylenders asked for too much interest. Then Raman suddenly turned up with all this cash in his bag. From where? Maybe some relative of Kumud's. Not that anyone on Kumud's side was moneyed. They did not have enough even to educate her past seventh standard. Laxman did not ask Raman where the cash came from. He didn't want to know. He did not want to feel beholden to any relative of Kumud's. Laxman took the bag and was consumed with guilt for having demanded so much from his younger brother.

'You can count it,' said Raman. 'It is exact. One-third dowry price.'

'No need, no need,' said Laxman, his mouth dry. 'Tea? Coffee? Campa Cola?'

'I already said tea,' said Raman, wondering why it was always so difficult to communicate with his brother.

Laxman leapt up and clapped his hands, shouting for the servant boy to get tea for Raman.

'Of course, we have been pushing ahead with all preparations. Sudha has been very busy and—'

'I know, I know,' said Raman. He had not come to accuse Laxman of not going ahead with the preparations, he had come strictly to talk business. And he continued without beating about the bush. 'Now the only thing is to sort out the wedding jewellery. Kumud is very . . .'

Laxman jumped up again. 'But, no, I insist, brother. Let me deal with that. All the jewellery I can provide. No need for you to worry about it. Good contacts I have with jewellers, I can handle.'

'I have already—'

'No, no. I will not hear of it.' Laxman squeezed Raman's arm. 'What else can I do for my nieces but find beautiful jewellery for them? It is my duty.'

'You are doing too much already.'

'Not enough. Not enough. It is the duty of the eldest brother always to look after the whole family.' And he jumped about pulling saris from the shelves, beautiful silks from Kanjeevaram, Banares and Mysore, of lush hues with richly embroidered borders. 'How about this sari for Meera–Mamta and this, so beautiful, no? And this . . .'

Raman quietly sipped his tea as Laxman brought out first one gorgeous sari and then another, each one a dazzling sample of shimmering silk. Now Laxman could afford to be as generous as he wanted. Sudha-with-Pension could not now say they were doing too much, more than their fair share. Raman had managed one-third of the dowry as they had demanded, and now they all owed it to him to give Meera and Mamta the most lavish wedding they could muster.

54

MOHINDER PATWARI, ADVOCATE, SAT BEHIND A HUGE BARE DESK. HE WAS
swatting flies with a red fan, and the desk was littered with the carcasses of
dead insects.

'What can I do for you?' he enquired mellifluously if insincerely,
leaning his elbows on his desk and clasping his hands.

'I wish to update the deeds of my late father's property,' said Laxman
looking at the dead flies with distaste.

Laxman had been overwhelmed by Raman's diligence in scraping
together the dowry money, itself no mean sum. Raman had shown he could
be a responsible father. He had not squandered the family fortune as the
brothers had feared but lived modestly within his means in the lychee garden
bungalow. The least Laxman could do was transfer the garden to Raman, so
that in old age both Raman and Kumud had some solace and stability.

Mohinder Patwari called his clerk to find the file. 'So, what is to be
done?'

Laxman explained. 'After my father's death, the property was divided
among we three sons. But the deeds were never regularized.'

'It often happens. There is a family dispute now?'

'No, no, no,' said Laxman. 'Just, I am thinking it is better to regularize
as per my father's wish.'

Patwari leafed through the file. 'The property is all in your name. Papers are tip-top.'

'Yes, yes. Just the lychee garden should be transferred to my younger brother.'

'Sometimes it is better to keep things in your own name until there is some dispute.'

'Please transfer to my brother's name,' said Laxman steadfastly.

'Of course you can give this property to whomsoever you wish but, well, I would not advise.'

'It is what I want.'

'I am only a notary,' Patwari shrugged. 'What is the exact name of the beneficiary? Spell please.'

Patwari scribbled a short note and handed the file back to his clerk. 'No problem, we will adjust and certify.'

That evening the clerk fed a sheet of paper into an old Remington typewriter at the end of a monotonous and continuous day's work which strained his eyes, his wrists, and his back, and typed the document. Slowly and laboriously, his mind dulled by a lifetime of documents and files, he rifled through the file, peering at each paper through his thick glasses. He thought for a while, drummed on the table, then in quiet exasperation he stood up and went in to see Mohinder Patwari.

'The paper, the one on which you wrote the name. Where is it?'

Patwari could not at first remember which name the clerk was referring to. He could not be bothered with such detail. 'No matter,' he said finally, finding nothing. 'Copy from the other document.'

'Oh yes,' said the clerk, remembering the document that had been lodged there just a week ago. He returned to his desk and found it.

'Write it exact,' said Patwari. 'Just as it is written under "titleholder of property".'

The clerk looked down the document. It was a mortgage document signed by Raman. He looked under 'titleholder' and copied onto the new document in a beautiful italic hand the holder of the title deed: '*The Writer of the Book*'.

The clerk blew gently and lovingly on the document and then carefully dabbed it with blotting paper. Patwari signed it without even looking at it, and applied his notary's seal as he did to dozens of legal documents everyday.

55

RAMAN CRAMMED AS MANY POTATOES AS HE COULD INTO A CLOTH-BAG, then removed some so that he could hold the bag handles with ease − he did not want to drop it. Despite the bulges there were deceptively few potatoes − the bag was mostly taken up with what was left over of the mortgage cash after paying his one-third share of the dowry.

Raman walked awkwardly down to Kumar Junction, but instead of his usual route to PTI he walked past the Vishnu Narayan temple to Sohan Lal & Sons. The shop was boarded up. He stood for a few seconds in the dim light then descended the creaking staircase. Out in the sunlight he blinked and hired a rickshaw in the direction of Laxman's house. He did not stop at his brother's bungalow but went on to the older part of Merchants' Colony, once one of the wealthiest quarters of Mardpur. In recent years the old trading wealth of Mardpur had been divided up and redivided between sons and grandsons, leaving little of the old ostentation. At Madan Lal's old bungalow, Raman paid the rickshaw-wala and alighted.

The jeweller was on the verandah, looking over his unkempt garden in much the same way that Raman tended to look out over the lychee garden. He was pleased when he saw Raman. Recently he had not had many visitors.

'Good morning, Ramanji. You should not have troubled yourself to come so far.'

'Oh no, no, not at all. I was visiting my elder brother only. It is no trouble.'

'You have been to the market? How much a kilo did you find the potatoes?' enquired Madan Lal with interest. He was not very good at haggling and always feared he had been given a bad deal.

Raman neither wanted to discuss the price of potatoes, which he did not know, nor did he want to disclose so early in the proceedings what else was in his bag. Instead he took a seat beside Madan Lal, without being invited, and began, as if delivering a speech.

'As you know, Madan Lalji, my daughters are getting married very soon. And I am looking to buy wedding jewellery. I have consulted Satyanarayan Swami and today is an auspicious day for any transaction.'

'Yes, indeed, Venus is high in the heavens. But Ramanji, are you sure it is wise while Mercury is in retrograde?'

Raman had not expected to find an astrologer in Madan Lal. 'Satyanarayan Swami's opinion I respect. There is no greater astrologer,' he said.

'Only the great Pundit Mishra, *rajguru* in ten states,' said Madan Lal dreamily.

'The husband of Amma? But he is gone. Now there is only Satyanarayan,' said Raman, a trifle irritated that Madan Lal had sought to imply that there was one greater than Satyanarayan.

'Oh yes, yes. Of course,' said Madan Lal, suddenly becoming very attentive. He looked at Raman expectantly. 'If Satyanarayan says it is auspicious then it is, most certainly it is.'

'Good,' said Raman, pleased to have Madan Lal in the right frame of mind. He coughed and began: 'Like you, Madan Lalji, we are a very old trading family of Mardpur.' He paused to ensure his words were having impact. Madan Lal blinked, and Raman continued. 'Only the best and oldest jewellery will do.'

'I have shown you some of my best pieces, Ramanji,' said Madan Lal, 'but you know they are most expensive.'

'What is expense when it is investment we are thinking of? Money sitting at home is doing nothing. We are an old family. We are not needing more land or property. Why not jewellery? Daughters must benefit too. It is not only sons who should inherit.'

'Yes, indeed,' said Madan Lal carefully. 'It is a pity more people are not thinking like you.'

'Well, I ask myself why should that princely fellow be so interested in these jewels? The princely families are knowing about investment. With so much money in their hands they can buy anything, property, land, anything. But he was looking for old jewellery. He is well informed, I should say.'

Madan Lal nodded. 'Yes, yes, indeed. He would pay any price for such jewels. He is not buying for a wedding. He is buying for investment. Yes. Investment.'

'Well, I am not just buying for a wedding. This wedding has given me the idea only. It is for the future I am investing.'

'Good idea,' murmured Madan Lal encouragingly. If he was wondering how Raman suddenly had the wherewithal to buy such sumptuous jewels, he did not reveal it.

'Such people like the princely fellow can buy anywhere,' said Raman dismissively. 'But I am coming to you because you are an old family and we are an old family. And we are both from the same town. Why should I go elsewhere? Why should I trust anyone else? You I have known long time. So let us make an auspicious transaction on this auspicious day.'

They talked and haggled and Raman persuaded and haggled. And at the end of an hour, Raman had secured the best pieces in Madan Lal's royal antique collection.

And Madan Lal somehow felt pleased that the jewels were going to one of the old families of Mardpur and not to some unknown prince, even if that prince would have paid him a better price for them. That prince had been so keen, he would be quite disappointed to find the jewels had gone. Madan Lal agreed with Raman that no one should know to whom the jewels had been sold. Who knew what petty jealousies lurked within the breasts of the people of Mardpur? It was better they kept such matters strictly between them.

Madan Lal agreed to bring the jewels back to his house in the evening and from there Raman could pick them up whenever he next was visiting his brother.

56

DEEPA WATCHED USHA REMOVE THE RAT FROM THE RAT-TRAP. USHA HELD
it by the tail as it swung violently, emitting a high-pitched squealing noise
as it tried to get free.

'Are you going to kill it?' Deepa asked, looking at the animal in horror.
It was not a large rat but it was plump and seemed strong. It would not be
easy to kill it.

'If I do not, it will come back again into our kitchen,' said Usha.

'How will you kill it?'

Usha considered this, watching the animal swing violently, then put it
back in the trap, slamming the door till she could decide what to do.
'Cannot beat it with a stick, it will just run away,' she said, squatting in
front of the trap, her arms folded on her knees, contemplating what
would be the best course of action.

Deepa bent over the rat, which was running hither and thither, looking
for a way out of the cage. 'It is not even afraid.'

'Maybe it knows it will not die.'

'You will not kill it?' said Deepa in some surprise.

'Maybe I will have to get rat poison,' said Usha thoughtfully.

'In Jindal's you can get it,' said Deepa.

'But will it eat?'

'If you put inside the cage, why not?'

'If it is a clever rat it will refuse to eat.'

'Maybe after few days it will be so hungry . . .'

'Then maybe we just let it starve,' said Usha.

'It will take too long.'

'What is the hurry?' Usha said, and stowed the trap behind the bucket-stove to deal with later. She glanced into the courtyard and as she did so she saw the regal-sahib enter and address Amma.

'It is the prince,' she hissed to Deepa.

'My goodness!' Deepa whispered back. 'What should he want here again? Amma has said she will not let him see the treasure.'

'Maybe he has come to marry you, then he will get the treasure.'

'I wish!' said Deepa, discerning the mocking tone in Usha's voice.

'Usha! Ohey Usha! And where is Deepa also?' called Amma.

'Coming!' called Deepa, and hurried out of the kitchen, closely followed by Usha.

The regal-sahib did not even throw Deepa a second glance.

'I cannot understand it,' he was saying. 'When last I went to Madan Lal the jeweller and he showed me the pieces, the old pieces from the courts of the kings, he showed them to me as if they were all for sale. Now he is saying they are all sold. So I have come to you again.'

'All the pieces?' said Amma, surprised at the news. Who in Mardpur could afford to buy them? She remembered how Madan Lal had looked at them dubiously so many years ago when she had taken them to him.

'I cannot sell such beautiful pieces here,' Madan Lal had said. 'Who will buy?' But he knew he would have to take them, just so that he could admire them himself.

'Who knows, maybe one day some very rich prince will come by and want them,' Amma had said.

'Who should come here?' said Madan Lal. But he bought the jewels, leaving himself short of ready cash ever since. It was one reason why his bungalow in Merchants' Colony had become so dilapidated.

'All the pieces?' repeated Amma. She sensed the regal-sahib's anger; his disappointment; his determination to possess such jewels at any cost.

'All the best pieces. Only a few small ones are left.'

'Well, many pieces Madan Lal did not have anyway.'

'So you have much, much more than what I saw at the jeweller?' said the regal-sahib, seizing upon her words.

Amma sensed the desire to possess swelling in his chest. 'Of course. For many years I worked alongside my husband at the courts of the kings. We were rewarded for our work.'

'Now I have only one possibility, that you show me the pieces you have.'

'They are not for sale,' said Amma. 'Did you not ask Madan Lal who had bought? Maybe the new owner will sell to you.'

'He would not disclose that information,' said the regal-sahib thoughtfully. 'He said only that it was a very old friend.'

'Maybe for a wedding,' surmised Amma. Then, thinking aloud she said, 'But for a wedding someone would buy only one or two sets, or a few pieces at the most. Madan Lal had much more.'

'He did not say,' said the regal-sahib, agitated at the mystery he had failed to get to the bottom of. 'Whoever it was would have to make a major investment to buy so many good pieces.'

'Just as you were thinking to do,' said Amma pointedly.

'Well, yes,' admitted the regal-sahib. 'But most people prefer property these days. Land in Mardpur is becoming very sought after.'

'Jewels are a better investment,' said Amma emphatically.

'It is a matter of opinion.'

'For a woman, definitely it is the *only* investment. We cannot wear land around our necks and our brothers would not want to wear our necklaces and earrings. These jewels should stay in a woman's hands,' said Amma.

'I do not dispute that. That is why I am here. Because I also believe jewels are a good investment.'

But Amma knew that was not what drove the regal-sahib. He had so many opportunities to invest. He wanted the jewels simply because once he wanted something he had to get it.

'They are a good investment, but no one else has come to me asking for the jewels, only you,' Amma continued.

'I should consider myself lucky there is no competition in that quarter,' said the regal-sahib with a voice heavy with irony.

'Madan Lal's pieces were on the open market, he could sell to anyone who asked,' Amma pointed out, and repeated, 'Mine are not for sale at any price.'

'Just show me what it is I am missing, then I can go,' the regal-sahib cajoled.

Amma shook her head. 'You are missing nothing. While these jewels remain hidden they will be missed by no one. Don't worry, for I will not sell to anyone else either. These jewels have no role to play until the right time comes.'

The regal-sahib sighed and shook his head in exasperation, then stood up to go. 'I do not wish to trouble you any more.'

'Do not go so fast! Take tea,' said Amma quickly. She had no reason to be rude to the regal-sahib. 'This is the second time you have come to me and I have not offered you anything. Usha! Ohey Usha-ay! Where is that girl? She is hiding! Run and look for her, Deepa.'

Deepa looked reluctant to go. She could not take her eyes off the regal-sahib. She was riveted by his speech and his mannerisms, the graceful way in which he sat on the edge of the *charpoy*. She had never seen anyone so refined in his movements. She thought of him as the most beautiful person she had ever seen, or was ever likely to see. There was no one in Mardpur like this. She wanted to remain in his presence for longer. Oh to be carried off by such a prince!

'Don't bother,' the regal-sahib said, addressing Deepa. 'Really, I have to go.' Deepa read kindness and concern into his voice. This gentle, smooth, refined voice, with such elegant speech. Even Dr Sharma did not speak like this, nor Govind.

'It is very rude of me . . .' Amma insisted.

'No, really, it is not necessary. Another time perhaps.'

'There will be no other time,' said Amma.

'There is no reason why I should not come again? Or will you refuse to let me in?' said the regal-sahib with some charm.

'You are welcome to come again whenever you feel like. But I will not be here.'

When the regal-sahib had left, Amma sent Deepa to look for Usha. Deepa wandered about the house calling Usha's name and then climbed up onto the roof, a place she rarely went in the heat of summer. There she found Usha hiding behind a pile of buffalo dung pats, neatly stacked to dry in the sun. The servant girl had quickly pulled some pats around her but Deepa spotted her faded blue *salwar-kameez* between the discs.

'You can come down. He is gone and you have made Amma angry by hiding,' Deepa said sternly.

Usha peered out. 'I do not like that man.'

'You are *baoli*,' said Deepa. 'He is very handsome. I think he is a prince. Did you see how he walked? So smooth, like Rama walking through the forest.' Deepa gracefully mimed a walk such as would have been portrayed in a dance.

'He does not walk like that,' said Usha dismissively.

'And his hair.' Deepa made as if to push back an imaginary shock of hair falling on her forehead. 'His fingers are so long and slender.'

Usha looked at her, incredulous. She had missed all this detail in regarding the regal-sahib.

Deepa sat back on her haunches and said dreamily, 'Such a prince I would like to marry.'

'Such a prince will ask too much dowry,' said Usha.

'He is asking for all Amma's treasure.'

'It is greed only.'

Deepa came back to earth. 'Of course I will have to marry who my ma says. But if I could find the treasure . . . It is, after all, the treasure of kings, I can take it to the prince, and . . .'

Usha emerged from her dung pile and looked at Deepa strangely. 'The treasure should be for you to keep; even if you are marrying you cannot give it to him. It is for your daughters, like Amma kept it for your ma and for you.'

'What use is the treasure to me, then, if I cannot marry whom I please?' Deepa wanted to know. 'Anyway,' she continued, 'I will never find it. Amma will not tell me where it is.'

'He will come and look for it when your Amma is dead,' whispered Usha.

'Where will he find it?'

'He will dig here and dig there and pull down all the walls of this house.'

'It cannot be,' said Deepa, 'for Amma has always said that only I can find it, and you, Usha, can help me protect it.'

'I do not know where it is,' shrugged Usha.

'But you can tell all your *bhooth* friends to look after it for me and to let no one else near it. You are friendly with these *bhooths*, they will listen to you.'

'Even *bhooths* do not know where is this treasure,' said Usha with conviction.

57

A COOL, SOURISH SMELL FILLED THE COURTYARD AS USHA CHURNED THE buttermilk. The ropes whirred rhythmically as Usha pulled them from side to side, winding and unwinding around the churning stick. Deepa sat on Amma's *charpoy*. A new notebook lay open in her lap. Not a word was written in it. Amma was splitting pea pods and the peas tinkled into a metal bowl. A small breeze picked up. Deepa felt it caress her hair, then rustle the dried *tulsi* leaves that Usha had strung across the doorways. The smell of ripening pickles wafted through the courtyard and chased the dust into the surrounding rooms.

Amma sighed and lay back as if tired even from the easy task of splitting pods. Deepa looked at her in concern and alarm. She put aside her notebook and lay beside her grandmother.

'Are you not feeling well, Amma?' said Deepa, touching Amma's wrinkled brow. It felt warm like Amma always felt warm, but not feverish. Lying so close, she could smell the sweet mustard oil on Amma's *dhoti*.

Amma said, 'Let us go to the temple. For some time I have not been there. Every day I am sitting here in the house only.'

'But you are tired,' protested Deepa.

'Tired only of sitting always in the same place. Here I am sitting always on the same *charpoy* and what am I remembering? How I travelled this way and that, seeing so many different parts of the country. But how long can I sit and dream of the past? I must come out and feel some other breezes, hear some other voices.'

'You should not exert.'

'There is something calling me to the temple,' said Amma, holding up her head and sniffing.

Even Deepa, used as she was to Amma seeing and feeling things from afar, wondered if one could smell a call. She felt an irrational twinge of fear, and wondered whether Amma's sudden idea to go to the temple was like the desires of old people she had heard about. They wanted to see familiar things, and have familiar faces around them before, finally, departing from earth. Deepa looked at her grandmother, eager and ready to step out and see the familiar places she had not been to since her accident, and pushed the small fear to the back of her heart, willing it away.

'Call Usha,' said Amma resolutely. 'Tell her to run to the grey trunk and find me a clean, white *dhoti*.'

Deepa leant against the wire netting of the kitchen door and watched Usha's plait slither from side to side across her back as she pulled first right, then left, her feet braced against the sides of the terracotta urn. The smell of buttermilk was strong and sour, overwhelming the more familiar smell of pickles.

'Amma wants to visit the temple,' said Deepa, addressing the slithering plait.

'In one minute the butter will be ready,' said Usha, without interrupting her rhythm. She did not seem to think that Amma's request was in any way out of the ordinary. Perhaps, thought Deepa, it was not. She tried to relax, squatted beside Usha, her arms folded on her knees, her chin on her arms, listening to the milk sloshing this way and that.

'Tell me a Baoli story.' She said it as though it were a command rather than a request.

'There is no time if Amma wants to go to the temple,' said Usha without turning around.

'Until your buttermilk is ready,' Deepa cajoled.

Usha gathered her thoughts for a few moments and then began: 'One day Baoli saw Jhotta was not producing milk, and that she was getting thinner and thinner. That Jhotta is going to die, she said to herself. I must get another one. But before she got another one Jhotta died. And Baoli went *baoli* with grief. "You stupid Jhotta, why did you die before I had bought a new buffalo?" she cried, and Jhotta's *bhooth* answered, "It is your karma to grieve for me." But she was so lonely, and she went out to look for another buffalo but she thought she could not be as happy with any of them as she had been with Jhotta. So she became more *baoli* with sadness and died.

> *'Baoli Maai, Baoli Maai,*
> *Kahan se aai?*
> *Koi jan na paai.'*

'Is that the end?' said Deepa.

'Yes.'

'But maybe Baoli's *bhooth* will meet Jhotta's *bhooth* and be happy again,' said Deepa.

'No,' said Usha. 'It is not like that.'

'Why not?'

'Because Baoli is *baoli* and does not want to be happy.'

Deepa sat there a little longer. 'It was Baoli's fate that her first Jhotta died, but it was for her to be happy. That is not decided by God.'

'Some people are always thinking that this person or that person is more beautiful than another person. Even if they are not. So you are thinking that prince is a handsome man, and you cannot be without him. So Baoli could not be happy without her beautiful Jhotta.'

'And what if there was no replacement for her Jhotta? No other buffalo. Then she could never be happy.'

'There is always a replacement,' responded Usha.

For my Amma, there is no replacement, thought Deepa, and wondered how she could possibly be happy if her grandmother passed away.

When the butter was ready, Usha went to the grey trunk and fetched the clean *dhoti* for Amma. Deepa watched Amma wind herself into her *dhoti* with a curiously graceful movement as she pleated and tucked, draped and arranged the length of cloth with hands that knew where each fold should fall. Deepa centred a large red *bindi* on Amma's upturned forehead between her fluttering, unseeing eyes.

'Is it in the middle?' asked Deepa, turning her head to the side to gauge whether the dot was equidistant between Amma's thin eyebrows.

Amma wrinkled her brow in all directions as if to feel the edges of the small circle of felt, then for good measure she rolled the tip of her index finger over it. 'It is perfect,' she pronounced.

Usha helped Amma put on her *chappals*, first straightening Amma's toerings before guiding the *chappals* onto her sturdy feet. Then, while Usha ran off to call a cycle-rickshaw to the door, Deepa waited with Amma on the *charpoy*. She noticed the abandoned notebook and picked it up.

'We have written nothing today.'

'I sense that Raman is too busy with other things. That is why we are going to the temple,' said Amma cryptically.

'Will Bharathi's father be there?'

'Yes.'

Deepa was beginning to understand. Something was blocking the messages from Raman. Amma needed to get closer. But Deepa, who so enthusiastically aided her grandmother with the writing and rewriting of the story of Jagat Singh, held back. What was the hurry? Every new notebook brought them nearer the end of the story. And Amma had said when they came to the end, her work on earth would be finished.

'Amma . . .'

'Yes, *beti*?'

Deepa thought, She must know what I am about to say. 'What happens if we do not finish writing before . . . ?'

'Before it is my time to go?'

She *did* know. 'Yes.'

'It will be finished, because that is what I am in this life for.'

Deepa looked at her. Compared to the strong and active grandmother she had once been, she now seemed old and frail. How could it be that the purpose of her grandmother's life now was to complete this task?

'Why should you be here only for this – this story, but not to stay here for me?'

'Your life will not be with me. But this story will not be written without me.'

How can a story be more important to Amma than her own granddaughter, Deepa wondered. 'Bharathi's father can write it himself! I do not care for this story any more!' Deepa's voice rose as the fear emerged from her heart again.

'He cannot write it without us, and we cannot write it without him.'

Deepa felt the tears prick her eyes. She picked up the notebook and ran to the red trunk to stow it away.

As she stood in the dim light of the shuttered room, bent over the red trunk full of notebooks and school texts, it was Govind she suddenly thought of. She saw his face again watching her as she danced. She heard his voice again in their discussions about Dasji's death. Govind understood what death must mean to someone like her. How it would once again cut loose her anchor, her anchor to Mardpur, and throw her to the mercy of her karma. Then Govind's face changed, taking on the beauty and the sophistication of a prince. He had turned into the regal-sahib. If only Govind were a prince, *the* prince, she thought.

Usha ran in to announce that the rickshaw was waiting outside. Deepa chided herself for even thinking such thoughts. *Dhut*, she said angrily to herself. What is the point of wanting anything, when in the end I will be left with nothing? And she wiped away the single tear that she had allowed to break away from the corner of her eye.

58

HUGGING THE CLOTH-BAG CLOSE TO HIS CHEST AFTER LEAVING MADAN
Lal's house, Raman hailed a rickshaw. He ordered the rickshaw-wala to
follow a circuitous route through Merchants' Colony to avoid his
brother's house, and then on to the Vishnu Narayan temple. Raman
would run to the deity to seek its blessings before going home. He would
not even stop to talk to Satyanarayan. Or, at least, not for long. Only long
enough for it not to seem unusual for him to be hurrying off.

Raman paid the rickshaw and hurried up the temple steps. He could
hear Satyanarayan and another older, familiar voice, paced and gentle. He
stole a look at the banyan tree. It was indeed Amma seated opposite the
Brahmin. This was highly unusual. It was some time since Amma had
been seen out and about in Mardpur. Her seclusion enhanced her status as
a feared *Bhootni Maai* – although for Raman such fears had now entirely
faded. He regarded her as an earthy, even warm individual with no hint of
ghostliness about her. He knew she was a recluse by necessity rather than
nature.

'What I want is a *puja* I can remember into my next life, for I am nearly
finished with this one,' Amma was saying.

'Ammaji,' Satyanarayan said, as stern as he allowed himself to be to an
elderly woman who had outlived her husband, the great *rajguru* and a

respected Brahmin, 'what you learn in one life and carry over to another is in the hands of the gods. I cannot help you with that. We are reborn in order to erase what went before and to be given another chance to learn all the lessons of life. Even if it means repeating the same mistakes again. This is what our scriptures are telling us. When you are reborn, you are starting afresh.'

'You are right. For what are we needing memories in our next life?' said Amma smiling inwardly.

'And,' continued Satyanarayan, 'if there were a *puja* so memorable, why would you come back again? Every evening I am doing *aarti* here for those who do not want to remember the last one.'

'So I should have a *puja* that I can remember for the rest of today,' said Amma, still smiling.

'For that I need camphor,' said Satyanarayan, knowing that inhaling the fragrances of the ritual was important for Amma. 'It is not often I am using it. Inside the temple I have some. I will go and fetch it.'

He got up inelegantly, straightening his Brahmin's thread, and headed towards the small out-building behind the temple which served as both his humble abode and a general store for all the implements of rituals, whether Vedic, Ayurvedic or astrological. Raman stood aside and let him pass. But this courtesy was barely acknowledged by the priest in a hurry.

As Satyanarayan's strong, charismatic presence retreated, Amma felt the stirring of Jagat Singh, a character who was not real but who was determined that he should not be ignored. It was a sure sign that Raman was near at hand. She knew even before the emergence of Jagat Singh in her consciousness that there was someone there, even though Raman had not spoken. She could smell the bag of potatoes, starchy and mingled with fresh earth, and she was slightly puzzled. But there was something else – old, tangy and metallic, yet mellower than iron or steel. Gold. Old gold, for there was a certain mustiness about it. As Amma thought about the smell of gold, she could sense the radiance of coloured light shining out towards her, so strongly that she thought she could catch the beams in her hands. These were gems, she thought, of such intensity and brilliance that they could only be from the courts of the kings.

So strongly did these jewels reach out towards her that she understood that, even after these years when they were no longer in her possession, they retained something of her. These were the jewels that she had sold to

Madan Lal. So the regal-sahib was right. Someone else had acquired them. And that person was standing very close.

'Ramanji! Are you not missing my Jhotta's raita these days?' she called out.

'Oh yes, every day I am thinking about it,' said Raman, who had been quietly hugging his bag. He was wondering whether to address her, but held back, saying to himself he should not alarm her by suddenly speaking out. The blind do not appreciate it, he told himself. They like a forewarning, a rustle, a cough, the scratching of a nail on the calloused skin of a heel. He should have realized that Amma was always forewarned by her own sensitivity to what was around her, and even to many things that were not around her, or not yet, anyway.

'Come then, and take some from my house. We are having too much!'

'I will,' promised Raman. He tried not to let his reduced enthusiasm for raita be too apparent.

'Why not today?' said Amma. 'For what are you waiting? We have too much every day, come, share with us.'

Raman could not think of an excuse. He could not tell her about the jewellery, even though ostensibly they were alone now – he had seen Deepa wandering a bit further away among the trees, but out of earshot. He wanted to take the jewels home and stow them safely in the cavity under his *palang*. He did not want to wander about Mardpur with the precious bag in his hands.

'Your wife must also be missing raita. Where will she go to get such raita? In the bazaar they are always mixing water,' continued Amma, gently persuasive.

It was true, Kumud had mentioned it a few times. Nagged, even. Raman shivered slightly. He felt the superficiality of their dialogue, not just because he had ceased to believe in the power of raita – indeed he had not thought of it for days – but because he felt that behind Amma's words there was another intention.

'Ramanji, can I ask you what you have in your bag?'

It was so sudden that Raman was caught unprepared. He looked down at his bulging bag, potatoes on top and velveteen-covered boxes with protruding corners underneath, and knew this was one person from whom he could not keep his secret.

'Potatoes only, Ammaji,' he said carefully, wondering if Amma's vision had already penetrated to the bottom of the bag.

'Potatoes only?' Amma echoed. She nodded. That was the earthy, starchy smell all right. But there was more. 'And inside the potatoes?'

'What should be inside?'

'Let us say only it is good that you have these jewels, you and not that stranger who thinks he is a prince, who has arrived in Mardpur in search of I do not know what.'

'The stranger?'

'I do not know what he will do to get his hands on the treasure of the courts of the kings. He is not used to not getting what he wants. He is not used to caring about people. What he might do I do not know.'

Raman began to feel fearful. 'He does not know . . .'

'I will tell no one,' said Amma, and then lowered her voice, 'but what are you intending to do with these jewels, Ramanji?'

'I do not know.' Raman was unhappy. He barely understood his own actions. It was madness, or folly, or both, for him to have given out such a huge sum of money for these jewels when Laxman had already agreed to take on the responsibility of buying the wedding jewellery for Meera and Mamta. He had convinced himself for a while that the jewels were for his twin daughters, as his duty as a father demanded. He had convinced himself that by buying these jewels he would not let Kumud down. But in reality these were not the reasons why he had mortgaged the lychee garden to buy them.

'I will keep, as an – an investment,' said Raman. His explanation seemed lame, even to him, although it was, strangely enough, the truth, for he found it difficult to lie in front of Amma. Would she understand what he meant? No one felt it unusual that he should pay out a huge sum in dowry. So many families gave out even bigger sums in dowries for their daughters and no one considered them madmen or fools. Yet to pay out a large sum to invest in these jewels was surely the act of a demented man.

Amma nodded. 'They are a good investment.'

Any moment, Raman thought, Amma would ask him from where he had obtained so much money to buy such treasures, and he did not know what he would reply.

The thought crossed Amma's mind, as it passed through Raman's, but she thought better than to ask. It would seem too impertinent to question him directly about his financial wherewithal. Instead she said chattily, 'And Ramanji, what about that Jagat Singh? After the *morcha* have you sent him to jail? After all, he has killed a man.'

'I am not knowing what the inside of a jail is looking like,' said Raman apologetically. But it was true, he had been planning to have the smuggler incarcerated. He did not like to tell Amma that he no longer needed to write the book now that he had paid his share of the dowry. Maybe Amma knew already, he thought. But Amma gave no signal that she knew any such thing. She pressed on with the details of Jagat Singh's adventures, drawing Raman back into the story he had been hoping to abandon – drawing him back in despite himself.

'Very dark, the light is coming through small window very high in the wall. Imagine some rays of sunshine coming in . . .'

'I am beginning to imagine,' said Raman, intrigued. Just by talking to Amma he felt the urge to move on with this story. Only recently he thought he had no more reason to write. Amma had stirred something in him again. He listened to her, eager for more. But she had hardly started when she broke off.

'Here is Satyanarayan,' said Amma as she felt Jagat Singh fade again.

Raman looked up surprised. He did not see Satyanarayan. It was only a moment later that the Brahmin emerged from the out-house and made his way towards them.

'Come to my place, and we will discuss. After all, we should not talk about jail in God's house,' continued Amma. She knew that now, with these jewels in Raman's hands, the story of Jagat Singh would be completed more swiftly than she could have imagined, more swiftly than with the to-ing and fro-ing of the *baltis* of raita, which had only very faint traces of Raman's thought patterns on them. Now, she would be able to read Raman's mind like an open book. Through the jewels she would reach him.

For just a few seconds more, she felt the stirring of Jagat Singh as Satyanarayan settled down to prepare the *puja*, until the lighting of the camphor-cube filled the air with such a pungent head-clearing aroma that it drove any other thought from Amma's mind, just as it was intended to, and drew her full concentration to the ritual in hand.

Raman watched the ceremony. Usha and Deepa, who had been wandering about the garden, also came running when they saw Satyanarayan light his lamps. The cool, fresh aroma of burning camphor calmed them all, as did Satyanarayan's droning chant and ringing of a small, tinny-sounding bell. It was only afterwards as Satyanarayan offered them flower petals to take inside the temple to throw over the gods that Deepa spoke to Raman as they walked towards the temple.

'Raman Uncle, you have not finished writing your book?'

She seemed worried, frightened even.

'With the wedding coming . . .' Raman began, trying to find an excuse.

'There is still much, much more then?'

'Not so much,' said Raman, realizing as he spoke that indeed there was not much more before his story was complete. There was no reason not to press on with writing it.

Deepa and Raman showered the deities with petals, and were in turn showered as Amma stood behind them, unable to judge the distance.

'But it will be done,' murmured Raman. 'It will be done.'

Despite the money he had acquired from mortgaging the lychee garden, which he had expected would absolve him of the task of completing the book, Raman knew it would be done. He looked sideways at Deepa, hoping that he had reassured her. But she stared up at him wide-eyed and fearful, the pink flower petals falling gently to her feet from her limp hands as she forgot the gods who were watching over her.

59

RAMAN PONDERED WHETHER TO ENLARGE THE CAVITY UNDER THE *PALANG* or dig another quite separate one. Whatever he did about hiding the jewels properly, in any case it would have to wait until after the wedding. Mistry, the carpenter, had been conducting repairs around the bungalow. What if he should look through the bedroom window and see Raman digging and scraping in the bedroom? Anyone would know right away that he was intending to hide something valuable. And then there was Kumud. He did not feel ready to tell her about the jewels just yet. He wondered where Amma kept her own treasure that no one could ever guess where it was. Here he was in possession of a great treasure that she had once possessed, and yet he had none of the aura and mystery that Amma had! There was more to the old woman, he knew, than just her treasure.

In the meantime, Raman removed the jewellery from the velveteen boxes. He wrapped each piece carefully in tissue paper and then in silk remnants he sometimes brought home from the Sari Palace for Kumud to stitch things with. The silk felt cool in his hands, the jewels heavy. He loved the feel. He placed the silk bundles in the hole – bundles of bright, rich colours: magenta, cobalt blue, turquoise, golden yellows and ochres, lush emerald greens, much more befitting of the treasure than the dull velveteen boxes which he now hid in the back of the wardrobe until such a time when he could find space for them in the hole. He replaced the tile and slid back the bed.

That afternoon Raman acquired his new bicycle. He puttered down to Jetco, riding behind on Gulbachan's scooter which protested and barked and sputtered even worse than during the heaviest rains. A number of times Raman nearly jumped out of his skin as the scooter let off a loud bang and shuddered. Gulbachan took it in hand, keeping it on the road and in a straight line, more or less, despite its coughs and splutters.

'It is just an implosion,' Gulbachan joked, after one big bang set Raman's hair on end and forced him to hang on grimly to the PTI correspondent in order not to fall off with fright.

'In truth it should be me who is getting a new bicycle, my putter-scooter is not healthy any longer.'

'It is not so bad,' said Raman quickly, hoping this did not mean that Gulbachan had changed his mind about the bicycle and would use the money to buy a new scooter instead.

'My putter-scooter I took to Kushwant garage and Driver Tejpal is saying nothing is wrong,' said Gulbachan, swinging to avoid a buffalo as he crossed Kumar Junction and headed towards Jetco. 'I am saying, "But look how it is doing putter-putter. It is not good." And Driver Tejpal said, "Engines are going putter-putter like crows are going caw-caw. You can silence them only when they are dead."'

'It is new technology,' said Raman as another bang nearly shook him off the scooter and caused him to lose his train of thought which had something to do with one of Satyanarayan's recent lectures. He retained only the image of Satyanarayan from the previous thought and said instead, 'Maybe you should take this scooter to Satyanarayan for Ayurvedic *dava*!'

Gulbachan laughed heartily and Raman felt quite proud of his joke.

'Satyanarayan? Does he even believe in Ayurveda any more?'

'Satyanarayan is very learned in Ayurveda,' Raman assured him.

'These days I am hearing Satyanarayan Swami speaks only of progress for Mardpur. No more about the *shastras*, Vedas, enlightenment and *moksha*.'

'Progress is a good thing, no?'

'Is it not the Brahmin's job to preserve tradition? If he did not do that, why, you banias could also become priests, that would be progress, if

Satyanarayan Swami would permit it. Would he take your Shanker as a *chela*? Never! He is liking that power too much.'

'He is enlightened also,' said Raman in the Brahmin's defence. Gulbachan was beginning to sound like Vaman. 'Some are hungry for power and not even enlightened.'

'That is truly progress!' laughed Gulbachan. 'Satyanarayan is not getting enlightenment from his earthen lamps, he is needing power for such enlightenment!'

Raman was pondering how to defend Satyanarayan anew but a big bang blew the thought from his mind. The scooter shuddered to a halt and stopped. Try as he might, Gulbachan could not get it started again.

'Well, it is not so far to Jetco,' said Gulbachan wheeling his scooter. 'We will walk.'

'I do not mind walking,' said Raman. 'I am walking all the time.'

'It is a good thing man did not forget to walk when he invented bicycle, scooter, car and bus,' said Gulbachan. 'When you go forward and progress, you must not forget where you came from.'

Somehow Raman thought Gulbachan was still talking about Satyanarayan.

At Jetco they looked intently at several bicycles before selecting the tall black Atlas model. Raman rode away from Jetco on it, proud of it despite himself, leaving Gulbachan far behind, sputtering and coughing, trying to get the scooter to work.

Bumping over the loose stones and savouring the smooth feel of the well-oiled bicycle, Raman thought: Atlas is truly the best. There is no better. How had he managed for such a long time without? Of course there were the heavy rains when a bicycle is not much use, but he was enjoying the exhilaration of pedalling along in the shade of the trees and winding his way through the leafy part of Merchants' Colony.

From his vantage point, Raman spotted the familiar figure of old Madan Lal, heading back to Sohan Lal & Sons after his afternoon sleep, a newspaper under his arm.

'Ohey, Madan Lalji!' said Raman cheerfully, tinkling his bell and liking the clear new sound not yet dampened by rust.

Madan Lal looked up as Raman halted, steadying himself with a toe on the soft ground. The jeweller took in the bicycle in one quick glance, with its gleaming handlebars, the corrugated cardboard still protecting the crossbars, and the newly oiled bicycle chain.

'*Ram, Ram,*' Madan Lal greeted him. 'I think you are receiving big-big dowry, all the new purchases you are making! Are you sure it is not sons you are marrying off next month, instead of daughters?' he joked.

'Please,' Raman silenced him with a serious look, 'my investments must not be public knowledge. All my money I have put into investing.'

'Oh no,' said Madan Lal hurriedly, not wanting Raman to think he would ever betray a confidence. 'It is the bicycle I am talking,' he lowered his voice so that even Raman could barely hear, 'not the jewels.'

'This bicycle is paid from PTI kitty. I am grateful to Gulbachan for that.'

Madan Lal ran his finger along the exposed part of the crossbar and saw there was no dust. Raman had not even been home yet with this bicycle.

'What is Gulbachan wanting from you that he is suddenly giving brand new bicycle?'

Raman tried to laugh it off. 'Who knows?'

'Maybe I can tell you,' said Madan Lal. He brought out his newspaper from under his arm and opened it. He pointed to a small square advertisement with the heading, 'TALENTED WRITER REQUIRED' and, in smaller letters, 'with a sense of history'. Raman blinked as he read the full advertisement. How could anyone in Mardpur match up to such a description? There was no one who could meet such perfection but Gulbachan himself. Nonetheless, Raman knew that every graduate from the municipal college and the Mission college would apply for the job, just like they applied for every other job that appeared in the newspaper. He wondered how long it would take Gulbachan to sift through the applications, and whether he would actually go through the motions of interviewing several candidates. He had not expected Gulbachan to proceed so quickly. He handed the newspaper back to Madan Lal.

'So,' said Madan Lal, summing up the situation with remarkable accuracy, 'it looks like Gulbachan is retiring. Maybe he is giving you brand new bicycle for one big-big thank you present.' And Madan Lal chuckled, knowing just as well as Raman that it was hardly likely.

Raman permitted himself to smile wryly.

'It is a good job,' commented Madan Lal, shaking his newspaper. 'PTI bungalow is also there. It will attract many candidates. So many candidates post office is attracting and they are providing flats only, not bungalow.'

'Where is it saying about PTI bungalow?' asked Raman pointedly.

Madan Lal perused the advertisement closely from top to bottom and corner to corner. 'You are right. It is not saying. Maybe government is thinking to sell off bungalow. Everyone is selling property these days. Marwaris are buying all.'

'Government does not know about property situation in Mardpur,' noted Raman shrewdly.

'True, true. You are right.' Then Madan Lal sighed. 'There must be monkey-business going on. Some PTI rascal in Delhi has promised the bungalow to a relative.'

Raman said nothing.

'Without bungalow included there will not be so many candidates,' Madan Lal went on.

'Some young fellow still with his parents will apply,' surmised Raman.

Madan Lal clicked his tongue. 'It is not so good to work with a younger fellow than oneself,' he commiserated. 'But at least now you have bicycle.'

'The problem is we are always getting older, there will always be someone younger coming,' Raman said philosophically, and pedalled off towards Jindal Hardware.

60

SUDHA-WITH-PENSION SPENT SOME TIME AT JINDAL HARDWARE STORE, purchasing a long list of items. Her list started with curtain hooks and pins, and wound up with stainless steel pots and pans, a brand new set of *thalis*, and enough bowls for a banquet.

'So many things you are needing, Sudha *bahen*, you are having a wedding in your family very soon?' enquired Jindal, polite as ever in his curiosity.

'Yes, it is all arranged,' said Sudha-with-Pension with some satisfaction. 'I must clean up the house, for there will be many guests. From Ghatpur also: industrialists, merchants. All big-big people.'

'*Wah*, Sudha *bahen*! It is a good marriage you have arranged.'

'Well, we are good family in Mardpur, business is good and we have influence among sari traders in Ghatpur,' she said.

'There are many there,' observed Jindal.

'We know them all,' she boasted.

'And how is dowry? Excuse for asking. Everyone is complaining these days it is getting higher and higher, so many things boys' side is wanting.'

'Oh, very small dowry. Our girls are educated – convent school, you know. And Sari Mahal is well known even in Ghatpur,' said Sudha. 'They are asking for this match very desperately. Forcing us to say yes.

They are wanting our girls so much, how could we say no? I said to my husband, what is the hurry? Let us wait till they have finished college. But it is boys' side in Ghatpur who is pushing and pushing.'

'Many troubles in Ghatpur,' observed Jindal.

'Oh, it is all over now, everything is forgotten,' said Sudha quickly. 'Businesses burnt down even.'

'For that they are getting compensation from *sarkar*. *Lakhs*. *Crores*, even. With that they can start new business.'

'Starting new business is not simple matter,' observed Jindal. 'Well, at least your girls will be close by,' he added. 'Not far in bus. And now they are widening the road to Murgaon-Ghatpur.'

'They are?' said Sudha with some surprise. She had not heard this.

'Yes. Land after bus station is sold to Ghatpur Marwari industrialist for building.'

'What building?'

'Factory, houses, shops, schools. They will call it Jodhpuri Extension. After that Mardpur and Murgaon will be one town. Then only needing development other side of Murgaon and Mardpur-Murgaon-Ghatpur will be one big-big town.'

Sudha-with-Pension looked impressed. On the other hand, the thought of being one of many sari shops in the Mardpur-Murgaon-Ghatpur conurbation was not as attractive as being *the* sari sellers of Mardpur. It is good we are making this alliance, she thought; soon there will be more competition in sari business. Sudha made her purchases with even more vigour, thinking there may be some tougher times ahead.

'*Namaste*, Ramanji,' said Jindal half an hour later. 'Only just now your sister-in-law-with-pension was here making many purchases for upcoming marriage. Good family, small dowry. Congratulations! And you are also doing up house for big-big wedding? What you want? My store is yours.'

'Rat poison only,' said Raman, wondering if this was a ploy by Jindal to make him buy all sorts of unnecessary items that he did not need.

'Rat poison is good start,' said Jindal. 'Must get house clean for guests.'

'I have problem with only one rat who is too clever to go in rat-trap,' said Raman, not wanting Jindal to think the bungalow in the lychee garden was kept like a rubbish tip.

'Not going in rat-trap? Oho! Design of rat-trap must be faulty,' said Jindal.

'Rat-trap was bought here,' said Raman, trying to keep an accusatory tone out of his voice.

'Oh? Design of rat-trap must depend on what kind of rat you are having. Wrong design will mean no rat. So what kind of rat is it, please?'

'I don't know,' said Raman grumpily, 'I did not see the rat.'

'Did not see rat? Oh. That means it is a very fast rat. I know such rats. Cannot use rat-trap for such rats, they are running past rat-trap before they are even seeing it! Only poison will do.'

'Yes,' said Raman with relief, thinking that Jindal might try to sell him another rat-trap that did not work. 'It is rat poison I want.'

'Excuse me, but I am asking how big is this rat?'

'Big,' said Raman with conviction.

'Big-big rat or only so-so?'

'It is the biggest rat in Mardpur.'

'Oh, so. It is Old Lady poison you are wanting.'

'What?'

'Old Lady brand, it is coming from south. Very potent. Kill biggest rats.'

'Okay, okay,' said Raman impatiently, not caring where the poison came from. 'How much?'

'You will not be needing anything else? Big-big *karhai*, just arrived, for making wedding feast and sweets?'

Raman shook his head. 'Not till I get the money from my book.'

Jindal looked impressed. 'Book-writing is going forward? In bazaar it is saying was stopped.'

'Who said?' said Raman quickly.

'Satyanarayan Swami is saying. Swami is also trying to kill big-big rats. I am selling him also Old Lady poison.'

'There are rats in the temple?' said Raman with a trace of disgust.

'I am sure they are holy rats, blessed by Swami himself. Nothing to be afraid of. Ganesh was riding a rat. It is in the scriptures.'

'Oh sure,' said Raman, 'but how can he kill rats inside a temple? It is not allowed.'

'Oh, if you are Swami, can do what you like. After killing rat you are sweeping away carcass and cleaning while reciting prayers, it is easy! And he is not only one coming with rat problem. As far as Jagdishpuri Extension these big-big rats have spread. Only yesterday that girl-from-Amma is coming for rat poison.'

'Deepa?'

'No, Usha. Anyway she is saying, Jindal we are having big-big rat in our house. You got poison? Very strong type I want. I said Old Lady poison very good. She said Old Lady poison? It is exactly what I am wanting. I am saying oh, so it is a very old rat you are trying to kill. It is a joke, you see. And she is joking back, you did not think I am trying to kill an old lady, did you? So I am laughing too.'

Raman did not find the joke amusing at all. 'For what would she want to kill Amma?' he said sternly.

Jindal shrugged. He had not thought of that. 'For treasure?'

'There are many who have jewels,' said Raman dismissively.

'Too true,' said Jindal. 'When she is leaving my shop she is talking to jeweller Madan Lal in the street. But I don't think she would try to kill him,' he said with conviction.

Raman did not like this talk of people being killed for treasure or anything else, but Jindal was well into his theme.

'Then one princely fellow is also coming to buy rat poison. I am wanting to buy Old Lady rat poison, he is saying. He is one very educated princely fellow, already knowing the names of poison.' Then Jindal lowered his voice. 'I am hearing that princely fellow is trying to get hold of Amma's treasure.'

'He would not poison her to get it!' said Raman, annoyed.

'Anything he would do, to get it,' said Jindal. 'Maybe if he thought *you* had treasure he would poison even you. He must be knowing you are fond of *raita*. Maybe he has asked Usha to—'

'*Ram, Ram!*' exclaimed Raman, hurriedly paying for the rat poison.

'Have you brought a notebook?' said Deepa running to meet Raman as he disembarked from his bicycle. Raman stroked her cheek with his knuckle. She seemed almost worried he would say yes. It was a change, thought Raman; she had once been so eager for the story to be written.

'Not today,' he said, 'for I have had many tasks to do before coming here. When there is a double-wedding there is too much to do.'

Deepa nodded and seemed almost relieved.

'You were telling me about the jail,' said Raman once he was ensconced on the *charpoy* opposite Amma. He felt comfortable and at ease despite the fears Jindal had tried to instil. 'You have not been inside one, of course!' he said aloud.

'Of course,' said Amma, chuckling as she called Usha to bring tea. 'But one must be able to imagine.'

She could feel the story of Jagat Singh emanating from Raman stronger than ever. Before her she saw virtually the whole story. The book would soon be finished.

'I was having a problem with the jail,' Raman admitted. He found himself curiously drawn to the tale while he was in Amma's presence, and felt he needed to know how it would progress and end. Despite there being no urgency to carry on writing, somehow he could not let go entirely.

'It is the lighting you must get right, the atmosphere. That is all. For what is there to see in jail? Four walls only. Dirty walls. No, it is the feel. The light, the heat. In jail it is hot. Very, very hot.'

'It is true,' said Raman, impressed. 'I can see it already.'

'Usha!' called Amma, breaking off. 'Don't forget to put sugar in Ramanji's tea.'

Usha ran to get the sugar pot. Just as she was about to drop a spoonful of sugar into his cup, Raman remembered what Jindal had said. He held his hand over the top of his cup. Some sugar spilt over the back of his hand. Usha looked up in surprise.

'No sugar,' said Raman.

'But you cannot take tea without sugar,' said Amma.

Raman thought quickly to invent a plausible excuse. 'I am having some stomach pains and doctor has ordered not to take sugar.'

'It is not tasting so good without,' said Amma.

'It is true, but what to do?' said Raman, trying to sound regretful. Usha moved away but stood hovering with the sugar pot, uncertain what to do herself.

'As you please, Ramanji. Usha! Put sugar in my tea. It is not enough. What is it with this sugar? We are getting more and more sugar mills in Ghatpur and everywhere so close to Mardpur but the sugar is less and less sweet.'

'It is called double-refined, Ammaji,' said Raman, watching warily as Usha carefully spooned sugar into Amma's cup.

'Double-refined?'

'It is to make the grains more fine, the sugar more white,' said Raman. 'This is the way people are liking it now.'

'I cannot see how white is the sugar, so what is it to me whether it is double-refined? I am wanting only a good taste.'

Raman picked up his cup and put it down again abruptly. 'Is this milk all right?'

'What is wrong with the milk, Ramanji?' The milk smelt fresh to her.

'I am thinking maybe it is not so . . .' He looked into his cup with distaste, thinking that this may have been the opportunity for Usha to have slipped in the poison.

'It is fresh milk, from our Jhotta every day,' said Amma. 'But if it is not looking good, we can make another cup. Come Deepa, you make. Usha is sometimes a little careless. Maybe she was not thinking and was using old milk.'

Usha frowned at this, but was used to taking blame as a servant and hung her head.

Deepa ran off and came back with a fresh cup. Raman took the cup willingly from her. The whole time Usha had been standing silently by, which under normal circumstances Raman would not have thought anything of. But today he found it sinister. Was she there to slip poison into his tea by some sleight of hand while he was not looking? Who would see? Amma was blind and Deepa was more engrossed with her homework. Raman decided not to touch the tea any more, even though he felt he needed a strong, sweet draught.

61

AMMA WISHED TO VISIT THE VISHNU NARAYAN TEMPLE A WEEK LATER.
Deepa could see she was tiring too easily, but Amma had not lost any of
her determination.

'Look how I used to travel up and down the country, and now I
cannot even go to the temple? What are you saying?' said Amma as both
Deepa and Usha tried to dissuade her. But they were no match for her
when she had her mind set on something.

'You are not so young as then,' muttered Usha who was on one side of
Amma while Deepa was trying to support her from the other. They
virtually had to lift her into the rickshaw.

The rickshaw-wala, the same one who had sold his pump to pay for his
daughter's dowry, had to descend from the front seat to help. Only when
he had ensured that Amma was safely seated with Deepa and Usha on
either side did he head off, pushing his rickshaw along by the handlebars
and saddle for a few yards and jumping on as gracefully as a ballet dancer
when it had gathered speed.

Deepa waved to Jhotta as the rickshaw pulled away. Jhotta did not even
acknowledge her, she was far too busy trying to eat as many of her
favourite sugarcane tops as possible before Pappu came to take her for an
afternoon of grazing and wandering.

Just before the Old Market the rickshaw began to sway from side to side. Concerned, the rickshaw-wala dismounted and examined the wheels. The left tyre was flat. The rickshaw-wala, sweating profusely with the burden, pushed the swaying rickshaw, using his weight to keep it on course. He strained this way and that with his thin, lithe body but it was not enough against the weight of the rickshaw. Usha and Deepa dismounted to reduce the load, but it hardly made any difference.

'You should hail another rickshaw, Maji,' said the rickshaw-wala, stopping to catch his breath and wiping the sweat from his face and neck with his shoulder-cloth. 'Many punctures I am getting.'

'I am not in a hurry,' said Amma, waving aside the suggestion. 'Puncture is quickly mended.'

They stopped at the Old Market where Munnu, the puncture-repair boy, barely more than nine years old, sat by the road with his bits of rubber inner tyres, sticky plasters and glues. He had a small rusty tobacco tin full of souvenirs he had pulled from tyres: nails, bits of coloured glass, sharp stones. He kept them all, because he had heard of the boy who had pulled a piece of glass from a tyre only to find it had been a diamond.

'And now he is a *lakhpati*,' the urchins assured him.

'So much is one small diamond worth?' said Munnu.

'It was a small-small diamond only! And *lakhs* of rupees he got for it. Now he is a jeweller in Ghatpur.'

This piece of urchin-lore had its foundation in a tale of a man who had indeed extracted a precious stone from the tyre of his bicycle. But he was already a jeweller and knew at once it was a diamond. Nonetheless, Munnu was not taking any chances. He prised the inner tube from the tyre with his screwdriver held together with string, black and grubby with the sweat of his worker's hands. The rickshaw-wala squatted on the ground, picking his teeth with a nail as he watched him.

Munnu looked at the inner tube with the many plasters and repair strips, patches cut from discarded inner tubes and other bits of fabric. The puncture was caused by a cracking leather patch that had fallen off, the glue being of poor quality, hardly able to hold leather to rubber. Homemade with flour, reckoned Munnu, and clicked his tongue. 'It is a new tube you are needing.'

'Not yet, I cannot afford,' said the rickshaw-wala, 'just repair it now.'

The boy did his bidding but said in an almost adult way, as if offering expert advice to someone who would not otherwise know what to do, 'Too many punctures. This tube is rotten. Soon you will have to replace.'

'I know, I know.'

'What is wrong with your tyres?' enquired Amma, who was sitting on Munnu's low stool which he had offered her while he knelt in the dust to look at the rickshaw wheels.

'Maji, it is an old-old rickshaw, but it is all I have. But I must keep going because I have taken out a loan on it to pay the dowry of my second daughter. If I do not, how will I pay back the loan? Then I will lose my rickshaw,' said the rickshaw-wala. His tone was matter-of-fact.

'Who has given you this loan?' said Amma, puzzled. Such things had never happened in Mardpur before. No one offered such loans in the past, not ones where collateral was involved.

'Maji, a Marwari sahib is offering rickshaw-walas loans. He is saying put your thumbprint here and you can have money. Pay back only little by little. But I am explaining to my rickshaw-wala brothers, if you do not pay back on time, you will be losing rickshaw altogether. I cannot read, but my father is explaining to me these things. He was a farmer. A little land he had, just outside Murgaon, and he lost his land because he took a loan from a Ghatpur sahib and could not pay back. Two bad harvests there were. One after the other. You remember the hot, hot summer when heat was terrible? That was the time. Then one year after monsoon was late. How could he pay? So they took his land, and it was lost for ever. That is how I am a rickshaw-wala. I have worked hard to own my own rickshaw. If I am not paying on time I will lose everything.'

'If you know all that why did you take the loan?' asked Amma, perplexed that he should stake so much.

'Maji, my daughter's wedding cannot wait. It was a good match. Horoscopes were too compatible. It was for my daughter. Loan I can pay back in three years if I work hard. Even up the hill to the lychee garden I will go now for a few rupees more. Before I could say no.'

Soon the puncture was fixed and the rickshaw-wala helped Deepa and Usha to manoeuvre Amma into the back seat. He was pleased she had not abandoned him when his wheel had sprung a puncture. He accepted one rupee less than he originally asked for when they finally got to the Vishnu Narayan temple.

'For the delay,' he explained.

'What delay?' said Amma. 'I am only going to do *puja*.'

'Then please offer the extra rupee on my behalf to Lord Ganesh so that he can remove all obstacles creating punctures from my path!'

Amma accepted that and, assisted by Deepa and Usha, mounted the steps to the temple garden.

'I hope he does not lose his rickshaw,' said Deepa who had been listening to the story.

'He will not, because he understands what a loan is,' Amma said. 'It is those who do not understand who lose everything.'

It was usual for Satyanarayan to be away from the temple. But Amma was unhurried. She was happy to wait under the banyan tree. She sat cross-legged, tired but relaxed and serene, like a goddess. She felt the breeze around her – the smell of fresh *tulsi* and henna bushes, moist from the post-monsoon dew. Deepa, too, noticed the henna.

'I must pick some leaves,' she said, calling to Usha to help her. 'Soon it will be the wedding of Bharathi's sisters and I will be needing henna for my hands. Amma, your hands also I will decorate.'

'No need, *beti*. I will not be attending any more weddings.'

Deepa stood still. What was Amma saying? Would she be gone before the wedding of Bharathi's sisters? Or was she merely underlining that she was no longer as strong as she once was? Deepa stood, fear beating in her chest, her desire to gather henna leaves ebbing away with each heartbeat. She looked towards the henna bush and saw Usha, not gathering leaves but talking to Hari. A few minutes later, Hari, agitated, came up to Amma.

He prostrated himself at her feet and wailed. 'Beat me Ammaji!' he cried. 'Thrash me, anything you like, for I have lost what is yours.'

'What is this?' said Amma mildly. She did not feel she had lost anything.

'The book, Ammaji, I lost it,' wailed Hari.

'What book?' commanded Amma. She could not make sense of his wailing.

'The notebook Raman sahib gave me to give to you. I put it here under my vest to keep it safe. But at Kumar Junction the buffaloes were running loose. I was helping Pappu to keep them together and the notebook, it was lost. You can beat me Ammaji!' Hari started wailing again.

Amma could not understand the role of the buffaloes in the story, but she understood that Raman had entrusted Hari with a notebook to give to her.

'When was it, Hari?'

'It was the day the buffaloes were running around in Kumar Junction!'

'When was that?'

But Hari was too agitated to be more specific.

'Well,' Amma said quietly, more to herself than to Hari or Deepa, 'that means there are not as many notebooks to come as once I thought. One, maybe two more only. That is why I have not been feeling so strong.'

Hari did not hear. He was still blubbering at her feet, convinced he was to be severely punished. Amma told him to get up; she would deal with the loss, she said.

'The book must be somewhere. Did you go back to Kumar Junction to look?'

'Yes, Ammaji,' said Hari, deeply crestfallen but calmer now that he realized Amma was not about to fly into a rage.

'He has lost a notebook! There will be a gap in the story, how will we finish?' exclaimed Deepa. She felt a surge of elation. The book was lost and the story would never be completed. Amma would be saved. She would stay on this earth for ever.

'When was the problem with the buffaloes?' Amma asked again. 'Last week? Last month? Now think and tell me.'

'It was more than a week, maybe two weeks already,' said Hari.

'More than a week, you lost the notebook and you did not tell me before?' said Amma.

Hari hung his head.

'And Raman also you did not tell?'

'No, Ammaji. I was hoping I could find it. But I could not find. Up the hill to the lychee garden I walked to find. But it is gone. Vanished. *Goom.*' Hari threw his hands apart as if suggesting something disappearing in a puff of smoke.

'One-two weeks?' Amma was thoughtful. 'Yes, I was expecting something. It was the day I sent you with raita, no? It is good there has been no rain since then. If it is fallen somewhere it can be found. It *will* be found. I can sense it. Very close by it is. You are shouting and yelling too much. When you are quiet, maybe I will find where it is. I will see it.'

'Yes, it was in Kumar Junction I knew I did not have it any more. Very close to here.'

'Perhaps even closer, I think it is.'

Hari stood before her, drawing circles on the ground with his toe. 'I have asked all the bazaar boys but none of them have found,' he said helpfully.

Amma thought for a moment, but got no clear image. 'It will be found,' she said finally. 'Now is not the time, but it will be found.'

Hari shuffled his feet, waiting to be dismissed in disgrace. But Amma asked him merely what he was doing at the temple.

'I am with my *malik*, Ammaji; they are waiting for Swamiji to come back.'

Hari waved in the direction of the furthermost tree in the garden, forgetting that Amma could not see.

'It is the prince!' said Deepa, who could make out his unmistakable figure even from so far away. She had dreamt of him so often, she could not forget his sleek outline, his well-defined profile. 'But who is with him?'

'It is Man Singh,' said Hari.

Deepa stole away to get a better look.

'Who is this Man Singh?' Amma asked Hari.

'He is working for the regal-sahib family, find-an-shell adviser he is called.'

'I see,' said Amma. 'I thought it was only my treasure he wanted, but he does not need a Man Singh for that.'

'Man Singh is doing many things, organizing with Satyanarayan Swami only. They are offering big-big money to develop temple.' That much Hari *did* know.

'Hmm,' said Amma thoughtfully. In her mind she could already see the beautiful new temple extension that would be erected within eight years. 'It will be a centre of power, not of worship.'

62

DEEPA PEERED OUT FROM BEHIND THE HENNA BUSH AT THE REGAL-SAHIB and his mysterious financial adviser. They were talking in low voices. She hovered behind the bush, trying to get as near as possible. She took her handful of henna leaves and edged closer to the pair, stopping behind the tree right next to them. She sat, her back leaning against the trunk, and shut her eyes to better capture the voice that lured her. The clear ringing tones of the regal-sahib reached her ears and made her yearn for something, she did not know what. Something she knew she could not have. And then the much slower, deliberate speech of Man Singh became clear.

'I estimate several hundred lychee trees,' Man Singh was saying. 'The house is small, but it can be rebuilt. There is land. That is why I had no hesitation in agreeing to the loan.'

'Of course, we must be discreet,' said the regal-sahib.

'Everything is in my name,' said Man Singh, 'so that nothing is traceable to you.'

'Good,' said the regal-sahib. 'This is a small town. Why antagonize anyone?'

But Man Singh was much shrewder than the regal-sahib gave him credit for. He had every interest in keeping everything in his name. The law did not recognize the gentleman's agreement. As for antagonizing the small town, would it matter, once he owned huge tracts of it? His link with the royal family had served him well. It had helped him enrich himself substantially. And it was the royals who would be the losers, although the regal-sahib was not to know that. Not yet, anyway.

They fell silent. But the regal-sahib was merely gathering his thoughts.

'I can tell you, it is no secret. It may be good to get some land here, but what really interests me is not property but the jewels.'

Man Singh was less interested in the jewels. He did not intend to enrich himself that way. He reverted to his old role as the family's trusted financial adviser.

'It will not be easy with the old woman,' Man Singh said.

'I know, I know. But something must be done. Property is property; if you do not get it here, you can get it there. But the jewels, there is no match, no alternative. Outside the royal families who will keep such jewels for generations? This old woman is the only one who is in possession of such pieces.'

'Assuming such stories are true.'

'How can it not be true? I saw the jewels with my own eyes at the jeweller's,' said the regal-sahib. 'Who knows who has bought them now?' He seemed dejected, but then brightened up. 'But the old woman's treasure is still a possibility.'

'Most of it is in the form of jewellery, gold with precious stones. This much I found out from Madan Lal,' said Man Singh, who saw no reason not to indulge the regal-sahib's whims. It kept his mind off other things. If he were not so wrapped up in this treasure, he might be taking a closer interest in Man Singh's property transactions carried out on his behalf, including the Vishnu Narayan temple extension. And Man Singh did not particularly want that.

'Now, what ideas do you have about this old woman, Man Singh?'

'There can be only one place: the house. There is little point trying to purchase the house, the old woman is not going to sell it. We will have to wait till she dies.'

That at least was tangible. Acquiring the property, whether or not there were jewels there.

'It could take for ever,' said the regal-sahib gloomily. 'And then who knows what other male relatives she has.'

'There are none,' said Man Singh. 'Only one daughter and a

granddaughter. None are in this town except the granddaughter. And she is only twelve years old.'

'I have seen her,' reflected the regal-sahib.

'The old woman after all is blind. She could have an accident. Who is to know?' said Man Singh quickly.

'Hmm,' said the regal-sahib, scratching his chin thoughtfully. 'But suppose the old woman is dead? Then what? We are no closer to knowing where the treasure is.'

Precisely, thought Man Singh. Precisely. Far better to concentrate on acquiring other properties in Mardpur.

'But time is on our side,' the regal-sahib continued. 'And the old woman has very little of that.'

At that point Deepa could take no more. Her chest heaving with fear and confusion, she stole away and ran back to where Amma was sitting cross-legged, dozing or meditating. She knelt in front of her, her breath coming in short, frightened gasps. She did not know what to make of what she had heard. All she knew was her fear that Amma's life may be in danger. It was different from Amma herself saying she would not live long. This was a threat from outside.

She was shaking a little as she put one hand on Amma's knee. Amma stirred.

'What is it, *beti*? I do not feel that Satyanarayan is here yet.' She could feel Deepa's fear but said nothing, knowing that Deepa could not keep it in her for much longer.

'Amma, I fear your life is in danger,' Deepa whispered.

'You are wrong, Deepa. I am going anyway. When the last notebook is brought to me, Raman's last notebook, then I will go,' Amma replied calmly.

'How will you go?'

'I can will myself to go. It is a very powerful force.'

Deepa looked at the wisps of white hair that had pulled loose from Amma's bun. She gently smoothed them back behind Amma's ears.

'So no one can kill you?'

'No. I am safe.'

'But they may be planning—'

'They may try. But I will already be gone before they succeed. That is the way it will be.'

Deepa did not know whether to feel relieved or not. Certainly she admired Amma for being able to control fate, cheat it even, rather than be carried along by it, while she, Deepa, had little choice but to sit and wait for whatever was to happen.

Then Amma said: 'While I am sitting here, I am feeling the presence of Jagat Singh and the *goonda*, very strong.'

Deepa looked around expectantly. 'Bharathi's father is not here, I do not see him.'

'No, it is not that. It is the feeling I get when I am holding the notebooks he has written. Perhaps it is the lost notebook.'

'The one Hari lost at Kumar Junction?'

'It is closer. In the temple.' Amma put her hands to the sides of her head. 'Lift the mat, Deepa,' she said quietly.

'The mat?'

'In front of me. Is there a mat?'

There was only Satyanarayan's mat. Deepa lifted a corner gingerly. She was about to put it down again when she spied a brown corner of something underneath it. She pulled back the mat further, and there was Raman's notebook.

'It is there!' she breathed, pulling it out. 'It is the lost notebook.'

'Let me feel,' said Amma, putting out her hands. Deepa put the notebook, identical to all the others that Raman had brought to them, into Amma's hands.

'Is it the last notebook, Amma? Is it the last one?'

Amma did not speak immediately. Then she said, 'It is not the last one. There is still more.'

Deepa quietened her beating heart. 'What is it doing here, with Satyanarayan?'

'Satyanarayan Swami knows the value of writing,' said Amma cryptically.

'He must have found it in Kumar Junction and brought it here. Maybe he was waiting only for you to come, Amma, to give it to you.'

'Maybe,' said Amma. 'Well, at least now it is found.'

Deepa looked at Amma's bony fingers stroking the cover. She was saddened, yet she was beginning to understand the power of this story in Amma's life, stronger than any power that sought to do away with her grandmother to get the jewels. It would dictate how long Amma would stay on this earth. She had accomplished a great deal in her life but there was just one last task. Amma had said she was put on this earth until the story of Jagat Singh was completed. And Deepa knew that fate could not be changed. Just as the regal-sahib could not get the treasure because it was not in his destiny to do so, so Amma was free to depart once the story of Jagat Singh was completed.

63

THE BICYCLE INDEED CAME IN HANDY. ONE MONTH BEFORE THE WEDDING
Raman gathered a stack of wedding invitations to distribute around
Mardpur. One of the first was for Gulbachan, who was touched. Just the
day before, Raman had accepted his offer of the post of sub-correspondent, putting Gulbachan out of his misery and ensuring him a secure
retirement in the PTI bungalow. Gulbachan immediately declared that
Raman was entitled to one month's holiday for his daughters' wedding.

'And do not forget to bring to me your book when it is needing to be
published!' he said. 'Will you have time to finish it?'

Raman nodded. He knew that that task would soon be finished. 'It is
nearly completed,' he said, surprised at his own conviction.

'Many do not finish books they are writing,' commented Gulbachan.

'It is the last notebook I am writing,' said Raman. 'There is no more.'

Raman was not wrong. The unexpected holiday granted by Gulbachan
meant that, despite all the wedding chores he had to perform, he could still
find some time to write. He had surprised himself at how much he was
putting down, even though he had told himself that writing could wait till
after the wedding of his daughters, for now the dowry was paid and their
jewellery had been taken care of by Laxman there was no hurry. Yet he

felt a strange urge, spurred by Amma's descriptions of the jail. He had to write the scenes she had described but instead of stopping where she had left off, he carried on. Back to the caves where the smugglers had been, down the river courses where the *goonda* Kanshi had tried to escape the same fate as Jagat Singh and back into hiding in the forests. He felt that the whole story would soon be concluded. Jagat Singh was in jail, the *goonda* would soon be caught too, and that would be the end of the adventure.

A fortnight later, Kumud had been at Laxman's house for some pre-wedding rituals, rubbing turmeric and flour on the arms and face of her daughters and anointing them with almond oil and sandalwood paste. She hurried into the kitchen, accompanied by the sweet scents which lingered in Raman's nostrils and made him think how hard she had been working for her daughters. What a good mother, he thought. Devoted and loyal as a wife, too. And so busy she had been!

Kumud, for her part, had been surprised at Sudha's change in attitude in just the last few days. Her sister-in-law had become quite helpful and cooperative. She had insisted on taking care of the jewellery. The dowry had never been discussed between the women, and Kumud simply assumed it had been taken care of by the brothers. But the jewellery was another matter. That was the women's province.

That morning she had seen the pieces Sudha had selected from Madan Lal's ordinary collection. Kumud promised she would pay Sudha back once her relatives had arrived, embarrassed that Sudha should take such a task upon herself. Far from relying on Raman, she would ask her brother, her parents maybe, for a little money to pay for the jewellery. She did not like being beholden to Sudha for such things. Even as she had mentioned paying later, Sudha-with Pension had said, 'But no, sister, let us buy the jewellery. Meera and Mamta are like my own daughters.'

Kumud watched Sudha-with-Pension wrap the two identical gold necklace-and-earrings sets in silk and put them in their velveteen boxes. Then, on impulse, she pulled off her own bangles from her wrists – two each of the four she had worn since her own marriage to Raman – and laid them in two pairs on top of the silk. They lay there warm and gleaming, then Sudha snapped the boxes shut.

On her way home, Kumud could feel how light her arms were now. She had become so used to her bangles, her arms now felt strangely empty. She jangled the two remaining bangles and listened to the resonance. That felt different too. 'It is easier to work with lighter arms,' she said resolutely, and then put all thought of her bangles out of her mind.

When she got home she quickly changed her sari, tying the *pallav* around her waist, and became busy with cleaning and tidying. In a few days her relatives would be arriving and she wanted everything ready in time.

'We must have big-big marigolds for wedding garlands,' she scolded Raju one afternoon as Raman lounged on the verandah. 'At Jindal's you can buy fertilizer. What is the use of such a big-big garden when it cannot even produce flowers for my daughters' wedding? When I married, all the flowers were coming from this garden. Not one was from the bazaar. For the *mandap*, the garlands, and for the wedding bed also,' she said.

Inside the house, Kumud was busy. The rip on the sofa that had been there for so long was suddenly repaired. Bharathi and Shanker were sent on errands all the time. While Raman was lounging in his armchair one afternoon, Kumud moved him on to check whether the cushions needed repairing, or upholstering even. Then, taking to her old black Singer sewing machine, she stitched some new cushions in just one evening.

Raju-*mali*'s nephew was called to clean the windows and Raman was delighted at how light and bright the bungalow now seemed. Of course the light merely showed up how dusty and neglected the interior was, and Kumud set out to rectify this with renewed vigour.

'I want everything tip-top,' Kumud informed Mistry, the bow-legged carpenter. 'You can get plaster at Jindal's to fill cracks,' she said, pointing to the gaping zig-zags that had adorned the walls ever since they had moved in. 'Oh yes, and perimeter fence must be repaired. We had one buffalo that escaped already. We don't want more loss.'

Kumud came to Raman. 'We need paint from Jindal's. I will ask Mistry to paint the walls when he has finished plastering.'

'Why paint the walls?' said Raman, not wishing to move from his comfortable armchair.

'Oho,' said Kumud, exasperated. 'Our daughters are getting married. We will have my relatives staying here. Everything must be tip-top.'

'Who is coming?'

'Have you forgotten?' said Kumud. 'I have a mother and father also, and seven brothers and sisters, and nieces and nephews, and my cousins.'

'They are all coming to stay here?' said Raman, incredulous.

'Have they not been been invited?' said Kumud.

'How will we feed them?'

'I have already arranged for a cook for few weeks. It is a relative of Raju-*mali*. She will come from her village specially.'

Raman felt glum. Kumud had taken things in hand like he had never expected, but then there was less than a month to go before the wedding itself and it was bound to get even more busy before the relatives arrived.

He went to the gate to meet Mittal the postman, whose bicycle bell he could hear tinkling. There were many letters. All from members of Kumud's family.

'Memsahib is saying you are having double-wedding,' said Mittal conversationally. He wanted to catch his breath before starting back down the hill.

'Yes,' said Raman, examining the letters. There were some rather large, brown stains over some of them, as if they had fallen into a puddle. The envelopes themselves were quite soggy.

'My brother is owning a wedding *shamiana*. You can hire,' offered Mittal.

'Thanks,' said Raman, getting even more worried.

Mittal noticed his expression. 'Don't worry,' he said. 'Many relatives are not writing, they are just turning up. Letter-writing is taking too much time. If thirty are writing back you should prepare for fifty.'

'Fifty!' said Raman.

'*Shamiana* is good for sleeping under at night-time. You have big-big garden here. No problem. Can put two *shamianas*, even. But sorry, my brother is only having one. For second one I can ask my cousin . . .'

'It's all right,' Raman stopped him. 'There will not be many sleeping in the garden. There are too many mosquitoes. They will all go to my brother's house.'

'Always more are coming than you expect,' said Mittal cheerfully. 'All houses will be full. Yours, your brother's, your *mama*'s, your *chacha*'s. I know, I have married off three daughters already.'

Raman wondered where Mittal had got the dowry from. 'You have no sons?'

'No. Only three daughters more to marry.'

'That is a lot of dowry.'

'Dowry, sahib? Oh no, that is only for those marrying up.' Mittal pointed heavenwards. 'I am a simple man. Not greedy. And my wife is simple too. My sons-in-law are all uneducated. But my daughters can read, I taught them myself.'

What was the point of finding uneducated sons-in-law for educated daughters? Aloud Raman joked, 'That is fine, your daughters can teach their husbands to read, save their in-laws from paying school fees.'

Mittal grinned. 'Not even! For what they need to read? I have got them all jobs in the post office.'

Raman hid his disgust. No wonder mail does not get delivered if the postal workers are illiterate. 'How are they guessing the addresses?' he asked, feigning total amazement as if there was some trick to be learnt.

'Oh no, sahib, they are not working in postal delivery, like me. For that you are needing BA. They are making tea only.' Mittal pointed to a large brown stain on one envelope in Raman's hand that had virtually obliterated the address.

'You have BA?' said Raman, while also wondering how many tea boys were required at the post office.

'BA in English,' said Mittal proudly. 'It was my father who got me this post office job. He was Mardpur sub-postmaster. He was having a small bungalow. Of course, I am only getting small flat.'

'I see,' said Raman. He wondered what hope there was for Mittal's grandchildren. From sub-postmaster to postman and then to post office tea boy, there seemed to be quite rapid downward mobility.

'Of course my sons-in-law are quite lucky. Even tea-maker is known as junior post officer and getting government quarters, so at least I know my daughters have place to live,' said Mittal. 'Even school teacher is not getting quarters. I was not getting when I was school teacher.'

'You were a teacher?'

'Yes, sahib. At municipal boys' school. English and Hindi. But no quarters.'

Raman began to think that whatever his relationship with his brothers he was well provided for in having the lychee garden for his home.

64

JUST DAYS BEFORE THE WEDDING, THE STRAIN WAS BEGINNING TO SHOW ON Kumud. That morning she brought back some freshly made sweetmeats from Merchants' Colony, where a sweet-maker had installed himself in the garden, building a U-shaped stove with bricks and cow dung and balancing a huge black *karhai* on it. There, under the watchful eye of Sudha-with-Pension, he turned out high-quality sweetmeats. Once home, Kumud divided the sweets between boxes for distribution to neighbours and friends, people she thought Sudha-with-Pension would not think of.

'Not to trouble, Kumud Sister,' Sudha-with-Pension had said, 'I know you have no maidservant. I will distribute. Just give me a list.'

'You have too much to do,' said Kumud sweetly. 'Let me take that one task off your hands. Bharathi can help me, and now that we have a bicycle, I will send Shanker when he is home from school.'

That evening, worn out by the day's work, Kumud was preparing the boxes of sweets for distribution, to clear her kitchen before the visitors arrived and it was taken over by others. She felt harassed and irritable.

Shanker wandered in sniffing the air and picking up the aroma of freshly made sweets. 'Ma! I am hungry. Can I have a *rasgolla*?'

'Have you finished your homework?' Kumud demanded.

Shanker looked guilty.

'No?' said Kumud. 'Well then, no *rasgollas* for you! Go away. Come to me only when you have finished. For what are we paying all these fees-wees at Mission school? So that you can get fat eating *rasgollas*? Go away from my kitchen! I have too much to do.'

Raman came in, hearing Kumud raise her voice. He decided to take matters in hand.

'What has he done now?' he said, raising his own voice to show he was boss.

'What has he done? What has he not done? He is not doing homework and is coming in my kitchen asking for food.'

'Ma!' said Shanker, appealing to her to be reasonable. He felt the situation was getting out of hand.

'You donkey without shame! Son of an owl! Go to your work!' said Raman, trying to sound as busy and stressed as Kumud.

But Shanker looked sullen at the unfairness of it. Did they care if he starved? Clearly not. He would crawl away and die of hunger under some tree and then they would be sorry. 'I will run away!' he shouted, full of self-pity.

'Go, then. Go!' shouted Raman and lifted his hand to strike. 'Rascal, you dare to raise your voice to your mother?' Shanker deftly skipped aside and stood in the corner of the kitchen, panting.

'Don't be so harsh,' Kumud appealed to Raman, forgetting that it was she who had first raised her voice. 'If he goes what will happen to us in our old age? You have only one son, you know.'

Raman let his hand drop and Shanker looked relieved that his maleness absolved him of any crime. 'He is good for nothing,' growled Raman. 'Others want to be doctors, engineers, and this one does not even know what he wants. Don't expect your parents to provide for you, boy!' said Raman. But Shanker was already feeling he had got off lightly and was not so fearful any more. He merely shifted from one foot to the other listening to the lecture.

'Now, come out of my kitchen,' said Kumud, flapping at them. Seeing the crisis had subsided, she wanted to carry on with distributing her sweets. 'This is not the place for fighting with fire and boiling milk and God-knows-what. Leave my kitchen!' She shooed Raman and Shanker out.

'He has not even learnt not to be cheeky to his *maa-baap*! See where it will get him. Donkey! I will turn him out of the house and he can fend for himself if he thinks he is so clever,' said Raman heatedly.

Shanker went red. He had not been cheeky. He had only said he was hungry and then they all started at him. Even his sister was out to get him. 'So if you want to disown me you can. I don't care. I will go and live with Vaman Uncle, who has MA and a big house. And I will share a room with Guru. And play *carrom* every day.'

'Shameless creature!' thundered Raman.

'Shanker!' said Kumud tenderly, taking his head in her hands and pressing it to her heart. Shanker tried to struggle free. She was trying to stop him getting even more worked up.

'You are pampering that boy, that is why he is so spoilt!' said Raman. 'So send him to Vaman Brother. Let him see what it is like. We don't want him here. Let Vaman Brother pay for his education also. Let him be a burden on Vaman Brother as he is a burden on us.'

Shanker hadn't considered this part. He had not thought of the finances. He thought he had scored a point against his father, but now he was unsure. Would Vaman Uncle welcome him? Or would he see him as a financial burden? If at that point Shanker was about to waver, it was too late. Raman had rushed out and had come back with a small suitcase. He began to throw Shanker's school books into it, higgledy-piggledy.

'Where are your clothes?' he demanded.

Shanker was rooted to the spot.

'Shanker, say sorry,' implored his mother. 'Then everything will be fine.'

'No!' said Shanker. He felt he had nothing to be sorry about.

'See!' said Raman. 'Offspring of an owl, he is! Stubborn and unrepentant. He can see how he will get on in the world being like that. Bring me his clothes!'

Kumud had no choice. She went out, got a pile of freshly pressed school uniforms, and laid them carefully in the suitcase. Shanker was so aghast at his mother's treachery – he had expected her to stand up for him through it all – that he barely heard her say, 'Come, Shanker, just apologize and it will be fine.'

'No!'

Raman snapped the lid of the suitcase shut. 'Carry your suitcase,' he ordered. Shanker could hardly refuse.

Then Kumud remembered the tasks she had in hand. 'Wait, on the way to Vaman Brother, please take some sweets to Amma in Jagdishpuri Extension.'

'It is not on the way,' said Raman, distracted for a moment.

'You are going by bicycle, no? I will get the boxes.'

Kumud ran to the kitchen and returned with a box of sweets, the grease already turning the cardboard a translucent grey. Raman inhaled the sweet, heavy smell and calmed down a little.

'Wait. I have something to write.' He sat down at the desk, which just seconds before had been covered in Shanker's school books. He pulled out a clean sheet of paper from inside the desk and began to write with great flourishes of his fountain pen. They all wondered what he was writing.

'You still have time to apologize,' said Raman as he signed the paper with a dramatic flourish.

'I won't,' said Shanker.

'Shanker!' his mother cried.

'Here then. Read it.'

Shanker looked at the sheet of paper and was at a loss to know what to make of it.

'What is it?' said Kumud.

'It is a formal Declaration of Independence. Shanker, from today you are independent from us. It is a partition. Cut off. That's it,' said Raman. 'I will deposit this fool with his uncle.'

Kumud and Bharathi watched them as they made their way to the gate, Raman looking stiff and Shanker with his suitcase in one hand and the Declaration of Independence, the ink barely dry, in the other.

65

RAMAN AND SHANKER TREKKED DOWNHILL IN SILENCE. RAMAN WAS wheeling the bicycle. The light was beginning to fade and there was a red glow in the sky. As they turned into the bazaar area, the smell of kerosene stoves being lit for the evening meal filled the air.

Raman said, 'We will go to the temple and pray for this poor fool who is about to cut himself off from us.'

Shanker sank deeper into sullenness. He believed his father wanted to parade him in front of Satyanarayan, that pompous Brahmin that his father admired so much, to humiliate him some more. Satyanarayan loved to humiliate everyone, and he always got away with it because of who he was. How could anyone stand it? Why did everyone insist on allowing themselves to be insulted by the priest? Vaman Uncle was right, it was all hocus-pocus. They had no pride, these people who subjected themselves to Satyanarayan's bullying – and Shanker stiffened his resolve not to be like all these others. *He* had some pride. Anyway, he thought, it was Raman who had cut *him* off, not the other way around.

They arrived at the temple to find Satyanarayan sitting in his usual place outside. The evening *aarti* was not long over – the butter-lamps were still burning under the trees, throwing long, flickering shadows over the deities, and whirls of incense smoke rose from the black incense sticks.

Sitting in front of Satyanarayan, cross-legged on a small mat with an air of fear and humiliation, was a boy. He was about Shanker's age, but smaller in size, with his head completely shaven except for a sliver of a pigtail behind. And he was dressed like a miniature *sadhu*, in a saffron *dhoti*, a Brahmin's thread over his shoulder, and even marks of sandalwood paste on his forehead. Satyanarayan was making him recite couplets from the *Gita* and shouting at him whenever he got it wrong.

'*Om bhur bhua swaha, thatsavithur veraniam* . . .' chanted Satyanarayan in Sanskrit, and the boy tried to repeat the words but was distracted by the arrival of Raman and Shanker. Satyanarayan looked up.

'*Pranam* Ramanji. Say *pranam*, Bhole.'

'*Pranam*,' said Bhole, obediently.

'Touch the feet of Ramanji, please.'

Bhole got up clumsily and touched Raman's toes. Raman stepped back in some surprise. Then collecting his wits he put a hand on Bhole's head. 'Keep living, child,' he said in an ascetic tone and tried to look paternal.

'This is my nephew, Bholenath. So to say, my sister's son. He has been sent to me to learn the scriptures and learn the life of a priest. My sister has no other use for him,' explained Satyanarayan in a monotone, as if this was the hundredth person to whom he was explaining the presence of Bholenath.

'Why didn't you tell me you were collecting boys that parents have no use for?' said Raman. 'I have one here also.' He nudged Shanker. 'Show the chit,' he hissed. When Shanker did not move, Raman reminded him sternly of the declaration.

Shanker put down his suitcase and slowly retrieved the declaration from his pocket. Raman unfolded it and handed it to Satyanarayan, waving away the wisps of incense smoke so that they would not cloud Satyanarayan's vision.

'What is this?' said Satyanarayan. Bhole stared stupidly at both Raman and Shanker.

'It is a Declaration of Independence,' said Raman. 'A partition. From now on this donkey is going to live with his Uncle Vaman. You are witness, Punditji, he will no longer be with us.'

'What is the trouble, boy?' said Satyanarayan addressing Shanker sternly. 'Have you failed in your duty to your *maa-baap*?'

Shanker did not respond. He did not see that he had anything to explain to Satyanarayan.

'Well, he is clearly stubborn and disobedient,' concluded Satyanarayan.

'That is what happens if you insist on sending to Mission school. But why are you sending him to that godless Vaman where he will be learning even worse habits?'

Raman was uncomfortable that his course of action did not meet with Satyanarayan's full approval, but tried to cover it up by suggesting jocularly, 'Why not I leave him here? And he can join young Bhole in learning scriptures under your excellent guidance.'

'It is a good idea, Ramanji,' said Satyanarayan, stroking his beard, 'an excellent idea. But I can only manage one *chela* at a time. Too much service makes a man lazy. Why not send this boy to your elder brother Laxman? He is at least a God-fearing man. This boy –' he waved a finger at Shanker '– does not need to learn any more irreverence than he already has by staying with his Vaman Uncle.'

'Well,' said Raman, considering this. 'There is something in what you say. But Laxman Brother is already burdened with my two daughters Meera and Mamta. And I cannot burden him with this owl as well.'

Satyanarayan sniffed the air. 'What is it you are carrying? It is smelling like some very fresh sweetmeats.'

'Yes,' said Raman. 'I am taking these sweetmeats to Amma in Jagdishpuri Extension. It is only a fortnight before the wedding of my daughters.'

Satyanarayan nodded. 'Sudha *bahen* has already been distributing sweets to all. So everything is ready?'

'Yes, Punditji, everything is ready, all that is left is the fire ceremony itself and your honourable presence to preside over the Vedic rites.' And Raman suddenly felt proud. He was a father and his daughters would be married with a good dowry and jewellery they could keep for generations. He stopped to contemplate. This was an important stage in a man's life, to give away his daughters. He said this aloud.

'Yes, Ramanji, it is an important stage in a man's life to give away one's daughters, but at the same time you are giving away your son,' Satyanarayan responded, and he fixed a gimlet-like glance on Shanker, who shifted uncomfortably.

'Let us go, it is getting late,' said Raman. 'We will go first to Jagdishpuri Extension.' At that Satyanarayan appeared to lose interest, and turned back to his nephew. 'Now, Bhole,' he said, going back to the *Gita*. '*Om bhur bhua swaha . . .*'

Shanker was sullen. Sullen that he was having to walk all this way instead of being delivered into the hands of his uncle, who would no doubt make light of the whole thing and point out how absurd his father had been. Sullen that he had been humiliated in front of Satyanarayan by having the declaration shown to him. And sullen that his father had offered him up to Satyanarayan in place of that idiot-looking Bhole with his shaven head and pigtail and sandalpaste U on his forehead. Did that not prove that his father did not care for him at all?

So wrapped up were father and son in their own thoughts that they hardly noticed a white Ambassador stop before them. The regal-sahib got out and called to them, 'Can I drive you somewhere?'

'We are going to Jagdishpuri Extension,' said Raman awkwardly.

'I know. Satyanarayan told me. Jump in,' the regal-sahib said to Shanker, who was delighted to get such an offer. He had never ridden in a car before. Only buses. He climbed in with his suitcase, springing against the upholstery to test it, and seemed pleased at the effect, leaning back and then forward. When the regal-sahib shut the door, Shanker examined the levers. The tinted window rolled down and Shanker's face, with its pleased expression, peered out. The window rolled up and then down and then up again.

'We will put the bicycle in the boot,' said the regal-sahib as Raman stood there not knowing what to do with it. He was distracted, and at the same time fascinated, by the rolling window, which seemed to go up and down as if by magic. He wanted to peer in to see what it was that Shanker was doing that was making it do this. He completely forgot he was angry with Shanker and should be shouting at him to stop playing with the regal-sahib's vehicle in that disrespectful manner.

'In the boot,' repeated the regal-sahib, beckoning to Raman with a jerk of his head. Raman reluctantly trundled his bicycle to the back of the car.

'You are taking sweetmeats to the old lady?' said the regal-sahib as he stowed the bicycle in the back, the front wheel sticking out of the boot.

Raman was mystified that his movements should be the subject of discussion between the Brahmin and the princely gentleman. The whole of Mardpur might be knowing that Raman was going to see Amma to distribute sweets on the occasion of his daughters' wedding. Tomorrow would tell Gulbachan to prepare a dispatch for PTI, just to save Satyanarayan the trouble of broadcasting it further, thought Raman.

'I have also a present for the old lady. Can you give it to her?' said the regal-sahib. Raman noticed the regal-sahib was holding a cardboard box which he had brought out of the boot to make room for the bicycle.

From it he extracted two sweetmeats. He held them in front of Raman's eyes, so close that Raman had to draw back to focus.

'These are the ones for the old lady. Put them in your box,' the regal-sahib said.

It was an odd thing to do, Raman thought, to extract just two sweets from a box. Why not give the whole box? Raman looked at the two sweets with distaste, wrinkling his nose to sniff their odour. They did not emit the milky-sweet smell of fresh sweetmeats. Instead, it was rather an acrid smell. He remembered that smell. Old Lady rat poison. Raman drew back even further, as if he might be poisoned just by breathing in the fumes.

'Put them in your box, among the others,' said the regal-sahib in his cool voice, as if what he was asking Raman to do was the most normal thing in the world.

He could not refuse to do what the regal-sahib was telling him. Who knows what this man would do to him and Shanker in the middle of the night? Yet Raman did not want to contaminate his own sweets. He laid the regal-sahib's sweets on top of the tracing paper that covered the fresh sweets of his own box, whose strong, fresh, milky smell rose deliciously to his nostrils, yet instilled fear into him rather than temptation. There was no way he could just throw the whole box away while the regal-sahib was watching. He looked at his thumb and forefinger in terror: there must be traces of poison from handling the sweets. His mind was a whirl, the fresh milky-sweet scent and the acrid, treacherous odour mingling to create total confusion in his head. Amma will know, he thought, her sense of smell is tip-top. She will sense it coming, so well can she see the future. She will know to avoid these sweetmeats, he convinced himself. He had to rely on her using her gifts, for there was no other way.

Mechanically he followed the regal-sahib to the door of the car and climbed in. He felt like a rat entering a rat-trap from which there was no way out. The box of sweets on his lap was warm against his trousers. He lifted it a little, so that the grease from the box did not stain his pants, holding it gingerly in his two hands, so tensely poised that his elbows and wrists began to ache. Raman stared straight ahead, not wanting to look either at the box or at the regal-sahib, as they drove away towards Jagdishpuri Extension with Shanker happily whistling in the front seat.

66

'IT IS COMING NEARER, I CAN FEEL IT,' SAID AMMA IN SUCH A LOW VOICE that Deepa had to put her head close to her lips. 'I am waiting only for one last notebook.'

'Only one?' said Deepa, sitting down suddenly on the *charpoy* with shock. Deepa was holding a *balti* in both hands. She looked at the pure white yoghurt with its fresh sourness. Jhotta's yoghurt.

'Amma, what will happen to Jhotta when you are gone?'

Amma tried to summon some strength before answering, 'There are many who are wanting a buffalo producing such good milk as hers. She will find a good home.'

'But she will not be producing milk for ever.'

'It is her destiny to produce, so she will produce.' Amma paused to take a deep breath, willing herself to continue. 'Soon she will have another calf and then there will be even more milk. Much more than we are needing. Look how we must always give it away. To Raman, to Usha's ma. If she has another calf she can feed a whole large family. She is not having another calf yet because she knows for us there is no need. We do not need so much milk!'

Then she lay back, and Deepa stole away to let her rest.

Usha had heard what Amma said, and when Deepa persuaded her to tell her a Baoli story, she had this one to tell:

'Once Baoli and Jhotta were in the garden and Baoli said, "Jhotta, you are eating and eating and you are giving so little milk." Jhotta said, "But you are drinking only one glass in the morning and one at night. For what should I produce?" But Baoli said, "You are a *baoli* Jhotta. So much money I paid for you just because you were producing good milk, enough for ten people." The next week all week Jhotta produced no milk at all. "*Hai!* This *baoli* Jhotta, what is she thinking now?" wondered Baoli, and Jhotta said, "This week I will produce no milk to make up for extra milk I gave you before." Baoli was very angry and said, "Okay Jhotta, then I will give you less food to make up for so much food I gave you before." So she gave Jhotta less and less and Jhotta became thinner and thinner and died, and Baoli had no milk at all.

> '*Baoli Maai, Baoli Maai,*
> *Kahan se aai?*
> *Koi jan na paai.*'

Deepa went out into the yard and nuzzled up to Jhotta. 'Poor Jhotta, you are like me. You don't even know where you will be going. You have to wish for a kind master. And be kind to him and give lots of milk, not like that *baoli* Jhotta in Usha's stories.'

Jhotta blew at her hair.

'Are you worried, Jhotta? Are you sad?' Deepa enquired tenderly, trying to guess her thoughts by looking into her eyes. Jhotta did not look either sad or worried. 'You have nothing to do but be happy and give milk.'

Deepa patted the beast and stirred her feed lovingly; she would let Jhotta eat her favourite sugarcane tops before bringing her into the courtyard for the night. The light was already fading and the first stars were visible in the dark blue sky. And at that moment she heard the roar of the regal-sahib's white car. She looked up. But it was not the regal-sahib who got out. It was Raman and Shanker. Raman retrieved his bicycle from the back, and the Ambassador drove away.

Raman looked a little uncertain, she thought, but she envied him for he had been able to ride with the regal-sahib in his car.

'Is Amma in?' said Raman, a little on edge.

'Where would she go?' laughed Deepa.

'Well, sometimes she visits the temple.' He was hoping that she would not be there, then he could go and throw away the sweets.

Deepa nodded. 'She is here. But she is not strong. She is getting tired very easily now. Perhaps she will not be able to come to the wedding of Meera and Mamta.'

Raman knew that Deepa had spotted the box of sweets in his hand, which he was holding a few inches away from his body so that his clothes did not stain. He could not throw them away now.

'I will not disturb,' said Raman. 'I have something for you, Deepa. You will be pleased to see it.'

He leant his bicycle against the wall and held up the sweet box. With his free hand he unbuttoned his shirt and retrieved the notebook. 'This is for you.' He handed it to Deepa with a big smile on his face, momentarily forgetting the sinister behaviour of the regal-sahib. 'It is the last one.'

Deepa held the notebook gingerly and stared down at it. It looked no different from any of the others that she and Raman had bought at Ahuja Book Depot. Then she looked up at Raman with a look of deep concern on her face. 'Is it really the last one?'

'Oh yes,' said Raman enthusiastically. He pinched Deepa's cheek. 'You should be looking pleased it is the last one!'

'Maybe there is a little more to write still,' said Deepa, unable to smile.

'Even if your Amma is telling me, I will not write more. Jagat Singh is in jail, it is the end. I have put him away. I do not want to know any more about his thoughts or what he is plotting!'

Deepa turned away, weighed down by her heavy heart. Raman and Shanker followed her into the courtyard.

'*Ram, Ram*, Ammaji,' Raman said, now in a good mood from thinking about the task accomplished. He had expected more pleasure from Deepa, but it was late and perhaps she was tired.

Amma sniffed. 'You have brought something for me, Ramanji?'

'Some sweets I have brought for you, Ammaji,' said Raman cautiously.

'So the wedding is here at last!'

'Few more days only, but we are already too busy! The house will be full. So I have come early to give you sweets before my relatives refuse to let me come, so much attention they will be needing.' Once again, Raman felt the pride of a father whose daughters were getting married, and marrying well, at that. 'Of course you must come to the wedding itself, we have hired a big-big *shamiana*.'

Amma waved a hand. 'It is too confusing when there are crowds. I will sit here and think of how beautiful the wedding will be, just like I sat here and thought of the adventures of Jagat Singh from afar.'

'Ah yes, Jagat Singh. No more adventures he will have! The last notebook I have brought,' said Raman, pleased.

'Where is it?' said Amma, putting out her hands to feel for it.

Deepa gently placed the notebook in her hands.

'So it is finished!'

'It is a major work,' said Raman, feeling a sense of achievement. 'But now it is over. For now I must concentrate on my daughters' wedding.'

'And the jewels,' whispered Amma, a little hoarsely, once she had sensed that Deepa had moved away. 'You will give them to your daughters?'

'It was my intention,' said Raman, a little embarrassed. 'But Sudha Sister has already organized the wedding jewellery. For Bharathi now I will keep them.'

Amma lay back, tired again. 'It is as I thought. They will stay hidden in the lychee garden, just as they are hidden here. You must be careful, Raman, of that stranger-prince.'

Raman froze. She *did* know about the sweets.

'You will still need your book. It will bring you money. But use it wisely, to keep the lychee garden in your own hands, or the garden and the treasure will be gone for ever from your family.' Amma coughed a great hacking cough and rested back, wheezing. Deepa came running and made her drink some water. But Amma wanted to talk to Raman; she waved Deepa aside when she had drunk.

'So what will you do now, now that the book is complete?'

'Gulbachan has friends in Delhi who can publish,' said Raman. He remembered Gulbachan's offer and realized at that point there was no reason to turn it down. Gulbachan would keep the PTI bungalow, but why should Raman begrudge him that? Gulbachan had treated him well all these years.

'Really? Then we should celebrate this book. Let us taste your sweets now!' said Amma, clapping her hands for Usha. Raman looked around in panic and wondered how he could stop her.

Usha brought some small steel plates while the water was being boiled and Raman carefully laid out the sweetmeats. The two from the regal-sahib he took out first and put carefully on the first plate, intending to avoid giving them to anyone. But while he was distributing the others, Usha came up beside his elbow, picked up the plate quickly before he had time to stop her, and placed it beside Amma. He stretched out his hand as if to try to snatch it back but it was already out of reach and no words could come out of his mouth in warning. She must already know, he thought. He prayed that Amma knew. Her vision must not fail her, like it did not fail him. Right to the end, till his book was completed, her vision had served him.

The stress of thinking about the sweets made him restless. He felt he had to get away. 'I cannot stay for tea, Ammaji,' he apologized. 'I must take my son to my brother's house.'

Shanker all this while had been standing nearby with his suitcase. But with the fear of the regal-sahib and the poisoned sweets, all Raman's anger had evaporated. His heart was no longer on going to Vaman's house. He had forgotten why he was going there with Shanker and his suitcase. He just wanted to get away from this house in Jagdishpuri Extension.

Amma did not try to press Raman to stay. 'I am drinking tea anyway,' she said. 'Go if you have to, but I must try these wonderful sweetmeats.'

Raman crammed one into his mouth and stood up. She *must* know, he thought. She can smell everything.

'It is late already, and because the boy is with me it is different. Another time I will come,' he said.

He took Shanker by the hand, walked swiftly through the courtyard, unlocked his bicycle and pedalled away from Amma's house as fast as he could, with Shanker sitting on the back.

He had departed so fast he had not heard Amma say quietly, 'There will be no other time.'

'I can smell fear,' commented Amma when Raman was gone. She also sensed she should avoid the sweetmeats.

'I am not afraid, just sad,' said Deepa. She was looking through Raman's notebook. The last one.

'No. It is Raman's fear I can smell,' said Amma, breathing deeply and laboriously. But Deepa only looked puzzled. What should Raman fear? Surely he did not still think of the ghosts in her grandmother's house!

Usha brought Amma's tea. Amma took a sip and put her glass down abruptly. 'Not enough sugar! How many times have I said, Usha, there must be two spoons of this double-sugar! Go and get,' and with an angry sweep of her hand she indicated towards the kitchen.

Deepa caught the glint of the steel plate as it flew up in the air, twisting and turning, sparkling and flashing as it caught the light of the lantern, before clattering to the ground, the sweets spilling under the *charpoy*.

'*Baap ré*. What is that?' cried Amma.

'Only your plate,' said Usha, rushing to clear up. 'It is nothing. The box is full of sweets. I will give you fresh ones. Let me clean.' Usha fetched another plate and took out two other pieces from Raman's box.

'It is a waste. But these sweets are smelling even fresher,' said Amma.

'The ones on top are being exposed to air when box is opened each time. They are never smelling as sweet as ones underneath,' said Usha sweeping up.

'It is true what you are saying. But this one is tasting of delicious, pure ghee, the other did not smell so pure.'

'They are all the same sweet,' laughed Usha, brushing the broken sweet from the ground and onto a piece of cardboard.

When Deepa came to the kitchen, Usha was feeding a sweet to the rat in the trap.

'You still have that rat?' said Deepa in some surprise, taking a glass from the shelf and holding it to the earthenware urn with the spout. She tipped the urn and filled her glass with cool water, savouring the taste of red earth as she put it to her lips. All around was the smell of pickles, strong and fulsome.

'She is knowing me now,' said Usha poking the sweet through the bars and watching the rat nibble fearlessly.

'You were going to kill with poison,' Deepa reminded her, the glass held to her lips.

'You cannot hurt someone you know,' said Usha. 'Look! She knows me. Here, *chuhia*. Eat, it is sweet.'

The rat pricked up its ears and poked its snout out of the cage. 'See, she knows my voice.'

'Can she do tricks?' said Deepa, impressed.

Usha laughed. 'Soon I will teach her to count! It is a clever rat.'

'Let me,' said Deepa. She put her glass down and proffered some sweet to the rat. But the rat did not take it from her; instead it concentrated on the piece Usha had given.

'See!' laughed Usha.

'I am preferring buffaloes,' said Deepa, miffed.

'Every animal knows who likes them,' said Usha. 'That is why this *chuhia* will only take from me.'

'Jhotta will take from everyone,' said Deepa, 'but I know she loves me. It is more than just the one who gives her food.'

Usha smiled. 'Soon my *chuhia* will begin to understand the difference too. Love goes beyond favouring the one who gives you something, *chuhia*, do you understand that? Remember my voice. Even if I am giving you nothing to eat, I am different from the others even if they are feeding you. She has no mother to tell her, so I must.'

Deepa laughed and tried to offer the rat the sweet again. Still the rat did not take it.

'She is full,' said Deepa.

'No,' insisted Usha, 'she is still eating the food from my hand.'

'Tomorrow I will try again,' said Deepa, determined to make the rat recognize her too.

'It won't work, this *chuhia* knows me already,' cooed Usha.

'Will you keep her?'

'Of course.'

'But where? If you keep her in the trap then you cannot use it.'

'I do not need it.'

'Then what happened to the rat poison you bought from Jindal's?'

'It fell into the *nullah*.'

'But how?'

'Like Amma, I was waving my hand and it fell.'

Deepa was not sure whether to believe her. 'Maybe you threw it?'

'How it fell is not important. What is important is, it is not in the destiny of my *chuhia* to be poisoned,' said Usha with conviction, proffering another piece of sweet through the wire.

67

RAMAN RODE FAST THROUGH THE OLD MARKET, HIS BICYCLE SWAYING THIS way and that with the additional weight of Shanker behind. Shanker was no longer angry. His feelings against his father had evaporated completely, leaving him feeling small, insignificant and powerless. The small brown suitcase seemed ridiculous, and the Declaration of Independence in his pocket even more absurd.

Raman, for his part, could only think of the dark, underhand regal-sahib who, although richer than anyone in Mardpur, could think of doing away with the widow of the great sage-astrologer because of his desire for her treasure. And yet, the regal-sahib had not been able to procure the jewels. Not even those that had been in the hands of Madan Lal. It was fate, thought Raman. Fate was the reason that he had been able to acquire the jewels before the regal-sahib. The treasure of the courts of the kings was not for those who were consumed with greed. It would, Raman was convinced, be passed from Amma to her granddaughter to ensure a suitable match. And the rest, the jewels that were in his own hands, would ensure a match for his daughter Bharathi. If he did nothing else well in life, he wanted to be a dutiful father.

But there was something else bothering him. He had stood by and allowed the poisoned sweets to be given to Amma. Why, he had handed them to her himself! He had even placed them on the plates instead of throwing them into the *nullah* where they belonged. If Amma were to die, was he or the regal-sahib the murderer? If Amma were to die, it would be more than one hand that had killed her, just as it took more than one hand to write the story of Jagat Singh. Raman was so agitated as he pedalled towards the temple that he was almost upon the figure standing in the road before he saw him.

'Where are you running away so fast in the night?' said Satyanarayan sternly.

'I am late to see my brother,' gasped Raman. The nosiness of the Brahmin was the limit! Did he have nothing better to do but stand in the road in front of the traffic? No lessons to impart to Bholenath? No lectures to give those who came to the temple, just as he had lectured Raman for so many years on the importance of tradition, only to abandon it when it suited him? Just as Raman had recognized the greed of the regal-sahib in the distance it had taken to pedal from Jagdishpuri Extension to the temple, he had now also recognized the shallowness of Satyanarayan. He understood that wisdom lay not in what one said, quoting from the *shastras*, the Vedas or other scriptures, but in what one did. He, Raman, was neither wise nor learned, but he knew and accepted his failings. He knew that Satyanarayan would never know or accept his own. It was, after all, Satyanarayan who had informed the regal-sahib of Raman's intention to visit Amma with sweets. Was he in it too, the plot to do away with Amma? After all, had Jindal not said Satyanarayan himself had been buying rat poison?

Raman looked at Satyanarayan with new eyes, the eyes of a man who was about to fulfil his duty towards his twin daughters. He said haughtily, 'With my daughters' wedding, there is so much to do, everything cannot be accomplished in the hours of daylight.'

Whether it was because he had no proper reason to be standing there in the first place or because he detected in Raman's voice the tone of a man who was not in a mood to be trifled with, Satyanarayan let Raman pass. 'In that case, I should not delay you.'

And Raman pedalled off. Perched side-saddle on the luggage carrier behind, Shanker looked back and watched the *dhoti*-clad figure of Satyanarayan retreat and meet with another person who had emerged out of the shadows. Shanker did not know who it was, for he had never seen Man Singh before.

Raman pedalled on more slowly, his anger towards Shanker forgotten in his preoccupation with the larger issues of life. Yet he continued towards his brother's house, wanting to carry through his threat to Shanker out of pride. Just for a while, he would leave him there. Tomorrow he would retrieve his son, he thought to himself.

It was Madhu who let them in, although they banged on the door for some time before she came. There was such a noise going on inside, no one could hear them. To Raman it sounded like a political rally. One particularly loud conversation just by the door was debating the merits and demerits of being ruled by the same party since independence, and was getting quite heated. Raman was quite relieved when Madhu came: he was beginning to think the house had been taken over for a party convention.

'Raman Brother! We were all talking about you!' said Madhu. 'Your *chacha* has arrived all the way from Lucknow, and your *bua*! We have not seen her in nearly fifteen years. Meera and Mamta were not even born then!'

Raman and Shanker were pulled into the crowded household. Guru dragged Shanker away to come and meet their cousins who had arrived that day. Everyone was talking at once. There were relatives Raman barely recognized, others who had grown older, more bent. So many people at once, he felt quite overwhelmed. They came to congratulate him.

'*Wah!* Raman, to think you are the father of twins who are to be married! When last I saw you, you were refusing to study properly at college – how angry we all were! Your brothers were all calling us to talk to you!' Bua said.

Chacha greeted him. Leaning on an old stick, he could barely walk. 'Where is your wife? Her name I am forgetting, that seventh standard pass *chokri*. Pretty, though, at least I will say that. And your girls I have seen already. They are pretty too. But lucky they are more intelligent than their *maa-baap*.'

Vaman came towards him. 'It is good of you to come to greet your relatives. They were all wondering where you were! Chacha was even saying, "Just like Raman not to be there at bus station to greet us all. He had no manners as a boy."'

Raman thought this was a bit unfair. No one had told him when Chacha would be arriving, nor Bua, nor any of his cousins and nieces and nephews, and who knows who had arrived at Laxman's house, too!

'It is already house–full,' said Vaman cheerfully. 'Others are coming tomorrow. We are putting *charpoys* on the roof just like at Aurobindo Hospital. Kumud must be swept off her feet dealing with her side of family, no?'

Raman rather wistfully thought of the calmness of the lychee garden compared with the pandemonium here. He wanted to get away and savour the last evening of peace before Kumud's relatives began to arrive tomorrow.

'Come and tell Bua about the boys' family. She has been asking all along,' said Vaman. Madhu passed by in a flap. 'I knew I was not having enough sheets for all these people! Where am I to get now?'

'What need for sheets?' said Vaman. 'Just lie down on mats. It is the traditional way for wives, no?'

Madhu looked at him witheringly and jingled her bangles. 'Some modesty must be preserved in this house!' she said.

'Don't worry, don't worry,' said Vaman. 'So many *dhotis* we have in the Sari Palace. If it is only sheets you are needing, I will get. You can use *dhotis* to cover.' He turned to Raman. 'Did you see Chacha's son, our cousin Ramnath? He is owning a car even!'

Raman did not want to see Ramnath just at that moment. He tried to tell Vaman about Shanker, although he realized that there would be no room in Vaman's house tonight to keep his errant son. It was altogether a bad moment. Moreover, the whole clan would know he had fought with his son, and it would be discussed for weeks, even years.

'I want you to give Shanker a lecture,' Raman said. 'Tell him how to behave with his parents. He is the limit already. Even Guru is not so disrespectful as this one!'

'Oh, it is Madhu who is keeping them in hand!' said Vaman. 'She is far more strict than me. One word from her and they all shut up and throw themselves at her feet.'

There was a commotion as Madhu came rushing out after Guru. 'How many times did I tell you? Those sweets are not for touching! It is like talking to the walls. These boys never listen. Beating is no good, they just do it again!'

'Our sons are not as we were,' said Vaman ruefully. 'Guru is giving his ma a hard time. What can we do? Lecture-*baji* does not work. They will see in their own time when they have sons. Now come and meet Ramnath, you must find out from him how he made so much money! He is dying to tell.'

Ramnath was fat and prosperous and smoking a cigarette, puffing the smoke into the air. 'So-hey Raman! Long time no see. How did you pay dowry? Did you rob a bank? And we all thought you are penniless and having to be supported by your brothers' generosity. No, Vaman Brother?'

'Yes,' grinned Vaman, who had also been surprised to hear from Laxman about the payment but had had no time to talk to Raman about it. Organizing for a wedding took up so much time, especially with a sari business to run as well.

Raman had nothing to say to his cousin, who as a child had always been fat and bullied both Raman and Vaman.

'Still working for that PTI fellow?' enquired Ramnath. 'Work for yourself, I say! And where is your little wife? The quiet one?'

That was Raman's cue. 'I must run home,' he said. 'She is waiting for me and there is much to do before the wedding!'

'Much to do? But you were always the lazy one, Raman, leaving others to do all the work. But then double-wedding is lot of work even when you have two brothers to shoulder most of it! Now ask me how I made my money. I'll tell you it is not from being lazy.'

Raman looked around desperately for Shanker, grabbed his hand and apologized to Ramnath. 'We are needed at home. Tomorrow I will come.'

'Home? That mosquito-infested garden? I am sure the plaster is still cracking like the day you moved in.'

'It has become a valuable property, you know,' Vaman butted in. 'Marwaris are buying up too much property in Mardpur these days.'

'Oho?' said Ramnath, interested now. 'How much do you think it is worth then?'

'At least sixteen *lakhs*,' said Vaman.

'Sixteen!' Even Ramnath was impressed. 'It is wasted on Raman, then!'

Raman looked and felt quite sick, but not because of what Ramnath had said.

'You have not asked me about my latest venture, Raman!' said Ramnath.

'Ask him,' urged Vaman.

'What is your latest venture?' asked Raman mechanically as Shanker broke away from his grip.

'I have started a small publishing house. And you have a book ready to publish, Vaman is telling me.'

'After the wedding,' said Raman, feeling a little dizzy. He fanned his face with his hand.

'No hurry!' said Ramnath. 'But at least I can do that for you, Raman, publish your book. And this is Shanker? Send Shanker to me! I will show him how to make money – he will never learn that if he stays here in Mardpur. That much I will do for my cousin.' And he slapped Raman on the back.

'It is a good idea,' said Raman, edging away and forgetting that his intention had been to send Shanker to relatives to learn about the real world. Deftly grabbing Shanker's brown suitcase, which was still in Shanker's hand, he mumbled something about relatives arriving at the lychee garden and shot out through the door into the night air – cooler, less oppressive and peaceful compared to inside. Raman took a deep breath to savour the tranquillity, which he knew would be broken tomorrow, and clambered onto his bicycle. Shanker, who had not enjoyed being sized up by Chacha and Bua any more than Raman had, jumped on the back with his suitcase and they rode towards Kumar Junction, where they dismounted and strolled up the hill.

Kumud was pleased to see them. 'Is it that Vaman Uncle did not want you, either?' she teased gently. She knew they would be coming back. But she did not want to suggest openly that perhaps Raman had backed down.

'Boy has relented,' said Raman curtly. His face was stern.

'I knew he would,' said Kumud. 'He is not a bad boy at heart. His place is in our home, and we cannot choose the children we are given. We have to put up with them.'

And she welcomed her son back with open arms.

68

THE HOUSE IN JAGDISHPURI EXTENSION HAD NEVER BEEN SO FULL OF PEOPLE. Deepa sat impassively on Amma's *charpoy* in the courtyard and watched as they filed through the house all morning to pay their last respects. Amma was inside, out of the hot sun, calm and peaceful, draped in a red shawl. There she lay on the ground, one with the earth. She had gone when she said she would go, when her earthly tasks were completed.

It was Usha who had gone out early to call Dr Sharma before morning surgery. But both Deepa and Usha knew before he came to verify her death that Amma had passed away peacefully in her sleep, willing herself away, as she had promised Deepa that she would.

Usha had washed the body and anointed it, as if it was just another of her daily tasks. She dressed it and covered it in the red shawl. Usha always seemed to know what to do. She had even found a bottle of Ganga water to pour into the old woman's throat in the prescribed ritual. And she had climbed onto the low stool that usually stood by the grinding wheel, to reach the *tulsi* leaves strung above the doorway to the trunk room.

'What is it for?' said Deepa, watching her pluck down one of the dried leaves that had so often picked up the breezes that meandered round the courtyard.

'It must be put in her mouth, for purification,' said Usha.

Deepa wanted to know how she knew all this. Usha saw her watching her every move. 'My grandmother also died. I watched my ma,' Usha said quietly.

That night Deepa had lain down beside Amma to smell for the last time her strong pickle smell, and to fall asleep still with that sweet scent in her nostrils.

'I have finished my work on this earth,' breathed Amma to the sleepy Deepa. And that was the last thing she heard Amma say.

Now the body of Amma was laid out and Usha had burnt some incense. Amma's smell was no longer in the air. Amma was gone and her scent was gone. Deepa was alone.

Deepa watched the people solemnly invade the house. People she hardly knew, but who honoured Amma as the wife of the great sage-astrologer. How fast the news had travelled! Sudha-with-Pension, bustling and busy with a double-wedding almost upon her, came early in the morning. She saw Deepa sitting on the *charpoy* and took the edge of her plain cotton sari to gently wipe the tears she imagined she saw in Deepa's eyes.

'Poor child,' she murmured. 'What is to become of you? I hope now your ma sees her responsibility, for your sake.'

Some women were wailing and crying and hardly noticed Deepa at all. Others recited prayers or sang *bhajans* – Amma's favourite hymns. They were melodious, even though they were mournful. Deepa was used to hearing them being sung in Amma's cracked voice. The sound of the *bhajans*, familiar or not, did not fill the void that Deepa felt.

'He-ey Maha-de-e-va Mahes-wara . . .'

Deepa turned round. It was Usha singing the familiar hymn, Amma's favourite, as if to console herself.

The only constant was Usha, who went about her work and tended the body at the same time, straightening the sheet, brushing off the flies. She went out and bought fresh vegetables and lit the bucket-stove to cook them for Deepa, just as she had done when Amma was alive. Then she folded Deepa's clothes neatly in piles and prepared them for Deepa's departure. She showed signs of strain only once, when she came out of the kitchen with the rat-trap.

'My *chuhia* has died too,' she said quietly. Then she wrapped its body in newspaper and threw it outside into the sewer.

Then she began to prepare her own meagre belongings, laying them in a cheap tin trunk.

'Where will you go?' Deepa asked her.

'My marriage is already arranged,' said Usha without expression. '*Sagai* is next week. I must go back to my village.'

Deepa was surprised. Amma must already have known about it for some time, and Usha too had said nothing. When had Usha seen her husband-to-be? she wondered. Or had she seen him at all? Maybe Usha had planned to come back after her wedding, a married woman, to carry on working for Amma as if nothing had changed.

'It is good you will have someone to take care of you,' said Deepa.

Usha looked at Deepa with some surprise. 'When you marry, it is you who will look after your husband.'

Deepa said nothing. It was not what she meant. She meant that she would be on her own, whereas Usha would have her husband.

'Your ma will be kind to you,' Usha said, trying to reassure her.

Deepa thought about that. Perhaps it was the same. Usha would be looked after by someone she hardly knew and so would Deepa. But then, she admitted to herself, she did still remember her mother as loving and warm. How could she forget?

She watched Usha pack her few things – a comb with teeth missing, a spotted mirror, some ribbons.

Deepa went and brought down the small red trunk which held her school books. There on the top were her notebooks, filled with Raman's story, a patchwork of paragraphs from Raman, Amma and herself. And there were Raman's notebooks themselves. Deepa tied them neatly with string into two bundles and laid them aside. Then she arranged in the empty red trunk the clothes that Usha had folded and put aside. She was ready to leave.

In the afternoon, Bharathi came with her mother. Kumud laid her offerings at Amma's feet and Bharathi came in search of Deepa.

'Will you go back to your ma?' she whispered. She sat next to Deepa on the *charpoy*, stroking her hand. She could barely imagine what it must be like now for Deepa.

'I think so,' Deepa said.

'Do you love her?'

'Yes.'

'As much as Amma?'

Deepa did not know how to reply. Amma was part of her. She had not experienced life without Amma. It would take some time before Deepa and her mother went through the same amount together, but it would happen.

'Soon I will love her as much,' said Deepa confidently. She told Bharathi to wait. She ran back and got the notebooks, handing them to Bharathi in a cloth-bag. 'They belong to your father,' she explained.

Bharathi did not even look inside. Her concern was still for her friend. 'Deepa, is there a convent in Vakilpur, where your ma is?'

'I don't think so.'

'What if there is only a government secondary school?'

'Then I will go to that.'

'But without a decent education how will you marry a good man?'

'I will have to marry whoever wants to marry me,' said Deepa, who was not thinking about marriage or the future at all.

Bharathi was quiet, then started again: 'Deepa, ask your ma if you can learn to dance. I am sure there are dance teachers in Vakilpur. You move so beautifully. If there is one thing you will be able to do, it is to dance.'

Deepa nodded slowly.

'Promise me you will ask? If you do not want, you cannot get.'

'Yes,' promised Deepa.

'Everything will be different,' Bharathi observed. 'Are you afraid?'

Deepa shook her head. 'I will be with my ma.'

How could someone who did not think about the future be afraid?

For Bharathi it was heart-wrenching. She was about to lose her best friend. She whispered, 'I will never see you again. I will think of you. Will you think of me?'

'Always,' said Deepa, looking at Bharathi with affection. The two girls embraced, remembering the times of contentment when they had played together without a care.

Bharathi tried to hang onto those times with one last effort: 'Can you try and come back for my wedding, Deepa? Then we can talk again about so many things.'

'I will try, Bharathi. I will try my very best.' But Deepa knew it was impossible. Who would bring her here?

Then Bharathi said something strange. 'Do you love Govind, Deepa?'

'No,' said Deepa, who did not know what love was.

'Try to love Govind.'

'Why?'

'Then you can marry him and come back to Mardpur and we can still be friends.'

Deepa smiled. 'If I am married, then you will also marry and you will be gone from Mardpur,' she pointed out.

'Then I must marry Shyam!'

The two girls held hands and giggled.

Kumud came to look for Bharathi.

'Come,' she said to Bharathi. 'We must go to the bus station. My brothers will be arriving. It is the wedding of my daughters,' she said to Deepa, who of course knew. 'If you are still here, you must come. But I don't think you will still be here.' Kumud kissed Deepa on the top of the head. 'You will go back to your ma. She has not forgotten you. Just like I did not forget my Meera and Mamta even though they do not live with me. They are still part of me.' The tips of Kumud's fingers lingered on Deepa's cheek, cool from the wet flowers she had cast over the body of Amma. 'Do not be afraid,' she went on. 'Soon you will find your own strength. Remember how strong was your *nani*? Maybe she was not always so strong. She had to discover her own strength.'

'Dance, Deepa,' whispered Bharathi.

Deepa watched them go; Bharathi was swinging the cloth-bag. Deepa felt she had given something of herself away; something of Amma's away.

69

DEEPA WAS STILL SITTING ON AMMA'S *CHARPOY* WHEN HER MOTHER arrived. Deepa recognized her immediately. She was exactly as she had always remembered her. Just a little plumper, that was all. Deepa's heart jumped, and she knew she would be all right. Ma, too, saw Deepa and came straight towards her without hesitation. She embraced her daughter, holding her tight against her soft body which bulged between her sari and her blouse. Her shoulder was plump and warm and Deepa pressed her nose into her neck and inhaled her warm smell. Ma's gold necklace was the same as the one in the wedding picture on Amma's trunk. Deepa stroked it with her finger. It was from Amma. It was a piece of Amma. And she felt reassured at the familiarity of it.

'Come,' said Ma.

Deepa looked up and saw Ma's wet eyes. She took the edge of her mother's sari and carefully wiped away the tears that were forming. Then Ma took Deepa by the hand to look at Amma's body for the last time. Ma knelt on the ground by the body and cradled Amma's head in her arm so that Amma's nose pressed into her neck, an indentation where Deepa had pressed her own nose against her mother. Ma tidied the red shawl and smoothed it over Amma's shoulders while Deepa gathered up some fallen flowers and laid them on the body: deep orange marigolds, barely opened, and jasmine, still wet with dew from the lychee garden, pure white against the dark red shawl, the dew drops clinging precariously to the fine red wool.

Then Deepa picked up the red trunk and walked out to start a new life, holding her mother's hand.

Usha stopped her work only momentarily to watch her go, wiping her damp hands on her *kameez*. When she had departed, Usha laid her arms on her knees and sobbed quietly, curled up in a ball, still sitting on her plank, her shoulders heaving with grief.

Ma stopped at the temple. She stood for a long time in front of the many-handed deity, her head bowed. And then she went in search of Satyanarayan to arrange Amma's cremation in nearby Ghatpur, where the river flowed swiftly past the sugar mills across the Gangetic Plain gathering the ashes of the departed as it went.

'I must first take my daughter home,' she said to Satyanarayan.

'I will arrange everything,' promised Satyanarayan. 'The widow of the great *rajguru* must have a decent funeral.'

He did a short *puja*. At the end of it, he spooned milk and honey into Ma's palm and bade her drink it. Ma sipped, and passed her damp palm reverently over her head. Satyanarayan did the same with Deepa. Then he filled Ma's palm twice again. At the end of this ritual, when he saw that Ma was calmed, he ventured: 'What is to happen to the house?'

'The house in Jagdishpuri Extension? You wrote to me about a prince who is wanting to buy. But it is not a house for a prince,' Ma said.

Deepa looked from Satyanarayan to Ma and back again. They had talked about selling the house even while Amma was alive and she and Deepa were living there! She remembered the conversation between the regal-sahib and Man Singh which she had overheard in the temple garden, and her heart felt sick.

'Amma was having strong karmic link to the courts of the kings. Maybe it is this karma that is making this prince want to buy,' Satyanarayan said.

'Yes,' said Ma. 'She had a special talent. She could foretell the future. I do not like to know about the future. I like to live for the present only. Why should I worry about what is to come?'

Deepa looked at her mother. She was beginning to recognize some sounds of Amma in Ma's voice. And now she saw where her own fear of the future came from.

'But this prince . . . ?' Ma continued, more puzzled than curious.

Satyanarayan shook his head. 'He is gone for now.'

'Gone?'

'I must look in the charts, for Saturn must be strongly aspected. It is an auspicious night for deaths. The princely gentleman left this morning. His father also died in the night. With a telegram, postman Mittal came running. The regal-sahib came only a few hours ago to do *puja* in memory of his *baap*, and now he is gone in his car. I do not know when he will come back.'

'There is no hurry,' said Ma. The future of the house was not her main concern. Not on the day her mother had died.

They left the temple and Deepa never saw Raman arrive shortly afterwards, in a state of agitation. He did not seek out Satyanarayan but went directly to the inner sanctum of the Vishnu Narayan temple and prostrated himself at the feet of the many-handed deity that looked down on him benignly, to beg her forgiveness.

'Oh Ma!' he addressed the deity, distraught. 'Punish me in whichever way you like. For I have helped to kill an old woman. Let me do penance for the rest of my life. I will exile myself in the lychee garden for you and not show myself, for I am not fit to be seen.'

And he made his way round the inner sanctum three times, feeling his way against the walls as if blind, before returning to his home on the hill, his only sanctuary.

At the bus station, while Ma was getting tickets, Deepa saw Mallika. Mallika did not see Deepa at first, but she was searching for someone in the crowd and in her search her eyes met with Deepa's.

Mallika came running. 'I heard about Amma. What will happen to you?'

'I am going home with my ma.'

'Is she nice?' Mallika's voice shrank to a whisper, looking around for a glimpse of Deepa's ma.

'She is wonderful,' said Deepa with conviction.

'Try to be happy, Deepa,' said Mallika, clearly relieved to hear this. Deepa knew she did not have to try. She knew she would be.

'Will you come back?'

Deepa shook her head. 'I don't know.'

Then Mallika lowered her voice again. 'Did you find the treasure?'

'No,' said Deepa.

'Then you will be back!'

Ma came back with the tickets. Mallika stared hard at her, looking her up and down. Ma did not seem to mind. Then, when Mallika had satisfied herself, she said goodbye to Deepa and ran off in search of her brother.

'You have many friends,' commented Ma.

'Yes,' said Deepa. 'But only one ma.'

Ma smiled wanly. It was a trite comment, but she knew it was heartfelt. 'Soon you will make new friends. And you have sisters, too. They are all waiting for you in Vakilpur. They are curious to see what you are like. They have heard so much about you.'

Deepa wondered from whom they had heard about her. Was it Ma who spoke of her, with the love of a mother for her child?

'You will like our house in Vakilpur. You will not be alone any more,' Ma said.

'Can they dance?' said Deepa suddenly.

Ma looked surprised. 'They are young still. Do you like to dance?'

'Yes!' said Deepa.

'Then we must find a teacher for you. Are you fond of music, too?'

'Not as fond as of dance,' said Deepa firmly. She felt a thrill of excitement at the thought of being able to learn. It was the first time she would get something she wanted. Before, she had never dared to want.

Ma smiled warmly. 'I will arrange something. Of course you must dance. I can see it now. You are so graceful.'

Deepa sat by the window, watching the people getting on the bus. Ma said nothing. She looked sad. Maybe she was thinking of Amma, maybe even Dasji, Deepa thought.

The conductor banged on the side of the bus and slowly it began to move, gathering speed as it eased out of the bus station. When it slowed to turn towards Vakilpur Deepa noticed a slim, tall figure running alongside the bus, waving. With a shock she realized it was calling, 'Deepa! Deepa!'

She craned her head out of the window as the bus moved away, straining to hear.

'I will think of you!' he called.

She saw the long legs and dazzling white pants fall behind. Then the bus turned a corner into the bustle of Kumar Bazaar and she could see Govind no more.

Soon Kumar Bazaar was left behind and all she could see were fields on both sides, still lush from the recent rains, although they were less frequent now. The monsoon season was almost over, and with it would end the marriage season. Soon the dry season would set in, baking the earth hard and shrinking the pools of water to tiny mud-puddles, just enough for a buffalo to get its knees wet.

A herd of buffaloes came into view. She sat forward in her seat, seeking out Jhotta. 'Jhotta! Jhotta!' she called.

She could not see her among the herd. It was only some yards further that she spotted Pappu, the buffalo boy, watching over two buffaloes lounging in a ditch of water. It was the one enjoying herself, the one with the carefree look on her face – that was Jhotta.

'Jhotta! Jhotta!' called Deepa, waving frantically.

Jhotta did not even lift her head.

'I will think of you!' called Deepa.

And as the buffalo disappeared from sight, Deepa's tears began to fall, faster and faster, in mourning for everything she had left behind.

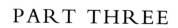

PART THREE

70

DEEPA KNEW IT WAS SOMETHING SPECIAL WHEN MA CALLED HER TO HER room – a sanctuary which Deepa had hardly ever penetrated since she had arrived in that large, sprawling house in Vakilpur. Ma liked to keep to herself.

When Ma came looking for Deepa that day, Deepa was doing her dance practice. Ma waited until she had finished, watching her daughter with appreciation and pleasure, before telling her to come to her room. Deepa took off her ankle-bells and laid them carefully in their box, replaited her long hair which had worked itself loose from the swings and sways of vigorous dance movements, and then went to Ma.

'We must cut your hair,' said Ma without any preliminaries. She already had her scissors ready.

Deepa submitted, without even asking why. She trusted Ma and loved her. Ma must know what was best. But she found herself biting her lower lip and fighting back the tears as she felt the clank of cold steel. She had allowed her hair to grow for dance. Dance was her whole life now. In it she played out all her dreams. She lived for nothing else.

Ma painstakingly cut her hair into a bob, making sure that the edges were straight and there were no straggling hairs. 'You'll be fine,' she said, patting Deepa's cheek when she was finished. 'You look very pretty.'

Ma held her by the shoulders and looked into her eyes. Then she took Deepa to her big trunk, the one that held only the most expensive and beautiful saris. She held various saris up to Deepa's slim shoulder.

'No,' Ma said, her head to one side, appraising the effect. 'Silk is too heavy for you. It makes you look older. And you are so slender and graceful.' She held up a chiffon sari of swirling pink and lavender hues. 'This is better.'

Then she wound it round Deepa's slim figure, finally pulling the *pallav* over her head. She tweaked the front over Deepa's forehead, pulled it down lower, shook her head and pushed it back. All this without a word to Deepa.

Ma put a very small hint of lipstick on Deepa's lips. And a *bindi* on her forehead. From her bangle box she picked some glass bangles that matched the sari, pushing them over Deepa's slender bunched-up fingers, the fingers of a dancer. All the while Deepa wondered but did not ask Ma where they were going. It could not be a wedding or her sisters, Geeta and Rita, would be getting ready as well. Deepa did not ask Ma much, ever. Although Ma was kind to Deepa, it was as if she did not know what to say to her daughter. Ma was not talkative and neither was Deepa. Perhaps Deepa had got the trait from Ma. Sometimes Ma would pat Deepa on the cheek as if she were a small child and say, 'So sad. Always so sad.'

Deepa did not feel sad. But she realized her quietness brought out people's sense of pity. There was not much she could do about that. Everyone knew her history and felt sorry for her. But why should they? She had been happy with Amma. And she was happy with Ma. Especially when Ma found her a dance teacher.

The highlight of Deepa's week was her dance class. She threw everything she had into it, all her passion, all her sensitivity. Perhaps after putting so much feeling into her dance, there was not much left for everyday discourse. Her sisters, used to their own company for so many years, never thought to include her in their games. They were younger than her by quite a few years but they did not venerate her particularly. They saw her as a kind of exotic intruder whom they did not understand. While they were noisy and disobedient, indulged by both their father and their mother, Deepa was quiet and compliant, helpful and considerate. Sometimes she helped them with their homework but rarely did they call on her company, and Deepa was left to her own devices much of the time. She did not mind. In Mardpur she had been used to that. Her stepfather was aloof by nature, although not unkind. But he felt insecure in Deepa's quiet, brooding presence. He was not really sure what kind of father he should be for Deepa, so he retreated behind newspapers and books while she was there but smiled and played with his younger daughters. The servants, who had not watched her grow up from babyhood and did not feel the bond of affection they felt with the rest of the family, neither teased nor chatted to her as they did with her sisters, filling the air with the giggling and laughter of shared childish jokes.

It was the dance master Shivananda, who, with his language of the hands, the feet and the eyebrows, spoke to her the most. He understood her inner thoughts, and knew for all the mystery that everyone else read into them that they were not that complex, really. They were not full of dreams and desires like other children; neither dissatisfaction nor distraction. He knew she lived for the present, and most importantly for her dance. He made her work hard but was never over-harsh, as he could be with some of his students.

In eight years, Shivananda had taught Deepa all he knew. And for some time now he had been trying to convince Ma that Deepa should be allowed to go all the way to Orissa to a *gurukul*, a residential school run by his own guru, Padmabhushan, whose sensitive interpretation of the Odissi dance style was renowned. At the *gurukul* there was no set time for dance. When the guru felt like it, everyone gathered. They imbibed his energy, his inner strength, his power of expression. This was the way for Deepa to learn: by watching and doing and feeling the atmosphere, the senses, around her.

But Ma said it was too far away for one so young. 'She needs some stability in life after all she has been through,' Deepa heard Ma say to Shivananda. 'How can we send her so far away?'

'Give it a rest,' Shivananda told Deepa. 'In one year's time I will ask your ma again.'

Deepa did not mind. She had so few expectations that she had few disappointments. She decided just to enjoy what she had. She had not lost the pleasure of the dances she already knew, for as she matured from girl to woman the range of emotions she was able to portray also developed, so that the dances she had learnt eight years before took on new life and intensity as she grew older.

One day, she believed, Ma would let her go to Orissa and that would be the right day. Until then she would give everything she had to her dance, in expectation of that day.

Geeta and Rita, for all their unruliness, sometimes stole up and watched her dance. Despite themselves, they became wrapped up in the myths and stories that Deepa's dancing evoked. When they watched her, they did not see Deepa, they saw Yashoda, mother of Krishna, angry but loving with her child, the gentleness of Goddess Parvati, the graceful gait of Rama. Deepa brought the whole pantheon alive with movement.

When she stopped Rita, brash and spoilt, could not resist saying, 'Why are you dancing so much? Do you imagine it will get you a better husband?'

Deepa thought, maybe it would. She had a dream that she was dancing in front of an audience and a prince came to her with a rose. That prince would be her husband. When she awoke she felt embarrassed to be dreaming about the regal-sahib. But he was the only prince she had ever met.

Sometimes Deepa suspected that Ma did not want her to go to Orissa in case it meant she would stay on and not complete college. But Shivananda had explained it would just be for a short while, maybe during the long summer holiday, when it was so hot in the plains. Who would want to dance in such heat? Then in Orissa it would be cool. How could Ma not agree . . . eventually?

'Your daughter has talent,' Shivananda told Ma.

'What will she do with such talent?' said Ma, pleased, but not sure what to make of it.

'Who knows what it will bring her?' said Shivananda. 'For now it is adding to her inner beauty.'

But Ma did not really understand. 'Dancing will not get Deepa a good husband. Boys want educated girls these days,' she said.

'You are always worrying too much about marrying your daughters,' Shivananda laughed. 'So many girls I have taught, and all their mothers are worrying about their marriages!'

'So why would I be different!' replied Ma with a smile.

Shivananda did not respond, he was not expected to. But later – some weeks later – he mentioned to Deepa with a sigh: 'I hoped your ma would be different, because she is educated.' He shook his head. 'But she is a true mother. Like every mother she is worrying about a match for you.'

After she had dressed Deepa Ma went to get herself ready, leaving Deepa sitting there on the edge of the bed, waiting, waiting she knew not what for – just as she had waited eight years earlier on Amma's *charpoy* for her mother to come and transport her to a new life.

Deepa got up and looked in the dressing-table mirror. She looked different. Thinner and older, with this short hair and *pallav* round her head. Like a young woman; not a girl any more. She thought the *bindi* was too big but she did not know in which drawer Ma kept her *bindis* and she did not want to rummage around her dressing-table. Her hair, a long, beautiful plait which used to swing as she danced, caressing her back, was wrapped in a piece of newspaper. Deepa could see it, still glossy, peering out of the newspaper which had been thrown in desultory fashion near the dressing-table. Discarded.

When Ma came back, she was dressed in silk. She looked very elegant, thought Deepa, smelling a whiff of imported scent wafting about Ma's plump arms.

'Come,' Ma said, beckoning Deepa. And they made their way to the bus station.

In her hand Ma had a small bag with towels and clothes, and it was only then that Deepa realized they were not going to see someone in town but further away and maybe for a few days.

In the bus Ma finally told Deepa the purpose of their journey. 'I have received a letter from a very good family. They want to see you with a view to marriage – if the boy likes you. It is the boy's choice. Very modern family. It is a good match for they are highly educated.'

Deepa had not expected her marriage to be settled so simply, so quickly. She had not seen anyone pore over her horoscope. No piles of letters with photographs and biodata of suitable boys. How much had been going on without her noticing? Then she thought, was she so wrapped up in herself that she had not even seen her own marriage being prepared?

Deepa looked at Ma. 'Will I be coming back? Or – or –' For the first time she felt fear. Was she to be attending her own wedding today? This was not how she had expected it to be. Surely there would be more preparations, more female relatives making a fuss? More ceremonies? Betrothal, anointing, all the rest? Was she to be married quietly, without all this? But most of all, she feared for her dream of one day going to Orissa.

Ma laughed. 'Of course you will come back. If they agree we must make the preparations for a fine wedding. They are a good family, and they are not asking for any dowry. Very modern. Very educated. Maybe even they will let you continue college after you are married. That is why I had to cut your hair. I know you like long hair, but it is not the modern way. And you look very pleasant now.'

Deepa wanted to say that she had been growing her hair for her dance, but what was the point? She could not now think of going to Orissa. When she was married, her in-laws may let her go to college. They may even allow her to dance, if it did not get in the way of the household chores. But they would not let her go to Orissa.

Deepa wanted to ask more about the prospective family but felt too shy, and Ma did not tell her much. She said only, 'They have a very beautiful bungalow. Brand new. But you will go to live where the boy gets a job. In some city, I don't know where. Bangalore, maybe Mysore. Even Delhi if you are lucky.'

Bangalore? Mysore? These were faraway places. Almost as far, Deepa thought, as Orissa. Were they close to Orissa? Could she travel there? Deepa tried to push the thought of Orissa from her head. She would be happy wherever she was, she insisted to herself. She would make a life wherever she went. Had she not been contented when she had come away with her mother? Deepa prayed as always that her future husband, whoever he might be, would be kind. And that he should let her dance. It did not matter if she could not go to Orissa as long as she could keep dancing. Ma said he was educated, and the family had a new house, so perhaps they were well off. But Deepa wished above all that he would be kind.

Don't wish, Deepa warned herself, in case you are disappointed. It is better not to want. Henceforth, she promised herself, she would dance only for pleasure. She would not use it to express dreams. But without wanting, you do not get, another voice said within her. You would not have been able to learn to dance if you had not wanted it. She remembered how eight years ago she had seen Mallika dance and felt the urge within herself.

'He is a scientist,' Ma said, and Deepa became attentive again. 'He could have been a doctor, even.' But she did not say why he had not become one.

A scientist, Deepa thought. Maybe he knows big words and I will not understand anything he says. Or maybe he will not talk to me at all. Deepa tried to stop herself thinking by imagining the footwork of the dance she had been practising when Ma came to find her to cut her hair. The fluid lines, the smooth patterns, the gentle movements, so calm. In dance it was all so easy, you could become a woman enticing a lover and you could be the lover in the arms of a woman, and there was nothing to be afraid of. Everything was choreographed. What differed was how much passion you put into each dance. The outcome – that the woman and the lover become one – was always the same. But life was not like that. In life, everything was unknown.

Ma dozed in the bus, and Deepa wrestled with her own feelings. Her eight years with Ma had been so tranquil, so uneventful, she hardly knew how to deal with the turmoil that had been stirred within her. Finally, tired with yearning and a confusion of thoughts, she sat back in her seat, watching acres of sugarcane and mustard greens flash by. For a long time they passed no village. But then they came to the outskirts of a town, sprawling but neat. The town did not seem familiar: it was very new, very clean. She became attentive suddenly when she began to recognize some buildings. Here and there was a landmark that jogged her memory and, if she obliterated the newer bits in between, she could form a map in her mind.

'Mardpur!' she breathed, and felt a surge of excitement in her breast. 'Mardpur!' She wanted to shout aloud. And then as a whole row of new houses flashed past, she felt a kind of foreboding that all would be different, everything would have changed.

71

'DO YOU REMEMBER THIS PLACE?' SAID MA, ALMOST AS IF SHE WERE ASKING herself. She was awake now and she looked out with a kind of detached interest, noting the many changes.

Deepa nodded, staring out of the window intently, willing the bus to slow down just a little so that she could take in the new Mardpur. But it did not, and she hung onto the edge of the window trying to catch and retain every familiar spot as it flashed past. There were many new buildings. But it *was* Mardpur.

'For so many years this place did not change, then after just eight I can hardly recognize it!' said Ma. She too was looking out at the new buildings, but with a curiosity that was different from Deepa's. It did not carry with it the same feeling of nostalgia and longing, and of belonging. She did not and could not form the same attachment to the small, modest bungalow in Jagdishpuri Extension built by Dasji, her dead husband. In the eight years that Deepa had lived in Vakilpur, Ma had never once mentioned Deepa's father.

'Will we stop here?' Deepa asked, barely able to believe she had returned. Her mind's eye flew back to her last moments in Mardpur eight years ago. *You will be back*, Mallika had said. And Deepa had never allowed herself to believe it. The longer she had been away, the less she believed she would return. Of course she no longer believed in Amma's treasure, but there was more to Mardpur than that.

'It is to Mardpur we are coming,' said Ma, and Deepa could hardly contain her emotions.

'Will we go to Jagdishpuri Extension?'

'It has been closed up. God knows in what state it must be. Since Amma's cremation I have not been there. I must decide whether to sell it or to keep. I was thinking to keep for your dowry. But family is not wanting dowry. It is your luck. Your fate.'

'No one is living there?' Deepa asked.

'Who should be there? I have already ordered Usha to come and work for a few days to sweep and clean so that we can stay tonight.'

Usha! She was still here. Deepa felt shy. What would she think when she saw Usha? Would she remember Deepa? So many new buildings, Deepa thought anew as they began to approach the bus station. The bus station had been on the outskirts but now there was so much new development it seemed as if it was in the heart of the city. When they got off the bus, Ma consulted a letter that she pulled out from her blouse.

'Jodhpuri Extension,' she told the rickshaw-wala.

'Jodhpuri Extension?' Deepa said.

'It is a brand new colony,' Ma explained. 'Built by a Marwari industrialist from Ghatpur. Even I have not seen it before. But you will see, Ghatpur is now almost part of Mardpur. Murgaon and Mardpur are already one. Mardpur has changed so much. You will hardly recognize.'

Deepa's eyes were wide. So much in such a short time! Mardpur was no longer a sleepy little town. It seemed to have taken on the bustle and thrust of Ghatpur, with which it had become joined. They travelled along the wide, well-planned streets of Jodhpuri Extension with new bungalows on either side. Some even had cars parked in front. Before, if there was anything in front it was usually a buffalo or a cow. The road was smooth, newly tarred, and not pitted by even one heavy monsoon. The rickshaw-wala pedalled effortlessly and the vehicle moved faster than Deepa had ever travelled in a rickshaw.

'Jodhpuri Extension is the best district in Mardpur,' said Ma. 'It is for those who are rich and with influence. You are very lucky, Deepa, that you should have a proposal from such a family. It is the reputation of your grandfather. My father was so well known in the courts of the kings. The Rajputs all remember him. And these are the people who are building Mardpur. You should be proud of his memory.'

Soon they stopped and Deepa looked up at the two-storey house, so new, and so clean. Deepa would not be living here, she knew, because Ma had said the boy would be working in another town or city somewhere south. But this was her in-laws' house.

Let them be kind to me, Deepa prayed as she walked through the gate.

When they entered through the door into the cool, marbled hall, Deepa kept her eyes on her feet. But when she heard the woman's voice, the voice of her future mother-in-law, the shock was so great she nearly turned around and ran away.

It was Mrs Sharma. Dr Sharma's wife.

'Oh, she has become so pretty!' said Mrs Sharma taking Deepa in her arms. 'You are like my own daughter.' She gently removed the *pallav* from Deepa's head and rearranged it on her shoulder, making her feel exposed. Her short hair made her head feel light, her shoulders bare.

'No need to hide from us!' Mrs Sharma said. 'We have seen you before.'

She led Deepa and Ma to the living room, a beautiful room with marble floors and polished wooden furniture. It was clean and sparkling compared to the cosiness of the dilapidated old home Deepa had stayed in when Amma had fallen and had to be taken to the Aurobindo Hospital. Deepa looked around. There was nothing familiar even about the few possessions displayed – shiny cups won for what, she could not tell. Sport? Debate? Small bronze dancing statuettes, tastefully arranged on a shelf. There were no flowers on the table, no lace doily.

'I must apologize,' said Mrs Sharma, a little flustered. 'The boy has become delayed because of a rail strike and will not be here till this evening, maybe not even till tomorrow. And Dr Sharma is delayed also. But that is not so serious – only at Cowwasji Hospital. He will be here soon. But come and eat, you must be tired after such a dusty journey. Nalini! Come, don't be lazy. It will be your turn next so you had better learn now how to serve. Mallika was married only this year,' she said to Deepa, knowing she would be interested. 'Two weddings in one year! So hectic it has been.'

Deepa stared at Nalini. She had matured into a lithe teenager, just beginning to blossom. Nalini peered back at her. 'You have not changed,' she said.

Deepa smiled at her. Neither had Nalini. She was still as outspoken.

'This is my youngest child,' said Mrs Sharma to Ma. And Deepa

realized that her mother had never met any members of this family that
was so familiar to her.

'It is so lonely without Mallika,' Mrs Sharma chattered away. 'She was
so lively, was she not, Deepa? You were very close to her.'

Deepa nodded. It was hard to imagine the household without Mallika.
But then the house had changed so much; it was much less haphazard,
more formal. It seemed the kind of place where liveliness would not be
encouraged as before.

'My husband is now the director of the Cowwasji Hospital,' Mrs
Sharma told Ma. 'Mardpur has really benefited from the new money.
Everywhere they have put money. You will not recognize the place, in
just a few short years it has been altered.'

She turned to Deepa and tried to make her feel at home with a little
joke: 'Some people are calling it Mar-pur. You know Mar, short for
Marwari! And one time we thought we were so backward compared to
Ghatpur. But now we are better than Ghatpur because we do not have
the factories.'

'Yes,' said Ma, overwhelmed by Mrs Sharma's chatter but feeling she
ought to say something. 'Mardpur has really extended.'

'You will not recognize it!' repeated Mrs Sharma, clearly proud of what
Mardpur had become. 'New colonies are everywhere. Anyone with land
has done very well.'

'Even towards the south?' said Ma. 'There was nothing there. Just fields
when last I came.'

'Oh yes, even south. The road from Kumar Junction is now a
pukka road. It is a very decent colony, out there beyond the old lychee
garden. Only the very rich are there. We are very pleased for
Bharathi.'

'Bharathi?' said Deepa eagerly. She wanted to know what had
happened to her best friend.

'What a nice girl! Her father is still there in the same old house in the
lychee garden. Imagine! He hardly comes out. No one sees him. Even I
have seen him only once since Bharathi's wedding. Still in that old
bungalow, even though now he has so much money he could build a
new mansion in that lychee garden. What will he do with so many trees?
And still living within those old cracked walls.'

'Some old people are liking their old houses,' Nalini broke in, in a way
that endeared her to Deepa.

'*Dhut!* Raman is not old. He is younger than me even,' scolded Mrs

Sharma. Then she turned again to Ma. 'Yes, they are a very rich family now. So we are pleased. They are rich from the book.'

'The book?' said Deepa in some excitement.

'You did not hear, Deepa? He was writing a book. I thought that was already before you went away, but maybe I am remembering wrong. But his book, it is so very popular. Who would have thought?' She turned to Ma. 'Even traders are writing books these days! And Raman, too. So much his brothers used to criticize him always! But now everyone is buying this book in Delhi and Calcutta. In Bombay they are making a film, even.' Mrs Sharma turned to Deepa again. 'It was a fantastic wedding, such beautiful flowers, all from the lychee garden. And the lychees – so good, so juicy. We are getting sackfuls every year!' Deepa realized she must be talking about Bharathi's wedding again. Deepa felt pleased for her friend. She began to relax in Mrs Sharma's effusiveness.

'Where is Bharathi living these days?' Deepa enquired, for if she had married she could not still be at the lychee garden.

'Why, Deepa, of course Bharathi is here!'

Deepa barely understood what Mrs Sharma was saying. The confusion rose in her breast and stuck in her throat.

'Bharathi!' called Mrs Sharma. She leant forward towards Deepa. 'She cannot know you have arrived or she would have come running!'

Deepa's confusion was such that she hardly dared look towards the door where the slim figure appeared, a happy smile on her face.

It was indeed Bharathi.

Deepa rose to embrace her and then froze. Beside her stood her husband. Unmistakably, tall and slim in his startling white pants, Govind stood looking at her with his sensitive eyes that still had the sadness that Deepa had always known in him. He did not flinch from her, but Deepa could not look back at him. Govind had married Bharathi.

72

DEEPA'S HANDS FLEW TO THE SIDES OF HER FACE IN EMBARRASSMENT AND consternation. She hardly heard Mrs Sharma speak.

'We are hoping Shyam will agree, Deepa. Then you will marry Shyam.'

'You will marry Shyam,' said Bharathi, gently taking Deepa's hands from her face and holding them in both hands. 'And you and I will be sisters! I am so lucky, Deepa. And so are you.'

Govind stood still silent, with the same look of pity on his face that he always seemed to reserve for her. But this time, for the first time, Deepa thought that maybe she deserved it.

'I had always wished for you to come back to Mardpur,' whispered Bharathi, who was radiant and beautiful next to Govind. 'You did not come for my wedding but I knew I would be there for yours, and I would bring you back to Mardpur.'

'Yes,' said Mrs Sharma, beaming. She was pleased to see so much affection between her daughter-in-law and Deepa. Deepa was a little reserved, she knew, but Bharathi would be able to communicate with her and bring her out of herself. Deepa would be happy in the doctor's family. 'It was indeed Bharathi who reminded us of you. But you were always like a daughter to us. And now we only have to await Shyam's decision.'

'It is such a problem with the trains,' said Bharathi, still holding Deepa's hands. 'Shyam is coming from Bhubaneswar, he is doing research there.'

'Bhubaneswar?' gasped Deepa.

'It is in Orissa,' said Bharathi.

'It is far, but I think you will like it,' said Mrs Sharma. 'We have not been there. But Shyam says he is happy. We are hoping he will soon have a posting to Mysore.'

Deepa and Ma took tea with Mrs Sharma, Bharathi, Govind and Nalini, during which Deepa and Govind hardly said a word while Bharathi and Nalini and Mrs Sharma chatted about all the changes in Mardpur and who lived in which new house.

'And the Vishnu Narayan temple you will not recognize!' exclaimed Mrs Sharma. 'A brand new extension is being built. It is almost finished.'

'You remember, Deepa, when we took Jhotta to the temple to cure her of her fever? So funny it was! The temple it is changed so. No buffalo could be allowed there now, all new and clean with marble and what all,' said Bharathi.

Deepa thought about Jhotta. The buffalo would not have liked the new Mardpur. But maybe she had found herself a small place to amble, and a nice garden in which to stand peacefully and chew cud. Jhotta would have found her own place to be happy, even if it were only a very small one.

After tea, Deepa and Ma took their leave of the doctor's family and hailed a cycle-rickshaw to take them back to Jagdishpuri Extension. It took a long time. And Deepa remembered with surprise how she used to walk across Mardpur. But now the streets were congested, not with the bustle and businesslike purposefulness that congested Ghatpur, but with a rapidly expanding population that filled the narrow roads. New stalls spilled out onto the streets. The shops extended onto the pavements, and hawkers from all the surrounding villages paved the residential areas selling their handicrafts and other goods which were rapidly being supplanted by the cheaper goods from the factories of Ghatpur. It was clear from the thin calves and emaciated shoulders and years of hard work etched on their faces that the villagers were not the ones who had benefited and prospered from the new wealth that had created the vast expanse that was Mardpur-Murgaon-Ghatpur.

The cycle-rickshaw edged forward, calling out to all ahead to make way, for his tinkling bell was inadequate in the mêlée. As they approached Kumar Junction, Deepa recognized the tall, white *gopuram* of the Vishnu Narayan temple shining against the blue sky. But the rest of the temple was now almost invisible behind the stalls attached to the temple wall.

Even Ma took note. 'Is that the Vishnu Narayan temple?' she called to the rickshaw-wala. She had to shout several times before he heard her.

'*Haan*, memsahib, it is the old one. It is the favourite of the Marwaris, they are building new extension on other side.'

'Are there no temples in Ghatpur?'

'This is the oldest one, memsahib. And land on other side is already belonging to temple. Extension will have biggest Laxmi-goddess. You want to see? I am charging two rupees for waiting.'

'No, no. Later perhaps. Now we must go to Jagdishpuri Extension.'

Deepa looked curiously at the many stalls, some selling garishly painted plaster of Paris images of Laxmi and Ganesh. The fragrance of the garland stalls wafted towards her, piled high with strings of marigolds, jasmine and roses. The ground was trampled with petals that had drifted away and fallen. In the old days, Satyanarayan Swami would sit and string the garlands himself, and any petals that fell he collected into a *thali* to be thrown over the deities by the worshippers.

'So many people must be coming to the temple now,' said Ma, making much the same observation as Deepa.

'*Haan*, memsahib, from all around they are coming. It is a place of pilgrimage. They are saying that miracles are being performed here, so they are coming to see.'

'What miracles?'

'Milk is flowing from the trunk of Ganesh idol that is sitting under the banyan tree in temple compound.'

Ma looked dubious. 'Have you seen it?'

'No, memsahib, I am just simple rickshaw-wala. Only the most devout and holy can see such a miracle. Satyanarayan Swami has seen it. He is a great man. And people who have given big-big donation, they also have seen. But we are lucky that Mardpur has been blessed with such miracle from the gods.'

'What next!' Ma said to Deepa. 'Always when there are too many people coming from far away it is easy to convince them of miracles happening.'

It was only when they came to the Old Market that things began to seem much as they were in the past. The vegetables were still laid out on the ground, on rush mats. The produce was wafted with reed fans – to keep off the flies – by the women who, adorned with all their wedding jewellery, silver anklets and toerings and noserings, pulled the *pallav* of their saris down below their eyes and haggled with customers wandering with their cloth-bags.

And Jagdishpuri Extension had not changed at all. Deepa felt a surge of excitement as they approached the familiar house; it looked untended, dirtier and with flaking plaster, but it was still the same. Deepa could smell its aromas almost before she entered. The pickle smell that had so pervaded it when Amma was alive was still there, struggling to burst free.

A maidservant came out to greet them. She was middle-aged and plump. Deepa did not recognize her. She strained to look past her, seeking out Usha.

'Is the room prepared?' said Ma.

'I have opened out the room and made up the beds. Are you wishing to eat, memsahib? Food is prepared.'

'Yes, Usha-rani, we will eat, and then we will rest.'

Usha! Deepa stared curiously at the woman but there was nothing familiar about her; this was a different Usha, someone else her mother had brought in. The Usha of the past had gone back to her village to marry. By now she must have several children. Maybe she had never come back to Mardpur. Deepa looked curiously at the new Usha and liked her nonetheless.

Only one room had been aired and cleaned and prepared with sheets. The maidservant had lit the bucket-stove in the courtyard and cooked outdoors. She prepared fresh chapattis, squatting a little way from them. Deepa and Ma also sat on the swept floor, on planks which made the house seem almost austere. There was no sign of the *charpoys* that used to be scattered in the courtyard in Amma's day. But Deepa did notice the corner where the grinding wheels had lain idle for so many years. The two low stools that she and Amma had sat on to grind, and later she and Usha, were still standing there, unmoved from that position. Every now and again Deepa would sniff the pickle smell wafting from the kitchen as if trying to escape. The pickle-pots are still there, she thought with some surprise, and the pickles had slowly matured. The smell of sweet mustard oil was strong and old. The pickles must all be ready, she thought.

After the simple meal Ma went to lie down. Usha-rani was preparing chapattis for her own meal, then she squatted by the smoking bucket-stove, eating quietly.

Deepa went to explore. There were padlocks on all the other rooms except the one that had been opened up for them. She went to the kitchen and threw open the door which still had the padlock hanging from it. She pushed aside the netting doors and found herself enveloped by the pickle smell, warm and enticing. It was stronger than she ever remembered it, as if by being pent up for so long it had become enriched and mellow, brewing into a stronger and stronger aroma of fermenting mangoes and limes. She opened the shuttered windows beside the door which looked out onto the courtyard to let in the light. The rays of light burst through with swirling dust and bleached the smell a little, letting in the clean, warm, neutral scent of the sun. In the light she saw the churning urn where Usha had used to sit in the morning. The rod was still in the urn, but laid at an angle, unsupported and unused. From it wafted a gentle earthy smell, soured by the yoghurt that had for so long resided in its pores.

Deepa came out and sat on the stool by the grinding stones, watching Usha-rani washing the meal-time *thalis* in two buckets of water. 'There is a tap in the kitchen,' Deepa said. They were the first words she had addressed to the homely maidservant.

Usha-rani shook her head. 'There is no water these days. For six hours a day it is switched off. Mardpur has expanded so fast there is not enough water for everyone. At night it is the same, the power is often going.'

'So many new people,' said Deepa. 'Where have they come from?'

'From the villages. The crops have failed for three years and everyone is running to Ghatpur and Mardpur and Murgaon to find work to feed their families. It is not the crops only. Ghatpur factories are producing many new things. People do not want things made in villages. It is harder and harder to sell. So now the artisans must also come to the towns to earn money.'

'Are you from the village?'

'Oh, I have been in Mardpur for many, many years,' said Usha. 'But my father worked so hard making mats and fans from grass. Like this.' She picked up the broken fan that she must have found in the kitchen and with which she had fanned the bucket-stove to get it burning brightly. She would not say much more about herself; instead she talked about Deepa. 'So you are to be married? Mardpur will be your home.'

Deepa did not say anything.

'It is a good family, that doctor-family. Very modern. Not thinking about caste or anything like that, only what is the boy's preference. Of course doctor-sahib would not allow boys to marry just anyone. Match for eldest son was with very rich family. But it was the son who chose the girl.'

Deepa was surprised to hear Bharathi's family being described as very rich. 'You mean Bharathi?'

'Yes, her father is very famous writer, from old Mardpur sari trader family. Rich from book-writing.'

'He has written many books?'

'Only one. But that is enough. They are living in the lychee garden on hill-top. Still in the old-old bungalow. He is never coming out of there. No one has seen him for a long time, even his daughter is hardly going there now that she is married. And the son is gone away to learn business from other family members.'

'And grandchildren?' said Deepa.

'There are some, I heard, living in Ghatpur.'

Those must be the children of Meera and Mamta, thought Deepa. 'The grandchildren do not come?'

Usha-*rani* shook her head. 'I have not seen. But the youngest daughter was married only last year. It is still early for grandchildren.' She continued to talk of the doctor's family. 'Now younger son must also choose. You are very lucky, if he chooses you, you will be in a very good family. Tomorrow he will come from Orissa. We must dress you in best sari and make you very beautiful so that he will want you.'

'If it is the son who chooses, then he must already want me,' said Deepa.

Usha-rani looked at her obliquely. 'I am hearing it was Bharathi who proposed you. Now the younger brother must see you and decide.'

Bharathi suggested her! Deepa did not know whether to be pleased or sad.

'Tomorrow I will bring yoghurt to put on your face. And *haldi-atta* for your arms. You will see, your ma and I will make you very beautiful. You are already very graceful, like a dancer.'

Deepa did not think of herself as a dancer, but others seemed to think of her as one. She merely nodded and listened to Usha-rani's plans to turn her into something that Shyam would not be able to resist.

★

When Ma awoke after her nap Usha-rani made tea. Ma sipped and sighed.

'There is so much to do with this house. I must clear out the rooms, for it should be sold. There is no point in keeping it if we will not be needing a dowry for you, Deepa.'

Usha-rani was listening, dunking her biscuit in her tea and chewing thoughtfully. 'Memsahib, I am always hearing there is treasure in this house. If you sell it what will become of the treasure?'

'What treasure?' laughed Ma.

'Memsahib, Amma, your ma, was having lot of jewellery from the courts of the kings which is still hidden.'

'Still hidden! The gossip of people here is terrible. They have nothing better to do! There is no treasure in this house. It is true my ma had jewellery but it was all given to me when I married. There is nothing here.'

Usha-rani dunked her biscuit. 'It is what people are saying, memsahib.'

'Let them say. There is nothing here. I will sell the house.' And Ma stared hard at Usha as if daring her to believe such tales.

But Usha-rani drank her tea, still deep in contemplation.

'But how will I sell this house?' Ma wondered aloud. 'Who would want it?'

She remembered her conversation with Satyanarayan eight years ago. 'Once a prince was wanting it. That was many years ago. And perhaps it is because everyone was buying land in Mardpur then, and he was wanting this house for the land only. Now who would want this place? Why should a prince want it, all old and broken, when he could have palaces?'

'Perhaps it is the treasure he is looking for, memsahib,' said Usha-rani.

'Usha, there is no more treasure here than there are miracles at the temple. If there were miracles at the temple more people would have seen them. No one has seen this treasure either. Even I have never seen.'

'Memsahib, some have seen the miracles. Those who are supposed to see them. Who are ready to see them. For the treasure it must be the same. Only those will find who are supposed to find and who are ready to find.'

73

HOW THE VISHNU NARAYAN TEMPLE HAD BEEN TRANSFORMED! IT WASN'T just the myriad stalls that signalled it to be a well-frequented site of pilgrimage in comparison to the sleepy shrine it had been when Deepa was a child. The simple stone deities that had once sheltered under the trees had all been removed, discarded for not being grand enough for a temple of such importance. No one knew where the old statues had been transported to in the dead of night. Satyanarayan had ensured that the secret was kept, for if the people found out it would surely have meant the spontaneous founding of a new temple on whatever land those deities happened to occupy. In the minds of the people, just because these stone idols had been moved away from the Vishnu Narayan temple did not mean they had lost their sacredness. And the proof that holiness, once endowed, could not be lost was that the temple garden trees themselves were still spattered with coloured powders and grains of rice as worshippers refused to break the habit of wandering among the arbours with their devout offerings.

Only a large marble elephant-god Ganesh sat under the banyan tree where Satyanarayan had once sat, while Satyanarayan had moved to a throne-like platform inside the new extension, from where he conducted the most important rituals.

This was the elephant–god that had miraculously spouted milk. It was a miracle that not only cemented the holiness of the new deity in the eyes of the people, but also the elevation of Satyanarayan himself as the person who had first witnessed the miracle. Even Vaman who did not believe in miracles was perplexed by the stories and went to see for himself, taking with him coconut and flowers to present to the new deity in the hope that he would perform the milk miracle for him. Such an act even by the unbelieving merely consolidated the impression that the deity was a supreme one. Which was exactly what Satyanarayan wanted.

'Well, did he perform?' Laxman had asked.

'No,' said Vaman with satisfaction.

'It is because you are not devout enough,' explained Laxman. 'Tomorrow I will make big-big donation to the temple and maybe I will see the miracle.'

'Good luck,' said Vaman. He had nothing against philanthropic gestures, but that did not mean one should believe in miracles.

Laxman made his donation, but was not honoured with the sight of any miracle although he sat before the deity all morning performing rituals, wearing nothing but his *dhoti*. 'I was not honoured,' he told Vaman sadly.

'Of course, because you are not Satyanarayan. Satyanarayan Swami, you may have noticed, takes all honours only for himself.'

But Vaman did note that the Ganesh deity, with its protruding belly and slightly supercilious expression, bore an uncanny resemblance to what Satyanarayan had now become: well fed, with glowing skin from a healthy diet as he lorded over one of the most important temples in the area with its new marble and silk idols.

There were other changes. What had once been called simply the Vishnu Narayan temple had now been renamed the Raja Man Singh temple. Man Singh, it was said, had made a huge donation for the renovation and extension of the temple. In actual fact it had not been Man Singh's money to donate. Only when the wily financial adviser to the kings fell out with the royal families of Rajasthan did they discover how much of their wealth was in his hands. They had allowed him such a free hand in their business matters that not only was he able to deprive them of huge amounts of money, but also of their name. For the most part, the royal families did not begrudge losing a fortune to philanthropic works, as most of the biggest projects happened to be. But they did resent not having their name all over the new institutions, hospitals and temple extensions.

Man Singh, for his part, had become quite renowned in the area for his generosity and he was awarded the honorary title of Raja, for a man who could give so much must surely be a great man. Few realized that none of the money was actually his. Those who did, like Satyanarayan, felt it would unduly complicate matters in the minds of simple people to reveal such a thing. As he saw it, all that had happened was that Man Singh had duped the rich to give to the poor. Satyanarayan, for his part, felt Man Singh was a useful person to have on his side, particularly when he provided not insubstantial funds for Satyanarayan's small campaign to establish a *panchayat* in the growing town and have himself elected as its head.

Dressed in a silk *kurta* with a fine poplin cloth draped over his shoulder, Satyanarayan was greyer, fatter, but not much altered beyond that. There were some, like Vaman, who would say his pompous air of the past had been replaced by a more overt arrogance, but that was perhaps a little unfair. Yet it was true that he now had little time for idle chit-chat and consequently no time to back up his opinions with quotations and citations from the *shastras*, so that his manner was extremely dogmatic rather than learned and scholarly.

The day that Ma and Deepa arrived in Mardpur, Satyanarayan had been doing what he did most days now: bustling around and supervising the building of the temple extension. The extension was a set of three tall ornamented pagodas, which would dwarf the old *gopuram* and house the new statue of Laxmi, goddess of wealth, whose importance in the minds of the people had increased dramatically. Before that, people did not really worry whom they were worshipping, as long as the deity looked familiar. After all, as Satyanarayan himself would say, every god is an *avatar* of another god. But for the new arrivals to Mardpur, the temple was too austere with its plain stone idols. A huge white marble Laxmi had been donated at great expense. Beautiful silks had been provided by the sari merchants, including Laxman and Vaman, to drape her, and fine jewels came from the jewellers of Ghatpur. Once the extension was built, the new Laxmi would be taken on a *yatra* to be anointed in the sacred river Ganges, in a procession led by Satyanarayan. Satyanarayan was excited about this prospect of being at the head of the rich and noble Marwari and bania families of Ghatpur-Murgaon-Mardpur. It would be like the Salt March, he imagined, remembering the stories that the journalist Gulbachan used to tell, and he spent many hours planning how he should dress for the occasion, either in just a plain *dhoti* and no *kurta*, with his Brahmin's thread across his chest, or in a silk *kurta*. He had not yet decided but he was coming down in favour of the latter.

Things had changed for Satyanarayan in another way. He had power as head of the *panchayat*. And there were often *panchayat* matters to attend to. He believed it was important for a *panchayat* to handle matters promptly, otherwise the local bureaucrats took charge of the matter and wielded the power. And there was little reason to allow the secular bureaucracy to handle matters when the Brahmin- and Marwari-dominated *panchayat* could do it just as well and swing things in their own interest.

All this left very little time for rituals, which simple people required to bring day-to-day solace to their changing lives. These he left to Bhole, his nephew, a thin, tall youth with a shaven head and a pigtail, and a huge U-shaped Brahmin mark on his forehead, without which it would have been very easy to pass him by without noticing him – he had none of the charisma of his uncle. That U of cool sandalwood paste marked Bhole out clearly like an advertisement and ensured that, with his mild manner and simple ways, people did not mistake him for a mere servant in the grandiose environment of the expanding temple.

When Deepa and Ma entered the temple, clutching their coconuts and flowers, they were hesitant. They were not sure where the heart of this new temple, the inner sanctum, was really situated. Satyanarayan was hurrying from giving an earful to the contractor building the extension. He had made him writhe and wriggle in terror and humiliation, making it easy to extract from him the confession that, yes, it was the contractor's fault that things were not going as they should. With this victory in hand, Satyanarayan was feeling particularly self-satisfied.

Ma stopped him with one hand on the sleeve of his silk *kurta*. 'Satyanarayan Swami, *Ram, Ram.*'

Satyanarayan looked down at his sleeve, concerned that a wrinkle had defaced it. Then he recognized Vimala, daughter of the great Brahmin astrologer of the courts of the kings, one of the very few men, most of them deceased, that he admired above himself, and he softened. Although he did not approve of Vimala's remarriage, his respect for her father, the great *rajguru*, was stronger.

'Oho! What brings you to this backward place?' He waved towards the extension. 'You see, we are trying to move into the twenty-first century, but these sons of owls have no brain! It is a job trying to keep an eye on them. They are eating my head every day.'

'I am here to arrange the marriage of my daughter,' Ma said.

Satyanarayan stared coolly at Deepa, sizing up her suitability as a bride. He showed no sign of remembering the twelve-year-old who had brought her sick buffalo to him for a cure. Deepa had no reason to avert her eyes.

'To whom is it arranged?' enquired Satyanarayan, as Deepa moved away to explore the temple grounds, much altered since her childhood.

'To the younger son of Dr Sharma,' said Ma proudly. 'It is a good match, they are not asking for dowry.'

'Ha!' snorted Satyanarayan. 'And to whom is their elder son married?' he said, unaware that Ma already knew. 'The daughter of that good-for-nothing Raman. The one who wrote the book and became rich. You know –' Satyanarayan lowered his voice '– I was always sure it was someone else who wrote that book, for he was an uneducated man and incapable of writing. But I was never able to prove.'

'Who should write for him?' said Ma. 'It is such a big job.'

'Write *for* him? No, no. He stole it from somewhere.' Satyanarayan gave Ma a sidelong glance, full of significance. 'It may even be Amma, your mother, who wrote it. The book should be yours. The lychee garden land also. Recently I have seen the deeds and it is clearly saying the estate is belonging to the one who wrote the book. So! It does not belong to Raman at all.'

Ma clearly thought any claim to Raman's wealth by her family a ridiculous notion. 'My ma? But she was blind for many years. She could not write such a book.' She shook her head. 'No, Swami, if someone else wrote it, it was not Amma.'

'The truth will come out,' said Satyanarayan grumpily. 'But you should believe me when I say you are perhaps entitled to this property.'

He had a plan up his sleeve which he was not ready to reveal just yet. But the anger of Man Singh still rang in his ears the day the financier-turned-raja came thundering up to the temple saying Raman had made not even one payment on the mortgage he had granted him, but there was nothing he could do because the deeds said the property belonged to the 'writer of the book'. The notary, one Mohinder Patwari of Ghatpur, a shrewd lawyer unimpressed by any raja-title that Man Singh could throw at him, had demanded proof that Raman was indeed the writer before proceeding against him and seizing the lychee garden on Man Singh's behalf.

'Bring me the manuscript of the book in his writing, that will be enough proof,' said Patwari, enjoying Man Singh's discomfiture. But Man Singh knew too well that there was no way he could get his hands on the manuscript.

'His name is on the published work,' he growled. 'Everyone knows it was he.'

'It means nothing, anyone can put their name to anyone's work, isn't it?' said Patwari with a penetrating stare at Raja Man Singh. 'Proof is needed.'

When Man Singh told Satyanarayan, the Brahmin consulted Laxman to see if the manuscript could be found. But he was foiled by Vaman. And it was Vaman who, not knowing why Satyanarayan sought the manuscript, said, 'It is not just Raman's manuscript but Amma's, now deceased, and Deepa, her granddaughter's.'

Vaman's aim was to deter Satyanarayan from interfering in the brothers' business. But instead this planted a seed in Satyanarayan's mind that he could not get rid of.

'You may be entitled to this property,' Satyanarayan repeated when he noted no look of surprise and amazement on Ma's face, only puzzlement.

'What will I do with this property?' said Ma. 'I do not need more property in Mardpur and I am content with what I have.'

Satyanarayan gave her another sidelong glance as if he considered this an odd statement. 'Everyone is needing money. Did you not say you were marrying your daughter?'

'Yes,' said Ma patiently, and repeated, 'The boy's side is not asking for dowry. Also I will be selling the house in Jagdishpuri Extension, for we do not need it any more. It is not a very big house but it will bring us something for jewellery and other expenses.'

Satyanarayan looked interested. 'This is the house with treasure?'

Ma laughed. 'Why is everyone always talking about treasure? There is no treasure there, Swami.'

Satyanarayan looked a little disappointed. 'Oho, so you have taken it away?'

'No, no. There was no treasure there ever. I have done nothing to the house, it remains as it was the day Amma died. But there has never been treasure there.'

'But even Amma was saying herself there was treasure there, and why should she tell a lie to everybody?' Satyanarayan persisted.

Ma shook her head. 'I do not know why she was saying that. Maybe she did not talk about it, maybe everyone is spreading the rumour only. Well, if there is treasure it is still hidden, and whoever buys the house will get it! But of course we know there is nothing.'

While they were talking, a young man had appeared in a white cotton *kurta*, looking very agitated. He was waiting patiently for Satyanarayan to be finished, because from years of experience he knew that Satyanarayan could get quite angry if interrupted.

Satyanarayan was getting quite distracted with his hovering, and he broke off his conversation with Ma to enquire: 'What is your problem, Guru? Why are you jumping up and down like an elephant on thorns? Can you not see I am talking to one very old Brahmin family of Mardpur? I have no time to deal with your thorns. Be off!'

Guru held his ground. It was too important. 'Swamiji, we are needing special *puja* today.'

Satyanarayan puffed up his chest. 'You know I am too busy. Bhole will do it for you.'

'Swami —' said Guru, looking very uncomfortable. 'This is very special, and my papa is saying—'

'You go back and tell that Vaman Father of yours, all *pujas* are special.'

'Yes, but Swami—'

'Go!' said Satyanarayan, swinging his arm in the air with an outpointed finger to indicate the direction in which Guru should head.

Guru did not move. He looked from Ma to Satyanarayan and at Deepa, as well, without recognizing her, and then blurted out, 'Swami, it is you who must come only. This morning, very early, Raman Uncle has expired.'

'Oho?' said Satyanarayan in some surprise. 'Was he ill, your *chacha*?'

'No!' wailed Guru. 'It was an accident. A stupid accident in a *tonga*!'

And his shoulders heaved with suppressed sobs.

74

WHEN RAMAN'S BOOK WAS PUBLISHED, WITH THE ASSISTANCE OF HIS cousin Ramnath, this story of Jagat Singh and the smuggler put Mardpur on the map.

A new school of novel-writing had been founded, the literary critics in Delhi enthused, and Mardpur, in the heart of the Gangetic Plain, was the birth-place of this new movement. They insisted that people had become tired of reading about politics, they had tired of the literary greats and were waiting for a contemporary voice. The voice from Mardpur was this voice.

When he realized that Raman with his bania-literature had brought Mardpur to the attention of the rest of the country, Satyanarayan set about ensuring, with renewed vigour, that Mardpur would be known for something quite different. It would be a place of pilgrimage. A centre of miracles. A focus of religion.

Satyanarayan was lucky. Man Singh had been at hand, financing the development of Mardpur, and above all the development of its temple. Satyanarayan was sure that the fame of Mardpur for its temple would long outlast the renown of Mardpur for pulp thrillers. He was not wrong. The newspapers that had heralded the dawn of a new era in book-writing waited and waited for more of the same to emanate from the same pen.

And when it was not forthcoming the enthusiasm fizzled out, the literary sections of the newspapers closed and the critics were assigned to film appreciation instead, or else became writers of radio-plays and were paid a pittance for their efforts.

But for all Satyanarayan's anger at Raman for having drawn attention to Mardpur through a piece of lowly fiction, he could not hold it against Raman for ever. In Satyanarayan's eyes, Raman had redeemed himself by not producing a second work of fiction in eight years, despite the clamouring of the literary establishment. Raman had realized the folly of his ways, Satyanarayan believed. True, he had had to make the mistake first, against Satyanarayan's better advice, but it was in the nature of less-learned folk not to realize true wisdom when they saw it, only to learn from their own hapless mistakes. There was another reason why Satyanarayan was willing to forgive. In the years since the book had been published, Raman, rather than basking in its glory, had curiously lived the life of a recluse, up there on the hill. He rarely stepped out of the lychee garden, almost as if he were ashamed of his success. And this suited Satyanarayan. Any possibility that Raman would upstage the Brahmin as a literary figure who was renowned up and down the country was prevented by Raman himself.

It was only at the wedding of his daughter Bharathi, to Dr Sharma's eldest son Govind, that Raman was seen in public: gauche and embarrassed by so many high-class guests who praised his book effusively, even if they had not read it. To them he had little to say in return.

It was a good match. Dr Sharma had achieved great status in the community. He had been selected to head the new hospital built with Marwari money. There was even talk of a new university and medical school, and Dr Sharma was on the planning board. He had been for more than seven years, and the university had not yet materialized. Nonetheless, Sudha-with-Pension had been particularly keen on the match between Bharathi and the doctor's son, for if there was to be a new university in Mardpur, the municipal college would surely fade into insignificance. Of course, Sudha could take her pension and leave. But in the new Mardpur, status had begun to count for something. In the new Mardpur you had to be invited to weddings, dinners and 'functions'. And to receive such invitations, you had to have some status.

When Sudha had discovered that Bharathi had seen Govind a few times, she engineered some more meetings. It was a delicate business, because the doctor's family were Brahmins and the sari traders were banias. But she also knew that the doctor and his wife were modern in the extreme and did not set much store by caste. Sudha was determined to exploit this. She took Bharathi under her wing when she reached college age. Raman had already achieved some fame by then and the money was beginning to come in. Bharathi was not a bad catch by any standards, and there was no reason, Sudha thought, why the rest of the family should not benefit from this by getting her married into a family of status. Particularly as the sari business was not what it once was.

Once Bharathi was under her wing, Sudha-with-Pension developed a sudden tendency to hypochondria. It was Bharathi she would send to the doctor's house, on the new scooter Laxman had bought for her, to find Dr Sharma.

'But Sudha Aunty, I am sure Dr Sharma will be at the hospital now,' Bharathi would protest.

'If he is, then his son Govind will go and look for him there. You must ask Govind to find him. Here, put on this nice sari and my jewellery you can have. If you are to meet Govind, you must look your best.'

Bharathi never let on whether she suspected her aunt's motives, but she did not object, and in time she became quite friendly with Govind's sister Mallika. Whatever Bharathi's own feelings about the matter, it was Sudha who one day approached Mrs Sharma with a proposal.

To Sudha's delight, Mrs Sharma did not immediately bring up the issue of caste. Instead she said, 'We do not believe in forcing anything on our children, it must be Govind who decides.'

Mrs Sharma quietly mentioned the proposal to Govind, who began to take more notice of Bharathi when she came to their home. It was some months before he gave his parents his decision, by which time Sudha-with-Pension was frantic. It made her genuinely ill, worrying whether her proposal would be turned down. Oddly, it was at this time, when she was getting all sorts of fevers from stress, that she stopped sending Bharathi to fetch Dr Sharma. Bharathi could not understand her aunt. When she was complaining about her headache, her back or her knees, there was nothing visibly wrong with her and she insisted on the doctor. But when she was lying in a feverish sweat, she refused to see him.

Sudha Aunty was so different from her own mother Kumud, who was straightforward and strong, and who contentedly ran her household. Sudha-with-Pension, who had lived many years in conditions far better than those of Raman's household, was constantly complaining and carping about her lot. Still, Bharathi had considerable freedom at her uncle's house, and was happy pursuing her college studies. She had no reason to complain. She liked to chunter around on her scooter and meet her college friends without having to feel that coming away from the lychee garden was a long trek. With her scooter she could head home whenever she wished to see her mother. The road from Kumar Junction was now paved, leading beyond the lychee garden estate to a small colony of large houses called Kumar Extension. There was more traffic on the road than in her childhood, but it was still a quiet backwater compared to the ageing Merchants' Colony where Laxman Uncle still lived in genteel dilapidation.

The wedding was a big event in Mardpur, even though it had to wait for the doctor's new house in Jodhpuri Extension to be completed. Satyanarayan had resided over the Vedic rituals. That was, Satyanarayan realized, the last time he had spoken to Raman.

Raman emerged from the lychee garden so rarely and the rest of the family, out of habit, was not inclined to go to the temple. Only Kumud came there sometimes, where she would meet Sudha-with-Pension and Madhu. And with Bharathi married and Shanker away learning a trade with his Uncle Ramnath, there was very little communication at all between the lychee garden and the outside world.

Deepa reappeared just as Guru was making his emotive announcement to Satyanarayan. She wanted to go up to him and ask about Raman, or at least offer her condolences. But she hardly knew Guru, except that he was the cousin of Bharathi, and it would not be looked on as proper for a young girl about to be married to address a young man of Guru's age. Guru, for his part, did not even look at her. He was too wrapped up in his own distress. Deepa turned away and followed her mother who had already begun to walk away when Satyanarayan was interrupted.

It was while Satyanarayan was hurriedly changing out of his cream-coloured silk *kurta* into more austere white homespun, more appropriate for the passing away of a member of one of the old trading families of Mardpur, that a familiar stranger appeared. Not the young man that he had once been, he was still slim and elegant, but without the fresh carefreeness of yesteryear. His gait was more stodgy, having lost its spring, and there was a slight heaviness in his heart that came from responsibilities he did not have in his youth. Satyanarayan recognized him, but knew Guru was waiting for him to take him to the lychee garden on the back of his scooter.

'It is a long time since you have been here,' said Satyanarayan, gathering together the things he would need for the rituals and stowing them in a cloth-bag.

'It is a few years,' agreed the regal-sahib. 'My father died, and then there were so many debts and family matters to attend to that I could no longer find the time and peace of mind to return. Many things change.'

'Everything changes,' agreed Satyanarayan. 'But you are the raja now.'

'You must know,' said the regal-sahib patiently, as if he had explained this to many others, many times before, 'there are no more rajas. There are no more privy purses from the government. We must make our own way.'

'Well, you have had a good start,' said Satyanarayan.

'You heard about Man Singh? How he cheated my family and other royal families too, and has acquired property and status?'

Satyanarayan suddenly became intent on adjusting his *dhoti*. He could not, after all, criticize one who had given so much to build a new temple.

'You will find he is not as you think.'

'No,' said the regal-sahib sardonically, 'he is not as we thought. I see his name is written up on the temple.'

'He is one donor. We have had many donations. This is to be a place of pilgrimage,' said Satyanarayan and swiftly changed the subject. 'What brings you here? The house with the treasure?' Satyanarayan prided himself on his long memory. 'Amma passed away a few years ago. Now you can buy it. Family is wanting to sell. They need it no more. I can arrange a meeting if you wish.'

The regal-sahib shook his head. 'Things have changed, Swami. I no longer have so much money that I can buy any house I like.'

Satyanarayan looked at the regal-sahib with surprise on hearing this; it seemed to him the only reason for outsiders to come to Mardpur was to buy huge chunks of it. 'Then for what are you here in Mardpur?'

The regal-sahib paused as if to consider this question. 'It is fate,' he answered.

Satyanarayan snorted inaudibly. He was a great believer in fate, but he also thought that fate did not bring one to any place in any aimless fashion. The purpose of fate must be evident at all times. He felt like saying this to the regal-sahib, but he was out of practice at giving people such advice, and feared that it would provoke the kind of discussion he no longer had time for.

'My car has broken down – it is a strange thing – on the same road it broke down before, eight years ago,' the regal-sahib said. His surprise at this coincidence seemed genuine but Satyanarayan, who had great experience in such things, saw nothing pre-ordained.

'Have you checked there are no nails in the road?'

'It was not the tyres.'

'Well then, you have been sold contaminated petrol at the last petrol station, same as before. These adulterators are the limit! They are giving Mardpur a bad name.'

'No. It is not that. I truly believe it was intended that I come here.'

Satyanarayan became very busy. He did not have time for those who were coming down in the world in a town where everyone was on the rise. And he did not have time to thrash out the mysteries of the regal-sahib's karma.

'Well, I must go. It is an important *puja* I have been called to. I wish you and your lady-wife good day.'

'Wife?' said the regal-sahib astonished. He looked behind him as if he expected to see a wife there. 'I have never married.'

Satyanarayan threw a cloth over his shoulder and picked up his bag. He said severely as if castigating a small child, 'You should have married when you were young and your father had status and wealth. It will be difficult now, even with your royal title. Who is wanting a poor prince, who is no longer even a prince, strictly speaking?'

'Poor? I am not exactly that. The debts have been paid off and the assets are secure. All I am saying is, it is not like before. I must make my own way like others around me.'

'Well,' said Satyanarayan, 'all the other royal families are in the same situation. Somewhere you can find a princess.' And he swept out of the temple with Guru, who had been waiting impatiently, but did not dare to break into the conversation. The regal-sahib watched Satyanarayan go, perched on the back of Guru's scooter, then left the temple himself. As he came down the old, cracked temple steps, he looked back and stared quietly at the board attached to the temple wall which heralded the work in progress. Raja Man Singh Mandir? What a person to name a temple after! It would be a temple to greed, he thought, bitterly.

75

DEEPA HAD NEVER BEEN TO GHATPUR. SHE KNEW THAT HER GRANDMOTHER had been cremated there on the banks of the river, but eight years ago she was just a child and had not been present. She remembered her mother had brought her to Vakilpur and then returned to Mardpur to organize the cremation, while Deepa shyly explored her new surroundings and got to know her sisters.

Thus, when Bharathi insisted that Deepa should be present at Raman's funeral, and, to Deepa's surprise, Ma did not oppose it, it was almost as if she were going on a pilgrimage to the place where Amma's ashes had entered the river.

For her part, Ma realized that being asked to attend the ceremony was a gesture of warmth. They were being invited into the family circle to share the intimacies including the sorrows. And so she accompanied Deepa on that short journey to Ghatpur.

It had not been easy finding a plain white sari. Deepa and Ma had come to Mardpur expecting to be dressed to impress and secure a match. They had not thought to pack plain saris or *dhotis*. And, because it was a member of the premier sari trading family of Mardpur who had died, the Sari Palace and Sari Mahal were securely padlocked.

'Where are the people buying saris these days?' Ma asked Usha-rani when they returned to Jagdishpuri Extension after an unfruitful trek from Kumar Bazaar.

'People are going to Ghatpur only for shopping,' said Usha, who was scrubbing the dishes with dung ash. 'Choice is better there. And there are many buses now. Few are shopping in Mardpur these days.' Usha shook her head. 'Laxman sahib and Vaman sahib were one-time very rich. But now sari business is having difficulties.'

'Not so much difficulties that they could not marry Raman's daughter well!' said Ma pointedly.

'Well, they are one old bania family of Mardpur,' Usha agreed. 'But Bharathi is getting a good marriage because Raman sahib is writing a book and becoming rich. Luckily older daughters of Raman sahib are married to sari trader family Ramanujans in Ghatpur and they are helping. Ghatpur sari business is good business.'

'Well,' said Ma, turning to Deepa, 'we will use old *dhotis* of Amma's; we cannot go to Ghatpur just to buy!'

'Everyone is doing it, *bahenji*,' Usha reassured Ma. 'Ghatpur is centre now for sari trade.'

Dressed in Amma's *dhoti*, Deepa sat by her ma and stared out of the bus window. There was no break in the buildings between Mardpur and Ghatpur. It had all merged into one town. And what of the buffaloes, Deepa wondered. Where were they to go? Her eyes searched for any patch of green where buffaloes might be grazing. She hoped secretly that she could spot Jhotta, convinced that she would recognize her immediately. But there was no *maidaan* and no buffaloes all the way to Ghatpur terminus.

The scooter-rickshaw they hired at the bus terminus shot skilfully through Ghatpur Bazaar and out the other side, buzzing and chirping with its high-pitched hooter as it careered along the road, past the sugar mills to the relative peacefulness of the *ghats*.

The acrid smell of burnt ghee mingled with the fragrance of sandalwood and the wood-smoke of previous cremations. Where the rickshaw dropped them off some pilgrims were bathing, oblivious of death around them. A funeral pile was being built, the contractor shouting as the workmen standing on top of the closely stacked pyre hauled up the scented sandalwood.

Some distance along the riverbank, Deepa and Ma saw a milling crowd around a large pyre. They guessed this must be Raman's, but realizing they might not be able to get near it, Deepa suggested they head away from the crowd and up some steps which led to a small temple overlooking the *ghats*. They climbed to the top and looked down on the people surrounding the large pile of sandalwood, the shape of a shrouded body discernible in its midst.

Deepa couldn't make out any faces from that distance, but intuitively she felt that the small sari-clad figure near the pyre was Kumud. Only one figure stood out, the rounded belly of Satyanarayan handing out red sacred thread. He was tying it around the wrist of a youth clad in a white *kurta*-pyjama, and Deepa imagined this must be Shanker.

'Palm-reading, *bahenji*?' said the fortune-teller, setting up his stool by Ma. He had followed them up the steps of the temple. Then, as Ma did not react, he looked out and took in the scene. 'It is the cremation of one Raman sahib, sari trading family of Mardpur,' he offered. 'He is writing one book. Many have come to have last *darshan* of great writer. People who are reading this book.'

'So many are reading?' murmured Ma.

'He was a great man,' said the fortune-teller. 'And I am only small man. Look, I am one reader and many palms; but for a writer it is one book and many readers.'

Chanting had started over the loudspeakers and Deepa saw Satyanarayan spooning ghee onto the pyre.

'From what did he die?' she asked the fortune-teller boldly. 'He was not old.'

'He was dying from lack of progress,' the fortune-teller said, pleased to display his knowledge of local events.

But Deepa looked quizzical.

'In Mardpur no one is using *tonga* now to travel,' the fortune-teller explained. 'Even in Ghatpur we are using scooter-rickshaw, cycle-rickshaw are only few. But Raman sahib is insisting on *tonga*. There is only one *tonga* with old-old horse. While Raman sahib is riding horse is rolling over and dying.' The fortune-teller rolled his eyes upwards and stuck out his tongue, leaning to one side. 'And *tonga* is rolling over also.'

Ma looked at the fortune-teller, stricken. '*Chup!*' she silenced him.

Deepa knew what her ma was thinking. How could she avoid thinking it herself – Dasji and baby Kamini underneath the *tonga* so many years ago? She was torn between wanting to know more about the circumstances of Raman's death and not wanting to sadden her mother.

But Ma pulled Deepa away. 'Do not listen to such *bakwas*. It is nonsense talking.'

'Palm-reading, *bahenji*,' the fortune-teller called after them hopefully as they moved further down the steps. But Ma ignored him.

'We must go down to the pyre,' she said.

'For what?' said Deepa in surprise. 'So many people are there. What will we see? From here we can see everything.'

'We are here so that we are seen, isn't it? Boy's mother must see us. Mrs Sharma must see that we are feeling part of the family.'

'But so many are here, not just the family!' said Deepa. Her words were lost. Ma was already heading down the temple steps and plunged into the crowd, pulling her reluctant daughter behind her. They wended their way through the crowd which was not as tightly packed as it appeared from the higher ground. It was mostly young men milling around, chatting and laughing, some of them holding copies of Raman's book, but all of them wearing white. Some of them leered and chirped at Deepa. She kept her head well down as she followed her mother, but she had noticed the red armbands worn by the men.

Ma and Deepa got to the front just as Shanker applied the torch to the pyre which, well soaked in ghee, burst suddenly into flames, pushing them back. She buried her face in Ma's plump arm and felt the heat of the fire against the side of her head as a cry went up: 'Raman *zindabad*! Jagat Singh *zindabad*!'

'We must find them,' Ma said, trying to lead Deepa around the pyre. But there was so much smoke Deepa held back, coughing.

'I cannot see them,' she said, trying to pull her mother back into the crowd.

'They must see us,' said Ma, her face already glistening with the heat. Dark patches appeared on the back of her blouse and at her armpits. The crowd had moved back a little.

'Too much smoke,' said Deepa.

Ma looked at Deepa and appeared to change her mind. 'Maybe it is not such a good idea, your face is shiny and there are black-black marks.'

Deepa wiped away some more ash, leaving another black smear.

'You are not looking your best,' said Ma; 'we should return.'

Deepa was only too happy to consent. They moved away, back through the crowd, and walked along the riverbank away from the pyre. An older man, wizened and stooped, was standing some distance away from the crowd with a middle-aged man.

'He was not so old,' the old man was saying, echoing what Deepa had said earlier.

Deepa strained to catch the reply.

'But he had already married all three of his daughters. His life's work was over. What else is there to do but die when your work is complete?'

Deepa could hear the crackling and burning, and the sound of Vedic chanting over the loudspeakers.

'Was it like this for Amma?' she said suddenly, turning to Ma.

Ma stopped and looked down at her in surprise. 'It was here, only,' she said, 'but there was no one. No crowd. Just a few relatives and Satyanarayan Swami.'

Deepa looked back and saw the flames rising above the crowd. Soon the ashes would be gathered and scattered in the river, just as Amma's had been, ending perhaps in the same place, after a separate long journey through life.

76

IT WAS ALMOST A FORTNIGHT BEFORE MA AND DEEPA WENT TO THE doctor's house again.

Ma chafed at the delay. Not knowing the sari trading family at all well, she had no reason to go to the lychee garden herself to pay respects, and it never occurred to her that Deepa had any reason to want to. The cremation had been enough for her. She was even more pleased she had been there, despite not being seen by any member of the family, when the Ghatpur ceremony became the talk of the town.

'Son came to light the pyre,' Usha told Deepa. 'Maybe he will have to come back to look after his ma now. All alone she will be in the lychee garden.' She shook her head. 'So much money and that house is still the old-old house. No money was spent on that old bungalow in so many years.'

'But it was a pleasant bungalow,' commented Deepa, remembering the happy, carefree days she had spent there. She had spent so much time in the garden that she had hardly noticed that the bungalow was lacking in anything.

Deepa contented herself with rediscovering the house in Jagdishpuri Extension, where the warm smell of pickles seemed to be getting stronger each day they stayed there. She went out into the yard where Jhotta had once stood, enjoying the familiarity of Jhotta's old feeding trough, empty and dusty with a layer of hardened mud at the bottom from several monsoons past. Deepa bent down to examine the scuff marks in the ground for any shape that might suggest Jhotta's hoof.

Ma called her in. 'Why are you making your sari dirty, Deepa? Come inside. If you stay in the sunshine so long your skin will become black. Then who will marry you? Not Shyam, for sure.'

'The doctor's family is supposed to be so modern,' murmured Deepa. But Ma did not hear.

Only Usha-rani heard. She said, 'Your ma is right. Modern families don't care about dowry and caste and all, but dark skin they do not like.'

Deepa just laughed, hitched her cotton sari between her legs and began her dance practice. She practised every day, the flowing gentle lines of Odissi, like a temple sculpture coming to life. She liked the courtyard with its shadows, and she danced in and out of them feeling the alternating coolness and heat of the ground with her feet. On the hot ground where the sun fell she danced fast, lifting her feet quickly; in the shade she danced slowly, cooling her hot feet.

Usha-rani watched her. She always cooked, washed and cleaned in the courtyard. She said she did not like the pickle smell in the kitchen.

'It is too strong. See, it is sticking to my clothes even,' and she sniffed the end of her *pallav* to show how persistent and clinging the smell had become. But Deepa felt energized by the pickle smell which reminded her of Amma. She danced to its scent, feeling its heady aroma as she moved.

'You are good at dancing,' Usha-rani said with appreciation. 'You must dance for Shyam. He will not resist.'

Deepa stood marking time with a few gentle steps, her arms on her hips, resting before the next sequence. 'In a modern match there is no dancing, no singing, no performance,' she explained to Usha-rani.

'No? How then is a boy to decide if he likes a girl? She must be accomplished.'

'In a modern match,' said Deepa dreamily, 'the boy and the girl talk, and if they like each other they agree to the match.'

'Oho? And what is it they are talking about?'

'Oh,' Deepa shrugged, herself unsure, 'about music, art, life.'

'Oho, talking about music and dance instead of watching it! And from that the girl and boy must know if they like one another?'

'There must be understanding,' said Deepa dreamily. 'A meeting of minds. You must not just like what you see on the surface, but look underneath.'

'So, everything is revealed by talking?'

Deepa did not respond. She launched into the next sequence of the dance: the smooth gait of Rama, pulling an arrow from his quiver, fitting it to his bow, and then launching it forth with a graceful spring. And then Sita with her perfect, coy beauty.

'*Wah!*' praised Usha-rani. 'Any prince would want such a Sita! From your dance any boy can see into your soul. For Shyam you should dance. He is not interested in talking. For what are you dancing, if not to get a good match? After you are married, you will not be dancing any more.'

'I will go with Shyam to Orissa, and I will learn with a guru,' said Deepa, and launched into a more energetic sequence of her dance.

Usha-rani carried on with her cleaning. Only when Deepa had finished, Usha-rani repeated, 'What is this modern way of a boy and girl talking? Do not talk to Shyam, dance for him.'

It was Bharathi who urged her mother-in-law to call Deepa to meet Shyam as soon as Raman's funeral was over.

'You should not worry about such things so soon after your father's passing away,' said Mrs Sharma. But Bharathi insisted.

'I need a sister,' she said. 'It would give me pleasure to have a sister like Deepa.'

'Very well, it is true they have come from far, and Shyam too. We should have a meeting now between them,' Mrs Sharma said.

Shyam was strangely reluctant. He knew only too well why he had been called home, but he had insisted he could not remember Deepa however much Bharathi, Govind, Nalini and Mrs Sharma tried to jog his memory.

'How can you forget a girl who stayed in your own parents' house?' exclaimed Mrs Sharma.

'I know the one you are meaning,' said Shyam sullenly – he had grown into a serious, studious boy. 'It was her grandmother who had *bhooths* in the house.'

'Shyam,' coaxed his mother, feeling the unwillingness in her son, 'those are children's stories. The grandmother died many years ago. There are no *bhooths* anywhere.'

Nalini teased: 'You think you will end up married to a *bhooth*!' She made a scary face at him then laughed wickedly.

'In the Mission school there were *bhooths*,' said Shyam grumpily.

Govind laughed. 'Where were the *bhooths* in the Mission school?'

Mrs Sharma was terse. 'Every *bhooth* was not Amma's doing. What did Amma have to do with the Mission school?'

Shyam was silent. The truth was, he did not feel ready for marriage. It had been sprung on him without any warning. It was Bharathi who insisted that Shyam should see Deepa so soon after his arrival. Shyam had not been blind to the way Sudha-with-Pension had pushed the match between her niece and his brother, and now he suspected some ulterior motive of Bharathi's in pushing the match between him and Deepa. Not that Shyam disliked his sister-in-law particularly, he just felt that Bharathi's family, a family of traders, had pushed their way into a match with the doctor's family in order to gain respectability. They had money by virtue of Raman's book, but they were still of the trading class, whatever their financial status.

Shyam was determined not to be used. He felt there were far too many social climbers in Mardpur since the town had become a centre for trade. The fact was, whatever Dr and Mrs Sharma liked to think about the way they had brought up their children, unhampered by caste prejudices, Shyam was not as modern as they liked to suppose. It mattered little that Deepa was actually descended from one of the oldest Brahmin families of Mardpur. To him, she belonged to this grasping, materialistic town which seemed to have forgotten its roots. And Shyam did not want to have anything to do with it.

Yet, it was true, he hardly remembered the girl. Only that she was quiet and strange and had not talked to him much when they were children. And now to be expected to marry this creature was too much!

'What is the hurry?' he said, when the family discussed Deepa again. 'I have just come from Orissa, I need a rest.'

'It is better you see the girl earlier and then spend the rest of the time deciding,' reasoned his mother.

'But it is so soon after a death. It is not decent,' protested Shyam.

'What to do?' sighed Mrs Sharma in exasperation.

'I have something to give to Deepa, from my father,' Bharathi said. 'It was his last wish, please call her here,' she pleaded with Mrs Sharma.

Shyam turned away. His mother always gave in to Bharathi. So keen was she not to appear the traditional, strict domineering mother-in-law that, in his view, she erred on the side of spoiling her daughter-in-law.

And so Deepa made her second visit to the doctor's family to meet Shyam, who refused to look at her, let alone say a single word in her presence. There was an embarrassed silence in the room, then Mrs Sharma suggested that she, Dr Sharma and Deepa's ma leave the younger people to, 'discuss things of interest to only themselves'. Shyam was still refusing to cooperate, despite the entreating looks from Bharathi to at least make an effort. Finally, tired of being put under such pressure, Shyam walked out of the room, leaving Bharathi and Govind embarrassed and Deepa slightly perplexed.

At that point Bharathi got up and came back with a cloth-bag. It was the same cloth-bag that Deepa had given Bharathi eight years earlier when Amma had died. She looked inside and there were all the notebooks, hers and Raman's. She looked curiously at the notebooks from Ahuja Book Depot and recognized her own childish hand. She looked at the notebooks that Raman had filled: the notebooks that had become the book that had brought wealth to Bharathi's family.

'They are for you, Deepa,' Bharathi said. 'They are yours, now.'

'Oh, no,' said Deepa, 'they are your father's. It was his story.'

'Well,' said Bharathi, 'he is no more. So I am returning them to you. What will I do with them? The house in the lychee garden will be taken over and who knows what will happen to these books then? They will be thrown out somewhere.' She had a significant look in her eyes when she turned to Deepa, as if there were more to tell but this was not the right time to tell it. Deepa said nothing and took the bag.

'You should take what is rightly yours,' Govind broke in. 'If you do not claim what is yours you will lose it.'

Deepa tried to avoid Govind's penetrating stare. You are marrying Shyam, she reminded herself. You are marrying Shyam.

Bharathi said in a low voice, 'It was you and Amma who helped my father with the book. Without the book he would not have had money. And I could not have married into such a good family. They are so kind to me, Deepa. That is why I want you to marry Shyam. I want you to be as happy as I am.' Once again she looked as if there were more she wanted to say.

★

Lunch was an uneasy meal. Shyam was still refusing to talk. He seemed angry and sullen. His puzzled parents and Bharathi did their best to cover for him, while the quiet ones, Govind and Deepa's ma, were polite and formal.

Ma was genuinely worried. She was not so sure it was such a good idea to consult Shyam so early in the proceedings. It would have been better if auspicious dates for the nuptials and other details had been fixed between the two families first, and then the girl and boy allowed to meet, knowing full well that the wedding would go ahead anyway. But to give so much power to the young man, who clearly did not know what he wanted, seemed wrong. Ma did not know where she stood. Mrs Sharma had written a letter to her expressing an interest in her daughter, and then it appeared it was the boy who must make the final decision.

It was towards the end of the meal that Shyam suddenly put down his spoon, cleared his throat and made his announcement.

'I have been thinking,' he said in a ringing tone, 'and I have decided I do not want this girl, Deepa, to be my wife.'

77

MA COULD NOT GET AWAY FROM THE DOCTOR'S HOUSE FAST ENOUGH. SHE urged the rickshaw-wala to pedal faster, faster.

'Memsahib, if I am going faster I will be crashing into rickshaw-wala in front. And he is of Latku gang.'

'*Chup!*' said Ma. 'What nonsense are you talking? *Jaldi karo!*'

'Memsahib, Latku gang is owning half the rickshaws in Mardpur and Murgaon. They will kill me and my sons and my son's sons if I am doing damage to their rickshaws.'

'Oh? And how do you know it is a rickshaw of theirs?'

'Memsahib, he is wearing red band.'

Deepa noticed it too, when the rickshaw-wala pointed it out: around the left upper-arms of a number of rickshaw-walas was tied a red kerchief. This was an aspect of Mardpur she had never seen. In the past all the townspeople had to worry about was whether there were ghosts in her grandmother's house. Now there were far more serious threats.

'Sometimes they are fighting for nothing, just creating trouble so that they can destroy our rickshaws, memsahib. If I knock the back of his rickshaw, that will be the end of me!'

'Okay, okay,' said Ma, silencing him. 'Just go quickly.'

Only when they were some way away from Jodhpuri Extension did

Ma say anything. 'He could not even wait to tell his *maa-baap* quietly after we were gone. No, he wanted to humiliate us to our faces,' she said bitterly.

Dr and Mrs Sharma had been extremely embarrassed and tried to excuse their son. 'He is tired from his journey, he does not know what he is saying,' said Mrs Sharma.

'Just wait, in a few days he will have had time to think and will change his mind,' said Dr Sharma.

But Deepa and Bharathi had no illusions. 'Deepa, I am so sorry, so sorry,' said Bharathi as Deepa was leaving. She looked so downcast, as if she had been the one rejected, not Deepa.

'I don't mind,' said Deepa, who was not sure if she did or not. The full impact of what Shyam had said had not yet hit her. She had heard his words, she knew they referred to her, but they had not sunk in. She was more worried about the humiliation her mother felt than her own. 'I did not want Shyam anyway,' she said resolutely. That at least was true.

Bharathi put her hand gently over Deepa's mouth. 'Don't say that. He may still want you.'

But Deepa shook her head. 'I don't think so.'

'Oh, Deepa! What will become of you?'

Deepa had no answer to that. Her dreams had evaporated, even her most cherished dream of one day going to Orissa to study dance.

In the doctor's house there was turmoil once Deepa and Ma had departed. Dr Sharma had retired with his newspaper, preferring to avoid conflict. But Mrs Sharma was angry.

'What was the need to speak out in front of the girl and her mother? They are one of the oldest Brahmin families in Mardpur and they are not good enough for you?'

'You said it was my choice,' Shyam said sullenly.

'But you know what we want. Why would we bring her here from so far away and you all the way from Orissa if we did not want this match?'

'You said it was my choice,' Shyam repeated adamantly.

'And what about the choice of the girl? She had chosen you already or she would not be here!'

Shyam sighed. He knew that underneath it all, he had not really had a choice and that his assent was a mere formality. But he did not regret what he had done.

Dr Sharma came out to tackle his son in his own calm way. 'So, what is your explanation, boy, for this behaviour?'

'It was my choice.'

'That is true. We always said it was your choice. But you must explain to us why you made this decision. You must make a choice but you must understand why you made it so that the next time you can make a better choice.'

Shyam shrugged; he knew that after the humiliation he had heaped on both families there was no repairing the damage. The match was well and truly out of the question, despite the pressure his parents were putting on him. He felt safe.

'So,' said Dr Sharma. 'What is your explanation?'

'I did not like the girl.'

'Is she not beautiful? She is intelligent. We know she is homely, did she not stay in our house?' said Mrs Sharma.

'She was my best friend,' added Bharathi, 'like my own sister, she is a good girl for you, my brother.'

Shyam sighed again. 'It is not what I want.'

'What is it you want?' said Dr and Mrs Sharma together.

Shyam shook his head. 'I want something more.' He hesitated, then continued, 'She should have some accomplishment, some talent.'

They were all leaning towards him to understand what he was trying to say. The parents were determined not to make the same mistake twice, eager to hear what their son wanted.

'What kind of talent?' said Mrs Sharma gently.

Then it came out in a rush. 'In Bhubaneswar there is someone I like.'

They drew back with shock. Their son was asking for a love-match! The questions tumbled out pell-mell. Who is she? What is her caste? What does her father do? Is she college-educated?

Shyam swept aside the onslaught. 'She is a dancer.'

'A dancer!' Dr and Mrs Sharma did not know what to make of this. They sat back and digested it.

But Shyam was rapt with the memory of the girl he had seen in Orissa. 'She is beautiful and graceful. And through her dance I can see her soul. That is the girl I want — expressive.'

Dr and Mrs Sharma were torn between urging Shyam to take time to reflect and get over his infatuation with this dancer, and making subtle enquiries about the girl herself and her family.

'In Orissa they are tribals, no?' Dr Sharma said to his wife.

'Is this girl a tribal, Shyam?' said Mrs Sharma severely.

'I don't know.'

'In Orissa they are dark-skinned, the girls,' Mrs Sharma moaned.

'Is she dark-skinned, Shyam?' Dr Sharma asked.

'Not for me,' said Shyam.

'Is she college-educated?'

'I don't know.'

'You don't know? How is it possible you don't know?' said Dr Sharma, exasperated.

'I have seen her only twice,' Shyam said defensively. 'I did not talk to her to ask her all these things. Both times she was dancing. There is so much you can learn from a girl dancing.'

Mrs Sharma snorted. 'So you are in love with the dance, that is all.'

'Well, Shyam,' said Dr Sharma, getting up. He thought it wise to leave matters to rest for a while. 'I am disappointed. There is no use hiding it. We have brought you up in a modern way but we did not expect you to run wild!'

'I will not have my son marrying a dancing-girl,' sniffed Mrs Sharma.

When Ma finally calmed down, once Jodhpuri Extension was well out of sight, she said, 'Let us go to the temple, Deepa, and pray for you.'

Deepa knew it was not so much for her daughter that Ma wanted to pray but for some inner peace of mind.

They stepped out of the rickshaw at the temple. For once it seemed quiet there, the vendors leaning against the walls, relaxed and lethargic. They did not even call out to Ma and Deepa to implore them to buy their wares. Ma bought some flowers. They entered the temple and together scattered the flowers onto the deity, forgetting the outside world in that simple act of offering.

Bhole proffered them *persaad* and they went outside to sit under the tree to eat it, under the gaze of the white marble Ganesh, the remover of obstacles, the performer of miracles. There in the cool breeze, Deepa and Ma felt healed again. Deepa wondered if they would leave Mardpur soon, now that the match had not materialized. She wanted to ask Ma. But she had sensed that Ma herself had not decided.

'Perhaps we will, after all, have to think of a dowry for you,' Ma said. 'It was too good to be true. Look at the luck of some! That Bharathi, daughter of a trader, marries the doctor's eldest son, with no dowry or anything. Her father was known as a good-for-nothing lay-about in Mardpur.'

'He wrote a book, Ma,' said Deepa. She still had the cloth-bag that Bharathi had given her. It did not feel as if it should belong to her. She had enjoyed helping Raman spin the yarn with Amma, but once the story was over, she felt no involvement.

'Anyone can write!' said Ma. 'Satyanarayan Swami is saying someone wrote it for him.'

'It was his own story,' said Deepa with conviction. She did not mention her own role, or Amma's, in the writing.

Ma sighed. 'Anyway, what good does it do us? We have still not found a boy for you. Let us go back to Jagdishpuri Extension. That house I must sell. It has brought nothing but bad luck ever since your father died.'

It was the first time Deepa had heard her mention him. 'Who will buy?' she asked. 'Everyone thinks there are *bhooths* there.'

'And there are some who think there is treasure,' said Ma thoughtfully. 'We have to sell to one who believes more in treasure than *bhooths*. Come.'

Deepa followed her dutifully, completely forgetting the bag of notebooks under the banyan tree.

78

MA AND DEEPA BARELY STEPPED OUTSIDE THE OLD COURTYARD HOUSE.
Deepa had no reason to go out, preferring the homely warm pickle smell,
comforting in its familiarity. Ma decided to sort through Amma's old
trunks.

'If the house is to be sold we will have to empty it of Amma's old
things. Who will want all this?' said Ma.

'Maybe the treasure is in there,' said Deepa, watching her open the first
trunks. They were full of embroidered tablecloths, napkins and other
linens. She examined the neat tiny embroidery stitches and realized with
some surprise that they must have been made when Amma's sight was still
very good. A very long time ago.

'You, too, are talking about treasure!' chided Ma light-heartedly.

'Then what happened to the jewels that Amma brought back from the
courts of the kings?' Deepa asked her mother. 'No one has seen them.'

'They were sold when I was married,' answered Ma, 'and some I took
with me when I married.' Her eyes clouded momentarily, for of course
she was thinking of Dasji. Deepa wanted to say, But there was much
more! And Amma has said I would find it, but she could see that Ma did
not want to talk further about it. It brought back too many memories that
she did not want to be reminded of.

'What to do with all those pickle-pots?' Ma said, her hands on her hips and her brow furrowed from staring up at the rows of terracotta pots on the high shelf in the kitchen. 'We cannot eat so much pickle. There is enough for eating our whole lives! For what was Amma making so many pickles?'

'She never gave them away,' remembered Deepa. She took the pickle-pots so much for granted it hardly occurred to her to think they would be a problem. 'Amma just made more and more!'

'They are good pickles, there is no doubt. I have already tried some myself while I have been here. A little bit of lime, a little bit of mango and even some hot chilli. Oho, it was sharp!' And Ma brought in her breath sharply as if remembering the hot chilli. 'But there is so much there! Some of it I will take back to Vakilpur. At Jindal's I will buy glass jars. Such earthen pots we cannot carry.'

Deepa nodded and the pleasant thought occurred that it would bring the pickle smell to Vakilpur and remind her of Amma. She liked the idea.

Meanwhile Ma made three piles of linen. One was for Deepa's trousseau. What Deepa did not need, she would keep for her other daughters in another pile. There was a third pile for things that would have to be discarded or given away – linens with black spots of fungus on them, from many years of storage, pillow slips with tea-coloured stains, old *dhotis* of Amma's, well-worn and frayed at the edges.

Deepa imagined Amma standing in her *dhoti*, feeling her way along the walls as she moved around the house. She picked up an old *dhoti* and sniffed. Among the mustiness and the clean smell of cotton thread were still traces of pickle smell, clinging to the well-worn fabric. She went into the courtyard and again examined the ground for Jhotta's marks.

'I'm back, Amma,' she whispered into the buffalo's old trough. 'I am here, but where is the treasure?'

She heard the faint echo of her own voice: 'Where? Where?' Then scolded herself. Stop thinking about treasure that is not there! Do not dream about things you cannot have! And she ran off to find her ankle-bells and practise her dance under Usha-rani's appreciative gaze. It was the only way she could stop herself thinking about the past.

In the trauma of being spurned by Shyam, Deepa had completely forgotten the bag of notebooks. She had even forgotten that Bharathi had ever given it to her, let alone that she might have left it somewhere. Then one day, a week after they had left the doctor's house in that hurried fashion, a young, goat-faced messenger arrived at Jagdishpuri Extension. He was a kind of dogsbody at the temple.

'Satyanarayan Swami is calling you to be present at one very, very important meeting of the *panchayat*,' he announced to Ma in a state of some excitement. 'Satyanarayan is important member of the *panchayat*,' he added in case Ma was not aware of the Brahmin's elevated status. 'He is the one who decides everything.'

'What does the *panchayat* have to do with me?' said Ma, perplexed. 'I have no complaint against the government or municipal authority. I have no dispute with family members over property. I am not demanding for a road to be built or a rubbish dump to be moved away from my house.'

'Have you not been reading the newspaper, memsahib?' goat-face said in astonishment. He did not read the newspaper himself, for he could barely read, but everything everyone said in Mardpur these days was prefixed with the qualification that it was in the newspaper, and that, from what he could make out, made it true. Everything else was mere hearsay, gossip. He knew Ma was an educated woman and could not believe she was ignorant of the story the whole town had been talking about for some days now. Jagdishpuri Extension was not the centre of town, but it was not *that* far away.

'I do not read the newspaper,' said Ma. 'It is full of bad news of floods and droughts.'

The goat-face contemplated this with interest; he would repeat this to the next person who asked him if he had read the newspaper. He had never known what to say before.

'It is all being written about in the newspaper,' he said importantly. 'Mardpur is being thrown upside down, the newspaper said.'

Ma had not noticed that Mardpur was any different, although she had to admit that she had hardly stirred outside the house in Jagdishpuri Extension.

'Why?'

Goat-face was so excited, he hardly knew where to start. 'It was the death of Raman sahib only last week. The one of the lychee garden on the hill above Kumar Junction, the place that is now called Kumar Extension.'

'What of it? It is known to all. He was young. He should have lived for another twenty years. But at least he had married his daughter and married her well. And he has a son who will look after his widow. He must have died in peace.' Ma said this without rancour, despite her feelings about the doctor's family, who she knew was related to Raman through Govind's marriage.

The boy was so excited now that he was stuttering, 'He – He, that is Raman I am talking – did not write the b-book that has made him so famous. It is what the newspaper said.'

'That is not new,' said Ma dismissively. 'Others have been saying. But I do not believe it.'

'But now it is different,' said the boy. 'Now notebooks have been found in which it is all written.' He waited for this to sink in and then added, 'And it is not all in Raman sahib's handwriting.'

Even Ma became curious. 'Whose writing is it?'

'You have not heard?' said goat-face, clearly enjoying telling the story with a measure of suspense.

'Where should I hear?'

'*Everyone* is talking in Mardpur,' said goat-face. 'Old-old notebooks were found in the temple by Satyanarayan Swami. It is one more miracle happening in the temple, Satyanarayan Swami has said. It is he who is saying it is not Raman sahib's handwriting.'

'Then whose?'

'It has not been discovered. But some are saying it is Deepa *bahen*'s.' The boy stepped back to survey the impact of his words on Ma. But he was disappointed in not getting a more dramatic reaction from her.

Ma smiled. 'Deepa wrote the book? I don't think so. How can it be? She was a child at that time. When I took her away from here she was only twelve and she has not been back since then.'

'Memsahib, that is why there is a special meeting of the *panchayat*. To find out who is the writer.'

'But the book is already published, so what is the necessity?'

'Well,' said the boy, hardly containing his excitement, 'Satyanarayan Swami is saying the person who wrote the book will own the lychee garden. Satyanarayan Swami is saying that today. He was standing in the temple telling many-many newspaper-walas. I have seen it! So many newspaper-walas are coming from everywhere to write about this special *panchayat* meeting. From Delhi also. Everybody is waiting for the arrival of Deepa *bahen*. If she is the one writing the book, she will be the owner of the lychee garden!'

Ma did not know what to make of this. It sounded so far-fetched, and she did not see the connection between the book and the lychee garden. She looked at the note, an officious-looking missive which asked that

Deepa, not Ma – even though it was addressed to her – should be present at the *panchayat* meeting in the temple extension that afternoon. It gave no hint of what the meeting was about.

Ma gave the goat-face a coin and sent him off. She glanced at Deepa, wrapped up in her dance, her body swaying from side to side, her head swinging. Ma realized with regret that if she had not shorn Deepa's hair in the modern way, there would be a long plait swinging there behind her shoulders adding to the graceful effect. Deepa was not beautiful in the classical sense, but she was graceful and expressive. She was certainly a dancer who did not fail to draw the attention of those around her.

Ma called Usha-rani. Usha-rani knew everything that was going on in Mardpur.

'Usha, what is it everyone is talking about in Mardpur these days?'

'The price of ghee, memsahib. It is going up and up—'

'No, no. Not that. Something else.'

'The price of gold. Per *tael* it is—'

'No, Usha,' said Ma patiently. 'There is talk about something completely new since Raman died, the one of the lychee garden.'

'Oho!' said Usha-rani, slapping her forehead in exasperation that she did not realize before what Ma was asking. 'Yes. There has been too much talk.'

'What are they saying?'

'They are saying he did not write the book that made him so rich.'

'Then who wrote it?' Ma looked closely at Usha-rani.

'Some are saying Deepa *bahen* wrote it, but of course I know it cannot be true. Only a child she was at that time.'

'And others are saying what?'

'Others are saying even Amma wrote it.'

'Amma?' said Ma in some surprise.

'Your ma. Dictating to Deepa *bahen*, they say, for she was blind.'

Ma shook her head in disbelief. 'I do not know who is inventing these tales. It is the same people who are inventing the *bhooths* and the treasure.'

'But *bhooths* and treasure is different,' said Usha-rani.

'How?'

'There is nothing to be gained from *bhooths* and treasure. But Satyanarayan Swami has said the person who really wrote the book, if it is proved, must get the lychee garden.'

'How can they give? The land is belonging to the sari trading family.'

'Papers were found in one notary office in Ghatpur. These papers are saying lychee garden will belong to the one who wrote the book. Satyanarayan Swami is saying this. He is telling the newspaper-walas and they are writing it. That is what everyone is reading.'

'How can Satyanarayan Swami say this, it is not his land to give away!'

'He is saying if Raman sahib did not write the book, he has stolen it from someone so the land is also stolen and must be given back.'

'So? That is the business of the family of Raman. Not of Satyanarayan.'

'Everyone's business is Swamiji's business,' said Usha-rani with equanimity.

Without denigrating Satyanarayan's accomplishments, Ma thought the priest was not exactly a good thing for Mardpur. But she kept her thoughts to herself. It was not good to criticize a Brahmin before a servant.

'Why did you not tell me all this before, Usha?'

Usha-rani shrugged. 'I was not believing it. How could Deepa, who is such a beautiful dancer, write such a book? I am hearing the book is about smugglers and *goondas*.'

'There are *goondas* in Mardpur,' said Ma, thinking about the rickshaw-wala's fear of the Latku gang.

'Back then, when the book was written, there were none,' said Usha-rani. 'It is only now that these *goondas* are here.' She sighed. 'Mardpur has changed too fast. It is not good. When I go back to my village there is nothing to do there. All the old cottage industries have died because of the factories.'

Ma did not think it was the right time to listen to Usha-rani on the subject of the economic development of Mardpur. 'I should go to buy the newspaper,' she said. 'This afternoon Deepa and I must go to a special *panchayat* meeting. We must be prepared. In the Old Market I shall find the newspaper. It is not so far. I could walk, even. But there is so much traffic and dust, I will take a rickshaw. Tell Deepa I will be back soon. I will not disturb her dance practice.'

Usha-rani ran to hail a rickshaw for Ma and then went back to finish her tasks as Deepa danced around her, oblivious of what was going on.

Shortly after Ma left, a scooter chuntered towards the bungalow and stopped outside.

'Bharathi!' cried Deepa when she saw her. They embraced.

'Your dancing is beautiful, Deepa. I have never seen it before.'

Deepa laughed. 'I am lucky to have a good guru.' She sat in the shade to take off her ankle-bells, patting the ground beside her for Bharathi to sit. Bharathi smoothed her sari beneath her so that it would not get crushed before sitting down. She looked sad.

'You are sad because your father died,' said Deepa, struggling with the knot of her ankle-bells. 'I was not able to pay my respects to your family in person.'

'Many people came,' said Bharathi, with a faraway look on her face. 'But now no one wants to know us. Ma is crying every day. She does not know what the future will be.'

'But she has the lychee garden. And Shanker will take care of her.'

'No, Deepa. You have been away for so long you do not know what is happening here. Papa died only one week ago and already they are wanting to take away the lychee garden. What will my ma do? Where will she go?'

'Who will take it away?'

Bharathi sighed. 'I will tell you the whole story. When my sisters Meera and Mamta were to be married, Papa took a loan. It was for the dowry. Ramanujan family was asking very high price, for their business was a very important sari business in Ghatpur. But Papa did not pay one *paisa* back of this loan. And now he is gone. So now the man who is giving the loan is asking to take the land to get back the loan money. And now the notary is saying the land does not belong to Papa, but the writer of his book.'

'So the person who wrote must pay all the loan money or lose the land?' said Deepa, trying to follow this complex tale.

'Yes. That means that whatever happens, Ma will lose the lychee garden. Where will she go?'

'But the writer of the book was Raman Uncle!' said Deepa.

'Some are saying it was not Papa,' said Bharathi. She took Deepa's hand. 'Deepa, we were friends together for so long. I saw how that book was written, with you and Amma. Amma has passed away, but you also were the writer. And you see, that is why I wanted you to marry Shyam.' Bharathi paused to wipe her tears and Deepa put her arm around her friend's shoulders and squeezed them, to let her know she did not hold against her what had happened with Shyam.

Bharathi went on: 'Just before Papa died, Govind and I went to the notary in Ghatpur to sign some papers for a small piece of land that Govind's father was giving to us as a marriage gift. There we discovered about the deeds for the lychee garden in Papa's file. You see, the notary at first thought the land was coming from Papa and not Govind's father, so he brought out the wrong file. We had already seen the papers inside before we told him his mistake.'

Bharathi stopped again, pensive. Finally she said, 'I knew with you as my sister the lychee garden would be safe. Ma could stay. Everything would be fine. But then Papa died and it has become known to everyone about the garden.'

'How did everyone know?'

'It was Satyanarayan. He knows everything in Mardpur.'

'Who has told Satyanarayan?' said Deepa.

But Bharathi did not know, and seemed less concerned about such details than what would happen in the future. 'The garden is yours, Deepa! You are the writer of the book!'

'No!' said Deepa.

Bharathi did not hear her. 'They were so pleased about you, but Shyam—' She shook her head at the memory of it. 'Now I do not know what will happen to the garden and my poor ma.' She held Deepa's hand with both her own. 'Promise me, Deepa, promise you will not turn my ma out from her home.'

'What are you talking, Bharathi? How can I do it? Kumud Aunty is like a mother to me. But you are wrong. I did not write this book. Raman Uncle wrote it. It was his book. It was his own thoughts that he wrote. Amma could read his thoughts for she had such a talent, but she could not think of such a book. And I had no thoughts at all about this book, I was writing only what Amma was telling, because she was blind. It was not my book and not Amma's book.'

'You are being called to stand before the *panchayat* and tell who wrote the book,' said Bharathi pointedly.

Deepa had not heard about this, but it changed nothing. 'No matter,' she said, 'I will say what I have said to you. And you must keep the lychee garden and pay back the loan so that Kumud Aunty can stay there in peace.'

'Even if she can stay, how will we pay so much loan and eight years' interest? The garden will be gone! But if the garden is yours, you can find the treasure of Amma and the loan can be paid!'

It was easy to dream, Deepa thought ruefully, but there was no treasure. 'Bharathi,' she said gently, 'you must understand: I am not the writer of the book.'

'Today only the *panchayat* is calling you. They will prove. They have the notebooks, and I have seen inside these notebooks for they are the ones I gave you. Someone has taken them from you. Your writing is inside, everyone can see.'

'*Baapré*,' breathed Deepa. She remembered only then the bag of notebooks Bharathi had given her. She had not brought them home, she realized, but had left them somewhere. And now they had been found.

79

SATYANARAYAN WAS PLEASED THAT THE TEMPLE EXTENSION HAD BEEN finished in time for such an important event. The Brahmin donned a freshly pressed cream silk *kurta* over his *dhoti* and surveyed the hall with the kind of satisfaction afforded a king surveying his private domain.

The deities at one end of the large hall had been curtained off with thick, luxurious velvet donated by a Ghatpur textile magnate. Sheets donated by the Ghatpur textile mills were laid on the ground, spotless and uncreased. The hall was well lit by fluorescent tubes donated by Jetco, wiring courtesy of Jindal. All these people would have their names written in gold below that of Satyanarayan Swami as 'Founder', on a marble plaque which was still being chiselled by a stonemason in a village on the outskirts of Vakilpur. It had been a difficult task to find a stonemason. They had all disappeared. No one wanted to work these days, thought Satyanarayan.

Once they found a stonemason, old but still able to carve beautifully, Satyanarayan himself travelled there to supervise the chiselling and ensure that the names were in the right order with the most important, the really big donors, at the top.

Everyone had wanted to give something for this new temple extension. Yet strangely enough no one had yet given their name to this beautiful new hall. Never mind, thought Satyanarayan, soon it would enter common parlance as Satyanarayan Hall; after all, was it not he who had done so much work to ensure it happened? Satyanarayan deliberately avoided urging the temple committee to think of a name. He had already begun to prime Bhole to think of it as Satyanarayan Hall in asking for donations.

'A little extra donation for the hall, *babu*?' Bhole would say after each small *puja* ceremony he conducted.

'What hall?'

'Why, the Satyanarayan Hall, the extension to the temple. Have you not seen? Go, go now and look at this beautiful building donated by the people of Mardpur. Satyanarayan Swami you will find there, directing the work.'

Impressed, they referred to it thereafter as Satyanarayan Hall.

Satyanarayan had been hard at work badgering the labourers to finish the extension on time. He feared Deepa and Ma would return to Vakilpur if it were delayed any longer. Deepa's presence was crucial.

Really, he had intended to open the extension after the *yatra* to the holy city of Hardwar where the goddess Laxmi would be dipped in the river Ganges and blessed by the high priests before being brought back to Mardpur to be permanently installed in the temple. All that would have to wait, thought Satyanarayan. In this modern age pragmatism was the key. Orthodoxy had also been known to block progress.

When Deepa and Ma arrived in the afternoon the hall was already crowded and abuzz with chatter. Even neighbours hardly had the time nowadays to meet and talk to each other. For that matter there was not much entertainment in the town, and, if nothing else, this gathering was expected to be quite entertaining.

Deepa drew back on entering the hall. She did not like large crowds, but Bhole was promptly at her side and led her to the front where she would sit to the left of the *panchayat* members, he explained.

Once settled, Deepa began to pick out some of the people she knew. There was Madhu, thinner than ever, with Sudha-with-Pension, plumper than before and with a glint in her eye, looking angrily towards her. Deepa withdrew her glance.

She was too far away to hear Sudha say haughtily to Madhu, 'There she is, the one who is trying to steal away our property from us. The cheek of it! She was such a simple girl. I am sure it is all her ma's doing. Anyone who can go away and find a second husband must be cunning!'

'She is pretty,' said Madhu, shaking her gold bangles which now stretched almost to her elbow, and glancing at Deepa. She was thinking what a fine bride she might make for Guru. Of course that was out of the question now, with the dispute over the book and the property, and there was also the question of caste: not everyone had the amazing luck of Bharathi to be able to hook a husband from a superior caste. Madhu was secretly quite admiring of Sudha-with-Pension for having engineered that one. But then anyone who allowed their son to take full responsibility for the decision on the match was easy prey. It was simple to entice a young man, unlike parents who would be looking out for all sorts of things like status and money and caste and what all.

'Pretty?' snorted Sudha. 'If she is so pretty, why was she rejected by Shyam in front of everyone?' Sudha had already heard the story from Bharathi and had relished telling the rest of the family. 'Shyam must be knowing about her cunning character for she has stayed in their house as a child. He must be knowing how she has an eye on our family property.'

'If he is knowing that,' reasoned Madhu, 'then he should be wanting her more. Our family property is something no young man would want to resist getting his hands on. Mardpur is getting so crowded these days and look what a beautiful garden is there on the hill. Has anyone such a garden? Property is more precious than gold these days!' And she shook her bangles again to reassure herself.

'Dhut!' scolded Sudha. 'Are you saying that girl will succeed in stealing our property away from us?'

'It is Satyanarayan's idea to give away our property,' Madhu reminded her. She did not repeat the words of her husband Vaman, who had been almost apoplectic with rage when he heard what Satyanarayan was up to:

'That Brahmin! He has always had a grudge against our family! What right has he to decide about our family property? If anyone feels it is their book, let them come to us and we will come to some arrangement. I will get a good lawyer, then let us see how that clever-clever Brahmin schemer can defend.'

'You cannot blame a Brahmin for the mistake of the notary. Such illiterates are becoming clerks these days and making such mistakes!' said Sudha, rattled at such venom being poured on a priest. She was, after all, quite devout, even if Vaman was not.

It was then that Satyanarayan called the meeting of the *panchayat*. He entered the crowded hall, raising his hands to silence the chattering masses. He sat at the front with a number of other notables who had used their status and friendship with Satyanarayan to negotiate a place on the council. Among them was the principal of the municipal college, who had feared a loss of status because of the planned new Mardpur university and was intent on using his position either to block it or, even better, to secure himself the post of vice-chancellor of the university. Also on the board was the head of the Aurobindo Hospital, who had feared the same when the sparkling new Cowwasji Hospital was being built. He was a much more humble man than the principal of the municipal college because when the new hospital had been built he was not chosen to head it. That honour had gone to Dr Sharma. Worse, Dr Sharma, when he was offered a seat on the *panchayat*, declined it, saying he did not have time for such matters. Running a hospital was a major job, Dr Sharma maintained. Others on the board included Mr Joshi and Mr Mishra, academics and leading lights in their field, proposed by the principal of the municipal college. It could be said that they constituted the beginnings of a power base for the principal, who had not inconsiderable political ambitions. The fact that they were all Brahmins was mere coincidence. But it had not been lost on Vaman.

'Have you noticed how the *panchayat*, a society of Brahmins, is trying to take away the property of a bania to give to another Brahmin?' Vaman complained to Laxman who was sitting beside him.

'The outcome is not certain,' said Laxman mildly. 'They must prove that this girl, who was after all only a child then, wrote the book.'

'You don't think that scheming Satyanarayan has fixed it by some devious means? Who knows what he has up his silk sleeve.'

'Satyanarayan is a holy man, why should he scheme?' said Laxman. 'He has nothing to gain. God will do the right thing. I came to the temple to pray this morning, and I believe God is with us.'

'I hope you are right,' said Vaman sardonically. 'But I don't think we need God on our side right now, we need this Satyanarayan. And all I can see right now is that he is not.'

Laxman hushed Vaman as Satyanarayan began to speak, explaining the purpose of this most important *panchayat* meeting since the *panchayat* itself was formed as a result of his own proposal. It was, in fact, one of the most important meetings since the one that had decided to build this beautiful temple extension they were all now sitting in, also incidentally proposed by himself.

Vaman groaned. 'Someone please go and pat his back so that this poor fellow does not need to do it himself.'

Laxman hushed him.

Satyanarayan explained how Raman, 'a man of little education and even less brain', had become rich from writing a book.

'We all knew this Raman as a child. He was the lazy one of the three brothers, who could not even do anything as simple as run a sari shop. So he was taken out of the family business. And he had a job at PTI as a clerk from which, after so many years, he did not progress. This is the man who is said to be the author of this book.' Satyanarayan held up a copy of the book with its garish cover. Necks stretched and craned to catch a glimpse of the book. Few in Mardpur were inclined to literature. They were seeing it for the first time, the book that had made Mardpur famous.

'Then suddenly in the temple, eight years later, I find this, as if placed there by God for me to discover.' Satyanarayan held up the cloth-bag and retrieved from it one of the notebooks containing Deepa's handwriting. 'It is a miracle . . .'

He paused, as the hall was filled with thunderous applause. Deepa felt embarrassed. Clearly she had misplaced the bag somewhere and it had fallen into Satyanarayan's hands. Hardly a miracle!

'This is the original writing of the book. But look! Inside, it is not Raman's writing, oh no. It is someone else's.' And Satyanarayan opened the book and held it with both hands towards the audience, making a slow sweep from left to right. The audience gasped, although it was far from clear how much they could see from that distance, and anyway how did they know what Raman's handwriting looked like? A few people began to clap again.

'Now,' said Satyanarayan, closing the notebook and replacing it in the bag. He handed the bag to Bhole, like a magician finished with a prop. 'The question in all our minds is, whose writing is this? Who really wrote this book? Who is entitled to all the money that Raman, that good-for-nothing, earned by claiming authorship? And who is the owner of the property, the lychee garden so-called?' Satyanarayan sat down heavily and there was clapping and wild applause drowning out Vaman's comment to Laxman:

'The question in *my* mind is *why* should anyone want to write Raman's book for him?'

But Laxman laid a restraining hand on Vaman's knee. The first witness was being called.

80

THE FIRST WITNESS WAS THE BLINKING, SLEEPY RAJU, WHO, AS HE GOT older, found that he needed even more sleep than in his younger days. It hardly mattered now, for several *malis* tended the lychee garden under the watchful eye of Kumud. Under her guidance, the lychee garden had been restored to its past glory – full of colourful flowering plants all year round. It was now so lush and well tended that many coveted that garden. Out of greed, or weakness or sheer ignorance, others had sold off their parcels of idle land – they had never known to what use to put them. But when they heard about the beauty of the lychee garden, they were filled with regret that they had not turned their own land into something equally worthy of admiration. Raju's job was to nurse the marigolds which grew from the terracotta pots, some thirty of them, dotted about the garden. Originally intended as water pots, they had been put to good use in the garden full of flowers and trees. That job kept Raju occupied for the full extent of his waking hours, which, it must be said, was not very long.

Raju, it was clear, did not really understand what the *panchayat* hearing was all about, although it had been Bhole's job to painstakingly explain to him what it was he was required to do – and Bhole was unusually patient. Whatever Raju's misgivings, he told himself, the *tamasha*, or show as many called it, was being held at the temple and he felt there could be no threat to himself, particularly with so many people watching. He stood under the long-stemmed ceiling fans, his unkempt hair whipped into an even more dishevelled mop. His yellowing *dhoti* was dirty with earth. He had not bothered to change it. His clean chequered *kurta*, which he had bothered to change, nonetheless showed its age. Raju-*mali* wore a pair of muddy leather shoes without socks and, inexplicably, he carried a grimy cloth-bag slung over his arm, as if he were hoping to squeeze in some shopping since he had been allowed a rare afternoon off work. It was not that he appeared disreputable, he was too simple-looking for that, but he did not resemble one who was in touch with the world outside the garden.

The people looked expectantly at this unexpected first witness. They had been hoping for a glittering show befitting the garish grandeur of the new temple extension where they had assembled, blinking against the white fluorescent light which bounced off pillars inlaid with a swirling mosaic of coloured glass.

As Mardpur had developed, so had their expectations. They did not want to be reminded that in the new, thrusting Mardpur, the likes of Raju-*mali* still existed, toiling away as they had always done in the past. The people of Mardpur had come to see the personalities they had heard about; real personalities, important people. Yet here was a grubby unkempt simpleton who seemed completely out of place.

Satyanarayan, full of energy, and a zeal he had been building up specially for this event, was unaware of the disappointment of the gathering. He was determined his own performance should not disappoint. He came at Raju aggressively with one of Deepa's notebooks.

'Raju, you worked in Raman's household for many, many years. Look at this notebook.'

Raju, taken aback at this attack, first looked everywhere but at the notebook and then, when Satyanarayan waved it before his nose, Raju looked at it intently as if undergoing an eye-test. 'Is this Raman's writing?' Satyanarayan demanded.

Raju looked more intently, blinking the sleep from his eyes. Satyanarayan held it closer, thinking the fellow was short-sighted. The *mali*, believing Satyanarayan was handing him the book, took it from Satyanarayan's hands and examined it carefully, turning it upside down then the right way up. He held it far away from his nose, then up close. Satyanarayan allowed him his time but then began to get irritated with these antics.

'Well?' he bellowed, making Raju jump. 'Is it his writing?'

Raju stuttered, fearing he had done something wrong, 'It could be that it is . . .'

Satyanarayan looked as dark as thunder, and snatched the notebook away to ascertain if it was indeed one of Deepa's he had handed to him and not one of Raman's.

'On the other hand it could be that it is not,' said Raju, turning one hand over the other in nervousness.

A titter went through the hall. Satyanarayan was sweating a little. He should have known better than to have called this imbecile, this peasant, this owl of the first order, as the first witness. Well, it was too late now. He tried to regain control of the situation.

'Well, which is it? Does this look like a man's writing to you?'

'Objection,' said the principal of the municipal college, holding up a finger. 'Do not suggest the answer.'

Raju looked at the notebook again. His expression was somewhat stupefied. 'I could not know, Punditji. I have never seen Raman sahib's writing.'

'Never?' said Satyanarayan, incredulous. 'But you worked there since – em—'

'Never, Punditji, I am illiterate.'

'Go,' said Satyanarayan, dismissing Raju abruptly. The Brahmin was not happy. He had attempted to create the atmosphere of a courthouse to give the hearing an air of importance and authority, but he had not reckoned on such stupidity. Raju thankfully stumbled from the dais.

'Whoever thought Raju would have his uses?' murmured Vaman, enjoying Satyanarayan's discomfiture. He fanned himself with a news-paper. It was not a hot day – the morning had been quite crisp – but the heat of so many people breathing in the hall made the atmosphere quite stifling.

Gulbachan was called. Gulbachan was nervous; the untimely death of Raman had made his own future in Mardpur somewhat uncertain. Raman had accepted the job of sub-correspondent, allowing Gulbachan to stay on in his government bungalow to enjoy his retirement. They had a pact. Raman never bothered to go to the office, and Gulbachan wrote what little there was to write in Raman's name, coming to the lychee garden from time to time on his putter-scooter for Raman's signature on any necessary documents. What would now become of this cosy arrangement and his continued happy retirement was anyone's guess. It was, of course, of great concern to Gulbachan. He had no view either way on the fate of the lychee garden. It made no difference who owned that land. He, Gulbachan, would still be left homeless. Still, he felt a certain loyalty to Raman, for having agreed to the arrangement in the first place and for continuing it even after Raman had no need of a job.

'This is Gulbachan, former PTI correspondent, now retired. Raman's former boss,' the principal of the municipal college announced, referring to the sheaf of notes carefully prepared by Bhole and handed to him by Satyanarayan before the hearing began.

'Do you recognize this writing?' said Satyanarayan, jabbing the book in Gulbachan's face.

Gulbachan, intent on singling out his friends and acquaintances among the assembled correspondents, did not even look at the notebook.

'Who would go on the Salt March if Gandhiji were not leading it? Did I tell you about when I went on the Salt March?'

'Please refer to the question, Mr Gulbachan,' said Satyanarayan, his teeth on edge. After the disaster with Raju he did not want any more setbacks.

'Who would go on the Salt March if Gandhiji were not leading?' Gulbachan repeated. 'By the same token, why are we all here if Raman is not the writer of the book?'

Satyanarayan, who prided himself on his intelligence, did not understand the analogy. 'Are you saying . . . ?'

'Of course Raman is the writer. There is no other in Mardpur.'

'The people will decide the outcome, Mr Gulbachan. What we want to know from you are the facts,' Satyanarayan said.

'Certainly,' said Gulbachan, undeterred. 'The facts are that Raman wrote the book and the book was written by Raman. Satisfied now?'

'Where is the proof of this?' said Satyanarayan.

'Well, at the time, I recall Raman spoke about this book with me, and, I believe, with you, Swamiji. No one else spoke about writing this book, otherwise I would have known about it. After all, I was Chief Correspondent of PTI. So it is clear to me, who else could it have been? Unless, of course, Swamiji, you are hiding some important facts from us all and someone else was coming to you at that time and saying they were writing a book. Now tell us Swamiji, did anyone else come to you at that time?'

'I do not recall—' said Satyanarayan before he realized that Gulbachan had turned the tables and was now interrogating *him*.

'What a shame!' said Gulbachan. 'I believe almonds are very good for the memory—'

'Thank you, Mr Gulbachan,' said Satyanarayan, dispensing with him as fast as he could.

Vaman clapped hard. 'Only a reporter would know how to interview a politician and put him in a tight corner!'

'Satyanarayan is not a politician,' commented Laxman, full of misgivings at what he was seeing and hearing.

'He is not?' said Vaman, his voice heavy with irony.

'No. He is judge and prosecutor all at once.'

'And legislator,' said Vaman. 'He is setting his own rules.'

Usha was the next witness. Deepa felt excited when she recognized her after so many years. She stared hard at her as if willing Usha to look at her. But Usha did not; she seemed quite calm and poised. She wore a simple cotton sari. The end of the *pallav* was tied around her as if she had just been scrubbing floors; it failed to conceal a growing bulge around her middle, the bulge of mid-pregnancy. With her was a small, dark-skinned boy aged about five, his eyes ringed with kohl. Usha held his hand, preventing him from wandering off. He wriggled and pulled at his mother's hand, but this did not distract Usha.

Satyanarayan came at Usha with one of the notebooks almost as aggressively as he had with Raju and Gulbachan. But Usha seemed unperturbed.

'Do you recognize this handwriting?'

'Yes, Swami.'

'Whose is it?'

'It is Deepa's, granddaughter of Amma of Jagdishpuri Extension.'

'Are you sure?'

'Yes, Swamiji,' said Usha. 'I was often watching her do her homework. And look, she has even written her name on the cover.'

Satyanarayan looked at the cover, pleased. He had missed that detail himself. He showed the audience the cover.

'What is written in this book?' said Satyanarayan, handing the notebook to Usha to examine.

'It is the book of Raman sahib,' she said immediately.

'The book of *Raman* sahib? In Deepa's handwriting?' said Satyanarayan loudly and clearly in a voice loaded with significance. 'Explain to us how this can be.'

'I don't know, Swamiji,' shrugged Usha. 'Sometimes Raman sahib was writing, sometimes Deepa. Both wrote the book.'

'*Both?* But a book can have only one author.'

'I know nothing about books, Swamiji,' said Usha. 'All I know is that Amma was sometimes telling the story, and sometimes Raman sahib was writing, and sometimes Deepa was writing.'

'So Amma had a hand in it too?'

'She was telling the story, to Raman sahib and to Deepa.'

'So it was Amma's story, and Raman and Deepa were only noting it down?' said Satyanarayan triumphantly. But the audience were already feeling confused. It was not clear now who had done what.

'It was *also* Amma's story.'

'Also?'

'It was Raman sahib's, and Amma's and Deepa's story.'

'There can be only one author of the book!' shouted Satyanarayan.

'That was how it was written,' said Usha, standing her ground. 'Three of them wrote it.'

'All three?'

'Yes, Swamiji.'

'Then,' said Satyanarayan, almost hoarse, 'how did the whole book come to be in Raman's hands? And published in his name?'

'We will come to that in a moment,' said the principal of the municipal college. 'We are still trying to ascertain who exactly wrote the book. Then we will find out how Raman got hold of it and published it.'

Satyanarayan reluctantly agreed to let Usha sit down. She was not only an important witness, she was unusually clear-headed for a servant. But she had made things confusing for the audience. Who could understand this story of three people writing together?

The audience was tittering. They did not like the scene before them of the well-fed Brahmin bullying the pregnant servant. It seemed unnecessary. She had committed no misdemeanour. And, they had now realized that the case was not a clear-cut one. They had imagined that the hearing would be short and dramatic and at the end of it the land would be awarded to Deepa. They had not bargained for such complexities.

Mr Ahuja was called.

'Did you sell Raman these notebooks?'

'Yes.'

'Did you sell Deepa notebooks?'

'Also,' confirmed Mr Ahuja.

'For what did they require these notebooks?'

'I did not ask them,' said Mr Ahuja loyally.

'Did you sell anyone else notebooks?'

'Yes.'

'To whom?'

'The students of the Mission school, convent school, municipal college—'

'Objection,' said the principal of the municipal college. 'Mr Ahuja sold everyone notebooks. At that time Ahuja Book Depot was the only one in Mardpur.'

Mr Ahuja was allowed to go.

Hari was called. He testified that Raman went frequently to Amma's house at the time the book was being written.

'For what?'

'For raita.'

'That was clearly an excuse,' said Satyanarayan, waving it aside. 'What else?'

'Just raita. Raman sahib was believing raita would help him write. He even one day stole Amma's buffalo while she was in hospital.'

'Oho!' said Satyanarayan, seizing on this slur on Raman's character. 'Indeed I witnessed this event myself. He was plotting something. Why did he steal the buffalo?'

'Because he wanted the buffalo for himself.'

'Yes, yes, why?'

'Because he thought the buffalo would help him write the book.'

The hall filled with laughter. Hari grinned, but Satyanarayan was not amused.

'This is a serious hearing,' he castigated Hari.

'Don't tell me,' grinned Vaman, enjoying himself hugely, 'we are to give over our property to this buffalo now!'

But Laxman was worried. There was no one to defend Raman. However amusing, it was all too one-sided.

'I am telling the truth, Swamiji,' said Hari earnestly. 'It was the buffalo-milk raita. Raman sahib thought it was magic and would help him write. He called it writer-raita.'

Everyone laughed except Satyanarayan. He dismissed Hari and tried to clarify matters in his wake.

'Let us not be confused. We are trying to find out who is the real writer of the book. The buffalo is neither here nor there. What Raman believed is neither here nor there. What we want to know is what he *did*. The fact that this Raman felt he needed a magic potion, this writer-raita, shows he was having trouble with writing. He could not have written the book by himself!'

Gulbachan objected, remembering his own belief in the raita. He raised his hand and spoke without being invited. 'It could mean that the raita merely *helped* him to concentrate on writing. It got the creative juices flowing—'

'You may speak only when called upon,' castigated Satyanarayan, not wanting things to be complicated more than necessary.

The principal of the municipal college held up a restraining hand. 'Gulbachan was merely clarifying, Punditji. These things may not be obvious to all.'

Satyanarayan grunted and turned to consult other members of the *panchayat*. After much discussion and a great deal of nodding and jiggling of heads, during which time the audience became quite restive, they concluded collectively that the buffalo was an irrelevance.

Seeing the audience distracted and chattering, Satyanarayan decided it was time to take a break. He did not want the audience overwhelmed.

'Let me summarize,' he said, clapping his hands above the din. 'We have ascertained that notebooks in Deepa's handwriting have been found. It is clear Raman *may* not have written the book. *At the very least* he had help. Tomorrow Deepa, granddaughter of Amma, will clarify her part in this drama.'

And with a wave of his hand he declared the hearing over for the day. The crowd began to file out, disappointed that it had been so short and that they would have to go back to their workplaces after all. Still, they had something to look forward to the following day. The star witness would appear. Many had wanted to catch a glimpse of this girl Deepa, who was said to be an orphan girl who had become a great dancer. It was also said she had performed in Bombay, Calcutta, Delhi and Madras. The men were swooning at her feet. She must certainly be beautiful as well as talented.

For Ma, it was embarrassing to be the focus of so much attention. After the hearing people stared at her and Deepa with curiosity.

'It is not good,' sighed Ma, 'to stand up in front of all these people and speak. It will not get you a husband. Perhaps tomorrow you should not come.' She paused. A thought had struck her. 'Unless, of course, you become the owner of the lychee garden. Then everyone will want to marry you!'

'Oh, Ma!' said Deepa.

'It is not a bad piece of land.'

'It is not mine,' said Deepa. 'I am going to the *panchayat* tomorrow so that everyone will know the truth.'

Ma shook her head. 'I do not know why it is so important who is owning the lychee garden: if there is such a big loan on it, it will be forfeited anyway.'

It is for Amma, thought Deepa. It is for Amma that I must tell the truth. She was put on this earth with this great gift, and this was her last major task, to help Raman Uncle with his book. She would have wanted it this way, so that everyone would understand her gift and that she was no ordinary woman. And only if they understood that Raman Uncle wrote the book would they understand her gift.

Ma went to offer flowers to the deity, but Deepa did not want to push her way through such a crowd and stood waiting outside. She stared up at the familiar white *gopuram* of the Vishnu Narayan temple, soon to be dwarfed by the triple pagoda of the Raja Man Singh Mandir. Her sari flapped in a gentle breeze, and she smoothed it onto her shoulder. Then she caught sight of Usha, with her black-eyed son still straining against his mother's hand. She wanted to run up to her but knew she could not. Usha had been Amma's servant. And maybe, thought Deepa, Usha wanted to speak to her but likewise was held back by convention which dictated a certain distance between them. Instead Deepa studied Usha's familiar movements, her calm voice as she warned her son from straying away. Then some people moved across Deepa's line of vision and she lost sight of her.

All at once she felt a tugging at the *pallav* of her sari. It slithered from her shoulder and she moved swiftly to rescue it before it fell to the ground, turning round to find Usha's son looking up at her. He had broken away from his mother and run towards Deepa. He recognized her as someone special. The one about whom everyone was talking. He looked up at her in the disarmingly trusting way of a child without fear and offered her his toy as a gift, reaching out to her on tip-toe with his arms outstretched. Clutched between his brown fingers was a wooden figure. He wanted her to have it.

Deepa accepted the toy, a small wooden buffalo roughly carved except for its smooth belly and rounded horns, painted black all over. She bent down towards the child.

'It is your buffalo,' she said, holding it out for the child to take back.

'Yes,' said the boy earnestly. 'Her name is Jhotta.' He kept his hands firmly behind his back.

'Jhotta. It is a nice name for a buffalo.'

'Yes,' agreed the boy. 'But she very *baoli*.'

Deepa smiled. '*Baoli*? Why? She looks to me like a very good buffalo.'

'Yes. But she gives milk no more. So I punish her.'

'It is not nice to punish.'

'No,' agreed the boy. 'So I give her away to you. Maybe for you she produce milk.'

'Thank you,' said Deepa, charmed to have been selected in this way. 'But Jhotta will miss you, no?'

'No,' said the boy with conviction. 'She too *baoli*.'

'Or maybe you will miss her?'

'No. She is leaving behind her *bhooth* with me!' And he held up another roughly hewn buffalo, almost identical to the first except that it had not been painted, the natural sisal wood pale against his brown hand.

'Naveen! Naveen!' Usha was calling.

The child looked towards his mother and darted away, leaving Deepa still holding Jhotta in her hand. The conversation between herself and the child went through her mind, and then she smiled to herself and whispered to Jhotta:

> '*Kahan se aai?*
> *Koi jan na paai!*'

81

WHEN THEY RETURNED TO JAGDISHPURI EXTENSION, MA RETIRED FOR A short nap and Deepa fetched her ankle-bells.

She threw herself into a gentle, flowing dance of Krishna stealing the butter and his mother Yashoda scolding him with motherly affection.

'*Wah!*' said Usha-rani. 'I can see the butter. It is glowing gold in your hand!'

Deepa smiled gently without breaking her step, coaxing the naughty Krishna with her hands and knitted brows. Gently she turned and swayed, graceful and controlled, rhythmically beating the steps.

'That butter, I can smell,' said Usha-rani. 'Even that pickle smell is not so strong when I am watching you dance!'

'I will do vegetable shopping,' Usha-rani told Deepa as she paused between dances. 'I will be back when your Ma wakes up to make tea.'

After a short rest, Deepa started again with the dance of the *gopis* playing with Krishna, enticing him on and then running to hide.

It was only when she had finished that she looked up and saw the figure of the regal-sahib, in his cream poplin shirt, leaning against the wall at the entrance to the courtyard, watching her intently and with pleasure. She flushed and busied herself with her ankle-bells.

'Is the mistress of the house . . .' The voice was enticing and smooth as ever.

'Ma is resting,' said Deepa quickly, hardly daring to look at him.

He stared down at her. 'I was at the temple today. I saw the notebooks. The writing in the book was yours.'

Deepa shook her head.

'If you say that to the *panchayat* you will lose the lychee garden.'

'It belongs to Raman Uncle, just as the book belongs to him,' Deepa said without looking up.

'It is in your hands to make a claim on that estate. The estate which, after all, was mortgaged to one Man Singh who has cheated many and who will become the owner if the loan is not paid.' His voice had changed. It was harsh, angry. Deepa looked up and saw an expression on his face that was so ugly it distorted his fine features in its intensity.

'And if the garden is mine, how would *I* pay the loan?'

'You could sell this house,' said the regal-sahib, looking around the courtyard.

Deepa laughed. 'This house will not pay for the lychee garden!'

This house with its treasure, the regal-sahib meant. But he let it go unsaid.

'I could help you.' His face was neither benign nor benevolent, despite his offer.

She looked at him intently, wondering at his intentions.

'If you tell the *panchayat* that it was you who wrote the book, I will help you rescue the lychee garden from the hands of Man Singh.'

'Why are you interested?' said Deepa, emboldened.

'Why should yet another property fall into the hands of Man Singh?'

'You mean instead of *your* hands?'

The regal-sahib said nothing. His eyes narrowed. 'It is too easy. Just say you are the writer. Who cares for Raman? He was always seen as a good-for-nothing. No one could understand how he could write such a book. Everyone will be willing to believe it is you.'

'And you? What is there in it for you?' said Deepa quietly.

'Me?' said the regal-sahib. He laughed a tinkling and melodious laugh. 'Then I will marry you. Who would not want a prince?'

Deepa put her head down, feeling dizzy. Was she dreaming this? Even for the treasure, the regal-sahib had not taken it seriously when Amma had said he would have to marry her. But now, to save the lychee garden from Man Singh, he was willing to do just that. She breathed deeply and then looked up again.

'I can only do what is right,' she said.

'And that is?'

'Tomorrow you will see,' she said softly.

'So I can hope?' He was coquettish, handsome, enticing.

Deepa shook her head. 'There is no hope,' and she squeezed her eyes shut to try to keep in the dream that was slowly draining away.

He half knelt, half squatted beside her, his hand resting lightly on his knee, bejewelled with rings. 'I hope you will change your mind,' he said quietly, caressingly.

'I cannot. I cannot. I cannot,' said Deepa, drawing up her knees and burying her face in them.

When she finally looked up, the regal-sahib had gone. Had he ever been there? Had she imagined it all? She slowly unwound the bells from her ankles, lost in thought.

She was still sitting in the same place staring into space when Usha-rani came back from shopping.

'Why, Deepa *bahen*, you are looking like you have seen a ghost!'

'It is said often that there are *bhooths* in this house,' replied Deepa.

82

DEEPA TOLD NO ONE ABOUT THE REGAL-SAHIB'S VISIT. SHE HAD SERIOUS
doubts herself whether he had really been there. Only her imagination
could conjure up such a vision, she thought. Yet in her imagination the
regal-sahib was always handsome and enticing. The impression he left
behind from his visit was unsavoury. Still, she hardly had time to dwell on
what had become of the person that had figured for so long in her dreams.

Usha-*rani* was fussing around her. 'I can hardly work with this pickle
smell,' she complained. 'It is getting too strong.'

'The glass jars I have ordered from Jindal's,' said Ma. 'Tomorrow they
will come. Then we can put the pickles in the jars.'

Usha looked a little hesitant.

'I will do it, Ma. I *like* the pickle smell. I have lived with it all my life,'
said Deepa.

'But your hands, Deepa!'

'The sweet mustard oil will make them soft, Ma,' Deepa assured her.

The following morning, Usha-rani laid out Deepa's sari with care and
attention. She knew it was an important occasion.

'You will look beautiful in lemon chiffon,' she said.

'Why do I need to look beautiful for the *panchayat*?' said Deepa.

'Everyone will be watching,' said Usha-rani. 'Who knows, there may be a future husband who sees you. All the rich people will be there. A prince, even.'

'A prince!' Deepa wondered if she knew about the regal-sahib.

'You should not trust a prince,' said Usha-rani. 'Sometimes they are marrying two-three times.'

'I could not be a second wife,' said Deepa, aghast.

'They make friends with each other,' said Usha-rani. 'Like you and Bharathi, like sisters. And then when their husband dies they do *sati* together.'

That was when Deepa realized that whatever her dreams, she could never die for Govind, nor for the regal-sahib. Suddenly, looking at Usha-rani smoothing the creases from her sari, she felt free of her old dreams. She could leave them behind and go forward unencumbered. She could start afresh.

That afternoon, Ma and Deepa arrived at the temple extension to an even bigger crowd. Photographers and reporters were jostling for space, trying to get close up to Deepa. She allowed them to photograph her, blinking at the white flash.

Bharathi came up to her, pushing through the crowd with Govind behind her, and squeezed her hand. 'We are relying on you, Deepa,' she whispered.

Deepa said nothing but looked up at Govind, the same expression of pity on his face as always. And Deepa thought, Govind would always have such a look of pity. Even if she were happy. It was not pity for her. It was pity for himself. Deepa watched Bharathi and Govind move away to find a seat. Bharathi had got her prince, Deepa thought, and now she, Deepa, was about to lose everything. Through the crowd she caught sight of the regal-sahib, jewels flashing on his fingers. She would lose everything but it would be of her own doing. For the first time she would be in control of her own fate. Govind had no reason to pity her. And the regal-sahib – she stole another glimpse at him and realized that amidst the new wealth of Mardpur he no longer stood out as he had done once. His glowing freshness, which once had seemed so attractive, had, with the passage of a short space of time, faded just a little. The regal-sahib, who thought he could get whatever he wanted, would not get her. He would not get the lychee garden, just as he had failed to get anything from Amma. He would not get Amma's treasure.

Deepa looked at Ma. The years of living with her mother made her realize how much like her she was: quiet and passive. She loved Ma. Ma wanted the best for her. Ma would understand. If it hadn't been for Ma, Deepa would never have realized what she herself was like.

From now on, thought Deepa, she would be more like Amma. And Amma had not given in to all around her. She was not dependent on others, despite her blindness. She had even stood her ground against the regal-sahib. Amma could see something in the regal-sahib and had known she must not give in to him. She had that special gift.

Bharathi would be sad, and Deepa would have to explain to her. How would she explain she had lost the lychee garden? Even if the *panchayat* awarded Deepa the lychee garden it could still be lost to the regal-sahib. The regal-sahib would try to possess her, as he had once tried to possess the treasure. And Deepa had nowhere to hide, not like the treasure!

Ma smiled at her, thinking she must be frightened. But Deepa realized, perhaps for the first time, that there was nothing about life to fear.

'Silence!' shouted Satyanarayan, sitting on the dais with the dignitaries of the *panchayat*. The hall hushed. The sound of the ceiling fans could be heard in that large room, lit by fluorescent tubes despite the bright sunlight outside. At the end opposite the dais the deities had been curtained off again, as if they should not witness what was about to happen.

'We call Shanker, son of Raman!' said the principal of the municipal college. There was some restlessness. The people had been hoping it would be Deepa straight away.

Shanker came to the dais. He was a thin youth, with a slightly sullen air, as if he did not believe from the outset that he would get a sympathetic hearing. In fact, that is exactly what Shanker *did* think: he had never had a sympathetic hearing, not at home, from his father, nor from anyone else and certainly not from Satyanarayan.

'You accompanied your father many times to Amma's house. For what was he going there?' said Satyanarayan.

Shanker scowled. How was it Satyanarayan's business? Anyone can go to anyone's house without being questioned in this manner. He said merely, 'He liked to walk in the evenings.'

Satyanarayan looked at Shanker in disbelief. It was an obvious lie. But he could not say that in front of the *panchayat*. 'He liked to walk in the evenings?' Satyanarayan snapped. 'All the way to Jagdishpuri Extension and back? For what?'

Shanker raised his voice. 'He liked to walk,' he insisted. 'You must be knowing, for a long time he had no bicycle and no scooter. He walked everywhere.'

Some people laughed but Shanker was not joking.

Satyanarayan chose a different tack. 'And when your father got to Jagdishpuri Extension, what did he talk about with Amma?'

'I don't know. Old people's talk.'

'What kind of things are discussed in old people's talk?' growled Satyanarayan.

'Marriage and things. I don't know. Why should I be interested in such talk? I was only a boy.'

The principal of the municipal college intervened. 'Clearly Shanker cannot remember, we cannot force him to say if he does not recall.'

Shanker was allowed to go.

'For once it is useful that Shanker is uncooperative,' commented Vaman with a laugh.

Laxman sighed. Did they honestly expect the son of the deceased, the inheritor of the land, to say anything that would jeopardize his ownership of the property?

Bharathi was called. She stood nervously, not knowing where to look.

Satyanarayan asked her who she thought had written the book.

'It was Deepa who wrote the book!' said Bharathi, and everyone clapped and cheered.

The principal of the municipal college leant forward. 'So how is it that the book was in Raman's possession?'

'When Amma died, Deepa was giving me the notebooks for safekeeping. I gave them to my father.'

The audience was tittering; here was the daughter of Raman standing up and saying the book was written by Deepa. She was, in effect, giving away her family's property to this Deepa. It must be true. Flashbulbs went off as the reporters got excited.

Vaman groaned. 'You see, if you marry one daughter off to a Brahmin she will disown you in no time. She does not want to admit she comes from a bania family.'

Laxman said sadly, 'Then maybe it is true. Raman did not write it. But where will Bharathi's mother go if the garden is lost? Surely Bharathi has thought of that.' He was fond of his niece despite everything. He wanted to think the best of her, but even he could not understand why she had spoken this way when it was so simple to keep quiet. Perhaps Shanker's approach was the right one: give nothing away if it is not in your interest to.

A little further away, Sudha-with-Pension glared angrily in the direction of her niece. After all she had done for her, found her a fantastic match, this was the way she showed her gratitude. Madhu blinked, completely incredulous. She thought she must have missed some detail. Things seemed all topsy-turvy. Kumud was not present, it was too soon after Raman's death, but if she were, how would she have felt as a mother? Madhu thought that it was a good thing she herself only had sons. Daughters could be so treacherous.

Satyanarayan was ecstatic. It was perfect. As he had predicted, it was an auspicious day. Mars and Jupiter were high in the heavens. It was bound to herald a positive outcome.

'We will call the most important witness: the girl who may rightly claim the property,' Satyanarayan said.

'Objection,' said the principal of the municipal college. 'It has not been decided, yet. This *panchayat* will decide precisely that.'

Deepa, unlike the others, was given a chair. She wondered if this was an indication of a lengthy interview. She sat on it, confident and serene.

Satyanarayan waved a notebook in front of her face, but not as aggressively as he had done to the other witnesses the day before. The lemon chiffon that fluttered under the ceiling fans had a calming effect. It made the coloured-glass decor seem ostentatious and out of place for a solemn hearing. There was something incongruous about this girl in yellow and that brightly lit hall.

Even Satayanarayan felt the impact of the gently billowing yellow. It was a sacred colour and he could not be so disrespectful to someone who had come dressed simply in yellow. Besides, he knew that everything hinged on what this girl would say. He did not want to frighten her.

'This is your notebook, is it not, with your name on it?'

'It is.' Deepa was calm and poised and it was catching: the hall was hushed.

'And this is your writing?'

'Yes.'

'So you are the writer of the book!'

'It is a notebook with my writing like many notebooks I had. They were to do my homework in. English essays and other writings.' These included, but she did not say so, Amma's memories, that she had written down as Amma had related them to her.

There was a laugh in the audience. But others were serious. Everything depended on this girl, lemon-fresh in chiffon. They expected her to claim this estate for herself, and they wanted this girl to be the owner of the estate. But could she prove that she had indeed, by some miracle, been able to write a book when she was only a child? The people wanted a miracle. They wanted to see a talent in their midst. They willed Deepa to stake her claim.

The principal of the municipal college looked at Satyanarayan. 'Have these notebooks been read to see if what is written is indeed parts of the smuggler book or just homework jottings? We should check.'

Satyanarayan handed the notebooks to him. The principal said, 'While we are checking we must clarify, if these are her books how did they fall into the hands of Raman?'

Satyanarayan turned to Deepa. He wanted to save time. He wanted the hearing to be over quickly so that the townspeople did not have time to develop divergent views, discussing every detail, every pro and con. He decided to do as the principal said, but he did not like it that the principal was beginning to take the initiative. He had been only too happy to leave everything to Satyanarayan the day before.

'So these are your notebooks, and you lost them, and Raman found them?' Satyanarayan continued.

'No,' said Deepa. 'I gave them to him.' Her *pallav* flapped under the fan and embraced her jaw and nose. She carefully prised the lemon chiffon from her skin and smoothed it down onto her shoulder. Mardpur watched her every move. She looked so pure, bathed in pale yellow light.

Laxman's heart sank; so Bharathi had been telling the truth.

'When were they given? Can you remember? You must remember exactly.'

'I remember exactly. It was the day Amma died. When the last word had been written. I handed those books to Bharathi on the day of her death.'

Satyanarayan looked triumphant. 'The granddaughter says she *gave* the notebooks. But grieving for her grandmother she did not know what she was doing. When Raman demanded the books, she gave him all.' The harshness of his tone contrasted with the coolness of the chiffon-clad apparition. The atmosphere that Deepa had created had been broken.

The people of Mardpur tore their eyes from Deepa and landed back on earth.

'Objection,' said the principal. 'We do not know what Raman said. And why should he demand?' The principal looked at Deepa, pretty and gentle, and was taken with this girl, just as the people of Mardpur were taken by her presence. She seemed so honest and clean, the product of the old Mardpur. She should not be given a hard time, he thought.

Satyanarayan started again. 'You understand we are trying to find out the writer of the book, so that we can ascertain to whom belongs the lychee garden? It is a big-big estate, with one house and one small bungalow.' He said this more for the audience than for Deepa. It heightened the drama.

'Yes,' said Deepa. 'It is quite clear.'

'So this is your handwriting?' He held out another of her notebooks.

'Yes,' said Deepa.

'Then you wrote the book.'

'I wrote a few things, but writing a little does not make a book. The thoughts were not mine. It is the thoughts that make a book.'

'They were your grandmother's!' Satyanarayan was almost shouting.

'She was seeing what was in Raman Uncle's mind and telling me.'

'How could she see?' He was gritting his teeth now. Everyone on the dais and in the hall was leaning forward with interest.

'She had a gift,' said Deepa. 'That was why she was so successful in the courts of the kings. She could foretell the future and she could read the minds of some people. Raman Uncle was one.'

'This is nonsense!' shouted Satyanarayan.

'Let her speak, Punditji,' said the principal. 'Why should she tell a lie? It is not in her interest. She is saying she is *not* the writer of the book. She is not trying to claim the big-big lychee garden estate, even though it would be so easy for her to say it. She is saying that her grandmother's gift helped her to write what was going on in Raman's mind. So she is right, that makes it Raman's book!'

This was the kind of summary Satyanarayan had not wanted. The whole hall was tittering.

He tried just one last time. 'You wrote this?' he said, but even he realized the fight had gone out of his voice. And indeed, it should not have been *in* his voice if he had wanted the people of Mardpur on his side. Who would fight with lemon chiffon? It was unprovoked aggression of the first order.

'I did some writing, that was all. It does not make a book. Raman Uncle wrote the book. We did not know even when it would be complete, Amma and I, only when he told us did we know,' Deepa said calmly.

The principal had decided to take matters in hand. He was touched by this young lady with such poise, whose father had taught at the municipal college and had died so tragically when she was so young. He had been a colleague of Dasji; that was long before he had become a principal. He had admired Dasji for his integrity. It was such a tragedy. And this was the daughter. He felt he had to protect her.

'We only need to know who is the writer of the book,' said the principal. 'And the young lady is saying it is not she. Do you have any other person who could be the writer?' he said turning to Satyanarayan, virtually terminating the interrogation of Deepa.

Satyanarayan gave him an angry look and shook his head. He now knew he had made a mistake. He should have worn his saffron *kurta*, or even the light yellow homespun one. They were holy colours and had all the moral force of religion behind them. Cream silk was altogether the wrong thing, one could not stand out in cream-coloured silk. It did not command the same attention as saffron.

'So the writer is indeed Raman!' pronounced the principal. And people in the hall began to clap.

'The writer was Raman Uncle,' said Deepa, her voice ringing throughout the hall, clear as a bell. 'Amma was reading his thoughts, and because she was blind I was writing them down. That was how it was written.' And she closed her eyes to the blinding flash of bulbs as a crowd closed around her. The hall was in uproar. People were clamouring for more. Some had not understood and their kith and kin were trying to explain what she had said.

'Amma was reading his mind . . .'

'Deepa was only writing . . .'

'It was Raman's thoughts . . .'

Laxman and Vaman thought it prudent to push their way out, signalling to Sudha and Madhu as they went.

And then someone cried, 'It is not the Ganesh miracle we should be bowing before, it is the miracle of this girl Deepa and her Amma! She is a goddess and her Amma was a goddess! *Jai Devi! Jai Devi-Amma!*'

There was such a commotion that Deepa hardly knew what was happening. Everyone was pushing to catch a glimpse of her. They may not have understood what she had said, but they understood that she had been instrumental in what was nothing short of a miracle. The creation of a book.

Satyanarayan was shouting for people to move back. It was Bhole who came and rescued Deepa, finding a way out of the confusion. He led her towards the exit and out into the old temple garden. Deepa sat under a tree, wondering where Ma was, when she saw Bharathi and Govind approaching. They stood before her.

'You are too generous,' Bharathi said without rancour. 'You let everything be taken away from you. Oh Deepa, when will you begin to control your own destiny? I fear for your future. I want you to be happy.'

'What will happen to your ma?' said Deepa, less concerned about herself.

'Ma will have to fight to keep the property, and Shanker, too. We will try to help them and Laxman Uncle and Vaman Uncle will also try to help. They are happy that Papa is proved to be the owner, but they do not know about the loan yet. Because of the loan we will have to fight. But there are new people here in Mardpur, and they do not care about the old Mardpur. They just want everything they can get, and those are the best lychee trees in the whole Gangetic Plain! You could have helped us, Deepa, but you are too simple.'

Bharathi said all this without accusation, just with a great deal of sadness.

Govind merely said, 'You could have claimed what was rightfully yours. Now you have nothing. You will always have nothing.'

Bharathi continued, 'You will leave again with your ma, Deepa, and we will continue to fight for our land. That Man Singh is so crooked and Satyanarayan is supporting him because he is building the temple. What chance have we against people like that? What chance do Ma and Shanker have against them? Ma is only seventh standard pass and Shanker . . .'

'No!' said Deepa, silencing her. 'Do not say that about your ma. She is so strong. She is stronger than me or you. She is as strong as Amma was. She will fight. The lychee garden will not be lost.'

Bharathi sighed. 'Can you tell the future? Like you said your Amma could tell? And did you ever find the treasure that your Amma said was for you and no one else? No! It is not fate that decides what you get. If you sit back you will get nothing. You must fight such people who are trying to take everything away.'

Govind tugged at Bharathi's arm and Bharathi bade Deepa farewell. 'I must go now, Deepa. You are still my friend, I want you to be happy, just as I have been made so happy.'

She meant, of course, her marriage to Govind, but Deepa saw only sadness in her eyes. Deepa remained sitting under the tree, her yellow chiffon sari being picked up in the breeze. She could hear the birds in the trees. Strangely, the clamour that was still continuing inside Satyanarayan Hall did not carry as far as the old temple garden. Here was peace. She sat quietly for a few minutes and then she heard a familiar voice behind the old henna bush.

'Naveen! Keep still only!'

'I want a Baoli story, Ma!' Naveen wailed.

'Not now. Soon we will go home.'

'Baoli story, Ma!'

'All right, because you are eating my life with your asking! But only one small one.'

Naveen climbed into her lap.

'Once there was a Baoli and she had a Jhotta. That Jhotta was also *baoli*. And one day Baoli and Jhotta had a fight, because Baoli said, "Jhotta! You are not producing milk. I am giving you food and I am giving you love. But no milk you are giving me!" And she turned her out of the house and let her roam in the streets. One day Baoli met Jhotta roaming and she said, "Are you happy Jhotta, without me?" And Jhotta said, "Yes I am happy. But no milk I am producing." And Baoli said, "Aha, it is because you cannot produce milk on your own. You need me also to give you food and give you love and to milk you every day." And Jhotta said, "No! I can produce milk by myself." And she wandered off. And Jhotta never again produced milk. And Baoli became *baoli* because she missed her Jhotta.

> *'Baoli Maai, Baoli Maai,*
> *Kahan se aai?*
> *Koi jan na paai.'*

'Another, another!' cried Naveen.

'No time, now,' said his mother.

'I want, I want.'

So Usha started again: 'One day, Baoli found a treasure and she hid it because she had no need for treasure, she only needed her Jhotta who gave her milk. But the Jhotta was a *baoli* Jhotta and saw her hiding the treasure, and the Jhotta said, "Unless you give me the treasure I will not give you milk." Baoli said, "You *baoli* Jhotta. What will you do with treasure? You do not need it!" But the Jhotta was insisting and refused to give milk. So Baoli went *baoli* and died.

> *'Baoli Maai, Baoli Maai,*
> *Kahan se aai?*
> *Koi jan na paai.'*

'She not die! She sell the treasure, buy food!' said Naveen.

'No. Because she cannot find it after she has hidden it. She is too *baoli* to remember.'

'I want the treasure!' insisted Naveen.

'It cannot be. You cannot have. Baoli also cannot have and Jhotta cannot have.'

'Who can have?' demanded Naveen.

'The treasure is only for the one who takes fate into her own hands.'

83

DEEPA AND MA RETURNED TO JAGDISHPURI EXTENSION BY RICKSHAW.

'It is good it is over,' said Ma, who seemed quite unaffected by the proceedings. She discussed none of the arguments, marvelled at none of the surprises that had come out of the hearing and seemed not to have an opinion on the issue at all.

'I was afraid this hearing would continue for a few days. We must finish clearing and packing and tomorrow we will return to Vakilpur. It is not good to stay, look how everyone is staring at you!'

'Let them!' said Deepa, and Ma looked at her, surprised at her new-found confidence.

'But I am glad you explained to them about Amma. No one understood her gift. Only my father, your grandfather, understood her, and supported her. But he was a very special man. I am proud that you were able to tell about Amma's gift.'

Deepa looked at her mother and embraced her there, in the back of the rickshaw, realizing that though her mother never said very much, she knew far more than she ever gave away. There was so much that was unsaid. Deepa hugged her, pressing her chin against her mother's necklace, which was studded and bejewelled from the courts of the kings.

★

The glass jars bought at Jindal's had been delivered and stood in a row in the courtyard, upside down. While Deepa and Ma had been at the temple Usha-rani had washed them all and they were ready to be filled with the pickles.

Deepa changed her clothes, tucked her plain Rajasthani cotton tie-and-dye sari around her waist, and helped Usha-rani lift down several of the pots from the high shelf in the kitchen. They brought them down, Deepa on the one side, Usha on the other, gingerly, gently, so that the mustard oil that filled them to the brim would not spill. Deepa marvelled at the weight of these earthen pots, but Usha-rani averted her face as the powerful aroma burst from the porous sides.

'It is the strongest pickles I have ever smelled!' she exclaimed.

'It is because there are so many pots in one place,' said Deepa.

'So much pickles, for what was your grandmother keeping?'

Deepa laughed. 'She had a vision for the future. She liked to prepare for the future.'

Deepa and Usha-rani brought down ten pots – the largest and oldest ones – and arranged them in the courtyard by the inverted glass jars.

Usha-rani held the end of her sari over her nose and said hurriedly, 'I will help your ma to pack the linen she is wanting to take back to Vakilpur.'

'It is okay, Usha,' said Deepa. 'I can manage.'

She took off the lid of the first pot, prising off the wax which sealed it with a knife, and began to spoon the ripe pickles, using a large ladle with a long, curving handle, into the first glass jar. The aroma was indeed strong. It invaded her nose, rising to the back of her head so that her eyes almost watered. The fermenting mangoes were giving off such vapours it was almost suffocating. From the glass rim the golden, syrupy oil dripped down towards the bottom of the jar. Deepa paused to watch how it trickled, slowly, pungently, in a viscous cascade, mingling with whole cloves and coriander seeds, mustard seeds and whole chillies. Everything was covered in thick, golden oil.

Deepa continued to ladle, marvelling at the amount that one terracotta pot could hold. The glass jar was almost filled and she was nowhere near the bottom of this pot. She ladled some more, then she screwed on the lid of the first glass jar and wiped the drips of oil from the outside with a rag Usha-rani had given her. So many glass jars we will need! she thought. We will have to hire a truck. Just like harvest time in the lychee garden!

She paused to think of Bharathi. *I hope Bharathi can be happy. After all, she has Govind.*

And for once she was able to think of Govind without any embarrassment.

She turned the second glass jar the right way up and dug the ladle into the coagulating pickle-mass in the terracotta pot. Most of the soft brown mango, soaked in oil, was at the bottom, getting thicker and thicker the further down she got. When she had taken the lid off the terracotta pot there had been several inches of pure golden mustard oil on the top, so clear she could see the pickle below. Now her ladle was getting heavier and heavier. She leant it against the rim of the glass jar as she dropped the heavy pickles inside, and she rested more frequently between ladle-fulls, massaging her arm. Then, so heavy were the pickles, the ladle snapped. She would have called Usha-rani to fetch another ladle, but she was reaching the bottom of this pot; she had emptied its wide belly, and it was narrowing towards the base. It would soon be empty.

She abandoned the ladle and scooped up the pickles in her hand, the mustard oil trickling through her fingers. The sides of the pot were smooth with oil. Her hand was submerged up to the elbow. She felt around, her fingers scraping the bottom from time to time; it was smooth but hard.

Then she felt something hard and pointed. Very hard. She curled her oily, dripping fingers around it. It slithered into her hand like a snake – several times she snatched at it and it slipped from her grasp. Then finally she pulled it up. It made a kind of sucking noise as it emerged from the oil and pickle. Deepa withdrew her elbow from the darkness of the pot and held up her hand to look at this thing clenched in her oozing fist. Her eyes opened wide. Her mouth opened wide. And then her face broke into a smile.

Her fist gleamed golden and red. There in her hand was a necklace of rubies, gleaming unmistakably through the oil that dripped away. The sun sparkled on the viscous fluid and flashed on the stones that shone beneath.

Holding the necklace aloft, Deepa peered into the pot, into the dark recesses of the bottom, and there, sparkling among the remainders of the pickles and oil, were four gold bangles and some gold chains.

It was Amma's treasure. Pots and pots of it.

GLOSSARY

aarti – evening prayer ritual with lamps or candles
arré – exclamation approximately equivalent to but or goodness!
Arya Samaj – reformist Hindu organization
avatar – reincarnation
baap – father
Baapré baap – my God!
bahen(ji) – sister
bakri – goat
baksheesh – tip or bribe
bakwas – nonsense
balti – small bucket
bania – merchant class, lower than Brahmins and Kshatriyas in the Hindu hierarchy
bansuri – gourd pipes
baoli – crazy
Baoli Maai – crazy old woman
barfi – sweet made of flour, coconut and milk
bat-cheet – chit-chat
beti – daughter
bhai – brother

bhaiya – brother
bhajan – devotional song
bhangra – exhuberant harvest dance from the Punjab
bhooth – ghost
bidi – kind of cheroot, cheap tobacco rolled in leaves
bindi – forehead dot worn by women
bua(ji) – aunt (father's sister)
carrom – board game
chacha(ji) – uncle (father's younger brother)
chai-khana – tea house
chalo – go
chamars – leather workers (outcastes)
chamra – leather
chappals – slip-on footwear
charpoy – string bed
chela – disciple
chini – sugar
Chini – Chinese
chokré – lad, urchin
chokri – wench, lass
chuha (m), *chuhia* (f) – mouse
chunni – shawl worn over breast and shoulders
chup! – be quiet!
chup-chaap – very quietly
crore – 10,000,000
dai – midwife
darshan – paying of respects by going to see someone, audience granted by king
dava – medicine
dharamsala – hostel for pilgrims
dhobin – washerwoman
dhoti – length of cloth wrapped around the waist and brought between the legs (for men), plain cotton or homespun sari (for women)
dhun – tune
dhut! – (onomatopoeic) threatening sound as if to silence someone
didi – older sister
doodh, *doodh*-wala – milk, milkman
Ganesh – elephant-headed god, remover of obstacles
Garuda – bird-god

Ghalib – Mirza Ghalib, famous Mughal poet
ghas – grass
ghats – riverbank area with steps leading to the river, usually where cremations are carried out
ghee – clarified butter, used in fire-rituals. The rising price of ghee is often a measure of inflation
ghungrus – ankle-bells used by dancers
Gita – holy book
goom – disappeared
goonda – thug
gopura/gopuram – arc-like temple pagoda
gurukul – residential school presided over by guru
haan(ji) – yes
haldi-atta – turmeric paste applied on the skin to enhance beauty
hartal – strike
haveli – ancestral mansion
Hai Ram! – O God!
Hé Ram meré! – O my God!
hundia – earthenware pot
huzoor – sir (often used in royal courts)
Jai Devi! – praise to the goddess!
jaldi karo – be quick
jalebis – sweets made of sugar syrup
jhotta – buffalo calf
kajal – black substance used to line the eyes (make-up)
kameez – long shirt worn over baggy pants
karhai – pan for frying, like a wok
karhi – sour yoghurt curry
karma – destiny, cycle of birth and rebirth based on one's actions
Kathak – classical dance form from northern India
Kshatriya – warrior caste, just below Brahmins in the caste hierarchy and above banias
kurta – smock-like shirt worn over *dhoti* or trousers
lakh – 100,000
lakhpati – millionaire
lathi – heavy bamboo cane carried by police
Laxmi – goddess of wealth
loo – hot wind, can cause severe dehydration and death
lotta – small metal pot for carrying water

maa-baap – parents
maidaan – field
mali – gardener
malik – boss, owner
mama(ji) – maternal uncle (mother's brother)
mandap – canopy erected over four pillars under which wedding ceremony is conducted
Marwaris – Rajasthani traders originally from Marwar
Meerabai – famous devotional singer of the last century
mela – fair
moksha – salvation
morcha – demonstration or march
mundan – hair-shaving ceremony for boys, usually at age twelve months
murti – stone idol
namaste, namaskar – greeting with palms together
nani – maternal grandmother
neta – leader, lit. patriot, often refers to leaders of the independence movement
nullah – open sewer
Odissi – classical temple dance from the state of Orissa
paan – betel
palang – bed
pallav – part of the sari worn over the shoulder or head
panchayat – village council
panir – unfermented cheese
paratha – flat fried bread commonly eaten for breakfast
persaad – offering to devotees handed out by a priest, usually some kind of sugary snack
phut-a-phut – quickly, snappy
pranam – greeting in Sanskrit, extremely formal
puja – prayer ritual
pukka – refers to brick-built buildings and tarmac roads, otherwise meaning strong or ripe, often used for emphasis
pundit – scholar, teacher
raga – melody
raita – yoghurt snack
rajguru – scholarly adviser to the kings
rajkumar – prince
rajkumari – princess

Ram, Ram – familiar greeting
Ramayana – religious epic
rasgolla – sweetmeat made of condensed milk
rasta do! – make way!
sadhu – religious mendicant
sagai – engagement ceremony
sala – brother-in-law, but commonly used as an insult
salaam – greeting (usually Muslim greeting but also used in imitation of court practice)
sant – saint
salwar-kameez – baggy pants and tunic
sarkar – government
sati – immolation of widow on husband's funeral pyre
satyagraha – non-violent resistance espoused by Mahatma Gandhi
shabash! – well done!
shamiana – large tent
shastras – ancient texts laying down laws and principles
shikar – hunting
swami – religious sage
Swatantra Party – Independent Party (existed for a short while in the 1960s and 1970s)
tamasha – show, entertainment
teel tal – three-beat timing in music
thali – steel plate
thoor dal – nutty-flavoured dal
tilak – religious mark applied to the forehead
tiffin – meal or snack
tonga – horse-drawn transport still in use in rural areas
ustaad – maestro
Vedas – ancient texts
wah! – exclamation of appreciation
yaar – used in familiar speech: mate, man
yatra – journey or pilgrimage
zari – gold or silver thread embroidery or weave often used for the borders of saris
zindabad! – long live!